Praise for DRAGONSBLOOD

"Compelling characters, both human and dragon, and a tightly woven plot make this tale of courage, sacrifice, and love a priority purchase. . . . Highly recommended."
— *Library Journal* (starred review)

"*Dragonsblood* is cause for celebration! A worthy addition to one of the grandest traditions in the literature of the fantastic, this is a lock-the-door, take-the-phone-off-the-hook, send-the-kids-out-to-play, curl-up-and-enjoy adventure!"
— DAVID GERROLD, author of *Blood and Fire*

"McCaffrey convincingly spins a dramatic, thoroughly captivating tale, steeped in the lore and well-drawn characterizations of the people and the dragons for which the Pern novels are prized. Fans old and new will be delighted by his continuance of a beloved saga."
— *Booklist*

"Todd McCaffrey does something I didn't think anyone could do: he writes Anne McCaffrey's Pern. Not just a novel set *in* Pern, but Pern. The people, the places, the characters and challenges. This *is* Pern, in the hands of a new master-grade harper, carefully trained in the old traditions but scoring his own ballads. May the saga continue!"
— DAVID WEBER, *New York Times* bestselling author of *The Shadow of Saganami*

"Master fantasist Anne McCaffrey passes the torch to her son Todd, who breathes refreshing life into the ongoing saga of the world of Pern. This stand-alone story fits seamlessly into the long and complicated history of Pern, and McCaffrey expertly mimics his mother's style."

— *Romantic Times*

"A strong, lively story, with vivid, interesting characters and plenty of exciting action. Todd has captured the tone as well as the familiar settings of the Pern books. Pern fans (and newcomers to the Pern universe) have reason to rejoice."

— ELIZABETH MOON, Nebula Award–winning author of *Engaging the Enemy* and *The Speed of Dark*

"The torch has been passed and burns more brightly than ever in this latest chapter of the venerable Pern saga. . . . This stand-alone tale fits beautifully into the existing history and style of earlier books while still breaking new ground."

— *Publishers Weekly* (starred review)

"For Pern lovers, the good news is that Todd McCaffrey has inherited his mother's storytelling ability. His dragons and fire-lizards, his harpers in Harper's Hall, carry on the great traditions—and add much to them. Huzzah, Todd! You have learned wisdom indeed."

— JANE YOLEN, award-winning author of *Briar Rose*

DRAGONSBLOOD

By Todd McCaffrey
Published by Ballantine Books

DRAGONHOLDER
DRAGONSBLOOD

By Anne McCaffrey and Todd McCaffrey

DRAGON'S KIN
DRAGON'S FIRE

DRAGONSBLOOD

TODD McCAFFREY

BALLANTINE BOOKS • NEW YORK

Dragonsblood is a work of fiction. Names, places, and incidents either are products of the author's imagination or are used fictitiously.

2006 Del Rey Books Mass Market Edition

Copyright © 2005 by Todd McCaffrey and Anne McCaffrey
Introduction copyright © 2005 by Anne McCaffrey

All rights reserved.

Excerpt from *Dragon's Fire* copyright © 2006 by Anne McCaffrey and Todd McCaffrey.
All rights reserved.

Published in the United States by Del Rey Books, an imprint of The Random House Publishing Group, a division of Random House, Inc., New York.

This book contains an excerpt from the forthcoming book *Dragon's Fire* by Anne McCaffrey and Todd McCaffrey. This excerpt has been set for this edition only and may not reflect the final content of the forthcoming edition.

DEL REY is a registered trademark and the Del Rey colophon is a trademark of Random House, Inc.

Originally published in hardcover in the United States by Del Rey Books, an imprint of The Random House Publishing Group, a division of Random House, Inc., in 2005.

ISBN 0-345-44125-7

Printed in the United States of America

Map by Joan C. Symons

www.delreybooks.com

OPM   9 8 7 6 5 4 3 2 1

For my sister,
Georgeanne Kennedy
Brave, strong, courageous

INTRODUCTION

Anne McCaffrey

WHEN SHELLY SHAPIRO, our Del Rey editor, asked me to write this intro, I hemmed and hawed because, let's face it, I'm compromised on several counts. One, it is my world Todd is writing in; and two, he is my son.

However, he comes from quite an authorial background. His great-grandfather was a printer-engraver. His grandfather, Colonel George Herbert McCaffrey, wrote many reports to the government dealing with the occupation of countries; his uncle, Hugh McCaffrey, wrote about his experiences as a military adviser to Thailand when they were training their border police corps in a book called *Khmer Gold,* published by Ballantine Books in 1988. His grandmother dabbled in writing murder mysteries, but with three kids to raise and my father to contend with, she never went as far as writing them down. And then there's me, his mother, and him growing up while I was writing the Pern series, which I've been doing since 1967.

They do say that teenagers are very impressionable. And as he was born in 1956, he was certainly immersed in the Pern experience at exactly the most tender time. Grown up, he has helped me work my way through scenes. He has put his military experience (he was in the U.S. Army), his flying experience (he holds a private pilot's license), and his knowledge of spaceships (he has a graduate credit in spaceship design) to good use in advising me and sometimes even contributing whole scenes to books like *Pegasus in Space, Freedom's Challenge,* and *Nimisha's Ship.*

Todd has published a number of short stories—some even

without the editors realizing his maternal connection! And he collaborated with me to write the recent Pern novel *Dragon's Kin*—an experience that proved both gratifying and fun for both of us!

So he is well qualified to write this book. He is also a damned good writer, as *Dragonsblood* will confirm. Perish forbid you should take my word for his abilities. But you should.

You see, I've always been paranoid about people writing in my world. If you'd seen some of the lovingly but inaccurately written stories I've seen, including a film script that had me cringing in fear that it would be produced, you'd understand how I feel about having my literary child misrepresented. But Todd was in at the beginning, and he *knows* Pern as well as he knows the innards of his computer (and as a computer person by nature and by education, he *knows* his computer!). And I knew he could write well. So I knew—well, to be honest, I *hoped*—that he was right for Pern.

Todd's insight into the world and its culture is well-nigh perfectly Pernese. He also had some of my strongest and most reliable Pern fans, like Marilyn and Harry Alm, go over the manuscript, so it isn't just Momma encouraging her child. They were harder on him than I ever could have been. Not that I didn't watch him closely! I couldn't let him make mistakes, and we did have a couple of arguments about scenes, but I am happy to admit that *Dragonsblood* is a good yarn, fitting perfectly into the Pern series, yet something I don't think I would have thought up myself.

Enjoy, as I did, another point of view about Pern. And thanks, son, you done did good and me proud!

DRAGONSBLOOD

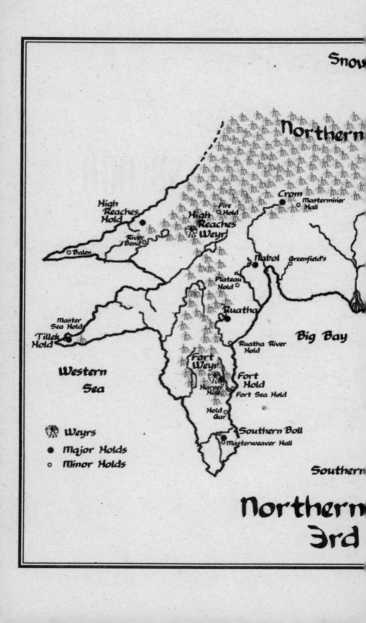

Snow

Northern

Crom
Mastermine
Hall

High
Reaches
Hold

High
Reaches
Weyr

Fire
Hold

River
Bend

Balen

Nabol
Greenfield's

Plateau
Hold

Ruatha

Master
Sea Hold

Tillek
Hold

Big Bay

Ruatha River
Hold

Western
Sea

Fort
Weyr

Fort
Hold

Harper
Hall

Fort Sea Hold

Hold of
Gar

Southern Boll

Masterweaver Hall

🌸 Weyrs

● Major Holds

○ Minor Holds

Southern

Northern

3rd

Red Star at night:
Firestone, dig,
Harness, rig,
Dragons take flight.

Chapter One

Fort Weyr, at the end of the Second Interval,
After Landing (AL) 507

FOUR MEN STOOD in a knot around the Star Stones of Fort Weyr. The sun was just above the horizon, casting the harsh shadows of early dawn at winter's end. Each man wore the prestigious shoulder knots of Weyrleader. Their warm wherhide jackets proclaimed them the leaders of Benden, Fort, Telgar, and Ista Weyrs.

K'lior, Fort's Weyrleader, was host and the youngest present. He was also the newest Weyrleader, having gained his position less than a Turn before.

He glanced back to the Star Stones—to the Eye Rock, which bracketed the Finger Rock, which itself was lit by the baleful Red Star. Thread was coming. Soon.

The air was made more chilly by the steady breeze blowing across the plateau where Fort's Star Stones were placed. K'lior suppressed a shiver. "Fort is still wing light. We've only had the one clutch—"

"There's time yet, K'lior," C'rion, Ista's Weyrleader, judged. He pointed at the Red Star and the Eye Rock. "Thread won't fall until after the last frost."

"There's no doubt, then, that Thread is coming," K'lior said, wishing the other Weyrleaders would disagree with him.

For over two hundred Turns, the planet of Pern had been free of the threat of Thread falling from the sky.

Now that peace would end.

The Red Star's return would bring the Thread that would try, once more, to devour all life on Pern.

For the next fifty Turns, the dragons would rise to the skies, flame Thread into lifeless char, or, failing, watch in horror as it burrowed into the rich soil of Pern to destroy all organic material with mindless voracity.

"Telgar's ready, K'lior," D'gan declared. He turned back from the Star Stones and the dawning light to gaze at the others, who were obscured by the sharp shadows of the early morning light. His words were firmly emphasized by the distant rumbling of his bronze, Kaloth. "My wings are at full strength and I've two clutches on the Hatching Grounds—"

One of the other Weyrleaders cleared his throat loudly, but D'gan's fierce glare could not pierce the shadows to identify the culprit.

"Yes, we were lucky," he continued in answer to the unknown heckler, "but the fact remains that Telgar will be wing heavy when Thread falls. And our holders have tithed fully so we've no lack of equipment or firestone."

K'lior shifted uneasily, for he had been frank in relaying his difficulties in getting Fort's full tithe. "But you don't agree to pooling resources?" he asked again.

He had called this meeting of the Weyrleaders to propose just that. As none of them had ever fought Thread, K'lior felt that his notion of "fly together, learn together" had merit, and would promote communication among the Weyrs. He was shocked when D'vin of High Reaches had refused the invitation and was even further shocked by D'gan's attitude. Telgar's Weyrleader was Igen-bred, after all. K'lior had hoped that D'gan's experience would have made him more amenable to working together, not less.

D'gan favored the wiry Fort Weyrleader with a superior look. "If you're still wing light when Thread falls, K'lior, I'm sure I could spare some of my own."

"I'll bet they're all bronzes," a voice muttered dryly. It came from the direction of the Benden and Istan Weyrleaders.

The implication that D'gan might want to reduce the competition for Telgar's next mating flight was obvious. Not that D'gan's Kaloth had to fly *all* Telgar's queen dragons to remain Weyrleader—just the senior queen.

D'gan stiffened angrily at the remark, turned to K'lior, and said, "I've a Weyr to attend, Fort. I must return."

"Let me call someone to guide your way, D'gan," K'lior offered pleasantly, worried about slippery walkways under unfamiliar feet.

The offer annoyed D'gan, who snapped, "I can find my own dragon well enough, Fort."

K'lior jogged after D'gan, still hoping to soothe the other's foul mood.

"C'rion, you *know* he's got a thin skin. Why do you insist on pricking it?" M'tal asked the Istan Weyrleader in exasperation.

C'rion chuckled at the Benden Weyrleader's remark. "Oh, you know, M'tal, he's not all that bad—when he stops taking himself so seriously. I feel it's my duty as an older, more experienced Weyrleader, to spill the wind from his sails when he takes on airs like that."

"D'gan *is* the sort to swear his Egg cracked the wrong way," M'tal agreed.

C'rion snorted a laugh. "I suspect that D'gan will be a lot more acceptable after his first dose of numbweed. And K'lior will steady up after his first Threadfall."

M'tal pursed his lips thoughtfully. "I'm not so sure about D'gan."

C'rion shrugged. "I've been worried ever since it was decided to abandon Igen Weyr and incorporate those dragonriders into Telgar."

"It made sense at the time," M'tal said, "what with the drought in Igen, the death of their last queen, and the good harvests at Telgar."

C'rion raised a hand to ward off further discussion. "All true. But D'gan himself worries me. He drills his riders

hard. Telgar Weyr has never lost the Games since he became Weyrleader—but will all that be worth anything when
Thread comes?"

M'tal nodded emphatically. "If there's one thing I could
never imagine, it would be D'gan shirking his duty. We
dragonriders know what to expect when Thread comes." He
waved a hand at the Star Stones. "And we know it will come
soon."

"I hear your queen laid a large clutch last week," C'rion
said, changing the topic. "Congratulations."

M'tal laughed. "Are you going to make me an offer like
our esteemed Telgar?"

"No, actually, I was going to offer a trade," C'rion said.

M'tal motioned for him to continue.

"Two queen eggs, by all accounts," C'rion said. "That
would make four queens all told."

"No, one of the eggs is a bronze," M'tal said. "We'd hopes
at first, but Breth nudged it back with the others." The queen
dragons always pushed their queen eggs into a special spot
on the Hatching Grounds, which they carefully guarded.

"All the same . . ."

"Are you looking for new blood, C'rion?"

"It's the job of every Weyrleader to see to the strength of
the Weyr," C'rion agreed. "Actually, I was thinking that to
honor a new queen requires a good selection of candidates.
I'm sure you'll want to Search for a proper Weyrwoman."

M'tal burst out laughing. "It's J'trel, isn't it? You want to
pawn that old scoundrel off on us!"

"Actually, yes," C'rion agreed with a laugh of his own.
"But he's not a scoundrel. *And* it's no lie that his blue has an
eye for good riders, especially the women."

"Which is odd, considering his own preferences," M'tal
remarked.

"Well, you know blues," C'rion agreed diffidently. As blue
dragons mated with green dragons, and both were ridden by
male riders, the riders themselves tended to be the sort who
could accommodate the dragons' amorous arrangements.

"And you want to get him away from Ista so he can forget

about K'nad," M'tal surmised. K'nad and J'trel had been
partners for over twenty Turns.

"K'nad went quickly," C'rion agreed, "it was a blessing.
He was very old, you know."

Less than a dozen Turns older than you, M'tal thought to
himself dryly. Somberly he also realized: And only fifteen
Turns older than me.

Aloud, he said, "So you want J'trel distracted by new duties?"

C'rion nodded. "It would be easier for us at Ista, too.
Thread is coming. It's going to be hard on the old-timers."

There was an uneasy silence. M'tal shook himself. "I'll
have to talk it over with Salina and the Wingleaders."

"Of course," C'rion replied. "There's no hurry."

Curious, M'tal asked, "Where is J'trel now?"

C'rion shrugged. "I don't know. He and his blue took off
after the ceremony for K'nad." He frowned. "He had that
look in his eyes, the one he usually gets just before Ista finds
itself with a whole bunch of the biggest fresh fruit you've
ever seen."

"He hasn't been going to the Southern Continent, has he?"
M'tal asked with a frown of his own. Dragonriders were dis-
couraged from venturing to the Southern Continent with all
its unknown dangers.

"I've made it a point never to ask," C'rion answered dryly.
"You *really* have to try the fruit."

Lorana sat on her knees, ignoring the hot sun beating
down on her, all her attention concentrated on the tiny creature in front of her. Sketching swiftly, Lorana used her free
hand alternately to keep the little thing from moving away
and to keep her sketchbook from sliding off her lap. She ignored the beads of sweat rolling down her face until one
threatened to drop in her eye, at which point she broke from
her task long enough to wipe it away hastily.

The creature, which she dubbed a "scatid," took that moment to burrow quickly into the dry sand. Lorana examined
her sketch and frowned, trying to decide if she needed more

details—the scatid was smaller than the tip of her thumb, and its six limbs had never stopped moving.

Grenn, the littler of Lorana's two fire-lizards, cocked his head at the retreating insect and then looked back at Lorana with an inquiring chirp.

"Of course it ran away," she said with a laugh in her voice. "You're ten times its size."

The fire-lizard pawed at the hole, looked up at Lorana, and chirped again.

"I'll know it if I see it again," Lorana replied, pushing herself up from her knees and stretching to relieve her cramped muscles. She stowed her sketchbook in her carisak and slid her sun hat back on her head—she'd slipped it onto her back when its shade had interfered with her view of the scatid. She added thoughtfully, "Unless you want it?"

With a squawk, Grenn jumped back awkwardly from the hole. Lorana laughed again. "I'd say that was a 'no.' "

Behind her, golden Garth squeaked an agreement.

"You've both been fed, so I know you're not hungry," Lorana said, half to herself. She peered down at the burrow and then at the irrepressible brown fire-lizard. "*Would* you eat it?"

Grenn examined the burrow for a moment, then dropped down on it and pawed at the hole, widening it. When the scatid was again uncovered, Grenn peered at it until the scatid's diggers snapped at him—whereupon the fire-lizard gave a startled squawk and sprang away.

"You would eat it, then," Lorana decided. "You're just not hungry enough." She glanced thoughtfully at the sun overhead. "Or you're too hot to eat anything."

Grenn chirped in agreement. Lorana nodded, saying, "J'trel will be here soon enough."

The little fire-lizards, distant cousins to the huge firebreathing dragons of Pern, trilled happily at the thought of seeing their large friend again.

"In the meantime, we can walk toward the beach again—there should be a breeze," Lorana told them.

The fire-lizards chorused happy assent and disappeared,

leaving Lorana to traipse along after them on foot. She *heard* Garth formulating some plan as the little queen and her consort went *between*. Deciding that the two fire-lizards were not getting into too much trouble, Lorana stopped concentrating on them and focused her attention on the path she was following.

Her clothing was not meant to cope with the hot Igen sun, but Lorana had done the best she could with it, loosening her tunic and rolling up her sleeves and trouser legs. Her outfit would be perfect once onboard the ship, and was almost warm enough for the cold *between*.

Halfway to the beach, she sensed a sudden exultation from Garth and felt the two fire-lizards go *between*. In no time at all, they reappeared high above her, chirped a warning, and dropped what they had been holding between them. Lorana held out her hands and caught a good-sized roundfruit. She laughed and waved at them. "Thank you!"

The fruit was delicious and moist, easing her dry throat. Energized, she picked up her pace to the shore.

Grenn swooped low over her and let out a querying squawk, curving back around toward her, eyes whirling hopefully.

"No," Lorana said, "you may not perch on my shoulder. You need to stretch that wing now that it's healed. Besides, between the carisak and our gear, I'm carrying enough, thank you."

Grenn gave her a half-sad, half-wheedling chirp and beat his wings strongly to regain his lost altitude. High above him, Garth gave him an I-told-you-so scolding.

As he climbed sunward, Lorana noted that in his antics there was no residual sign at all of the broken left wing that had nearly cost his life—and had completely changed hers. With a frown Lorana forced the memory away and continued on to the beach.

"Why didn't you wake me, you silly dragon?" J'trel grumbled, pulling off his riding helmet and running his hand through his stringy white hair as he searched the darkness below for any sign of Lorana. "You *knew* I'd had too much wine, but you went off sunning yourself on some rock and fell asleep, didn't you? Poor Lorana! Waiting and waiting for us . . . only *we* were asleep."

Talith took J'trel's moaning in good part, knowing that the old dragonrider was merely practicing his excuse on him. Talith *had* been tired and the sun had been so warm. J'trel had needed a rest himself and the wine at Nerat Sea Hold had been so inviting . . . and they had worked hard all these many days helping Lorana with her explorations.

We were tired, Talith told his rider. *The sun, the wine, were good.*

"Ah, but while we were sunning ourselves, Lorana was doubtless being fried in the heat or was bitten by one of her subjects, or—it's turned so cold, Talith!" J'trel said, pulling his riding helmet back on. "Almost as cold as *between.* What if—"

She is down there, Talith said, tightening into a steeper dive. J'trel craned his head out over Talith's neck and saw a small fire below on the beach.

"She's probably half frozen," J'trel chided. "This will never do."

Lorana leapt from her place at the fire and rushed to greet the old rider as Talith settled. Grenn and Garth chirped cheerful greetings to Talith, who rumbled back.

We fell asleep in the warm sun, the dragon told Lorana, *and now J'trel is afraid that you are cold.*

"The fire's warm, J'trel," Lorana said, beckoning eagerly, "and there should be enough light to see by."

"See what?" J'trel asked, his earlier excuses forgotten in the heat of Lorana's excitement.

Lorana held up a hand. "I can't tell you, I have to show you."

"Well then, let's get to that fire."

When he was settled by the fire, angled so that its warmth was on his back and its light good for reading, Lorana opened her sketchbook and passed it to him.

"Look at this one for a moment," she said, pointing to one of her earlier drawings.

J'trel took the book and peered at it. His eyes weren't good close up anymore; he moved the book farther away until the image came into focus.

"Hmm, ugly little beastie," he muttered to himself, then hastily added, "but you drew it well."

With a polite nod, Lorana took the book, flipped the pages to one of her more recent drawings, and thrust it back in the dragonrider's hands.

"Now look at this, please."

J'trel frowned, and examined the drawing more carefully. "Why it's almost the same—but different! I can't quite see what, though."

Lorana leaned forward and pointed. "Here—the back legs have none of the fur of the other ones." She flipped back to the first drawing. "But see how the front digger legs are much thinner on this one than on the other? I think that this northern one needs the thinner diggers to burrow in the wet earth, while this little beastie needs wider diggers to push the sand away. See?"

"Almost," J'trel said with a frown. He shook his head. "My eyes are too old, and it's too dark."

Lorana laughed. "I suppose the light *is* too bad! But I've been looking at these pictures for hours." Catching J'trel's grim face, she added hastily, "Oh, don't worry, J'trel, I was quite safe—Garth and Grenn kept watch."

She glanced back at her drawing and then eagerly back to J'trel. "Did you have any luck finding a ship? I'd love to see if there are any different sorts of scatids in Tillek, not to mention the other beasties I've found."

"A ship, she asks!" J'trel exclaimed. "Oh, Lorana, did I find the most beautiful vessel for you! Fit for a Holder this one is—in fact it's *meant* for a Holder—none other than the Lord Holder of Tillek, the Masterfisher himself, designed it, and it was built—ah, it's just finished in the yards and will sail with the tide!"

His beaming smile suddenly vanished.

"J'trel, what's wrong?" Lorana asked.

"The tide!" J'trel wailed. "Oh, Lorana, that dratted dragon of mine—we've missed the tide!" He turned to his dragon. "Talith, why didn't you wake me?"

"I'm sure you were *both* tired," Lorana said in a reasonable voice. "But, J'trel, what does it matter that we've missed the tide?"

"*Wind Rider* sailed with the tide, Lorana. The ship's gone!"

There is plenty of time, Talith said soothingly. *I know when we should meet the sailing master. You have given me a very clear image.*

J'trel brightened. "Of course!" he agreed. "Lorana, gather your gear and I'll have you on the good ship *Wind Rider* before she sails!"

Between only lasts as long as it takes to cough three times, Lorana reminded herself silently as Talith rose high above the Igen shoreline and the faint traces of her campfire blended into the darkness far below them.

Since meeting J'trel and his blue dragon, Lorana had been *between* several times as they had gone from their unmarked camp to various points on Pern. She had become mostly used to the chill and dead silence of the nothingness that was *between* one place and another.

It may take a bit longer this time, Talith warned her. And then they were *between.*

The warming comfort of Talith's presence steadied her. Lorana counted slowly to herself: *one, two, three, fo—*

The sun shone high in the sky as Talith appeared over Ista Sea Hold. Garth and Grenn arrived moments later right above the dragon, chittering their pride in following the larger dragon *between.*

Talith nimbly deposited his riders before the main entrance to Ista Sea Hold and told J'trel he was going to look for a nice warm resting spot.

"Just don't fall asleep again," J'trel warned, slapping the blue dragon's neck affectionately. As the blue dragon became airborne, he gave a soft cough.

Lorana looked at J'trel, with her brows raised. "I don't recall him coughing like that before."

J'trel waved a hand. "He's old. Sometimes a thick lungful of air will make a dragon cough. His lungs aren't like they used to be."

"Do dragons cough often?" Lorana asked, with natural curiosity—her father had been a beastmaster and had even tended people in emergencies, and she had learned much of his craft.

J'trel shrugged. "Dragons are very healthy. Sometimes they seem to get a bit of a bug, and sometimes a cough." He made a throwaway gesture, saying, "It doesn't last long."

"What about the Plague?" Lorana asked with a faint shudder.

"The Plague affected people, not dragons, and the dragonriders were careful to keep safe." J'trel's face took on a clouded look. "Some say we were too careful."

Lorana shook her head emphatically. "We *have* to have dragons to fight Thread, and they *have* to have riders to help them."

J'trel smiled and wrapped an arm around her shoulder for a brief hug. "That's the spirit."

Because she was with a dragonrider, Lorana was not jostled by the crowd: People cleared out of their path. J'trel took this deference by the seaholders as a dragonrider's just due and set a brisk pace to make up for his earlier tardiness.

Lorana struggled to keep up with him. J'trel noticed and gave her a worried look. "Are you all right?"

Lorana flushed and waved his courteous inquiry aside. "I'm just a bit tired, is all. Maybe I've been walking too long."

You have never gone between *times before,* Talith told her with a yawn of his own.

"*Between* times?" Lorana asked aloud.

"Shh," J'trel said suddenly, holding a hand up warningly. Then his eyes narrowed as he considered what she'd said. "Why did you say that?"

"Talith told me," Lorana said.

J'trel sighed. "We had to get here before *Wind Rider* sailed," he explained.

Lorana motioned for him to continue. Leaning closer to her, he lowered his voice. "Dragons can not only go *between* from one place to another, but from one *time* to another," he explained. "When we jumped *between* we also jumped back in time. In time for you to catch the *Wind Rider.*"

"That's amazing!"

"It has its price, though," J'trel added, wearily rubbing the back of his neck. "It takes a toll on dragon and rider—and any passengers."

Lorana gave him an inquiring look.

"Right now you're here at Ista Sea Hold and also on the Igen seashore," J'trel explained. "How do you feel?"

Lorana thought about it. "I'm tired," she said after a moment. "But I thought that was from all the excitement."

"That, *and* timing it," J'trel said. "Some people feel stretched and irritable after they've timed it. It gets worse the longer the jump, the more a person's in two places at once."

"So dragons don't time it that often?" Lorana asked.

"Dragonriders are *never* supposed to time it," J'trel replied. He wagged a finger at her. "Let it be our secret."

Lorana nodded, but she had a distracted look on her face. J'trel had seen that look before on others and had worn it himself when first confronted by the dragons' amazing ability, so he waited patiently for the question he knew she would ask.

"J'trel," Lorana began slowly, her expression guarded but hopeful, "could we go *between* time to when my father was with that herdbeast and warn him?"

J'trel shook his head and said sadly, "If we could have, we already would have."

Lorana raised her brows in confusion.

"You can't alter the past," he told her. "As long as it never happened in the past, it never *can* happen in the past."

"Why not?"

It cannot be done, Talith said. *A dragon cannot go to a place that is* not.

Lorana looked puzzled.

"I tried once," J'trel said, shaking his head at some sad memory. "I couldn't picture my destination in my mind."

It is like trying to fly through rock, Talith added.

"I wanted to go back to when my mother was still alive," J'trel said. "I wanted her to see that I'd Impressed, that I'd become a dragonrider. I thought it'd make her happy." He shook his head. "But I couldn't do it. I couldn't see her and the place clearly enough in my mind to give Talith the image."

You had not done it, so you could not, Talith explained with draconic logic.

Lorana shook her head, mystified. "Maybe if I think about it long enough, it'll make sense," she said, but her attention was already caught by the tall masts of the ships docked just ahead. Swarms of seamen and landsmen bustled about, loading and unloading carts, ships, and conveyances. "Which one is it?" she asked J'trel.

"The shiny new one!" he told her, gesturing with a flourish. "The good ship *Wind Rider,* readying for her maiden voyage."

Eyes widening, Lorana grabbed her book and stylus from her carisak and began sketching furiously.

A sea voyage would do her good, J'trel mused, watching her draw. It would give her a chance to take stock, see more of the world, and maybe learn to see herself as she really was. She thought too poorly of herself.

He remembered how he had first met Lorana. It had been late and dark, and he and Talith had been cold and feeling old . . . lost.

His partner, K'nad, had succumbed to his ailment, and K'nad's green Narith had departed forever *between* a sevenday before. J'trel had summoned his courage and done everything to make K'nad's passing easier for everyone in the Weyr.

Then he had gone to tell K'nad's kinsfolk, at the Hold where he had been born and raised. Carel, Lord Holder of Lemose and K'nad's younger brother, took the news silently,

inured to death from the great losses of the Plague twelve
Turns before.

After an uncomfortable dinner, Lady Munori saw J'trel to
the great Hold doors.

"He has buried his grief so deep that it no longer shows,"
she said of her husband, as an apology to the dragonrider.
She touched his arm consolingly. "He was always proud of
K'nad."

J'trel nodded and turned to leave.

"Dragonrider! My lord!" someone called out of the night.
"A moment, please." There was a note of panic in the voice.

J'trel turned to see a young woman rushing toward him. She
was tall, still gangly in her youth, and not very pretty.

"Your pardon, my lord," she said. "I was hoping to speak
with you before you left."

"This is Lorana," Munori said to J'trel, her voice tinged
with sadness. "Her father, Sannel, was a beastmaster who
bred for us, as well as Benden and Bitra." She grimaced.
"One of our beasts got crazed and kicked him in the head."

"To be in demand by three Holds—your father must be
sorely missed," J'trel said, looking at Lorana more closely.
He revised his first impression. Her dark hair and almond
eyes were set in an expressive face that was, at the moment,
quite somber. He wondered what she would look like when
she smiled.

Lorana nodded. "I was wondering if I could ask your advice," she said after a moment. "The beast that killed my father also snapped the wing on Grenn, one of my fire-lizards."

"I'm sorry," J'trel replied, guessing at the nature of her
request. "I'm afraid I haven't heard of any new clutches recently. But if I do, I'll be sure to put your name in for a
replacement egg."

Lorana shook her head. "He still lives."

J'trel was amazed. "Usually a fire-lizard suffering such a
wound will go *between,*" he remarked. "Often forever."

A brilliant spark of determination flared in Lorana's eyes.
"I wouldn't let him."

"It was the most amazing sight," Lady Munori added.

"You could even see them breathing together, her and her fire-lizard, as she fought to keep him here."

Intrigued, J'trel said, "I should like to see this fire-lizard."

"Thank you," Lorana said, dipping a slight curtsy to the dragonrider.

Lady Munori accompanied them. "You should see her drawings, too, J'trel," she said. "Lord Carel has two hanging in his chambers."

J'trel cocked an eye at the young woman. "A healer and a harper! You are a woman of many talents."

Embarrassed, Lorana ducked her head.

Silently, she led them to one of the guest rooms and gestured politely for J'trel and Munori to precede her.

A fire-lizard's chirp challenged them as they entered.

"They're friends, Garth," Lorana called out.

"You've two!" J'trel exclaimed as he caught sight of the beautiful gold fire-lizard posting guard over the injured brown.

"I tried to get Coriel . . ." Lorana began defensively.

"How many times do we have to tell you that you've nothing to apologize for?" Munori asked in exasperation. She explained to the dragonrider, "Lorana was watching the eggs for my daughter when they hatched and, well . . ."

The brown fire-lizard gave a plaintive sound. Seeing that his wing was splinted and immobilized, J'trel began crooning reassurances.

"There, lad," he said. "Let's have a look at you." He moved closer, but stopped when the little queen gave him a haughty and challenging look.

"Talith, could you—?" J'trel said aloud to his dragon.

The gold gave a startled squawk as the dragon spoke to her. Then, with a very dignified air, she moved away from her injured friend.

"I've never seen the like," J'trel said admiringly, examining the splint. "A break like this . . ."

"I did my best," Lorana said.

"You did the best I've ever seen," he told her. "Our Weyr healer could take lessons from you."

Gently he spread the wing, examined the splint, and then returned the wing to its original position. "How long ago did this occur?"

"About a sevenday," Lady Munori told him. "When we first came upon the three of them, we thought we'd lost them all, father, daughter, fire-lizard. But then that one—" She pointed at the gold. "—started squawking at us, and we realized that her Lorana was still alive."

"Will the wing heal?" Lorana asked, worried that she might have condemned her fire-lizard to a fate worse than death.

"The bones are aligned properly," J'trel judged. "And he seems well-fed," he added, with a grin at the brown's bulging stomach. "I'd say that his chances are good." Privately, though, he wasn't so sure.

"Is there anything else I should do?" Lorana asked. "And when will it be safe for him to fly again?"

J'trel pursed his lips thoughtfully. Something in the girl's demeanor, in her worry and her determination, sparked his compassion.

"Why don't you come with me and we'll take him someplace safe and warm where he can rest until his wing is healed," he suggested.

Lorana's eyes grew round with surprise.

"But wouldn't the dragons at the Weyr—"

"I wasn't thinking of the Weyr, lass," J'trel interrupted. "I know a very nice warm place where dragons—and fire-lizards—can curl up and rest all day long." He wagged a finger toward the brown fire-lizard. "I think the best thing we can do is encourage this one to rest and *not* to fly until his wing is healed."

Lady Munori beamed at Lorana. "You can't go wrong with an offer like that."

Lorana smiled at the dragonrider, a smile that lit her face. "Thank you!"

It took a month of careful attention for Grenn's wing to heal in the warmth of a southern sun. During that time, J'trel was pleased to provide Lorana with pencil and paper to sketch upon—and amazed when he saw the results.

They had been together in the sunny warmth for two sevendays before Lorana really opened up to the old dragonrider. It happened the evening after J'trel had announced that he was certain Grenn's wing would heal. Lorana had just finished sketching the splint design she'd put on Grenn and started a new page. J'trel hadn't been paying attention until he heard her stifle a sob. Looking over, he saw that she was drawing a face.

"Is that your father?" he asked. He had guessed that, as soon as she knew her fire-lizard was safe, Lorana would allow herself to grieve.

Lorana nodded. Haltingly, with J'trel's gentle questioning, she told him her story.

Lorana had been helping her father since she could toddle; indeed, since the Plague took the rest of her family—mother, brother, and sister—she had been his only helper.

She recounted huddling amongst the cold bodies while her father stood in the doorway shielding them from the outraged holders who feared his roaming ways had brought the Plague with him. It was only when they discovered that nearly all the bodies beyond him had gone cold that they relented.

Lorana had used all her wits—particularly her skill at drawing—to bring her distraught father out of the despair that overtook him after that fateful day. Since then, Sannel had used her ability in drawing, tasking her with registering all the marks and conformations of their various breedings, and taking her everywhere he went. When he died, she had been devastated.

When J'trel looked over Grenn that evening by the campfire, he was very pleased to be able to give Lorana some good news. "I think we should try to see if he can fly tomorrow morning," he announced. "When the air is cold."

"Because the air is heavier then, right?" Lorana asked.

"Exactly," he agreed. "And, if he's all right, I'll take you back to the Weyr with me."

Lorana's face fell.

J'trel gave her an inquiring look.

"I don't know if I belong there," Lorana admitted. When J'trel started to protest, she held up a restraining hand. "I don't know *where* I belong."

J'trel bit back a quick response. He gave her a long glance and nodded slowly.

"I think I see," he said at last. "In fact, I feel somewhat the same myself."

"You do?" Lorana asked, taken aback.

"Not about you," he added hastily, pointing a finger toward his chest. "About myself."

Lorana was surprised.

J'trel let out a long, slow sigh. "I'm old," he said at last. "I can't say that I'll be any credit when Thread falls again. And I'm tired."

"Tired?"

"Tired of hurting," J'trel admitted. "Tired of the pain, tired of memories, tired of not being able to move the way I used to, tired of making compromises, tired of the looks the youngsters give me—looks *I* used to give old people.

"It was different with K'nad," he continued softly, almost to himself. "Then I had someone to share with. We would groan when our joints hurt and laugh about it together."

He shook his head sadly. "I hadn't planned on anything beyond saying good-bye to K'nad's kin," he admitted. "And then I met you."

Lorana shook her head, trying to think of something to say.

J'trel waved her unvoiced objections aside. "I'm not complaining," he assured her. "In fact, I'm glad to have met you." He grinned at her. "I've never met a woman more fit to lead a Weyr."

"Lead a Weyr?" Lorana repeated, aghast. "Weyrwoman? Me? No, no—I—"

"You've more talent than I've ever seen," J'trel told her. "Half the Istan riders of the past thirty Turns were searched by me and Talith."

He smiled briefly in pride. "And you can talk to any dragon!" he exclaimed.

Lorana crinkled her forehead in confusion. "What makes you say that?" she asked. "I've only talked with Talith."

"While it's true that a dragon can talk to anyone he chooses, only riders bonded to a dragon can address one—and usually only their own. No rider can talk to another dragon unless he can hear *all* dragons. Do you know how few can do that?"

Lorana could only shake her head.

"Torene is the only one I can think of," J'trel said. "And I don't think she had your way with them. It's more like you *feel* them than talk to them."

"You don't?" Lorana asked in surprise. She looked out to Talith and smiled fondly at the blue. "I'm sorry, I—"

"Lass, when are you going to stop apologizing for your gifts?" J'trel interrupted her gently.

"It's just—it's just—" Lorana couldn't continue.

"I see," J'trel said to stop her from tearing herself apart. He grimaced. He had seen this behavior in many of the survivors of the Plague.

The Plague had come up suddenly twelve Turns earlier. Some said it had started at Nerat Tip, others said Benden Hold, still others said Bay Head. Wherever it had started, it had spread quickly, if sporadically, across all of Pern. While the Holds of Benden Weyr—Bitra, Lemos, and Benden—were hardest hit, no hold from southeasternmost Nerat Tip to northwesternmost Tillek Hold had been spared.

In less than six months the Plague had passed, leaving grieving holders and crafters to recover—and wonder why the dragonriders hadn't helped out sooner. Help from the Weyrs had come, but only when the worst of the Plague had passed. J'trel knew why: He'd heard from his Wingleader, J'lantir, of the bitter arguments amongst the Weyrleaders over whether to aid the holders or preserve their own numbers to fight Thread that was due to fall in the Turns to come.

In some places, one out of three holders had perished. In

others, only the very youngest and the very oldest had been affected. Some outlying holds had been left empty, devoid of all life, and everyone had at least one close relative or friend who had succumbed to the Plague.

When the Plague had passed and the dragonriders had come to help, they'd found fields untended, men and women sitting listless and vacant-eyed. The few healers who hadn't themselves fallen to the Plague explained that these people were in deep shock. It took days of comfort and caring for the survivors to recover.

Everyone felt the same nagging loss, the same wonderment mixed with shame at their survival—the sense that they were not worthy of their existence.

"What would you like to do?" J'trel asked her.

Lorana shook her head. "I don't know," she said. "I just don't think that I'm ready . . ."

"Perhaps you aren't," J'trel agreed. "You could always go back to Lemos—"

"No!" Lorana exclaimed. She took a deep breath, then continued more calmly. "Please, Lemos holds too many sad memories—I don't want to go back there."

"Very well," J'trel said. He pursed his lips. "Perhaps we should look at your skills . . . ?"

"Well, I guess I'm not bad with broken wings," Lorana allowed, with a glance toward the sleeping Grenn.

"And you can draw very well," J'trel said. He yawned. "Perhaps we should sleep on it."

When the sun woke him the next morning, J'trel was struck with an inspiration. He knew that Lorana would overcome her grief more easily if she had something to engage her attention, and he recognized that her eye and training put her in an excellent position to categorize the various species on Pern.

"No one's ever drawn all the different creatures of Pern," he told her. "You could be the first."

Lorana was intrigued.

"But how can I get all over Pern?" she asked. "I couldn't ask you to take me everywhere."

"I shall have to ponder that," J'trel said, admitting, "at some point I'll have to get back to my own affairs."

Then he stood up, slapping his legs with his hands. "But now, I think it's time to see whether our charge is ready for his first flight."

It was only a few moments before the fire-lizard came back down squawking loudly in complaint.

J'trel looked surprised. "I don't understand."

"I do," Lorana said with a laugh. "We've been stuffing him so much, he's too fat to fly!"

"J'trel?" Lorana's voice drew the dragonrider back from his reverie.

She handed her book to him nervously, pointing at her latest sketch. J'trel could see that she'd done several in rapid succession.

"Is this Captain Tanner?" she asked, pointing to her latest effort.

"That's him, indeed!" J'trel agreed enthusiastically. "Let's go aboard, so you can meet him."

Aboard, J'trel led her to the stern of the ship. Lorana's eyes darted all about, taking in the activity and the sights with relish.

Suddenly they stopped.

Captain Tanner was opposite her. Next to J'trel was another seaman. Two others stood on either side of Captain Tanner.

Lorana was surprised to realize that Captain Tanner was the youngest of the men. She guessed that he was near her own age of twenty Turns. The other seamen all looked older, sea-grizzled, and not nearly as wholesome, wearing grubby clothes and frowns.

Captain Tanner's honest brown eyes met hers in quiet appraisal.

"Here's your ship's healer, Captain Tanner," J'trel said, "as promised."

Tanner's eyes widened as the words registered. He turned

to Lorana, his expression bleak. "My lord J'trel did not mention that you were a woman."

"Show him your drawings," J'trel said.

Numbly, Lorana extended her sketchbook to Captain Tanner. Tanner took them politely and glanced down at the first
drawing.

"Have you ever drawn a ship?"

"Just now from the docks," she said. "If you turn the
page . . ."

Captain Tanner did so and gasped in awe. The sailors near
him drew closer for a better view.

"I'm also interested in the fish and the birds at sea," Lorana said.

"That's why Lorana wants to journey with you on the
Wind Rider," J'trel put in.

"And you'd draw them, as well?" one of the older men
asked. Lorana nodded.

"And if we caught them, would you give us a drawing of
that?" another asked. Before Lorana could answer, the third
seaman guffawed, "As if you'd ever catch anything, Minet!
You and that old rod of yours!"

"Aye, a net's the only proper way to catch fish!"

"There are no nets aboard *Wind Rider*, you git!" Minet
replied. Lorana could tell that there was no real rancor among
the three.

"*Wind Rider* is a schooner, Baror," Tanner said. "She's
built for speed, not trawling."

The seaman named Baror looked away from Tanner, face
clouded. Lorana wasn't sure she liked that look.

"They say it's bad luck to have a woman aboard a ship,"
Baror muttered. Beside him Minet nodded.

"I'd say it's worse luck to travel without a healer," J'trel
observed. Captain Tanner nodded.

"Did you say the *Wind Rider* was built for speed?" Lorana
asked, looking at the other ships in the harbor for comparison.

"Aye," Minet told her, "Lord Holder Tillek—the Masterfisher himself—had her built here special, for fast runs between Thread."

"If it ever comes," the third seaman growled.

"It'll come, Colfet, it'll come," Captain Tanner replied, casting an apologetic look toward J'trel.

Colfet seemed to realize his gaffe. "I meant no disrespect, dragonrider."

J'trel didn't hear much apology in the northerner's tone but let it go. "Then I'll take none, seaman."

Tanner decided to change the subject. "J'trel says you've also got a way with beasts."

"My father worked with them, yes," Lorana replied.

"Do you suppose you could splint an arm or tend a scrape for a person?"

Lorana shrugged. "It's not much different. More than a scrape or a break and you'd want to get a proper healer."

The seamen all nodded in agreement.

"None of the lads are likely to get themselves hurt on a milk run like this," Colfet growled. "Just down to that new sea hold and back here."

Captain Tanner told Lorana, "I'm only captain for *Wind Rider*'s shakedown cruise. After these three get the feel of her rigging, they'll be taking her on up to Tillek."

"But I'd like to go to Tillek," Lorana said.

Colfet glanced at the other Tillek men, then said, "For that you'll have to get my approval." He took a long thoughtful breath. "Let's see how you are on this run down to this new Hold, first."

"We'd better be moving then," Tanner said, turning to the others. "The tide doesn't wait."

J'trel shook her hand and then grabbed her in a hug. "You watch out for yourself, youngster. I'll want to know how you get along."

Lorana gave him a smile. "I'll do that, J'trel."

The *Wind Rider* was everything Captain Tanner had said it would be. Lorana stowed her gear in the healer's cabin and then joined the crew on deck as the ship was nimbly warped out of Ista Harbor. The schooner heeled as the wind caught her quarter, and the helmsman cursed as he struggled to control the wheel.

As the ship heeled into a new wave and burst through the other side, Captain Tanner said to Colfet, "What do you think of her now, Mister Colfet? Is she fit for your Master's fleet?"

"She grabs the wind well, Captain Tanner," Colfet admitted. "But it's early days, early days. I'd like to see her in a blow."

Tanner laughed and pointed to the confused seamen above in the rigging. "Not before this lot get themselves sorted out, I hope."

Colfet gave him a sour grin. "No, not before." He glanced at the setting sun over the taffrail. "And tomorrow will be too fair for a strong wind."

"What makes you say that?" Lorana asked.

"Bad weather coming, probably a blow," Colfet answered, as if that were all the explanation needed.

Captain Tanner raised his monocular to his eye. "Lorana, look there! It seems we're getting a send-off!"

Lorana looked where Tanner pointed and could see a dragon and rider in the distance waving at them. She laughed and waved back.

J'trel says safe voyage, Lorana, Talith told her.
Thank him please, Talith.

High up in the sky, Talith relayed Lorana's reply to J'trel.

"You're welcome, lass," J'trel said to himself. "Did you hear that, Talith? How many can speak to other dragons? How many Weyrwomen can do that? Not one, I'm telling you. She'll ride gold, and she'll be the best Weyrwoman Pern's ever seen."

-ome (suffix): (i) the biological portion of an ecosystem. (ii) the material and genetic information required to re-create the biological portion of an ecosystem. Examples: the "terrome" refers to the biological portion of the Terran ecosystem; the "cetome" refers to the biological portion of the Cetus III ecosystem; the "eridanome" refers to the biological portion of the Eridani ecosystem.

—Glossary of terms, Ecosystems:
From -ome to Planet, 24th Edition

Chapter Two

Fort Hold, First Pass year 42, AL 50

WITH ANOTHER wordless cry, Wind Blossom rolled out of her dreams into the new day. It was always the same dream. Only—different this time. Something had woken her early.

Even with the dream interrupted, as if against her will, Wind Blossom remembered her mother's last words: "Always a disappointment you were to me. Now you hold the family honor. Fail not, Wind Blossom."

Wind Blossom had had the same dreams for the last forty years.

The sound repeated itself: a dragon bugling in the sky above.

Her mother, Kitti Ping, had created the dragons. Kitti Ping, famed Eridani Adept, who had saved Cetus III from the ravages of the Nathi War was also Pern's savior with the creation of the great, fire-breathing, telepathic dragons.

Wind Blossom was credited with—blamed for—the creation, through similar genetic manipulation, of the photophobic watch-whers. On the starships' manifests Kitti Ping and Wind Blossom had been listed as geneticists. That title conveyed only a small portion of the full Eridani training Kitti Ping had received and had passed on to her daughter, Wind Blossom.

"Always a disappointment you were to me," her mother's calm, controlled voice came to Wind Blossom's mind—a memory over forty years old.

They had come to Pern fifty years earlier, thousands of war-weary people seeking an idyllic world beyond the knowledge of human and Nathi alike. They had been led by such luminaries as Emily Boll, famed Governor of Tau Ceti and heroic leader of Cetus III, and Admiral Paul Benden, the victor of the Nathi Wars.

Instead of finding rest and a pastoral, agricultural world, they discovered that their lush planet Pern had an evil stepsister—the Red Star. Its orbit was wildly erratic, coming through the solar system on a cometary 250-year cycle, dragging with it the mysterious peril of Thread.

Eight years after the colonists landed on Pern, the Red Star came close enough to unload its burden on its sister-planet. The Thread, mindless, voracious, space-traveling spores, ate anything organic—plastics, woods, flesh. The first Thread-fall on the unsuspecting colony was devastating.

Galvanized by this new threat, Kitti Ping, Wind Blossom, and all the biologists on Pern dropped their work in adapting terran life-forms to life on Pern to concentrate instead on creating a defense against Thread.

From the native flying fire-lizards, barely longer from nose to tail than a person's arm, Kitti Ping created the huge fire-breathing dragons, able to carry a rider, telepathically bound to his mount, into a flaming battle against Thread. And so humankind on Pern was saved.

It was the sound of a dragon's bugle that had disturbed Wind Blossom's dreams. Through the unshuttered windows, she could make out the beat of the dragon's wings and heard it land in the courtyard outside the College.

Shouts and cries reached her window with emotions intact but words incomprehensible. The dragon alone was indication enough of something extraordinary, and the voices confirmed that there was some sort of emergency.

The voices in the courtyard moved inside.

Her room smelled of lavender. Wind Blossom took a long, deep lungful of the smell and turned to look at the fresh cutting on her bedside table. Her mother's room had always smelled of cedar. Sometimes of apple blossoms, too, but always of cedar.

Perhaps some arnica would help, Wind Blossom thought as she summoned the strength to ignore the pain in her old joints and the weakness of her muscles as she sat up in bed and slid her feet into her slippers. Arnica was good for bruises and aches.

And some peppermint tea for my thinking, she added with a bittersweet twinkle in her eyes.

She walked to her dresser and looked impassively at her face reflected in the still water of the wash basin. Her hair was still dark—it would always be dark—as were her eyes. They stared impassively back at her as she examined her face. Her skin had the same yellowish tinge of her Asian ancestors; her eyes had the Asian almond shape.

Wind Blossom completed her inspection, noting once again that the muscles around her face, which had slackened thirty years before, pulled the corners of her lips downward.

Opening her dresser, she saw the yellow tunic at the bottom of her drawer and sighed imperceptibly as she had done at the sight of it every day for the past twenty years. Once, an accident at the laundry had left one of her white tunics with a distinctly yellowish tinge. No one had remarked on it. When the day was over, Wind Blossom had carefully put the yellow tunic away in her drawers. She had worn it again, years later—and no one had noticed. Now, as always, she carefully pulled out one of her scrupulously white tunics. From the lower drawer she pulled out a fresh pair of black pants.

Dressed, Wind Blossom turned her attention back to the noises that had awoken her. From the sounds outside, she suspected—

"My lady, my lady!" a girl's voice called. Wind Blossom didn't recognize the voice. It was probably one of the new medical trainees. "Please come quickly, there's been an accident!"

Although there was no one in the room to see, Wind Blossom did not let her face show her amusement at being called "my lady."

"What is it?" she asked, rising and moving toward the door.

"Weyrleader M'hall from Benden has brought in a boy," the trainee answered, opening the door as she heard Wind Blossom reach for the latch. "He was attacked."

Wind Blossom's heart sank. Her face remained calm, but inwardly she quailed. The look on the girl's face was all she needed to identify the attacker. The youngster continued resolutely, "It was a watch-wher."

Wind Blossom passed through the door and marched past the apprentice who, though much younger, towered over her. "Bring my bag."

The trainee paused, torn between guiding the frail old woman down the steps and obeying her orders.

"My bones are not so worn that I cannot walk unaided," Wind Blossom told her. "Get my bag."

There was only one clean room in the infirmary. It was too primitive to be considered anything like a proper operating room but it was well scrubbed.

Wind Blossom registered how the people outside it were grouped: Her daughter and a musician were in one group, M'hall and a man she thought she should know were in another group, and two interns were in a third.

The interns looked up when she arrived, but M'hall spoke first. "My lady Wind Blossom, my mother told me that you are the most skilled in sutures."

When had everyone started with the "my lady" 's? Wind Blossom thought acidly.

"How is the patient?" she asked Latrel, the nearest intern.

"The patient has severe lacerations on the face, neck, and abdomen," he answered quickly. Wind Blossom noted but did not comment on his ashen appearance and the way he licked his lips. Latrel had attended a number of major injuries—clearly this was worse. "He is a ten-year-old boy. He's been dosed with numbweed and fellis juice, and was suitably wrapped against *between* during the journey from Benden Hold. His pulse is thready and weak; he shows signs of shock and blood loss. Janir is attempting to stabilize—"

Wind Blossom interrupted him with an upheld hand and walked over to the large basin outside the clean room. She pulled back her sleeves. "Gown me, then scrub."

Latrel nodded, pulling sanitized gowns out of a special closet. Once she was robed, Wind Blossom started carefully scrubbing her arms and hands to clean off as many germs as she could. She motioned for Latrel to continue his report.

"We cannot type his blood—"

"It's O positive," the man beside M'hall interjected.

Wind Blossom turned to face him, her expression showing interest.

"I've been keeping track of our bloodlines; it can only be O positive," he repeated.

Wind Blossom matched his face to her memory of a young boy she had spoken with long ago. "Peter Tubberman."

The man winced at the name. "I am called Purman now," he corrected. "The boy is my son."

A crease formed on Wind Blossom's brows. Ted Tubberman had been considered a dangerous renegade in the early days of the Pern colony at Landing. He had "stolen" equipment to conduct biology experiments, one of which had killed him and orphaned young Peter at an early age. Wind Blossom could understand why Peter Tubberman would want to remove himself from memories of his father.

"Purman. Benden wines," she said to herself. "Modified vines, no?" She waited only long enough for his body language to answer her before she said to the other intern, "Purman scrubs with us."

She turned her attention back to Latrel. "The old needles, you kept them, right?" When the intern nodded, she said,

"Have them sterilized and bring them in. What about sutures?"

The young trainee—Carelly, Wind Blossom finally put a name to her—arrived, breathless with Wind Blossom's medical bag. "My lady," she gasped, and gathered in another breath to say, "there are no more in Stores."

Wind Blossom grunted acknowledgment. She looked at the Benden Weyrleader. "M'hall?"

M'hall approached the diminutive geneticist. He bent over her when she beckoned him closer.

"I have one set of sutures left. If I use them on this boy, others will die later. Probably dragonriders," she said in a voice that carried only to his ears.

M'hall nodded his understanding.

"I saw this day coming," she added. "We are losing our tech base. These sorts of wounds are rare enough that soon no one will even know how to treat them."

"Then let us use these sutures now," M'hall said, "while there is still someone with your skills."

Wind Blossom nodded. She turned to Carelly. "Go back to my room, girl, and bring down the orange bag."

As the girl ran off, Wind Blossom turned to Purman. "The last of the sutures and antibiotics are in my orange bag. Your son will be the last one treated with such medicines on Pern."

"For how long?" Purman wondered, as if to himself.

"A long time, I fear," Wind Blossom answered. "There are so few of us who have the skill and the knowledge. And now, without supplies, the skills will become useless."

In the clean room, Wind Blossom found that the boy's injuries were every bit as awful as she'd feared. His right forehead, nose, and left cheek had been opened by the three-clawed paw of the watch-wher. The claw-marks continued down the top left side of the boy's chest, near the shoulder, and into the biceps of the upper left arm.

Wind Blossom leaned closer to the boy's face. Before the incident, he had been as handsome as his father at the same age. Now . . . she shook herself and checked his pulse.

"He is in shock," she announced. Janir nodded, saying, "I've been keeping him warm, but he has lost a lot of blood—and going *between* . . . "

The doors to the ready room swung open as Latrel, Carelly, and Purman entered.

"He will need blood," Wind Blossom announced. She looked at Latrel. "Get the other bed set up close by." She turned to Purman. "He will need at least three units. You can only donate one." She patted the bed that Latrel brought up. "Get on it—you'll be first.

"Carelly, find Emorra and tell her we have need of her," Wind Blossom ordered. "And have someone make me some peppermint tea with a dash of arnica."

The young apprentice waved an arm over her shoulder in acknowledgment as she sped off on her mission.

Purman's face was clouded with fear. Wind Blossom explained, "We need to stabilize him, and irrigate the wounds to prevent infection."

She looked closely at the boy's nose.

"He has lost a lot of cartilage. Rebuilding the nose will be difficult."

She gestured for a probe from Janir. Gently, she examined the boy's cheek.

"The damage to the left cheek is severe. Immobilizing it while it heals will be a major concern." She continued her examination, adding, "Fortunately, there is no sign of damage to the underlying bone."

She sighed and looked at the boy's chest wound. "The chest cavity is intact—that is good. It is a flesh wound. We will have to leave it open and irrigated to ensure that there is no infection."

She turned her attention to the boy's arm. "Some of the muscle has been removed here," she said. She looked at Janir. "You will irrigate with saline solution and bandage here, too."

"Him? What about you?" Purman asked, sitting up on his bed.

"We need three units of blood," Wind Blossom repeated in answer. "You will give the first."

The door opened, and a competent-looking young woman entered the clean room, bringing with her the faint smell of starsuckle, the Pernese hybrid of honeysuckle.

"Emorra"—Wind Blossom nodded to the woman, and Purman was struck by their resemblance—"will donate the second unit, and I, the third."

"But—" Purman objected.

Wind Blossom silenced him with her upheld hand. "I will stitch his facial wounds before I give the blood." Her lips curved up in a shadowy grin. "It is fitting. Kitti Ping's daughter and granddaughter should help Tubberman's son and grandson."

"And," she added as Purman started another objection, "she and I are the only other two suitable blood donors available."

"You are too old, Mother," Emorra objected. "I shall donate two units."

"Who is too old?" Wind Blossom snorted. "What do you know? You never studied medicine."

"You know better," Emorra corrected. Carelly arrived with a tray and a cup of tea.

"That was genetics, not medicine," Wind Blossom said. Emorra's eyes flashed.

Purman and Janir looked askance at the two women. "Please," Purman said anxiously. "My son."

Wind Blossom spared one more moment to glare at her daughter. "Always a disappointment you were to me," she muttered before she bent over the boy. She worked quickly, starting with the lacerations of the forehead. Gently she teased the open wounds together.

She stitched the dermis and subcutaneous fat together with polydioxanone—a synthetic absorbable suture—and closed the epidermis with synthetic polyester sutures. She made her stitches small and as few as she could; there was even less suture material than she had feared.

Janir monitored the boy's vital signs, while Latrel supervised the direct transfusion of first Purman's and then Emorra's blood.

When both units had been transferred to the boy, Wind Blossom said, without looking up from her work, "Carelly, take Purman and Emorra out of here, make sure they both have wine and cheese, and take some rest."

An hour later, Wind Blossom laid aside her tools and walked wearily to the other bed. "My turn now, Latrel."

Janir and Latrel exchanged worried looks. "The boy is—" Janir began.

Wind Blossom cut him off. "He needs the blood. I don't."

Latrel pursed his lips. "Emorra may not have studied medicine, but I have. A unit of blood at your age is not a good idea."

Wind Blossom looked up at the young intern. "Latrel, there is nothing more I can teach you to do with the supplies we have left," she said slowly. "The boy's wounds came from a watch-wher, my 'mistake.' If it's to be, then nothing would suit me more than for my blood to redeem my error." When she saw that the intern still looked unconvinced, she added, "And it's my choice, Latrel."

"Very well," he replied, his tone resigned but his face showing his worry.

Wind Blossom winced as he inserted the needle into her vein. As her blood began to flow into the mutilated boy, she sighed, and remembered nothing more.

It was always the same dream.

"How could you say that the Multichord songbird of Cetus III is my greatest success?"

That honors had been heaped upon Kitti Ping for her work in developing the hybrid, which had so neatly averted the worst ecological disaster of the Nathi Wars, was not answer enough.

"When are we done?" Kitti Ping prodded when Wind Blossom would not answer her first question.

"Never," Wind Blossom heard herself dully repeating.

"Why is that?"

"Because today is the mother of tomorrow," Wind Blossom said, spouting another of her mother's sayings.

Kitti Ping's eyes narrowed. "And what does that mean, child?"

"It means, my mother, that our work today will be changed by what happens tomorrow."

"And only those who anticipate tomorrow will find rest in their labors," Kitti Ping concluded. She sighed, her symbol of utmost despair in her daughter. "The Multichord was *nothing* compared to the leechworm."

Wind Blossom schooled her face carefully to hide any trace of her thoughts: Here it comes *again*. Aloud she said, "I consider the Multichord the obvious representative of the entire symbiotic solution you created, my mother."

Kitti Ping allowed her gaze to soften—a little. "You are in error. The leechworm, the ugly eater of unwanted radiation, was the true solution to the problem. The Multichord was a felicitous symbiont embodying both a guardian for Cetus III's pollen-spreading systems, and a suitable predator for the leechworms, allowing us to quickly concentrate the deleterious radioactives in a controlled sector of the biosphere."

Wind Blossom nodded dutifully. Behind her eyes she remembered the awards citing the Multichord of Cetus III as the First Wonder of the Universe. They had been such an elegant solution to the radiation left by the nuclear horror that the alien Nathi had rained down upon Cetus III in their attempt to eradicate all humanity—an attempt that would have succeeded if not for Admiral Benden.

Wind Blossom remembered the marvelous multitonal choruses that had thrilled the night air and brought smiles to all the survivors of that horrible war, the sheer beauty of the rainbow-colored birds, built upon the original hummingbird genotype, as they flitted like the little bees they protected, from one plant to another, pausing occasionally to eat any stray leechworm that threatened to transport radioactives into those areas already reclaimed.

The dream changed. "Why did you make the watchwhers?"

Mother, Wind Blossom thought, you know why I made the watch-whers. They were part of the original plan.

"Why did you make the watch-whers, Wind Blossom?" The voice was not Kitti Ping's: It was deeper.

Wind Blossom opened her eyes. Sitting beside her was Ted Tubberman's son, Purman.

She sat up slowly. She was in her room. Purman was seated beside her bed, looking intently at her.

"Your son, how is he?" she asked.

Purman's eyes lightened. "He is recovering. Your Latrel had to dose him with fellis juice so that he wouldn't talk and dislodge the sutures in his cheek. His chest and arm wounds are healing nicely."

Wind Blossom raised an eyebrow.

"You have been unconscious for nearly two days," Purman told her. "You really were too old to be a donor."

"My daughter?"

Purman's face took on a gentler expression. "Emorra did not leave your side until she collapsed into sleep herself. I had Carelly take her to her rooms." His expression changed. "I think you treated her harshly. Was Kitti Ping like that?"

Wind Blossom examined his face before slowly nodding. "It is a great honor the Eridani bestowed on us."

"It's a curse," Purman growled. "This whole planet's a curse."

"How did your son come to be mauled by the watch-wher?" Wind Blossom asked, sidestepping his outburst.

Purman glared at her before answering, his lips pursed tightly.

"Tieran loved that thing. He played with her, and spent all his time with her," he replied. He sighed. "She was sleeping and Tieran came over to her and tried to scratch her head, like he'd seen M'hall do with his dragon."

Wind Blossom sat upright and tried to get out of bed, but Purman stopped her, looking at her questioningly. Her fatigue did not diminish the fire that fanned in her brown eyes, as she said, "That one must be destroyed. Immediately."

Purman recoiled. Instead of asking her why, he furrowed his brows in thought.

"An instinctive reaction?" he guessed. "Why?"

The door to her room opened and M'hall and Emorra entered.

"An instinctive reaction," Wind Blossom agreed. "I thought I had bred it out." She turned to M'hall. "That watch-wher must be destroyed before she passes on the trait."

M'hall shook his head. "Bendensk went *between* already, Wind Blossom."

Wind Blossom sighed. "She was very old." She looked at Purman. "Perhaps if she had been younger, she could have controlled herself." She looked up at M'hall. "How is the wherhandler?"

M'hall crossed the room and seated himself, frowning. "That may have been part of the problem, too," he said. "Jaran—now J'ran—had been Searched and Impressed the week before."

"The watch-wher would have been confused and seeking out a new wherhandler," Wind Blossom said to herself. She looked at Purman. "Probably your son."

"How is the boy?"

"He is doing well," Emorra replied. "Janir has him in a fellis-laced sleep."

"We shall have to wake him soon," Wind Blossom said, making a face. "And we must keep his jaw as immobile as possible."

"That will be hard on him," Purman said, flashing a smile. "He is a talker."

"Then someone who can outtalk him should be at his side when he wakes," Wind Blossom replied. She looked at her daughter. "Emorra, see to it."

"My lady!" M'hall protested, "Emorra is the administrator here. She should not be ordered about—"

"She is my daughter," Wind Blossom replied, as if that were enough. Emorra bit off a bitter response, nodded curtly to her mother, and left.

"Mother or not—" M'hall's indignation suffused his face.

Purman was unmoved. "Why did you send her out?"

Wind Blossom stared at M'hall until the Weyrleader let out an angry sigh. "How much has your mother told you, M'hall?"

M'hall shot a pointed glance at Purman. Wind Blossom motioned for M'hall to continue. The Benden Weyrleader relaxed, looking only at Wind Blossom.

"My mother," M'hall said, giving the second word slight emphasis, "has told me everything she knows."

"About what?" Purman asked, turning from one to the other, realizing slowly that the conversation was for his benefit.

"About the dragons, the watch-whers, and the grubs," the Benden Weyrleader replied.

"And now, Purman's vine-grubs," Wind Blossom added.

"Don't forget the felines in the Southern Continent," M'hall countered.

Wind Blossom cocked her head toward Purman. "How much can you tell us about the felines?"

Purman shook his head. "I don't understand."

"The dragons, watch-whers, and grubs are all modifications to Pern's ecosystem," Wind Blossom said, as if that were explanation enough.

Purman pursed his lips in thought. "The dragons fight Thread from on high, and the grubs catch it down low," he said after a moment.

"But the grubs do more than that, don't they?" Wind Blossom prompted.

Purman nodded slowly.

"My mother made the dragons and I made the watch-whers," Wind Blossom said. M'hall snorted derisively at her, but she held up a restraining hand. "That is what everyone has been told, M'hall."

Purman cocked an eyebrow at this exchange. "My father bred the felines and the grubs," he said after a moment. "The grubs protect Pern, so you were wondering if I knew the purpose of the felines?"

Wind Blossom nodded.

Purman shook his head, sadly. "My father never said," he

told them. "He was very excited with them, said that he would show everyone, but I was too little and he never tried to talk to me." He frowned at old memories.

"I don't think he trusted me to keep his secrets," he admitted.

"My mother believes that there are too many secrets on Pern," M'hall said, looking back and forth between the two of them. "She is afraid that something will happen and that vital information will be lost, to the detriment of all."

Wind Blossom had been scrutinizing Purman's face carefully while M'hall was talking. Now she shook her head. "M'hall, I don't think he knows."

"Knows what?" Purman asked.

Wind Blossom answered his question with a question: "When does it end?"

"When does what end?" Purman replied, irritated.

He thought he knew M'hall, and was accepted at Benden Hold for his valuable work in adapting the grubs in a tighter symbiosis with Benden's grapevines, but now he wasn't sure. He wondered if he was being mocked by these two for being his father's son. His life had been so hard as a youngster that he'd changed his name, making it more Pernese and less readily identifiable with the rogue botanist.

Wind Blossom sighed, shaking her head. She reached out to take Purman's hand in her own, soothingly. "I am sorry, Purman. I had hoped that your father had passed on his knowledge to you."

"He told me some things," Purman replied stiffly. "Other things I learned on my own."

M'hall slapped his leg emphatically, exclaiming, "There, you see! That proves Mother's point. There should be no secrets."

"I do not disagree, M'hall," Wind Blossom said. "But some things are pointless to know—like the knowledge of sutures—because the technology cannot support it."

M'hall nodded reluctantly.

Purman had been thinking while the other two were talking. Now he looked at Wind Blossom. "How similar are the watch-whers to the dragons?"

M'hall snorted and gave Purman a keen smile. "You see, Wind Blossom, Purman lends weight to my point."

Wind Blossom nodded and turned her head to face Purman. "They are very similar. I started with much of the same genetic base and the same master program."

"What is their purpose, then?"

She raised an eyebrow in surprise, then sighed. "Your training is sparse, Purman. You should have been taught that there should always be more than one purpose in introducing a new species into an ecosystem.

"In fact, the watch-whers were intended to solve several problems," she continued. "Dragons, by their nature, would associate only with a select few people. But they must become part of the human ecology, if you will. They must not be feared."

"So you bred the watch-whers as something that most people could see?" Purman sounded skeptical.

"And they're uglier than dragons, too," M'hall added. "If you were to try to tell someone who'd never seen a dragon what they were like, you'd say like a watch-wher but bigger and prettier."

"So their first purpose is psychological?"

"It is not their first purpose," Wind Blossom said rather tartly. "Unlike your wines."

Purman grunted in response and gestured for her to continue.

"I designed their eyes to be excellent in low-light situations," Wind Blossom said, choosing her words carefully, "and particularly tuned to infrared wavelengths."

"Don't forget that you designed them to be more empathic than telepathic," M'hall interjected. Wind Blossom gave him a reproving look. "Sorry," he said, chastened.

"I altered the design of their dermis and epidermis to incorporate more of their boron crystalline skeletal materials—"

"She tried to make them armored," M'hall translated. Wind Blossom nodded.

"It didn't work," M'hall added. Wind Blossom sighed.

M'hall waved a hand toward her in conciliation, saying, "But it was a good idea."

"Yes, it was," Purman agreed, "but why? Why not incorporate those changes directly into the dragons?"

"Two different species are safer," Wind Blossom said. "Greater diversity yields redundancy."

Purman nodded but held up a hand as he grappled with his thoughts. Finally he looked up at the two of them. "The watch-whers fight Thread at night?"

"By themselves," M'hall agreed, eyes gleaming in memory. "I've seen them once—they were magnificent. I learned a lot about fighting Thread that night."

"They breathe fire?"

"No," M'hall said. "They eat Thread, like the fire-lizards. They don't need riders, either—the queens organize them all."

"The queens?"

M'hall nodded. "Of course. They're like dragons, or fire-lizards for that matter."

"What about their wings?" Purman asked. "They're so short and stubby, how do they fly?"

Wind Blossom's eyes lit with mischief. "They fly the same way as dragons. I made the wings smaller to avoid Thread damage."

"Why keep this a secret?" Purman asked with outrage in his voice. "Everyone should know this."

"Why?" Wind Blossom asked. "So they'll never sleep for fear that Thread will fall at night? How many people are content to let only your grubs protect the grapevines?"

"It doesn't happen often," M'hall put in. "The oxygen level in the atmosphere shrinks at night, especially in the three thousand- to fifteen hundred-meter range, and the air's too cold to support the spores. A lot of them freeze and are blown all over the place as dust."

"But what about those that do get through?" Purman persisted.

"It's no different than dealing with the small amount of Thread that the dragons miss," M'hall said. "Hopefully, the ground crews find and take care of them."

"And they are fewer at night anyway, due to the cold." Purman pursed his lips thoughtfully. "But on a warm night?"

M'hall recrossed his legs and shook his head ruefully. "That's how I found out, Purman. I asked myself that same question, wondering how I could get my riders to fight day and night—especially as neither humans nor dragons can see that well at night."

A look of wonder crossed his face as he recalled the experience. "They swarmed in from everywhere, arranged themselves by their queens, and flew up to the Thread. I was above them, at first, and they came up at me like stars coming out at night. And then they were above, swooping and diving for the still-viable clumps of Thread."

"They see more in the infrared range," Wind Blossom said. "They can differentiate between the live Thread and the Thread that has been frozen by the night atmosphere."

"So they have night vision . . ." Purman breathed.

Wind Blossom nodded. "That is why their eyes are so bad in daylight: too much light for them."

"And Benden's watch-wher—why did it react to tickling?" Purman asked.

Wind Blossom shook her head sadly. "I wanted them to react if they were asleep and Thread fell on them," she said. "I had hoped to make the watch-whers tough enough to survive Thread and protect Pern . . . in case something happened to the dragons or their riders."

Purman sat bolt upright, shocked. He looked to M'hall for confirmation, but the Weyrleader only nodded. Purman asked him, "Do you think this could happen?"

"I'm not a geneticist, Purman," M'hall answered, "but I certainly hope not."

Purman gave Wind Blossom a long, searching look. Finally, he said, "I remember not too long ago I had a problem with one of the vineyards. Something I hadn't seen before. The grapes started going bad. I had to work hard to isolate the problem, and it turned out that the usual fungus that protected the grapes had been replaced by a new, more virulent strain. It took me months to finally develop a variant vine-grub to protect against that fungus."

While he spoke, he carefully watched Wind Blossom's reaction. When he finished, he knew. "You fear that something similar might affect the dragons, don't you?"

Wind Blossom nodded. "The dragons are derived from the fire-lizards. The parasites that prey on the fire-lizards could also prey on the dragons."

She frowned. "But just as you modified your grubs to aid the grape in fighting off that fungus, so the modifications to produce the dragons have rendered them immune to bacterial and viral vectors that affect fire-lizards . . . I hope."

"But time will generate mutations," Purman said to himself. He looked at Wind Blossom. "How much time? What sort of problems would the dragons have?"

Wind Blossom shook her head. "I do not know."

She sighed and lay back down in her bed.

"The Eridani like to take centuries to add a new species to an ecosystem," she continued. "At the least, even with all the urgency of Thread, my mother wanted to spend decades.

"As it was, we did not have time to research more than the most obvious disease vectors affecting the fire-lizards before my mother created the dragons."

Wind Blossom sighed again. "I had the advantage of somewhat more research before I created the watch-whers, but still . . ." Her voice trailed off.

"I must rest now," she told them, gesturing for them to leave. She smiled up at Purman.

"Go look in on your son," she said. "I would like him to stay here, so I can teach him all that you have not been able to."

She rolled over in her bed. "He must stay here a while, anyway, for his wounds to heal."

Wide ship, tall ship,
Tossed on a raging sea.
Fair ship, brave ship,
Bring my love back to me.

Chapter Three

Near Half-Circle Sea Hold, Second Interval, AL 507

THE AIR WAS COLD and moist with sea spray and it pressed Lorana's clothing tight against her body as she finished her climb to the top of *Wind Rider*'s highest mast. The sound of the sea and ship beneath her were all that she could hear— she could see little, for the stars were hidden by cloud and the dawn's light was still a while off.

From the moment *Wind Rider* had heeled over as it caught the wind and the swells outside of Ista Harbor, Lorana had wanted to do just this—climb to the highest point on the ship, wrap her legs around the mast and hold tight while she raised her arms to the wind and felt the salt air chap her cheeks. She'd had to wait though, until she'd overcome her fear of the heeling ship, and her fear of climbing the ratlines and then beyond the crosstrees to the highest point of the ship, and she'd had to wait until she was sure no one would be watching her, for hanging in the wind was only her first goal.

She dropped her hands to her side and gingerly brought the pouch she'd draped over her shoulder from her side to her front. She carefully pulled out the drawing board, already prepared with a sheet of paper, and found the charcoal stick she'd rigged by pulling on the string she'd tied between it and the board. And now, with gray all around her, Lorana quickly sketched.

The light from the rising sun gave Lorana a chance to reappraise the image in differing lights, and to compare her rendering with the sea's majesty. The sun was just over the horizon when she was finally satisfied that she'd got the best rendering she could. It was just as well, she decided: Her fingers were tingling with the early morning cold.

"Ahoy up there!" a voice called up to her. "What of the morning?"

"Light winds, scattered clouds, red skies," Lorana responded, stowing her supplies in her sack and starting back down the mast. She heard a groan rise up from the deck.

She made her way back aft to the tiller where Colfet had the watch. "Why the grumble on the weather?" she asked the grumpy mariner.

Baror made a sour face and spat over the rail. "Sailor take warning," he answered shortly. Lorana's brows arched a question.

Baror shook his head. "The old saying goes: 'Red sky at night, sailor's delight; Red sky at morning, sailor take warning.' There'll be a blow for sure, but I already knew that."

Lorana had heard from others that Baror had broken his arm years back and was convinced he could tell when the weather was going to change by the way it ached.

"I just hope we get into harbor before it catches us," he added, rubbing his arm.

Lorana sidled away from the sour seaman. Of the three mates, Baror was her least favorite. Lorana had never managed to catch him without a bitter or angry look on his face. For a while she had wondered if the old break in his forearm had left him in constant pain, but she had come to realize that Baror was simply the sort that could not pass up a chance to complain or moan.

Down on the deck, Lorana found that the sea spray had grown thicker, and she shivered from the chill. She started down below but stopped, glancing back at Baror. He was staring at her intently, as though seeing her for the first time. Quickly she turned and resumed her descent.

Captain Tanner came up the gangway opposite her.

"Good morning," he said.

Lorana nodded and started on her way, but as she did a loud thump on the deck above was followed immediately by a groan and a string of curses—first from Colfet and then from Baror.

"Lorana!" Baror called curtly. "Get back here; Colfet's done himself a mischief!" In a lower voice, which still carried, he muttered, "Who'll relieve me now?"

"Come on," Tanner told her with a jerk of his head.

"I'd better get my gear," Lorana said, dashing back down to her cabin.

"Good idea," Captain Tanner agreed.

Lorana was back on deck in less than two minutes, with her healer's bag and a warm coat. A bit of numbweed stilled the worst of Colfet's pain and grumbling, while a quick inspection showed her that the ulna was broken midway between elbow and wrist.

"Could be worse," Colfet observed when she told him. "And now *I'll* have a weather gauge."

"Come below to my cabin—I'll have to set it," Lorana told him.

Tanner looked alarmed. Catching sight of a seaman coming up on deck, he called, "Gesten, Colfet's broken his arm. Help him down below so that Lorana can go ahead and get set up."

"No, it's all right!" Colfet called back, putting his weight on Lorana, who nearly buckled in surprise. "Lorana's a stout lass, we'll manage. Besides, the weather's picking up—you'll be needing all hands to trim sail."

Getting the large seaman down below to her cabin was much harder than she'd figured, but Lorana felt that she'd proved herself "one of the boys" by doing so.

In the cabin, she threw her pack at the far end of the table and rummaged in the lockers for bandages and the other material she'd need.

When she came back and sat opposite to set the burly Colfet's arm—which she was sure would be child's play compared to Grenn's wing—she noticed that he was gazing intently at her. She felt her face getting hot as she reached across to gently roll the seaman's shirtsleeve up away from the break.

"You've a soft touch," Colfet said appreciatively. Lorana glanced up at him to gauge his expression. Feeling her face redden in the intensity of his look, she jerked her eyes back down to the break.

"You're lucky you didn't break the skin." She probed the break gently. Colfet winced. "Numbweed won't help, I'm sorry."

"Nor fellis," Colfet agreed grimly, dragging a lock of his cloud-white hair away from his face with his good arm. He drew breath over his teeth with a painful hiss. "No matter, do what you need. I'll keep my eyes on your drawings while you work, if that's all right."

Lorana had forgotten the drawings she'd hung in the cabin to dry out from the sea's damp. She'd nearly run out of paper with all the sketches the crew and Captain Tanner had begged her for. Not that she hadn't been eager to oblige; the journey in *Wind Rider* had given her many new subjects to draw. She had got good likenesses of dour Baror, sour Minet, and several of Captain Tanner—who, Lorana admitted to herself secretly, was more than a little rewarding to look at.

The only one she'd got of Colfet had been when he'd caught a fish. It wasn't her best, because she had to sketch fast to catch the action, but the seaman had been so impressed that he'd forgotten the fish in favor of finding a safe place for her drawing.

"A right fine likeness," he had said at the time.

With Colfet diverted by the drawings, Lorana could time her move to match the bucking of the ship. She eyed Colfet, eyed the break, felt the ship, and quickly jerked—

"Aaaaah! Shells, why don't you just break it again?" Colfet shouted, face red with pain. Lorana had just missed the motion of the sea, painfully jamming the two broken pieces over each other.

"I'm sorry," Lorana whimpered, tears starting in her eyes, "I tried—"

"Are you all right?" Captain Tanner shouted from above them.

"That's what you get for having a woman aboard," Baror added in a bellow of his own.

"Rogue wave!" Colfet called back, rolling his eyes at Baror's complaint. "Lorana didn't get the timing right."

He looked across at Lorana, licked his lips, and shouted, "She'll get it this time, I'm sure."

Lorana nodded fervently, "I will, I'm sorry, Colfet—"

"No need to apologize," Colfet said a bit brusquely. "Just do it right this time." The old seaman licked his lips.

Lorana bent her head over her work. Colfet studied her closely in the silence.

"There," Lorana said, deftly finishing the binding. "How's that?"

Colfet inspected the splints bound around his forearm. "Feels right." His face brightened. "You did good work, lass. You've the makings of a good healer."

"Now, how about some wine with a bit of fellis juice to ease the pain?" Lorana asked, rising from the table to pull a flask from the locker.

Colfet's face brightened at the thought of getting drunk for a good reason, but then shook his head. "You're a good lass, but the captain might need a hand, and we'll be in that new sea hold before nightfall. I can wait until then."

The old seaman's face grew thoughtful. He shifted his arm carefully.

"With this, I'll have to let Baror take first mate," he told her. "He'll be captain when *Wind Rider* finishes this cruise."

He pursed his lips, frowning. "You might not want to stay aboard, then."

"But I was hoping—"

"Baror doesn't like women," Colfet interrupted. "You know

that." He paused and leaned in closer to her. "He doesn't like dragonmen much, either. And for the same reason."

Lorana looked intrigued.

"His first wife ran off with a dragonman," Colfet told her. "I can't say as I'd blame her—he was never much to look at, and his idea of romance would bore a fish."

Lorana made to comment, but Colfet held up his good hand to forestall her.

"I suppose he might have changed his mind," Colfet went on, "if only his second wife hadn't died in the Plague. He blamed the dragonriders for not helping soon enough."

"Oh!"

Colfet nodded. "He found a third wife, but she hounds him unmercifully. I think that's why he was so happy to go on this voyage. Still, he's no reason to think kindly of women or dragonmen."

"Well . . ."

"You've nothing to worry about as long as Captain Tanner's aboard," Colfet assured her. "And maybe we can sort Baror out afterward."

Lorana couldn't think of what to say.

"Land ho!" The cry from above deck interrupted her thoughts.

"We'll be in port before noon, I expect," Colfet said.

Lorana nodded. "You should get the Hold healer to look at that."

Colfet started to say something, pursed his lips in thought, and nodded. "You're right," he said, adding with a grin, "but I doubt there'll be any complaints!"

As *Wind Rider* neared the coastline, she passed a number of trawlers on their way back to the new sea hold from their day's work. The trawlers all reacted in the same way: At first they turned toward *Wind Rider,* then they tried to match her course, and then they fell behind as the sloop's sails sent her swiftly through the waves.

The ship's crew grew more and more amused with each unsuccessful attempt at interception until finally even Colfet had a grin on his face and ruefully admitted, "I reckon she's faster than anything my Master has ever seen."

As the coastline drew nearer, however, the northern crew began to grumble about Captain Tanner's navigation.

"I heard it said that there's fickle winds out here," Baror said as he cast a suspicious look at the captain. "If one's not careful, a ship could get dashed on the coastline before she makes port."

Tanner ignored Baror's outburst and the others it inspired, contenting himself with a confirming glance at the binnacle. "We'll make the sea hold in the next half an hour," he said aloud for everyone to hear.

As the half hour crept to its end, with the sun just past its midday height, even Lorana was worried about their course.

"There's a huge cliff up ahead," the lookout shouted. "We'll hit it in—I don't believe it! There's a great big hole in the middle of it!"

"That's the port," Captain Tanner said, suddenly calling out orders to reduce sail and adjusting his course just slightly as the "big hole" came into view from the deck. He spared a glance at Baror, telling him, "Prepare to launch the skiff." To the crew forward he shouted, "Prepare to make anchor!"

Five minutes later *Wind Rider* was riding at anchor in the huge bay. To port they could see the great cavern that had been carved out of the coastline, while to starboard they could see miners and others laboring to carve a new hold out of the cliff face set just behind a pebbly shore. Lorana, Tanner, Baror, and Colfet were all eyes as the skiff sailed jauntily to the shore.

"Nothing like this at Tillek," Baror said when he found his voice.

"Nor Ista," Captain Tanner agreed. "It'll be safe from all but the worst winds—and that dock!"

A tall, thin man met them as they reached the shore. "I'm Trinar," he said shortly, "Dockmaster here. That your ship?"

"It is," Captain Tanner replied. "She's the *Wind Rider*, commissioned for the Masterfisher at Tillek and on trials from Ista Sea Hold."

Trinar was impressed. "I heard about it. She looks very pretty, very fast. Much room for fish?"

Colfet snickered. "She's built for fast runs of valuable cargo, not fish."

Trinar looked less impressed. "Well, if you want to stay the night, you'll have to unstep her topmasts and bring her to dock here in the cavern."

"That won't be necessary—we'll be leaving with the evening tide," Tanner replied.

"Very well then, I'll get someone to moor your skiff. See me when you're ready to depart," Trinar answered. "The mooring fee is two marks."

"Two marks!" Colfet hissed. "Didn't you hear the man say this is the Masterfisher's ship?"

"It's still two marks," Trinar said. He waved his hand and two burly seamen approached. "Jalor will take your skiff out, and Marset will show you up to the Hold."

Tanner held up his hand in an arresting gesture. "How much to put an anchor watch on *Wind Rider*?"

Trinar pursed his lips thoughtfully. "Reckon we could do that for four marks."

"Very well," Tanner said, passing over the marks. He turned to the skiff's crew. "This is the Dockmaster, Trinar. He's going to supply an anchor watch for the ship. You go back, work it out with the others, and you can all come ashore until the evening tide—how's that sound?"

Baror tapped Tanner's shoulder. In a hoarse whisper, the grumpy seaman asked, "What's to stop them from taking her?"

"She's one of a kind, where would they take her?" Tanner replied. "Besides, she's not your Master's ship yet. Until we've completed the trials, if anything happens to her it'll be on my head."

Baror grunted acknowledgment, still looking doubtful. Tanner turned to Marset. "We'd be glad to see your new hold."

"I'd like to see a nice glass of cold wine," Baror muttered.

Lorana spoke up for the first time. "And Colfet needs to see your hold healer."

Tanner looked chagrined. "To the healer first, then we'll see."

Healer Bordan was a short, elderly man with thick, bushy eyebrows and long white hair worn in a queue. He sniffed the cast carefully for any signs of infection, checked the bindings, spoke curtly to Lorana about the break, and finally pronounced himself well satisfied with the current cast.

"You were wise not to try a solid cast," Bordan told her.

"We didn't have the supplies to make it," Lorana replied. "But wouldn't it have been better?"

Bordan nodded. "Yes, a solid cast keeps the bones in place better, but on the sea where everything gets wet, you'd soon have nothing more than a mass of soggy wrappings. No, a well-wrapped set of splints will do fine." He gave Lorana a searching look. "Ever thought of turning healer?"

Lorana was stunned at the implied compliment and confused as she tried to construct an answer. Tanner saved her. "I'd say that Lorana has her work cut out with her drawings."

Bordan's bushy eyebrows rose to greater heights. "You draw, as well? Have you ever considered drawing for the Healer Hall? Have you a good eye?"

"Her drawings look so real, I'm afraid of falling into them," Colfet told him.

"Well, if you ever think so, I'll be happy to write the Masterhealer," Bordan said.

Lorana's eyes widened in delight. "Thank you! Thank you very much, Healer Bordan."

"Hmmph," Colfet grumbled. "Didn't I tell you there was no need to see the healer? But I'm parched, from all that poking about—begging your pardon, Healer Bordan."

Bordan snorted, smiling. "We've got some good Benden wine down in the cellars that would probably do wonders for your pains." He raised a cautioning finger. "But, mind you, drink enough water with it or your bones will feel it when the wine dries them out!"

The entire hold smelled of stone dust, a dry acrid smell. The Main Hall was large enough, but there were few in it, as even here the sound of miners carving out stone could be heard ringing through the air.

"You're off that foreign ship, is it?" a sturdily built woman asked as they entered. "Here for some wine and a bit of food, I'd imagine?"

"If we could, please," Lorana asked.

Lorana's politeness startled the woman, who reappraised the group. "Well, you'd probably be as bothered as the rest of us with all that hammering," she said and leaned closer to them. In a whisper she added, "Most of the lads are out in the valley where the noise is less. You'll find food and wine out there, too. It's a bit like a Gather."

The walk from the new hold to the valley inland was not long, but Lorana found the going difficult.

"You've still got your sea legs," Tanner informed her. "You'll be a bit wobbly for the rest of the day, probably."

Colfet looked at the sun and frowned. "Won't be much of that left, soon." He asked Tanner, "When did you plan to head out?"

Tanner considered the question and looked at the sky. "The offshore breeze won't start until after sundown," he replied. He held up a hand to forestall Colfet's protest. "I know it will be a rough night, but the winds in Nerat Bay can be fickle, particularly near the shore, and I'd rather get away while we can."

"You want to ride a storm out of here?" Baror asked in shock.

Tanner nodded. "After the storm there'll be days of wind-less dead calm and thick morning fogs," he told the northern sailors. "I don't want us caught in either."

Colfet considered what Tanner had said for a moment and nodded firmly. "Don't get much windlessness up north, but we know all about fog."

Baror shuddered. "I couldn't stand being stuck in the same place for days on end, praying for a wind."

Tanner nodded in agreement. "Then let's be off, get our Gather, and get gone with the night airs!"

"There it is, Talith!" J'trel called as they burst into the afternoon sunshine at the new sea hold. "Look down there, see it? That must be their Dock Cavern, and you can see all the tents—practically a Gather—of the people waiting to move into the new hold. And—look!—there's the *Wind Rider*!"

J'trel asked his dragon to bank sharply to the right on their way down, craning his head over the dragon's neck to get a better view of the hold. In his earlier conversation with Captain Tanner, he'd heard a lot about the new sea hold—it was all any of the seafolk would talk about—and some of what he'd heard had disturbed him.

Oh, he was sure that the Benden Weyrleader must have been told that Nerat was settling a new hold, and from what he'd heard about M'tal, he knew *that* Weyrleader would insist on all the proper procedures being followed in building and founding the new hold. But—where were the shutters for the windows? And didn't that main hold door look a bit too wide? What if the wind blew Thread up against the hold doors and someone opened them too early? J'trel shuddered at the thought.

"Talith, put me down on the sand, please," J'trel requested. Talith, who had *heard* more of J'trel's ruminations than the old dragonrider realized, rumbled in agreement and turned toward the widest part of the shore. "I want to see this hold and talk with its holder before I find Lorana."

At the hold entrance, J'trel was nearly bowled over by a group of lads trudging through with wheelbarrows full of chipped rock.

"Out of my way, you old git!" the first one yelled as he swerved to dodge J'trel.

The second one, following, went wide-eyed as he recognized J'trel's distinctive garb. "Genin, you fool! That was a dragonrider!"

Genin spared a backward glance at the dragonrider and

said loudly, "So? He's too old to do any useful work—probably doesn't even know how!"

Talith bugled angrily from the shore and Genin jumped, tripped over his feet, and toppled his wheelbarrow over. His face turned livid with rage as he sprang up, shouting at J'trel, "This is all your fault, old man! Why don't you go back to your Weyr?"

J'trel stopped and turned back angrily. He sized up Genin as he approached. The lad was burly and muscled from years working nets and hauling sail; cropped blond hair topped a beefy face with eyes set with the look of a bully.

As Genin rushed at the dragonrider, his cômpanion dropped his wheelbarrow and grated, "Genin, no! He's a dragonrider!"

"Stay out of it, Vilo!" Genin said, his voice rising as he threw himself at J'trel—

Who wasn't there. The bully fell with a jarring thud onto the hard stone as his lunge for the dragonrider met empty air.

With a tight grin, J'trel noted that the oaf had winded himself. In other circumstances, J'trel would have left matters at that, but a crowd was gathering. The dragonrider felt the heat of anger burning within him—and an echo from Talith at the shore.

Rough hands parted a way through the crowd and a dark-haired man appeared. "Hold! Enough of this—oh, dragonrider! I didn't know! I—"

"I will settle with this one," J'trel said, his words harsher and thicker than he had intended. The dark-haired man's eyes widened and he opened his mouth to protest. J'trel, hands raised in readiness, turned his attention back to the winded bully.

"Everyone stand back, give them room!" the dark-haired man shouted at the crowd, which obediently drew back.

What are you doing? Talith asked. *You are not young anymore.* J'trel could hear the dragon's wings as Talith launched himself into the air.

This is a question of honor, J'trel said. *Thread comes soon. Holders must respect dragonriders.* Talith accepted the answer reluctantly, taking station and circling watchfully high above the crowd.

The distractions had given Genin time to recover. Just as J'trel turned back to deal with him, Genin threw himself at the dragonrider.

Genin had heard enough as he was recovering to realize that he would be outcast from the Hold. Always quicker to anger than to thought, the bully roused himself to revenge. He grappled the dragonrider at the waist, intending to snap the old man's spine.

The shock of the assault took J'trel off his feet. He fell back under the weight of his attacker. Agony ran along nerves from his waist. With a shock, echoed high above by his bugling dragon, J'trel realized that the tough was planning to kill him. As Genin dragged him up in a bear hug, J'trel grabbed his head in either hand and dug his thumbs into the holder's eyes.

Genin dropped J'trel with a shriek, his hands covering his eyes. J'trel took a sharp ragged breath, stepped back, and shot a brutal kick to Genin's groin with his right foot. The impact staggered the holder. Landing on the foot he had kicked with, J'trel followed immediately with another kick to the chest. Pain lanced up the dragonrider's foot as the blow jarred through his body. Genin collapsed facedown into an inert lump.

Even though both his waist and foot hurt him abominably, even though he was sorely winded and dearly wanted nothing more than to sprawl on the ground gasping for air, J'trel forced himself to take one deep calming breath, stand squarely, and look commandingly for the dark-haired man.

"I am J'trel, rider of Talith," he said, turning slowly to catch the eyes of everyone in the crowd. "I request the courtesy of this Hold."

"I am Rinir, my lord," the dark-haired man said instantly, bowing. He frowned at Genin, and continued nervously, "I assure you—"

J'trel cut him off with a wave of his hand. "I am looking for someone off that ship. Where is the crew?"

"I met them earlier, my lord," a woman said, coming forward to stand next to Rinir. "They've gone over to the tents."

J'trel glanced skyward and ignored the crowd as Talith responded to his silent request. The crowd followed his glance and ran out of the dragon's way as Talith landed daintily beside his dragonrider. With a final, curt nod to Rinir, J'trel mounted and signaled Talith to take them to the meadow.

You're hurt! Talith complained. *You need numbweed and fellis. Let me take you back to the Weyr.*

No. I promised Lorana that I'd see her, J'trel replied. *If I go now, I don't know when I'll be able to return.*

Talith rumbled anxiously but flew on to the meadow.

"It's not right for a woman to be aboard a ship," Baror grumbled into his cup. He and Minet sat under an awning at the crowded vintner's tent.

"So tell the captain," Minet said, tired of hearing the same old moaning from Baror that he'd heard since *Wind Rider* had first set sail.

"Captain!" Baror snorted. "He's only the captain until we're finished our trials." He took another gulp and slammed down his empty mug. "Then it's me."

"Well, you've not that long to wait, then," Minet said. "And then you'll decide." He took a pull from his mug, frowned, and looked into it. His frown deepened when he saw that it was empty. "Still, she's a pretty one, isn't she?"

"She's a bit plain for my tastes," Baror grumbled.

"She'd keep you warm at night," Minet said suggestively. "Especially if you were the captain. She'd have no choice then."

"My missus would skin me," Baror grumbled. Minet knew that all too well. He was convinced that getting away from his wife was half the reason that Baror had agreed to this voyage.

"Your missus would skin you only if she found out," Minet said, his eyes glinting. "As you said, it's bad luck to have a woman aboard a ship. And accidents can happen."

Baror met his eyes with a thoughtful look. Minet nodded at him suggestively. Baror pursed his lips, then grinned.

"But," Minet cautioned, "you'd have to wait until you were captain."

"I could be captain today," Baror snapped back.

"And how do you suppose that?" Minet wondered.

"Accidents can happen," Baror replied, rising blearily from his seat.

"What about that dragonrider? You heard he killed one of the local oafs, didn't you?"

"I'll take care of him, too," Baror said, stalking off. "He'll be no trouble if he's in his cups."

The crew of *Wind Rider* had split up long before J'trel arrived. He found Lorana by herself, pretending not to look at some of the more beautiful fabrics on sale in the weavers' tent.

"They'd make great wear for a woman, wouldn't they?" J'trel asked as he walked up to her.

"J'trel!" Lorana threw herself into his arms for a hug. "Good to see you!"

"And you." Trying not to wince in pain, J'trel grinned at her. "The sea air seems to have done well for you." He grabbed her hand. "Let's go somewhere where we can sit— and drink."

"I know just the place." Lorana led him to a tent where they served cool wine and crusty bread. They found a table apart from the others and ordered their drinks.

"Where are your fire-lizards?" J'trel asked when he was sure they were out of earshot. "I've got something for them."

Lorana looked around to be sure no one was looking, then summoned the fire-lizards. Garth appeared immediately and chirped happily at the dragonrider. Lorana frowned as she concentrated on summoning Grenn. When the brown fire-lizard finally appeared, he chattered loudly at the two of them before Lorana could shush him.

"My! He's in a mood!" J'trel remarked with a grin. He

pulled forth two packets from inside his jacket. "Get these on them, and let's see how they look."

The packets turned out to contain beautifully strung bead harnesses. Lorana gasped as she saw the markings. "What's this?"

J'trel waved dismissively. "It was the beader's idea. I told her about Grenn's wing."

Lorana gave him an incredulous look. "Well, all right," J'trel confessed, "I did make some suggestions."

"Animal Healer-in-training?" Lorana asked as she deciphered the patterns in the beadwork. She got Garth's harness on easily and smoothed it out, but Grenn insisted upon fluttering about her.

"What's got him so worked up?"

Lorana held out a hand to the fire-lizard and coaxed him close to her. She concentrated, focusing to sort through his confused images.

"There was a fight," she said at last. Then she looked accusingly at J'trel. "You were in it! Why didn't you say something?"

J'trel waved a hand. "A lout learned a lesson in manners. It was nothing."

"Nothing! At your age!" Lorana started to say more but snapped her attention back to the fire-lizard. Her eyes grew wide and her face paled as she turned back to the dragonrider. "J'trel, Garth never saw the man get up again. She watched for a long time."

The color drained out of J'trel's face. Before he could say anything, a man approached him, clapping him on the back.

It was Baror. "Well done, dragonrider! I hear you put a lout in his place!" He leered at the two of them, his eyes glazed with drink, "And I'd say, well in his place!" He slapped his mug in front of the dragonrider. "Have a drink on me!"

The seaman pulled up a chair close to the table. "I never knew you had it in you, to be honest. Of course, I knew you dragonriders are a tough lot, but I figured at your age—well, drink up!"

Ashen-faced, J'trel took a deep gulp from the cup Baror

proffered. Baror turned quickly away from the dragonrider toward his friend, hiding a smirk. "So, Lorana, I'll have to watch out for you as well, I'm sure! You keep sharp company, and that's no lie!

"Another round here!" he called out to the barman. "Drink up, dragonrider, this one's on me!"

Baror continued to ply the dragonrider with wine and offer commiseration—"You wasn't to know. And he did have it coming, didn't he, dragonrider?"—until even Lorana, who had been careful with her drink, began to feel bleary.

J'trel was still upset over the fight and its outcome, but was finding it harder and harder to raise his glass. "I should be going—"

Baror gave a grunt and stood bolt upright. "I think I see Captain Tanner over there!" He looked at the two of them. "I'll be right back."

Lorana patted the distraught dragonrider on the shoulder, trying to think of something to say.

Baror came back, bristling with purpose. "We've got to go now, Lorana! I spoke with the captain, and we're to set sail as soon as we can."

"I'll stay here," Lorana replied, looking at J'trel.

"No, no, you've got to go!" J'trel said, heaving himself to his feet. "I've got to get back to the Weyr and—" He staggered, leaning on the table for support.

"You've got to get some rest and see a healer," Lorana replied.

J'trel straightened up and pushed himself away from the table. "And I can do that best at the Weyr," he said. "Go on, get! I'll be awhile mending. I'll look for you as soon as I'm done."

Baror took in their words with a hidden sneer. "Stay if you want, I'm going."

Lorana glanced at him, and back at J'trel. "Wait!" she called to the retreating seaman. She gave the dragonrider a gentle hug and said, "I've told Talith to watch out for you."

J'trel forced a smile over the grimace of pain that her hug had caused him. "He always does."

In the distance, the blue dragon coughed. Lorana frowned, adding, "And keep an eye on that cough!" She pursed her lips. "I swear it's gotten worse."

With one last wave at him, she started after Baror.

The seaman carefully led her out the far side of the tent to avoid the crowd that was slowly gathering around another seaman spread out on the ground, knocked unconscious by a hard blow with a rock that lay nearby. Baror wondered if he had killed Tanner with the blow, but he didn't really care.

"My lord?" a voice whispered nervously into J'trel's ear. "My lord, it's very late."

J'trel stirred, and raised his head from the table even while wondering how it had got there. Except for the light of the lantern the man carried, it was pitch-dark.

Emboldened now that the dragonrider had stirred, the man said, "I've got to close up now, my lord."

Talith? For a terrible instant J'trel feared that something had happened to his dragon and that he'd find himself left all alone, with neither partner nor dragon. The sense of loss for K'nad, which had engulfed him after Lorana had rushed away, enveloped him like a thick shroud. His sense of dread grew as he waited longer and longer for his dragon to respond.

J'trel? Talith's voice came back to him without its usual warmth and strength. *I don't feel right.*

Instantly J'trel heard and felt his dragon's distress. With a wordless cry, he lurched to his feet, against the pain in his battered ribs, the drink-induced nausea, and the muzziness of an incipient hangover.

"My lord, are you all right?" the tavern man asked, hands fluttering from gestures of aid to gestures of entreaty.

"I've been better," J'trel replied with a trace of his usual humor. "But I'm all right."

He swiveled blearily toward an exit.

Talith waited in a nearby clearing. J'trel bit off a gasp of pain as he climbed up the dragon's side. J'trel could hear his dragon's breathing and noticed how strained it sounded.

You're hurt, Talith noted compassionately.

And you're—J'trel was going to say *tired* but suddenly realized that he meant *old*—and was shocked into silence. But Talith, from Turns of intimacy, guessed both the original and substitute words J'trel had not thought. The dragon rumbled softly in gentle agreement, and the rumble turned into a sharp cough.

As the blue launched into the cold night air, J'trel reminisced on the past several months. He had only planned to notify K'nad's next of kin. The pain of his partner's loss and age itself had taken too much of a toll on the old dragonrider.

There was too much pain—and his duties had been discharged. Some dissenting thought crossed his mind, but he couldn't focus on it. Talith coughed again, painfully.

I have made you tarry too long, old friend, J'trel said kindly to his lifelong mate. *You are tired.* I *am tired.* Talith rumbled soft agreement. *It is time.*

For a moment longer J'trel reflected on his life. *Give Lorana my love, old friend. She will carry on without us, I'm sure.*

After a moment the blue dragon responded, *I have told her.*

J'trel nodded. "Good. I am tired and it's time to rest."

Together, dragon and rider flashed one moment in the pale moonlight and were gone.

It is the duty of an Eridani Adept to preserve their assigned '-ome'.
— Excerpt from the Eridani Edicts

Chapter Four

Fort Hold, First Pass, Year 48, AL 56

As THE SOUND of breaking glass reached her ears over the booming of the message drums, Wind Blossom paused in her slow, steady hunt. She sighed and bid silent farewell to yet more precious glassware. *I was never good at this,* she thought sadly to herself. *The boy was worse than Emorra had ever been.*

Wind Blossom took a deep breath and turned toward the noise. Resolutely she overrode the creaks of her joints and the complaints of her muscles. Time—and medicine—on Pern were not what they had been: At seventy-nine, she felt more like a doddering ninety.

The sounds of the drums died as the message was completed—and the noise of breaking glass diminished, but not before Wind Blossom had located its source. It came from her own room. She opened the door but did not enter.

Hunched over the remains of a cabinet at one end of the room, Tieran panted. Tears streamed down his face. Wind Blossom noticed with sadness that his hands were bleeding in several places—again.

"Tieran?" Somehow she managed to modulate her voice to more than a croak. *For such small things are we grateful,* she thought to herself.

The lad, rangy and awkward in the midst of adolescence, turned away from her, but he did not continue in his destruction. Instead, he started picking his way across the shard-strewn floor toward the door.

Wind Blossom sighed inwardly with relief as she noticed that he at least had his boots on. The damage to his hands looked minor as well, she noted clinically.

As always, almost instinctively, he kept the right side of his face—the "good" side—toward her and tilted his neck in such a way that the lacerations on his nose looked their best.

Of all his injuries, the damage to the nose was the worst—at least for a sixteen-year-old boy who had to endure the pitying stares of his elders and the taunts or the silent shunning of his peers.

Wind Blossom knew that it was possible to repair the damage, once his face had finished growing. If she could learn the necessary skills. If she could find the necessary materials. If she could keep the necessary medicines. If she lived long enough.

They were in a three-legged race: waiting for him to grow up, striving to keep the medical supplies necessary, and hoping that she didn't grow too feeble to perform the surgery.

And they both knew they were losing.

Latrel could have done it, but that lab accident had cost him the use of his left thumb and, without it, he couldn't operate. Carelly had never progressed beyond competent nurse. Wind Blossom felt that she could train Tieran to do it—he had the skill—but he could not be both surgeon and patient.

"Where is it?" Tieran demanded in a rough, torn voice. Wind Blossom raised an eyebrow.

"Where is the antibiotic?" He glared at her.

"It is safe," Wind Blossom said.

"I want it," Tieran told her. He held out a hand. "Give it to me—now."

"Why now?"

Tieran's face crumpled. "He—he—he was under that rock slide for two days! The sepsis had set in long before they found him. The fever took him before I got there."

Wind Blossom shuddered. "He was a good man."

Tieran glared at her. "Give it to me! I'm going to find

someone—M'hall, someone—and we'll *time* it—don't think I don't know—and we'll save him. I need that medicine!"

"You cannot break time, Tieran," Wind Blossom said softly. "Not even for your father. There is no way."

Wind Blossom had taught Tieran that dragons could not only go instantaneously *between* places but also *between* times. The paradoxes and rules of time travel applied to dragons as much as to anything else that existed in the space-time continuum. It was impossible to go back in time in a manner that could alter events that had already occurred.

"You can't alter the past," Wind Blossom said.

Tieran's face crumpled and he leaned over and onto Wind Blossom. "You said he'd always be there. You said we'd always see each other. You said . . . And I wasn't there! I couldn't help him, I wasn't there!"

Drawing on her inner strength, Wind Blossom straightened her spine and held the lad while his sorrow and anger poured out.

"I shall miss him, too," Wind Blossom said after a while. "He was a good man. A good botanist, too. With more training—"

"Training! Is that how you measure a man?" Tieran demanded. "Is that how you see me? No scars, only an apt student? And what am I learning? A lost art, a dying way of doing things—all for your pleasure!"

"Your father wanted you to—"

"My father's dead," Tieran cut her off. "And now it's only you who wants me to learn all this genetic foolery. Splicing genes we can't see—the last electron microscope failed last year, or don't you remember?—for ends we don't know. We could introduce mutations without knowing about it, and for what? For nothing. A might be!"

Brutally he pushed away from her and stormed off down the corridor. Over his shoulder, from his left side, he called back, "You can get Emorra to clean that up. After all, you treat her like your slave."

Wind Blossom straightened up slowly. With an eye to the glass on the floor she walked over to her cot and sat upon it.

With eyes that would admit no tears, she muttered bitterly, "Such a way you have with children, Wind Blossom."

"Mother! What are you doing?" Emorra demanded as she strode into her mother's quarters.

"I am cleaning up," Wind Blossom replied from her position on the floor where she was delicately picking up individual shards of glass and depositing them into a recycling container.

"What happened? Where's Tieran?" Emorra asked.

"Tieran happened, and I do not know," Wind Blossom answered. She looked up at her tall daughter, careful not to let any pride show in her expression. "His father was dead before he arrived. He wanted to *time* it with some antibiotic to save him."

Emorra gasped, eyes wide. "That can't be done, can it?"

Wind Blossom sighed, using one of her better sighs. "It cannot, as you should well know."

"At least not in any literature," Emorra replied, her face heating as she caught her mother's implied rebuke. "Mother, what's the use of learning about temporal paradoxes when they can't occur? It's more important to pass on a good fundamental knowledge than to deal with such esoteric issues." Emorra found herself harping on her favorite issue and discovered, as always, that she couldn't help it with her mother. "Songs that people will sing and remember—an oral tradition, that's what we have to rely on."

"What's wrong with books?" Wind Blossom quipped.

Emorra frowned. "Mother, you know I love books," she said with a deep sigh. "But find me someone who's got the time to make them. Bookmaking is a labor-intensive industry, from the felling of trees to the making of inks and the binding of pages—things that are impossible to do when Thread is falling."

"So easy it is to blame Thread," Wind Blossom said. "Nothing can be done, so we'll sing about it."

Emorra stifled a groan and waved her hands in submission. "Let's not go through this again, please."

Wind Blossom nodded. She gestured to the recycling container. "This one's full; get me another."

Emorra frowned and leaned down to pick up the bucket. After she left, Wind Blossom pursed her lips tightly and held back a heartfelt sigh. Pain, she thought to herself, pain is how we grow. Is this how it was for you, Mother?

"Is there anything else I can get you?" Emorra asked, as she heaved herself up from the floor and grabbed the last bucketful of broken glass. She surveyed the floor carefully, looking for the reflection of any last shards.

"No, thank you," Wind Blossom said. Emorra's nostrils flared at her mother's dismissive tone but she said nothing, nodded curtly, and left, closing the door quietly.

"Well-trained," Wind Blossom muttered to herself. She kept her gaze on the door for a few moments, assuring herself that Emorra had indeed departed.

Then—a subtle shift, a slight relaxation, and the merest hint of a smile played on her lips. It was short-lived, chased away almost instantly by a frown.

"Your face is like a window," Kitti Ping's voice echoed in her mind. "I can see everything you think."

You see what I *want* you to see, Wind Blossom thought back to the ancient memory.

She moved to her dresser and opened the drawer with her tunics. Gently she lifted them and found the yellow one. Yes, she thought to herself, Purman would like this.

She pulled the tunic out of the drawer along with the small bag she'd carefully hidden underneath it. She quickly shrugged off her regular tunic and pulled on the yellow one. Then she took the bag and walked over to the laboratory end of her room.

The room was huge and had been a supply room when the Fever Year had hit. Wind Blossom had occupied it in the haste of those deadly days and had never been asked to leave. She lived simply in the room, with only a bed, a dresser, and a bedside table for her comfort. The far side of the room was given up to her laboratory and studies. She liked the room because of the large windows running floor to ceiling on one side.

She opened a locked door in her tall cabinet and pulled out a crucible, ancient ceramic tripod, and grazier. She put these on the workbench along with the bag from her drawer and another bag she had pulled out from the cabinet.

She eyed a stool and shook her head slightly, grabbing her things off the workbench and putting them on the floor beyond it, concealed from the window by the large workbench.

She fished a small lump of charcoal out of the second bag and placed it on the grazier. She lit it quickly, her fingers well-practiced, and slid the tripod stand over it. Into the crucible she placed a selection of herbs from the bag she had taken from her drawer. After a moment, she pulled a number of strands of hair out of her scalp and curled them up into the crucible.

Satisfied, she placed the crucible on the tripod and let the flames of the charcoal lick at it.

I am glad you decided not to join us here at the College, Wind Blossom admitted silently to her memory of Purman. *You would have been welcome, but I do not know if you would have accepted the course I've chosen for us all.*

It will be thousands of years before our descendants will once more be able to bend genes to their will, she mused. *It would be a mistake to force our children to cling to our ways. They need to move on, to learn their own ways.*

"Make your own mistakes," Kitti Ping's voice echoed in Wind Blossom's mind.

The Eridani Way is not the only way, she thought, partly in response to her mother's words. *Their thinking is deep, but they never thought of war. They never thought of the Nathi. They never thought of a time when no one could twist genes into new shapes.*

Wind Blossom's eyes flicked to the crucible and she brought her thoughts back to Purman. *Your way, the way of breeding, will work on Pern for now.*

She sighed. It had been difficult to turn Emorra against her. So difficult that she had only half-succeeded: Her daughter had remained at the College and even become its dean. It had taken less effort to drive Tieran away from her, to quench his inbred curiosity about genetics.

In both situations, she had felt all the pain of a mother turning away her child. But Wind Blossom knew that if she taught them the joy she found in genetics, they would be enraptured—and stuck with knowledge they couldn't use. Committed, as the Eridani had always intended, to the Eridani Way, the way of countless generations husbanding species and planets, they would become incapable of developing solutions of their own.

Wind Blossom's head shook imperceptibly as she recalled her own internal conflicts, how she had determined that the future of Pern could not rest on the shoulders of a few, select bloodlines—the Eridani Way—but on the actions of all Pernese.

As the last of the smoke rose from the crucible, Wind Blossom wondered again if Ted Tubberman had thought the same thing, and if he had turned his son against him just as Kitti Ping had turned her daughter against her—and as Wind Blossom herself had tried to alienate Emorra.

"Shards!" Tieran groaned as he discovered that he had outgrown his latest hiding place. Hiding was second nature to him. He had always liked the caves and tunnels of his Benden Hold home, particularly when—he suppressed a pang of regret, fear, anger, sorrow—he had been with Bendensk, the watch-wher.

When he had first come to the College, it had been easier: He'd been small for his age and always won at hide-and-seek. Until one day he had realized that no one was looking for him anymore—that they were laughing instead. "Hide-away." "No-nose." "Scarface."

After that he had spent more time with Wind Blossom. Truth be told, he loved to learn all the secrets she had to teach him. He was one of only five people on all of Pern who had looked at human DNA under the electron microscope. And he was one of three—no, two, now—who could trace a

mutation back to its genes. Wind Blossom said that soon she
would start him on proteomics, the study of proteins.

Tieran snorted. As if *that* would impress anyone! In fact,
there was probably no one on Pern who knew what proteomics was, let alone what it was used for. It was all a waste.
He was only here because *she* wanted him to be here, waiting
until he was "ready" for the operations to fix his face.

The sob that threatened to break from his throat was throt-
tled in the harshest of self-control. The boys he could handle;
he'd learned enough of hand-fighting from M'hall and—he
grimaced—his father. But the girls—lately Tieran had noticed them. Noticed them and noticed how quickly they looked
away, walked away, grouped together, speaking in hushed
voices.

Admit it, Tieran thought, no matter how great a surgeon
you become, no matter what you do, even if Wind Blossom
can perform a miracle, no girl is going to look at you.

Except maybe to laugh.

And now his last hiding place was too small. Tieran stifled
a curse—not because he was afraid of swearing, but because
he was afraid the curse might come out as a sob.

Voices approached in the dark. Tieran pulled himself into
a shadowy nook.

"How did the boy take it, then?" Tieran recognized the
rich tenor voice as that of Sandell, a student musician. Some
Turns back they had played together—hide-and-seek.

"It was hard on him," Emorra answered. "It must be hard
to lose a father."

"Don't you remember yours?" Sandell asked.

"No." Emorra paused. "In fact, it's been Turns since I last
asked mother about him. She never told me anything."

Sandell laughed. "I'll bet he was a musician, and that's
why she hates us."

Emorra snorted. "That would explain where I got my talent."

"And your looks," Sandell added softly. From the sound of
clothing and the soft noises, Tieran guessed that Sandell had

taken Emorra in his arms. He peered around the corner. They were kissing!

Tieran ducked back again as Emorra pushed away from the journeyman.

"Not here," Emorra said. "Someone might see us."

Sandell laughed. "So let them!"

"No," Emorra said firmly.

"Very well, Dean Emorra," Sandell replied indulgently. "Your quarters or mine?"

Tieran relaxed as he heard them depart.

The loud sound of drums—he guessed it was Jendel up on the big drum—rattled out an attention signal. Tieran heard the response from the four outlying stations and, almost on top of their response, the College drums sounded out their message in deep commanding booms. It was the sign-off for the evening; no other message would go out until morning, except in an emergency.

Tieran listened to the details, his throat clenched as he heard the report of his father's death being passed on down to all the minor holds along the way equipped with either a drummer or a repeater station. The drums fell silent, were echoed by the repeater stations farther on and, very faintly, by the stations beyond those, and then the sounds of evening took over the night air.

With a quick breath and a determined spring in his step, Tieran turned to the Drum Tower—his new hiding place.

Fierce winds blow.
Seas roil.
Calm, wind. Settle, sea.
Let my loved return to me.

Chapter Five

On the WIND RIDER at sea, Second Interval, AL 507

THE WIND WAS gusting as they weighed anchor. When they cleared the harbor, *Wind Rider* heeled so much that Baror called for them to reduce sail.

With the sail reset, *Wind Rider* still heeled over at a fierce angle, her bow breaking through the waves as she sped into the moonlit night.

Within an hour the offshore breeze had been supplanted by gusting winds, and the moons were lost in a haze of clouds. Five minutes after that the first of the rain fell upon them.

An hour later the ship was in a full gale, heeling hard over with two men fighting the helm and four men struggling to furl sail.

Colfet found Baror at the wheel with another man he'd never seen before. He shouted over the roar of the wind, "Where's the captain? This sail's all wrong for this weather, we're heeling too hard. We need to alter course, too—see how she's digging into the waves? We'll broach to if we don't."

"The captain's not here," Baror replied, teeth wide in a grin.

"I can see that," Colfet responded irritably. "Where is he?" He looked forward. "Is he forward with the sails?"

"No, you git, he's not here," Baror responded, his grin disappearing in a frown. "Left me in charge, seeing as you've got that bum wing."

Another gust spun the ship and Baror gripped the wheel, calling to the other man to help out.

Colfet gestured at the new man. "Who's he?"

Baror grinned. "New man I signed on at Half-Circle." He waved at the new man. "Vilo's his name."

Another gust heeled the ship over as *Wind Rider* plowed into a wave.

"We've got to let her have her head!" Colfet called. "Get the sails off, put out a storm anchor, and ride it out!"

Baror shook his head. "No, we'll keep our course. I'll show that pansy Istan how real men sail."

Colfet started to argue, but at that moment two men climbed up the hatchway. Both looked green and unseamanly. He started to make a rude comment to Baror but stopped as he got a good sight of the second man.

"Who's on the pumps?" he asked.

"You might want to check on that," Baror replied, keeping his eyes on the two landlubbers as they made their way toward him.

"All right," Colfet said, heading for the hatchway. He nodded grimly at the two greenies as they passed him by. "Gentle night, isn't it?" he asked with wry humor. The two made no attempt to respond.

Once they were out of sight, Colfet's expression hardened. He paused at the top of the hatch, looking back at Baror and his cronies. "Baror!" he shouted. He had to repeat himself twice before he was heard. "We should trail the launch—in case anyone goes overboard."

Baror grinned evilly. "Anyone overboard in this'll stay overboard."

"All the same."

Baror squinted at him and then nodded. "All right. I'll get some men to it."

Colfet nodded and, watching his bandaged arm, plunged into the darkness belowdecks. Quickly and carefully he made his way down to the depths of the ship and sounded the well. He could hear the pumps in the distance and grunted with surprise as he discovered that *Wind Rider* had made less than a foot of water. Still, it wasn't all good news—he'd never seen more than an inch before.

Having satisfied himself that the ship wasn't going to sink any time soon, unless that fool Baror ran her under the waves, he made his way aft to the surgeon's quarters.

A cry, loud and inarticulate, pierced through the noise of the storm.

Colfet raced back to the surgeon's quarters. Inside he found Lorana, sprawled across her desk. Two fire-lizards chittered inside, their tone changing to anger as he entered.

"There's trouble!" Colfet said. Lorana looked up at him: Her eyes were full of tears. "Lass, what's wrong?"

"He's gone," she replied. "J'trel and Talith have gone *between* forever."

Wind Rider bucked abruptly as it plowed into a wave and rolled sharply as it paid off, throwing Lorana across the table and Colfet out of the cabin.

Colfet let out a curse as his full weight crashed against his broken arm.

"You're hurt!" Lorana exclaimed, trying to reach him.

"No time for that," Colfet said. "We've got to get to the captain's cabin."

"Why?"

"We've got to get you off this ship," Colfet said. "Baror's left Captain Tanner behind, and I can't think he means you well." He made a face. "Baror's got a nasty way with women. If you don't leave now, while he's distracted, you may not leave at all." He looked at the fire-lizards. "Can you make them wait by the launch?"

"What's that?" Lorana asked.

"That's the boat we used today to get to shore," Colfet explained. "Baror's going to lower it astern."

"Why would he do that?"

"I asked him," Colfet said, grinning. "In case anyone fell

overboard in this blow." His grin widened. "We'll just 'fall overboard' right now."

"Oh."

"Can you make them wait?" Colfet asked again.

"I can try." Lorana said, turning to the two fire-lizards. Garth and Grenn both chittered obstinately before Lorana overcame their disagreement and they disappeared *between*.

"Good, now let's get to the captain's cabin before Baror has a chance to send some men after you."

Lorana paused at the doorway. "What about you? Why are you doing this for me?"

Colfet gave her a measuring look. "You might say that I owe you, for fixing this arm. Or you might say that I won't let anyone be taken against their will. But mostly I'm thinking of my daughters."

Lorana didn't know what to say.

Colfet shrugged. "Come on, then, off with you."

The captain's cabin was the next cabin aft. The door was unlocked and they made their way through the fore cabin and into the after cabin. Colfet opened the shutters quickly and peered out. Seeing what he wanted, he grunted affirmatively and then looked around the cabin.

"We've got to find something to grab the line," he said.

"Grab the line?" Lorana echoed, looking at the opening. All she could see was rain and pitch-darkness. "What line?"

"The one for the launch," Colfet answered, upending the captain's chair. He reached out through the opening and hooked the rope with the seat of the chair, carefully angling to keep the rope from slipping off. Dragging it into the cabin he turned to Lorana.

"Now all you've got to do is climb down this rope into the launch."

Lorana eyed the bucking rope. "All?"

Colfet nodded. "It's that or wait until Baror and his mates have time to deal with you. You can't stay on this ship, they'll turn it upside down looking for you." He saw her blanch and added, "Look, all you have to do is grab it with your feet and your arms and scale on down. Don't let go until you're in the launch. The wind's fierce enough that it won't drop you in the water, I hope."

"And if it does?"

"Keep hold of the rope and climb aboard the launch," Colfet said. "But don't capsize it."

"All right, and then what?" Lorana demanded. "What about you?"

Colfet thought about that. "It'll be too tricky with my bad arm."

Lorana shook her head. "I don't know where we are, how to get back—anything." She looked frantically around the cabin, finally coming back to him. "Your belt! How about you tie on with that and come on down after me! It'd help when you have trouble with your arm."

Colfet smiled. "It would at that. You're right, it could work. Very well then, you first."

Lorana swallowed and reached for the rope. She climbed out the opening and jumped up, looping her feet desperately around the rope. For one sick moment she hung there, suspended by hands and feet on a wildly swinging rope, and then she gripped it tighter and started climbing down into the darkening sea.

It seemed to take forever. Suddenly a wave swept up at her, dowsing her backside with frigid water. She clenched the rope tightly, for fear of being pulled off. Then the wave was gone and she started down again.

Beyond her legs she caught sight of a blob in the distance. The launch. It seemed dragonlengths away.

Another gust came and a wave crashed around her, burying her in water. She held her breath, frantically hoping that she could hold on. Finally the water parted around her.

Her feet felt the hard wood of the launch.

Colfet's glib description of how she would get in the launch turned out to be completely inaccurate. Lorana had to pull her feet over the gunnels and into the cockpit of the launch, and then she had to grapple with the prow with her hands and turn herself over before she could kneel into the launch. It was a hideous maneuver and she nearly lost her last meal as her stomach roiled from the exertion and her fear.

Two encouraging chirps told her that she'd made it, and that the fire-lizards were nearby.

She waited for what seemed forever before she realized that she and Colfet had not agreed on any way to let him know that she was safely aboard. Hastily she grabbed the rope and gave it two sharp tugs. She waited and felt two answering tugs—Colfet must have got the signal.

Or *was* Colfet still there? What if Barór had gone searching for her and had found out their plan? What if it wasn't Colfet but someone else coming down the rope?

Lorana eyed the rope and studied how it was tied to the launch. She looked around and found a knife in the stores locker. If she had to, she could cut the rope in a moment.

Looking across the bucking sea to the high stern of *Wind Rider*, she saw the outline of a form climbing down toward her. Was it Colfet? She thought she saw his bandage, now hopelessly soaked. She peered forward, squinting. With a sigh of relief, she realized it was Colfet.

A wave crashed over him and he lost his grip on the rope. Lorana stifled a cry as he hung by his feet and his belt. In an instant Garth and Grenn launched themselves toward him, each grabbing an arm and flapping frantically to help him reach the rope again. A wave engulfed them.

For a long, terrible instant Lorana was afraid all three had been swept away. She imagined countless days adrift in the small launch with only that horrid memory to dwell upon. And then the wave broke and Colfet had his good hand back on the rope, and the two fire-lizards were circling above him, chirping encouragingly.

Lorana bit her lip as Colfet's legs came within reach. Belatedly she found some rope and tied herself to the launch. Then she moved forward and did all she could to help Colfet clamber aboard.

"There, that wasn't hard, was it?" Colfet said through gasps as he finally righted himself in the bow of the launch.

"Have you got a knife?" When Lorana nodded, he said, "Then cut that line and let's be out of here."

C'rion turned at the sound of feet entering the meeting room. The dragons had only finished their keening. J'lantir, ashen-faced, stood in the entranceway. Silently, C'rion gestured him in.

"C'rion, I'm sorry—"

C'rion shook his head. "He was old," he said. "I'm sure he wanted the rest."

J'lantir pursed his lips, still shaken. "If I'd kept a better eye on him—"

"You did the right thing," C'rion said. "J'trel made his choice."

J'lantir shook his head sadly. "I'm surprised, though," the Wingleader said after a moment. "He was quite enamored of his current project."

C'rion looked puzzled and made a "go on" gesture.

"Apparently he'd met some young lady—rescued her, in fact—and had taken a great interest in her drawing abilities."

C'rion raised an eyebrow.

"J'trel always appreciated women," J'lantir explained, "even if he didn't *appreciate* women."

"Just as Talith was the best on Search," C'rion agreed.

"Just so," J'lantir said, nodding. "Apparently he took this one under his wing and set her aboard that new ship, *Wind Rider.*"

"Why?"

"From what I've gathered at the sea hold, the girl was planning on drawing all the plant and animal life she could find from Nerat Tip to Tillek Head," J'lantir replied.

The Istan Weyrleader pursed his lips in a silent whistle. "That *would* be quite something," he said appreciatively.

"And she's good, too," J'lantir continued. "One of her drawings is on display at Ista Hold."

"Someone should find her and give her the news," C'rion said.

J'lantir nodded. "I'll take care of that."

"Good," C'rion replied. "And—I'm sorry. He was a good man."

J'lantir sighed. "He was old," he responded. "I don't think he'd want to be old when Thread falls again."

"Some of us have no choice," C'rion said softly.

Colfet's cry of pain startled Lorana from her half-rest. She pulled away from him, the cold fog digging deeper into her bones, and realized ruefully that she had been the cause of his discomfort. In her sleepy desire to get warmer, she'd wrapped her arm over his chest and had disturbed his broken limb.

The cold dug deeper into her, but Lorana forced herself to search out the fire-lizards before she settled, carefully, once more against Colfet. Garth and Grenn huddled miserably on the floorboards beneath them.

They looked only a little less wet and bedraggled than they had been in the worst of the storm. Lorana had pleaded, scolded, cursed, and shoved at them in a vain effort to get them to seek safety, but they had remained steadfast. They made her aware of their fear that if they left, they would not be able to find her again in the storm—and they would not abandon her.

Colfet's eyes fluttered open and he bent his head toward her, looking for a question.

"I nudged your arm," Lorana said softly. "Sorry."

He made a wordless sound through his shivers. He tried again: "C-c-cold."

Lorana snuggled against him, placing as much of her body as she dared on top of him, careful of the roll of the little launch and of his broken arm.

His cast had disintegrated before the first hour of the storm had passed. He had banged the break painfully as he'd wrestled a storm anchor over the stern. When the storm anchor had torn loose hours later, he had insisted upon bailing with both arms, as he and Lorana had fought to keep the launch from foundering.

He had so injured and worn himself out that by the time

they had bailed out the worst of the water, he was incapable of setting another storm anchor and had to shout instructions to Lorana until he lost his voice.

Lorana had made two mistakes in setting the new storm anchor: She'd used their oars; and she'd tied them to the tiller. When a particularly violent gust had nearly scuppered the launch, the resulting drag had torn not only the oars but also the tiller off of the stern.

When the storm broke and the fog had replaced it, Lorana had made a new storm anchor out of the launch's boom.

"Storm coming," Colfet said drowsily. "Two, maybe three hours away."

Lorana glanced about. Yes, there was a wisp of wind—and it was cold.

The storm engulfed the launch without warning. Lorana found herself grabbing the fire-lizards and shoving them down behind Colfet in a hectic instant, blinded by the sea spray and drenching rain. She barely had time to brace herself in the bottom of the launch before the little boat was whipped violently around by the fierce winds of the new storm.

After that, time ceased to exist. Lorana was tossed about, frozen, inundated with freezing rain and roiling sea.

When the water level got too high in the boat, she started bailing, desperately fighting the incoming rain and sea, all the while terrified that one more wave would sink them. When Garth and Grenn tried to help her, she cursed them.

"Go! Go!" she wailed at them. Garth's mouth opened in response but her voice was lost on the wind. Lorana didn't need to hear the fire-lizard to recognize her stubborn resolve. Grenn hadn't even bothered to slow down in his efforts.

Nor did Lorana. Still bailing, she grieved at the thought of her fire-lizards needlessly sacrificing themselves for her. Numbly she tried to organize new arguments to convince them to leave her.

"Lorana!" Colfet's hoarse voice barely rose above the howl of the storm, and the warning came too late for her to do anything. The launch heeled horribly, nearly capsizing as it was tossed by a sudden swell.

Lorana knew instantly that the sea anchor had torn loose. She dropped the bailer. The only thing left to use was the launch's mast. She bent down and started untying the stays that had kept it secure, all the while tossed horribly as the launch lurched on the sea.

Finally, she got the mast secured to the stern of the launch and was ready to place it overboard.

As she kneeled to push the mast out over the stern, another wave hit the bow of the launch and Lorana tumbled overboard.

In an instant the launch was lost from her sight. A wave crashed over her, submerging her. She returned to the surface gasping for breath, frozen to the core.

"Lorana!" Colfet shouted from the distance.

"No!" Lorana shouted back, but the wind whipped her words away.

Flitters of brown and gold appeared above her, battling the wind to avoid being slammed into the sea.

"Go away!" Lorana shouted at them. "Save yourselves!"

Garth and Grenn ignored her, diving to grab at her hair and yanking painfully on it. The pain was nothing compared to Lorana's outraged grieving that her two fire-lizards would waste themselves for her.

"Go!" she shouted again, trying to bat away their hold on her hair. Something bumped into her and she grabbed at it. It was the mast. Lorana closed her eyes against tears. Colfet must have cut the mast free, hoping it would get to her as a float. Her wail was inarticulate. He had thrown away his life for hers.

I'm not worth it, she told herself. He'll die, Garth and Grenn will die—all for nothing. Me.

Arms wrapped around the mast for support, Lorana caught her breath. The sea rose all around her. Lightning flashed in the distance. She was doomed.

"Garth," she said, her words a whisper echoing her thoughts as she tried to find the gold fire-lizard in the air above her. "Grenn. You must go. Leave me. Find someone else. I can't survive this and I can't bear the thought of you dying with me."

She felt a wash of steadfast warmth from the two fire-lizards in response. They would not leave her. They would not abandon her.

Anger shook her. They would *die* if they stayed with her. And it would be such a waste.

"You must go!" Lorana's voice carried above the roar of the storm. Feeling her heart stiffen, she hardened her will and thrust it at the two fire-lizards. *Go!*

Garth and Grenn shrieked in the night sky. A flash of lightning peeled across the sky. Lorana gathered all her strength, felt herself like a thunderbolt, and threw herself at the fire-lizards. *Go!*

Somewhere safe, Lorana thought. Somewhere where you'll be loved. Another flash of lightning lit the sky, and again she pushed the fire-lizards away from her. *Go!*

And they were gone. Lorana heaved a sigh that was more like a whimper and laid her head on the mast. Safe, she thought. At least I've saved them.

As she lay there, she felt the last of the warmth and comfort the fire-lizards had given her fade away, like a lost dream. And then, as she drifted into a numbed sleep, at the very end, Lorana thought she felt something—an answering warmth at the end of the long tunnel that connected her to Garth and Grenn. A frozen smile played across her lips. Good, she thought dimly, someone will take care of them.

Terrome: (i) the biological portion of the ecosystem of Terra, the third planet of solar system Sol; (ii) the information and materials required to produce a functioning ecosystem based on the Terran ecosystem. (See terraforming.)
—*Glossary of terms,* Ecosystems: From -ome to Planet, 24th Edition

Chapter Six

Fort Hold, First Pass, Year 50, AL 58

SUNLIGHT STREAMED through the room, bathing Wind Blossom's cot in warmth. Wind Blossom woke, startled by the sun. You should have been up hours ago, she chided herself.

Her old, stiff bones resisted her efforts to rise quickly. Wind Blossom forced herself up anyway. With a deep, relaxing sigh she began her morning exercises.

As she completed her exercises, the Drum Tower boomed out an alert. She wondered if the drummer were Tieran. She had only seen him fleetingly in the two years since his father had died and he'd fled to the Drum Tower. He'd be eighteen now, near his full growth, and quite capable of pounding the drums as loud as they were being pounded now.

Wind Blossom tensed, then relaxed again immediately as she recognized why she had slept so late: The Drum Tower had been silent. With this realization, she knew why the tower had been silent earlier and what its message now would be—Threadfall.

That also explained why her newest trainee had failed to wake her this morning: The young lady was helping prepare the HNO_3 tanks for the ground crews, whose job it was to search out stray Thread missed by the dragons and burn it before it could burrow into the ground.

Wind Blossom's place was in the infirmary, to deal with any mishaps beyond the expertise of her alumni. She changed with a conservative haste and proceeded down the stairs, clutching the railing carefully; it would not do to let rushing make her the first patient of the day.

One of the new trainees—Mirlan, Wind Blossom thought it was—saw her approach and strode over to offer a hand.

Wind Blossom snatched her own hand away from the proffered support. "I am not enfeebled, child!" she said, bitter that the whole effect was spoiled by her scratchy voice.

"I do need something to drink, however," she added as soon as she could trust her voice again.

Mirlan escorted her to Admissions and then hurried off for some food and drink.

Janir—when had he gotten so tall?—approached her.

"The current pool is guessing that there'll be two severe, one minor, and three stupidities this Fall," he said, his eyebrows quirking with amusement. Long ago Wind Blossom had started a guessing game with the students to help prepare them for those wounded in Threadfall. Long ago it had ceased to be amusing to Wind Blossom. But it was still educational, so she pretended to enjoy it.

"Two minor, two stupidities," Wind Blossom guessed. Janir pursed his lips speculatively.

"Is that a wager?" a new voice asked. Wind Blossom turned to see Josten, another of the new ones, appear behind her.

"If it is, it is between myself and the senior surgeon," Wind Blossom replied. She noticed that the room had fallen silent. Mirlan returned with some food.

"This Threadfall will last six hours, yes?" Wind Blossom asked rhetorically. Around her, heads nodded.

"Is all the equipment ready?" Again, heads nodded.

"Then is there any reason why you should not be studying?" she asked the collected group. Janir suppressed a grin of remembrance and added his scowl to hers. Hastily the others in the room filed out in search of texts or to work together in groups, practicing various injuries.

"I shall inspect later," Wind Blossom said. Janir's eyes darkened. Wind Blossom noticed it. "What?"

"Um, my lady—"

"Spit it out, Janir."

"Don't you remember?" Janir looked embarrassed. Wind Blossom frowned. "After the last Threadfall we had agreed that I should run the infirmary and you would consult."

Wind Blossom started to respond, then froze. After a moment she continued, "Of course. May I speak with you alone?"

Janir nodded and gestured to his examining room.

Once inside, Wind Blossom turned to him and said in a toneless voice, "Janir, it appears that I am beginning to exhibit signs of senile dementia. Do you concur?"

Janir closed his eyes briefly, a look of pain lining his face, then nodded. "My lady, this is the second time you've told me that."

Outwardly, Wind Blossom absorbed this news like a rock; inwardly she reeled like a reed in a storm. "I see. When was the first time?"

"Only last Threadfall, my lady," Janir replied. "Since then, you've exhibited no memory problems. Perhaps the stress?"

"Threadfall should not be stressful for me."

Janir disagreed. "Threadfall itself is not stressful but, as you yourself said, we must anticipate a number of injuries—I think that is very stressful for you, my lady."

"Yes, I believe that is so," Wind Blossom said. *My mind! I am losing my mind!* She took a deep, calming breath. "But I am alarmed at the possible implications."

Janir gave her an apologetic look. "We've been keeping an eye on you, my lady, to be safe."

Wind Blossom pursed her lips and nodded. "Thank you. I was considering the broader implication to our aging population. I had expected that we would retain our faculties well through the late eighties, perhaps even our nineties."

Janir nodded. "You said this the last time, my lady."

Wind Blossom was so troubled by that answer that it took her a second to regain her composure. "I have no memory of that. What else did I say?"

Janir sighed. "When we talked, we agreed that while some of the early-onset dementia might be due to increased stress, it was more likely that it was due to differences in diet."

"There could be other factors, too," Wind Blossom said. "Could there be environmental factors?"

"You were concerned that there might be trace elements present or missing in our food that might affect memory and neural function," Janir replied.

"We should perform some biopsies on any new cadavers," Wind Blossom said. Janir gave her a long, discerning look, and she shook her head. "I do remember that we do not have the facilities to maintain a morgue. But if we could get to a corpse early enough, we could obtain some samples."

"I agree, my lady," Janir replied. "Sadly, our older population was depleted during the Fever Years and reports of death usually come after the burial has already taken place."

"We would need to locate a cadaver nearby," Wind Blossom agreed.

"And if we did, my lady, what then?" Janir asked gently. "Do we have the equipment to identify the contributing factors?"

A number of scathing arguments sprang into Wind Blossom's mind. With a kick of her will, she disposed of them. She then spent some moments in deep thought. Finally, she answered, "I think you will say that our staff does not have time to do such extensive studies, and that we could gain more working on solving infant mortality problems."

Janir shook his head, a small grin on his lips. "Actually, my lady, you said that in our last conversation. I have to agree, however. Given our current population it is vitally important to ensure that it grows as rapidly as possible. Our biggest gains will be in improving survival through early childhood."

Wind Blossom nodded. "And while the young represent

new cultural capital, the elderly increasingly become a drain on our precious resources."

"You said that, too," Janir said gently. "But I would like to disagree with you on that score. I have always admired you and wished that I could learn more from you."

Wind Blossom smiled and patted his hand. "You were a good student, Janir."

"Thank you, my lady," Janir said, gripping her hand with his.

Wind Blossom turned to leave. "I think I'll review my notes in my room." As Janir nodded understanding, she added, "If you need me—"

"I will be sure to send someone for you, my lady," Janir finished. He bit his lip reflectively. "I hope you are not too concerned about the memory loss. It is concentrated in your short-term and recent memories." Wind Blossom turned back to face him as he continued, "Your knowledge of genetics is as good as it ever was and should remain so."

"Yes," Wind Blossom replied, turning back to the door, "but I am trying to learn reconstructive facial surgery, Janir."

She left before the embarrassed healer could form any reply.

Tieran leaned into his stroke as he beat out the all clear. He had filled out and muscled up from the awkward sixteen-year-old he'd been when he first joined the tower. Now, at eighteen, his body was lean and tightly muscled from daily work.

He grinned as he heard his drumbeats echoing back along the cliff wall that housed Fort Hold. The echo didn't mask the responses from the higher-pitched walking drummers in the surrounding minor holds and fields.

Jendel had been right to argue for siting the Drum Tower built between Fort Hold and the College. The shape of the cliffs made a natural reflector that concentrated the sound of his drum.

Because the location left the Large Drum exposed to all elements and particularly susceptible to Thread, it was secured in one of the rooms beside the Drum Tower during Threadfall. Jendel had made a habit of drilling his drummers in disassembling and reassembling the Large Drum. Tieran and Rodar, working as a team, had set the best time.

Tieran had come to the Drum Tower at a propitious time. The tower had only been completed a month before, and Jendel had still been experimenting with the best way to use the drums. Tieran had quickly learned the original code, mastered it, and developed a second, superior set of drum codes that Jendel and the rest of the drummers had enthusiastically adopted.

When Tieran had first escaped to the Drum Tower, he had expected to be unceremoniously hauled back to Wind Blossom. It had been half a year before he had allowed himself to believe that he had been left to fend for himself. It had taken him much longer to recognize that his place within the College was secure.

Tieran took advantage of his lofty and panoramic position to drink in the sights and sounds below him. When he was up here, two stories high and several dragonlengths from both the College and the Hold, no one could really see his face. From the heights of the Drum Tower, Tieran felt master of all he surveyed.

He saw Lord Holder Mendin on his way to the College— so soon after a Fall? Shifting his gaze, he saw Mendin's eldest son, Leros, hot and weary, trudging in from the fields surrounded by flamethrower crews, apparently doing the job that his father should have been doing. Studying the two, he failed to notice Jendel's jaunty step until the head drummer was halfway up the stairs to the tower.

"Tieran!" Jendel called out as he crested the stairs. Without pausing for breath, he continued, "You're needed back at the College. See Dean Emorra."

Tieran raised his eyebrows momentarily in surprise, then placed the huge drumsticks back on their hooks and reached for his shirt.

"Bring lunch for us when you come back," Jendel added

as Tieran started down the stairs. "And Kassa—you two will relieve us."

"All right," Tieran called back unheard over his shoulder with an acknowledging wave of his hand. There were always two on the Drum Tower.

Classes, Tieran guessed to himself as he crossed under the archway into the College. He made his way to the small classroom reserved for the drummers.

Emorra was waiting for him outside the door. "I want you to teach some of the youngsters drum code."

Tieran cocked an eyebrow at her. When he had first been asked to teach, just after he had proved the value of his new codes to Jendel, he had been afraid of standing in front of a group of people with his scarred face and gangly body. But the first group had all been older students in their twenties, and they had all been intent on one thing: learning the new codes. Once he realized that, Tieran had thrown himself with enthusiasm and creativity into the job of imparting the new codes to them.

After several classes, Tieran had realized that some of the drummers weren't learning the codes to work in the Drum Tower or in Mendin's outlying minor holds. Some of the older students had left the College, taking their knowledge of the drum codes with them.

Others had been even more enterprising. They had taken their knowledge of the drum codes and brought them back to the music that many considered to be the life and the soul of the College. Emorra had told him that his codes had not developed into a new form of music. Rather, the drumming had allowed musicians to create new works both of jazz and of traditional old-Earth Celtic music. Tieran had been surprised, then pleased, and, finally, an enthusiastic participant in the music that had resulted.

Emorra recognized Tieran's raised eyebrow with a nod. "I was wondering if working with drums and the drum codes might be a good way to teach musical beat."

Tieran nodded, trying to hide his hesitation, but Emorra noticed it.

"They're a good group; I just had them," she told him, handing him a small drum.

Tieran's heart sank as Emorra left. He hefted the drum, placed it under one arm, and absently beat out a quick tattoo— "trouble." Inspiration struck, and he quickly amplified the beat and modified it.

He entered the room still drumming and took his place at the front of the class. There were eleven students in the class. All of them were young—the eldest hardly looked eleven and the youngest was close to seven years old. This was the youngest class he'd ever seen.

He switched the beat, changed the rhythm, and started a new message, still while watching his students. Two or three were unconsciously trying to imitate his beat on their drums and all of them were attentive.

With a flourish, Tieran finished his message and set the drum down on the teacher's table. He looked at the youngsters. "Now that I've said all that, are there any questions?"

The eyes of the youngsters widened and there was silence in the classroom until one of the older girls raised her hand. Tieran grinned and nodded at her.

"What did you say?" she asked.

"I told you my name and welcomed you to the class on drumming, and asked you why you were here," he answered. "Would you like to learn how?"

Every head in the class nodded, eyes wide. Tieran kept his smile to himself and started teaching the basics of drumbeat and rhythm.

He was pleased to finish the lesson on a high note, having the class drum out the message "It's lunchtime" just in time with the sounding of the hour.

"And with that, class, I take my leave," he told them. The youngsters were very polite. Most of them came up to him and thanked him for the class and told him that they hoped he'd be teaching them again.

Emorra was waiting outside the class. She fell in with him as he walked toward the kitchen. "I take it you survived, then?"

Tieran nodded. "Nice kids."

"Would you be willing to teach them again?"

"Sure."

With a frustrated groan, Emorra whirled around in front of him, forcing him to stop. "And?"

Startled, Tieran's first thought was to realize suddenly that he was taller than Emorra—and that he liked that. "What?"

Emorra gritted her teeth, then sighed to regain her temper. "Every class is a lesson for the teacher."

Tieran nodded. "I've heard you say that before. I guess it makes sense."

"So," she asked with a tone of strained patience in her voice, "what did you learn today?"

"I guess that I might be able to teach younger students," Tieran said.

Emorra's eyes flashed. Tieran had seen that look before, and always when she was frustrated, usually in debates when she was about to make a telling point.

He raised his hands in surrender. "What do you think I would have learned?"

Emorra shook her head, dismissing his question. Ever since Tieran had hidden up in the Drum Tower he had become something of a project for her. The young man's rebellion against her mother had sparked Emorra's interest in him. Her interest had increased when she had learned that Tieran had developed the improved drum codes. When she had discovered how much his teenaged feelings of not belonging had been reinforced by reactions to his scarred face, she had tried to find ways to help.

Tieran's stomach grumbled. With an apologetic shrug, he stepped around Emorra and gestured for her to follow as he resumed his way to the kitchen.

"You're worried about me," he said after a moment's silence.

Emorra nodded. "I worry about everyone."

Tieran snorted. "Then you worry too much."

"It's my job! Like everything else on Pern, the College has to earn its keep. So the students pay tuition and the teachers are paid for their research. And any profits are put into new projects."

"Like the Drum Tower—I know," Tieran said.

They reached the kitchen. "I've got to get food for Jendel and the others and bring it to the tower."

"I'll help," Emorra offered.

"Thanks," Tieran said, surprised that the dean of the College would offer to do such a menial task.

Happily, Alandro and Moira were working in the kitchen that day. Alandro had been a fixture in the College's kitchen since the Fever Year, when he had arrived as a sick orphan. As soon as he recovered, he gravitated toward the kitchen, willing to do any job cheerfully. Now in his fourth decade, he was no less cheerful and not much slower in the kitchen than he had been when he first arrived.

Moira was a more recent arrival. She had started with the College as a fosterling but had refused to leave when she reached her majority two years ago. She said that nowhere could she find as good a kitchen as at the College and she refused to work with second best, even though every major holder had tried to lure her away.

"I need four lunches for the Drum Tower," Tieran told them as he stepped into the kitchen.

Moira's scowl—she was a fierce guardian of her domain— cleared when she identified him. "And in return, you'll . . ."

Tieran grinned and bowed low. "I shall sing your praises to each and every one of my fellow drummers."

Moira quirked an eyebrow at him and pursed her lips humorously. "Best not sing, Tieran. I still don't think your voice has settled."

"It has," Tieran corrected sadly. "It's just that's all there is to it."

She gave him a judicious look. "In that case—an hour's sculling after dinner."

Tieran considered the counteroffer for a moment before nodding. "Done! But only if you'll let me make meringues."

Moira's face brightened at the prospect. "Deal!" She

turned to her kitchen partner. "Did you hear that, Alandro? Tieran's doing the yucky dishes this evening!"

The large helper looked down thoughtfully at the small cook, then over at Tieran, who waved, and asked, "Meringues, too?"

"Yes," Moira agreed, "he'll make meringues." She found a soup ladle and waved it at Tieran threateningly. "Only no rose extract this time—costs a fortune and you haven't learned restraint."

Emorra smiled as she took in the byplay. She liked the way Moira went to the trouble of actually *finding* something to wave threateningly at Tieran. She was also relieved to see that Tieran was so warmly welcomed in the kitchen.

Of course, he'd be a fool to get on the bad side of the College's best cook—and it was becoming clear to Emorra that Tieran was no fool.

"Wait a minute," she said aloud. "Those are *your* meringues?"

Tieran nodded.

"They're good." Emorra gave him a longer, more appraising look. "You can cook, clean, teach—"

"No more hot boxes," Alandro interrupted her, pointing to two trays.

"Yes, the last of the thermal units cracked yesterday," Moira agreed sadly. "That's why I've put your soup in small bowls and made sandwiches. If you lot want hot food from now on, you'll have to eat in the hall."

"Are there any of the thermos flasks left?" Tieran asked. "It gets very cold on the top of the Drum Tower at night."

"I imagine it does," Moira agreed. "There are two, but they're both reserved." She smiled at Emorra. "One's for you, Dean, and the other's for your mother."

Tieran nodded as he picked up a tray. Emorra picked up the second one.

"Maybe you could rig up a fire," Emorra suggested as they made their way out of the College toward the Drum Tower.

"There's no place for it," Tieran replied. "Besides, I think it would be a fair bit of work to haul wood up every evening."

"Lazy!" Emorra teased. "Well, it's your bones that'll freeze."

The tower grew in Emorra's eyes as they approached it; she was always used to seeing it from the distance of the College. They walked and climbed in companionable silence until they were halfway up the steps wrapped around the outside of the tower and Emorra paused, gasping for breath.

"And *this* is why I'll keep my bones cold, thank you," Tieran said, pointing at the stairway and grinning as he waited for her to recover her breath.

"Yes, I can see that it would be a chore," Emorra agreed at last. Much more slowly they completed their ascent.

"Rodar, Jendel, we're here!" Tieran called as he crested the stairs.

"You're late!" Jendel retorted. "I just hope the food's good."

"It's cold," Emorra said as she set the tray down on the only table available.

"That's nothing new," Rodar said, jumping up to help her.

"Where's Kassa?" Jendel asked.

Tieran groaned and slapped his forehead. "I *knew* I was forgetting something!"

"It's my fault, I distracted him," Emorra said.

"Never mind—at least you brought food!" Rodar exclaimed.

"Poor Rodar's been up here since first watch," Tieran told Emorra.

"What's the soup?" Rodar asked, lifting a bowl and sniffing it.

"The last of the hot boxes failed, so it's all cold," Tieran warned.

Rodar had already dipped a finger into his bowl of the whitish soup and licked it. "Potato leek! Excellent."

Further investigation revealed a number of cold cuts, plenty of fresh-sliced bread, honey, mustard, and Alandro's own special invention, a sage vinaigrette that doubled as a dressing for the greens and as a condiment for the sandwiches.

There were no chairs at the top of the Drum Tower, but the lower parts of the crenellations were wide enough to offer comfortable, if sometimes windy, seating.

"Alandro's dressing is superb, as always," Rodar said to no one in particular.

"We're lucky to have it," Emorra agreed. Jendel raised an eyebrow at her, so she expanded her comment. "The botanists had a very hard time getting the sage to take."

"Why was that?" Rodar asked.

Emorra shrugged. "Mother said something about the boron uptake rates. In the end they finally got it to go by grafting it onto a native plant. Mother says it doesn't taste quite the same as the original."

"She's one of the few left who'd know," Jendel said.

"I like the flavor," Tieran declared.

"What's the difference?" Rodar asked Emorra.

Emorra shrugged. "I never asked her."

"The dean of the College not asking?" Rodar was amazed.

Emorra shook her head. "I was a student of my mother's at the time."

"Oh," Tieran said. He and Emorra exchanged looks of understanding.

"Did they adapt all the Earth fauna, or what?" Rodar wondered. He looked at Emorra. "Would you know?"

"Most of the adaptations were done before Crossing," Emorra answered. "But I believe that the botanists and Kitti Ping had to drop a few adaptations. Some of it was a question of resources."

"And some of it?" Rodar prompted.

Emorra grinned. "Some of it was by choice. Apparently there was something called okra that was dropped by mutual consent."

"I'm surprised they didn't drop spinach, then," Jendel noted sourly, pushing a few spinach leaves about his otherwise empty salad bowl.

"Ah, but that's good for you!" Tieran said.

"They were pretty selective about their animals, too," Rodar noted sourly.

"They had complete gene banks at Landing," Emorra said, adding dryly, "I think the original growth plans were interrupted."

"Did they have elephants in the gene banks?" Rodar persisted.

"Not that again," Jendel groaned. Tieran shook his head and smiled.

"Yes, they had elephants," Emorra said.

"We sure could use them," Rodar complained.

"As beasts of burden they are not as good as horses," Emorra said, ignoring Tieran's alarmed look and Jendel's agitated shushing gestures.

"Who wants beasts of burden?" Rodar replied. "Their feet were very sensitive to subsurface vibrations—"

"They could hear noise over thirty kilometers," Jendel and Tieran joined in chorus with Rodar.

"Oh," Emorra said, suddenly enlightened. "That would make them good for picking up your drum sounds, wouldn't it?"

"*If* you could train them!" Jendel said.

"They were very smart!" Rodar said.

"But how would they have got them from Landing to here?" Emorra wondered.

"On a ship," Rodar answered.

"How could you get an elephant on a ship?" Jendel asked.

"Once you got it on, how could you get it off?" Tieran added.

"And what would you do if it actually *liked* ships?" Jendel continued.

"I suppose you'd have to take it on a cruise around the world," Tieran finished with a laugh, which Jendel joined in, much to Rodar's disgust.

Tieran leaned to Emorra and confided, "We tried to warn you. Rodar's always going on about elephants."

"Anyway," Emorra continued, back on the original topic, "they couldn't take over the Pernese ecosystem completely—"

"Did they ever completely categorize the Pernese ecosystem?" Rodar asked.

Emorra shook her head. "Hardly. On Earth they had never completely categorized the ecosystem, and they had millennia."

Jendel rose from his seat with a shudder. "Oh, this is too much for a simple percussionist!" he said, waving the conversation away. "Tieran, seeing as you forgot to bring along your partner, how do you plan to run your watch?"

"I'll stay," Emorra offered. "You two can bring the trays back and send the other replacement over."

Jendel pursed his lips consideringly.

"She knows the sequences, Jendel," Tieran said.

"She does?" Rodar was surprised.

"Sure," Tieran said. "They're a fairly basic set of sequences, many of them modeled on genetic sequences."

"Genetic sequences?" Jendel repeated. "You never told me that."

He grabbed a tray, passed it to Rodar, and grabbed the other for himself, gesturing for Rodar to precede him down the tower stairs.

"All right," he said from the top step. "Tieran, you can use the small drum to drill her on some of the basic sequences just to be sure. You know, attention, emergency, stuff like that."

"Will do," Tieran said, throwing the chief drummer a mock salute. Jendel returned it with a nod of his head and began his descent.

Tieran dutifully drilled Emorra on the drum sequences, gave her a quick test, and pronounced her fit to take watch with him. The whole procedure took less than a quarter of an hour.

"That's twice in one day you've taught a class," Emorra remarked dryly. "Keep it up and we'll have to put you on the faculty."

Tieran didn't respond to her comment. Instead, he carefully hung the small drum by its harness on one of the small hooks pounded into the wall nearest the stairs. Then he peered out into Fort's lush main valley, watching people tending the fields.

Finally, he turned back to Emorra. "What did they have,
the settlers, before the first Thread fell? Eight years, less than
that, and then they had to abandon everything and come
here to the North."

Emorra nodded. With a sigh, she rose and walked over to
him.

"They didn't have any time to do a proper survey, did
they?" Tieran asked.

"Especially when you add the need they had to engineer
the dragons," Emorra agreed. "Mother would never tell me,
and the reports are very vague."

She frowned as she said that, wondering why her mother
hadn't insisted on making her read every report of the original landing survey.

"So what did they get? Five percent, ten percent?" Tieran
wondered.

Emorra shook her head. "The best I could ever discover
was about three percent."

Suddenly she realized why Wind Blossom hadn't told her
about the survey: Her omission had encouraged Emorra to
look up the information herself.

Mother, you manipulated me—again! Emorra thought angrily.

Tieran snorted, unaware of Emorra's feelings. "Three percent of the entire ecosystem, that's all?"

"They got a very good description of the fire-lizard
genome," she answered. "That's almost complete, say ninety-
seven percent or more. They mapped two or three other
genomes, including one of the more basic bacteria."

"What about Thread?"

"You know," Emorra responded. "Mother says that they
got a complete decode on the Thread genome—"

"—but it was lost in the Crossing," Tieran concluded. He
glanced guiltily at Emorra.

Everyone knew that Wind Blossom had been responsible
for a large part of the equipment and records that were lost
overboard on the storm-tossed ships bringing the survivors
north from the Southern Continent. He continued hastily,

"And the Fever Year was caused by a mutation of one of the viral strains from Earth."

"Yes, as far as we know," Emorra said. "It was far too early for any crossover infection."

"And when that comes?"

Emorra shrugged. "I can only hope that people on Pern will survive. For all that they had so little time, my mother and grandmother, and all the other medical people, did everything they could to adapt us to life on Pern—even before they arrived."

"Is that why you quit?" Tieran asked. "Is that why you left your mother? Was it the thought of just having to wait, having to hope that if any epidemic broke out it would come at a time when we could still identify it, still fight it, and come up with a cure before everyone on Pern was too ill to survive?"

"Is that why *you* quit, Tieran?" Emorra asked, deflecting his question.

Tieran nodded slowly.

"You lasted longer than I did, you know," Emorra admitted. "I could only handle four years before I fled. You stayed a whole six. After my mother, you are the best-qualified geneticist on Pern."

Tieran snorted. "That's not saying much!"

Emorra shook her head emphatically, flinging her braided hair in the breeze. "It's saying a lot, Tieran. You must know that."

Tieran brushed her comment off. "Why did you give up?"

Emorra pursed her lips for a long moment of silence, wondering whether she would answer him. At last she said slowly, "I quit because I wasn't good enough, Tieran. I knew that I couldn't be the sort of person my mother expected me to be, the sort of person my family traditions demanded that I be."

She swallowed hard. "I couldn't wait for the next plague, the next mutation, the next biological disaster, knowing that the tools we needed had either failed already or were going to fail any day—maybe the day before we needed them the most." She shook her head emphatically, looking miserable. "I just *couldn't.*"

Tieran reflected that while Emorra might have fled her responsibilities, she had only gone so far as to become the College's dean. It seemed to him that she would clearly be dealing with the impact of "the next biological disaster" in that lofty position.

"So how will we survive on Pern?"

"The best we can," Emorra answered. "When this Pass ends—and that'll be very soon—people will spread to every liveable corner on the continent. And they'll have children, lots of children, and those children will eat things they're told not to."

Tieran snorted in agreement.

"And some of those children will get sick," Emorra went on. "Some will die, and others will get better. Over time, people will learn what Pernese plants and animals they can eat, and what they have to avoid. With enough time they'll be able to develop a whole new list of ills and a pharmacopoeia of the herbals to cure them.

"And if worse comes to worst, then perhaps some isolated group of people will not get infected and the disease will run its course, and the isolated ones will survive and repopulate the planet.

"And that's what we hope for," she concluded.

Tieran looked doubtful. Emorra looked away, out toward the College.

"Is that person my replacement?" she asked, pointing to a woman walking briskly in their direction from the entrance of the College.

Tieran peered out, following her finger. "Yes, that's Kassa."

"She's pretty," Emorra said suggestively.

"She's seeing someone," Tieran agreed sadly.

Emorra reached up and ruffled his hair affectionately. "You'll find someone," she told him.

Tieran sneered, running a finger over the scar from the top of his right forehead to his left cheek. "Not with this."

Emorra held back a quick retort with a shake of her head.

The sound of someone climbing the stairs alerted them to Kassa's approach. Then Kassa arrived, breathless. "Sorry, Dean! I put my head down for a nap and completely lost track of time."

"No problem," Emorra said, taking her place on the steps. "I had a lot of fun."

She gave Tieran a cheerful wave as she left.

"The trouble with this job is that it's either very boring or very exciting," Kassa grumbled hours later as she and Tieran lounged under the waning sun.

"We've got only a few more hours to go," Tieran said. The last message they had handled had come in over an hour earlier, and had only been a simple inquiry from the southern Ruatha valley—just a communications check. Kassa had impishly drummed back, "What? You woke us up for that?"

Tieran had groaned when she sent the message, hoping that Vedric wasn't on duty at the South Tower or she'd get a scathing. Vedric had no sense of humor and didn't "appreciate levity when engaged in official duties"—as Tieran could attest with well-remembered chagrin.

She'd been lucky and there'd been no further response. They both agreed that the drummer was likely Fella, who still had problems with some of the more complex rolls, which explained why her message was so simple and also why she had made no reply.

After that they had been reduced to gossiping. Naturally, the first topic of conversation was what would happen with the Drum Towers at the end of the Pass, only a few months away. Kassa hoped that with no Thread falling, it would be possible to link up the various towers established at the Holds into a Pern-wide network. Tieran wasn't so sure and wondered if the dragonriders wouldn't fill in the gaps? Kassa thought that the dragonriders would be too busy with their own issues to be bothered. They both agreed that it would be far easier to set up Drum Towers than it would be to lay telegraph lines across the continent. "Besides, there are better uses for the metal," Kassa pointed out.

The conversation moved on to more intimate topics. Kassa admitted that she wouldn't mind being placed in one of the newer holds after the Pass. She was hoping to marry soon—she blushed in embarrassment—before she was considered a spinster. Mind you, she had said, she wasn't sure she could handle six kids as well as her mother had. Maybe four or five, but not six.

Tieran tried to steer the conversation in a different direction before he found himself having to deal with embarrassing issues. He had said that while it was important to increase the number of Pern's settlers until there were enough people to safely live and protect the Northern Continent, he wasn't sure that everyone absolutely had to have children.

"Are you nuts?" Kassa replied. "Everyone's got to have at least four kids or we'll be wiped out—as we nearly were—by the next plague that hits us." She narrowed her eyes at him and opened her mouth to continue heatedly, then closed it again with a snap.

Tieran flushed in embarrassment. "That number's an average. Some people don't have any, look at the dean . . ."

Kassa snorted derisively at him. "The dean? She just hasn't found the right person. I'm sure she'll have six or more when she gets the chance."

Tieran was shocked.

Kassa shook her head patronizingly, which further infuriated Tieran, as she was a full two years younger than he.

"Really, Tieran, you need to get out of this tower more," she said. "However are you going to find a mate if you don't keep up with current affairs?"

His anger inflamed him to respond. "No one," he said, pointing to his face, "is going to want me with *this*."

"Oh, I don't know," Kassa replied soothingly. "I'll bet there are plenty of girls out there who are willing to lower their sights."

At that point Tieran had stalked off, getting as far from her as he could.

Kassa didn't say anything for the next hour. When she finally spoke again it was only to say to herself, "Storm's coming. I can feel it."

Tieran heard her, as he knew she had intended. He was still irritated with her but grateful for the warning; early on it had been established that Kassa had excellent weather sense.

He looked around and saw only a few scattered clouds above. To the west he could see some cumulus clouds building up into larger thunder clouds. He sniffed the air; it was preternaturally clean, as though all the ions had been swept out of it—like shortly before a big storm.

"We should get word from the West Tower soon," Tieran said to himself, but also loud enough that Kassa could hear him.

Kassa disagreed. "It might slip north of them."

Tieran was about to turn around and engage her directly in conversation when a loud boom and a rush of cold air heralded the arrival of a dragon. A large, bronze dragon. A halo of condensed air swirled around it as it glided in low for a quick landing between the tower and the College.

Tieran had grabbed the small drum and was darting down the stairs, telling Kassa, "I'll go!" in an instant.

"Go, go!" Kassa had replied, a broad grin on her face. "I'll relay."

Tieran returned the grin with a wave as he darted down the tower's stairs. As soon as he reached the bottom of the stairs he broke into a steady, loping trot, deftly slinging the small drum over his shoulder without breaking stride.

The bronze dragon was Brianth and the rider was M'hall, Weyrleader of Benden Weyr. There were two other passengers—no, Tieran corrected his assessment as he got closer: one other passenger and a wrapped bundle. The bundle was a body. The passenger was Wind Blossom.

M'hall was helping Wind Blossom down as Tieran arrived. He grabbed the small woman from M'hall's hands and deftly put her on the ground.

"Get help," Wind Blossom ordered. "The body must go to the cold room."

"Body?" Tieran repeated even as he was rapping out a quick staccato on his message drum. It was answered by a rush of people from the College, and the shroud-wrapped figure was quickly carried away, Wind Blossom trotting alongside, snapping instructions.

There was another boom and burst of air, and a second dragon arrived. Tieran had pulled the small drum off his back and banged out his quick message to Kassa before he had identified the new arrival, who landed on his right.

It was M'hall on Brianth! Again. While the new arrival looked somber and time-pressed, the first M'hall was desolate and had tears streaming down his face.

"Don't do it!" the first M'hall shouted to the other.

Somber M'hall startled at the sound of his own voice coming to him. "You're from the future?"

The first nodded. "Please, don't do it. You'll regret it more than you can possibly imagine."

"We shouldn't be talking!" the younger M'hall said. He caught sight of Tieran and told him, "Send for Wind Blossom. Urgent."

"No!" the other yelled. "Don't do it!"

"You would make a time paradox?" younger M'hall's eyes were wide with terror and incomprehension that his future self would even consider such a dangerous suggestion.

The older M'hall's jaw worked but he was voiceless. Finally, he jumped back onto his Brianth, sobbing, "Go then! Don't say I didn't warn you!" The older Brianth gave a leap, one powerful downbeat of his wings and vanished *between*.

"Tieran!" the younger M'hall called to him. Tieran looked up. M'hall was clearly overwhelmed by his future self and dizzy with worry. "Don't say anything about this until I get back."

Stunned, Tieran could only nod.

Wind Blossom returned, escorted by a medical trainee. Tieran helped lift her up to M'hall. And for the second time in almost as many minutes, Brianth vanished *between*.

As though the dragon's disappearance had been a signal,

rain started falling. It went from a trickle to a torrent in no time. Lightning flickered across the sky and thunder boomed repeatedly. Tieran was surprised to realize how dark it had gotten. Dimly, he wondered if time-jumping acted like a lightning rod. He was drenched in seconds.

Genomics: The study of genetic material and the functions it encodes. See DNA *(deoxyribonucleic acid).*
—*Glossary of terms,* Elementary Biological
Systems, 18th Edition

Chapter Seven

Fort Weyr, First Pass, Year 50, AL 58

THE COLD OF *between* was still deep in Wind Blossom's bones as she and M'hall were escorted to the queen's quarters at Fort Weyr.

"My mother asked for you," M'hall told her as he helped her into Sorka's quarters.

"Is it her time?" Wind Blossom's voice was calm, flat. She had seen all her friends die, save this one.

M'hall's lips trembled as he nodded, and a deep anguished sigh passed his lips. Wind Blossom reached to take his arm reassuringly, but her grip was so weak that M'hall misinterpreted the gesture as need for support. He grabbed her and helped her to a chair.

"How did you know?" she asked. Then, taking in M'hall's exhausted pallor, she answered herself, "You timed it."

M'hall nodded.

"It drained you," Wind Blossom said.

"More than you can imagine, and please don't ask," the Weyrleader said, forestalling further questions. He turned to Sorka, lying half-asleep in her bed.

His mother must have felt his presence, for her eyelids fluttered open. "Did you bring her?"

"I'm here," Wind Blossom answered, rising from her chair

and kneeling beside Sorka's bed. The old Weyrwoman reached out a hand and clasped Wind Blossom's as she offered it.

M'hall dragged Wind Blossom's chair over to her. Thankfully, Wind Blossom sat. "Your son brought me."

"He's a good lad," Sorka agreed with a small smile. "He does as he's told."

The two elder women shared a secret pause, then smiled as the expected comment from Benden's Weyrleader failed to materialize.

"He has learned wisdom," Wind Blossom said. It was her highest praise, words she had never before uttered to or about anyone. "He is a good man. Like his brothers and sisters. Blood tells. You and Sean have everything to be proud of."

Behind her, Wind Blossom felt M'hall stiffen at the mention of his late father, who had led the colony's original dragonriders through their first and so many other Threadfalls with an iron will.

Even at the hale age of sixty-two, Sean O'Connell had retained his position as the first Weyrleader—and Weyrleader of Fort Weyr, despite every argument to the contrary. But he was too old. Badly scored when they failed to dodge an oddly clumped bunch of Thread, Sean and Carenath had gone *between*—and never returned. That had been over eight years ago.

In all that time, Faranth had never again risen to mate. No one had commented on it, considering it merely due to Faranth's age. Only Wind Blossom knew differently.

The reason was one of many secrets that she and Sorka had shared over the years, and a part of one of Wind Blossom's few true friendships.

As the first queen dragonrider and the most experienced geneticist, Sorka and Wind Blossom had maintained a working relationship during the years after the first Fall at Landing. But the creation of the watch-whers had soured most of the dragonriders on Wind Blossom, Sean in particular, and Sorka's dealings with her had become businesslike.

Wind Blossom maintained detailed records of all the

original dragons and their hatchlings, tracking growth and watching for any signs of genetic defects. When the colony reestablished itself in the north, and Admiral Benden redirected the technical staff away from her studies, Wind Blossom found herself without specific duties.

Admiral Benden had suggested publicly that she consider diversifying into the medical profession, perhaps considering nursing or technical lab work. And, the Admiral had added with a smile, Wind Blossom should remember her duty to the colony and her genome: Had she considered how she would fill her child-rearing obligations?

Wind Blossom's meek response was taken for acquiescence—and perhaps a tacit admission that her loss of valuable technical gear during the Crossing had made her a pariah.

She dutifully left her lab and took on a trainee role with one of Fort Hold's doctors, working hard to achieve her eventual rating as a general practitioner.

Still, Wind Blossom kept track not only of dragon bloodlines but also of the watch-whers and their progress. She was often asked for advice on the handling of "Wind Blossom's uglies," as they were called.

Emily Boll, in particular, expressed interest in the watch-whers. "I saw them fly the other night," she told Wind Blossom once in private. She smiled at the smaller woman.

Wind Blossom nodded. "I, too," she replied, suffused with pleasure at the memory.

Emily grabbed her hand. "It must be hard for you," she said with warm sympathy.

"It is my job," Wind Blossom replied with only the hint of a shrug. "I do what you and the Admiral ask of me; I carry the burden my mother has left me."

"Well, it seems damned unfair to me!" Emily declared, scowling fiercely.

Wind Blossom made no response.

"Oh, I know it's all part of the plan," Emily went on. "And how much we need it. You showed me the numbers yourself, but it still seems wrong that your contributions and efforts should either go unnoticed or vilified."

Again, Wind Blossom did not answer.

"Wind Blossom," Emily said, gripping her wrist tightly, "you can talk to *me*. I know all the plans. When we're alone, you can tell me anything. It's not right that you keep everything locked up inside you, and it's not fair. In fact, as Pern's leading psychologist, I say that for your own good." When Wind Blossom said nothing, Emily continued softly, "And I say it as one who knows how much you've suffered."

For the first time ever, Wind Blossom broke down and collapsed into Emily's arms. For how long she cried, she did not know. Afterward, Emily gave her one last hug and a bright smile, but they said nothing.

When the Fever had struck, Wind Blossom's skills as a doctor were in high demand. She drove herself harder than any other, often surviving for weeks on end only on naps snatched here and there. And she spent as much time as she could tending Emily Boll.

Wind Blossom and Emily were both too honest to deny that the old governor of Tau Ceti would not survive this infectious siege. Wind Blossom prescribed what palliatives she could and did everything in her power to make the older woman's passing as painless as possible.

Late in the night, when Wind Blossom and Emily had convinced poor Pierre de Courci, Emily's husband, to take some rest, Emily tossed fitfully on her bed.

"If I'm going to die, I wish I'd hurry up," she said bitterly after one more wracking cough had torn through her body.

"Maybe you will recover," Wind Blossom suggested. When Emily glared at her, she persisted, "It's possible. We don't know enough about this illness."

She regretted her last sentence even as Emily gathered about her the indomitable aura of "The Governor of Tau Ceti" and demanded, "How many have died, Wind Blossom? Pierre wouldn't tell me. Paul wouldn't tell me. Tell me."

"I don't know," Wind Blossom replied honestly. "They've started mass burials. The last count was over fifteen hundred."

"Out of nine thousand?" Emily gasped. "That's over one-sixth of the colony!"

Wind Blossom nodded.

Emily's eyes narrowed. "It's going to get worse, isn't it?"

Wind Blossom said nothing.

"The dragonriders? Are they all right?" Emily demanded. When Wind Blossom nodded, Emily sighed and lay back on her bed, eyes closed. After a moment she peeked up at Wind Blossom, her lips curved ruefully, and said, "Your doing, isn't it? The dragonriders? Some of that Eridani immune boost?"

"Only some," Wind Blossom admitted. Apologetically, she added, "There was not enough for you."

"I wasn't on the list," Emily said. "Paul and I had talked about this years back. Is Paul all right?"

"He fell ill last night," Wind Blossom told her.

Emily closed her eyes again—in pain. When she opened them, she told Wind Blossom, "Get Pierre. You will do an autopsy, find the cure."

Wind Blossom was horror-struck and for once it showed. "I—I—Emily, I don't want to do that."

Emily smiled sadly at her. "Yes, dear, I know," she said softly. "But I must ask it of you. I did not bring these people here to fall at the first—no, second—hurdle."

Wind Blossom reluctantly agreed. "It is my job," she said. "But please tell your husband, it would be too much for me."

Emily nodded. "I understand, and I'll do that," she replied. "Now, what to do for your future . . ."

"I shall go on," Wind Blossom answered. "It is my job."

Emily snorted. "Yes, your job, but what about your life? What about a family? Come to think of it, how old was your mother when you were born? How old are you now?" She paused, thoughtfully. "More Eridani genetic tricks?"

"Yes," Wind Blossom agreed, "more Eridani genetics. It is necessary."

"And secret, no doubt, or I would have heard more sooner," Emily commented. "Where I am going, no one will ask me anything. Would you be willing to satisfy my curiosity?"

Wind Blossom shook her head. "No, I do not want to do that."

Emily's eyes widened in surprise. "Well, I can't force you," she said.

Wind Blossom nodded. "It would be painful for me."

"A pain-induced block?" Emily barely contained her revolt at the concept.

Wind Blossom shook her head. "No, nothing like that. To talk about it—I am shamed."

Emily's eyes narrowed. "Not about your uglies? Not about the last batch of dragons?"

Wind Blossom waved those examples away with a gesture of derision. She looked Emily squarely in the eye. "Do you know how badly we have failed?"

"Failed?" Emily shook her head. "All your work has been brilliant."

Wind Blossom was silent for a long while. When she spoke again, her voice was quiet, near a whisper. "In the Eridani Way we are taught that harmony is everything. A good change is invisible, like the wind. It belongs—it seems like an obvious part of the ecosystem.

"You remember the ancient tailor's saying: Measure twice, cut once?" she continued.

Emily nodded.

"The Eridani would say measure a million times, then a million times more and see if you can't possibly find a way to avoid the cut. 'A world is not easily mended,' they say.

"It is drilled into us." Her hands fluttered upward, as though to talk on their own, only to be forced back into her lap with a sour look when she noticed them. "It was drilled into my mother. Into my sister—"

"You had a sister?" Emily interrupted. "What became of her?"

"She is back on Tau Ceti, Governor Boll," Wind Blossom replied flatly.

"I *was* governor of Tau Ceti," Emily said. "Here, I am just Emily, Holder of Boll.

"So, you left a sister on Tau Ceti," she mused. She narrowed her eyes cannily. "To watch the Multichords?"

Wind Blossom shook her head. "To watch the world."

"So every time an Eridani Adept adds a new species to an ecosystem, a child must stay behind to watch?" Emily's voice betrayed displeasure.

"No," Wind Blossom corrected. "Every time an ecosystem is altered there must be those that watch it and bring it back into harmony."

"More than one?" Emily asked.

"Of course."

"But here, on Pern—Tubberman?" Emily was surprised. Then she grew thoughtful. "I'd always wondered why it was so easy for him to gain access to such valuable equipment. I realized that the Charter permitted it, but it had seemed odd at the time that no one had been guarding the equipment more zealously."

Wind Blossom agreed, secretly relieved that the conversation had turned in this direction. She discovered, in talking with Governor Boll, that she was not ready to reveal all her secrets.

Pierre came back with a tray a few minutes later and the conversation lapsed, failing completely when Emily choked on a bit of food and slipped into a coughing fit as her tortured lungs protested the extra effort.

Pierre looked at Wind Blossom. "Is there anything you can do?" he implored.

"I have some medicine that can help the pain but—"

"She told me about the casualties, Pierre," Emily interrupted her.

Pierre bit his lip and gave Wind Blossom a bitter look.

"I asked—it is my duty, you know."

Pierre looked into Emily's eyes, then nodded sadly. "At this time, I would have preferred to keep the pain from you, love."

"I know," Emily said. "And so did Wind Blossom. But I had to know. It helped me to make a decision. Two, in fact."

Both Pierre and Wind Blossom looked at her.

"I have already asked Wind Blossom to perform an autopsy on my body," Emily said.

"I do not want to do this," Wind Blossom told Pierre. His

eyes wide, he looked long at her face, saw that her own eyes were rimmed with tears, and nodded.

"Anything that can help the rest of you," Emily said. "It is my job, my last duty."

"I see, *ma petite,*" Pierre responded. "It shall be as you ask. And the other decision?"

"You can help, here," Emily said. She looked at Wind Blossom. "Is it true that we don't have a complete knowledge of the Pern herbal remedies?"

"We have none!" Pierre exclaimed, only glancing at Wind Blossom for confirmation. "You are not suggesting—"

"It is a bad idea," Wind Blossom interjected. Emily and Pierre both gave her startled looks. "I appreciate the thought, but how would we know if a herbal was exacerbating the illness or helping it? Also, in your state, it would take too long to determine if the herbal was having any positive effects. It would be bad science, Governor."

"Even to try palliatives?" Emily asked in a small voice. "You see, I just don't think it's fair to give me the painkillers when you could give them to others who might survive."

"You've earned the right to them!" Pierre protested.

"That's not the point, love," Emily said, dropping her voice and reducing the tension in the argument. "Again, if I can't be saved, why should we waste valuable painkillers on me and not on others?"

"What you say is true," Wind Blossom agreed, earning a withering look from Pierre. "But, as I am the doctor on scene, triage is *my* responsibility."

"But you have admitted that I am not going to survive," Emily protested.

"How do you think we will feel if we have to watch you die in great pain?" Wind Blossom asked softly. "It is not only your decision."

Emily threw open her hand in a gesture of defeat. "But," she tried one last time, in a small voice, "there are *children*—"

Wind Blossom leaned over the bed and grabbed Emily's open hand in hers. "I know," she said, the iron control over her voice threatening to break. "I have held their hands as they . . ."

Pierre leaned across and laid an arm on her shoulder. "I am sorry, Wind Blossom, I did not think—"

Wind Blossom straightened up, her face once again mask-like. "I cannot save them if I surrender to grief."

"My point exactly," Emily persisted, a look of triumph flashing in her eyes.

Wind Blossom nodded. "There are some infusions we make now, like the juice of the fellis plant—"

"I have some here," Pierre said.

"If you would agree, we could substitute those known herbals for our standard medicines."

"I like that," Emily said. "We could test dosage levels while we're at it, couldn't we?"

And so they arrived at the treatment. Wind Blossom wrote the original prescription and Pierre filled it. Once Emily had taken her first dose, Wind Blossom begged other duties and left them.

She returned three more times during the night. The first time she returned, they agreed to up the dosage and added something to ease the cough. The second time, Emily seemed asleep.

"She is in a coma," Wind Blossom told Pierre after she took Emily's vitals.

"I was afraid of that," Pierre said. "She has been so hot."

"We don't know if the fever kills or is just an immune response," Wind Blossom said. "Pol Nietro and Bay Harkenon's notes show that they tried cold water immersion with no success."

"Her temperature's not that high," Pierre said.

Wind Blossom nodded. "Her pulse is low and dropping. It's almost as if her heart were—" she broke off abruptly, and collapsed to the floor.

"Are you all right?" Pierre rushed to her side, lifting her up and putting her into a chair. Her skin was pale; Pierre put her head between her knees. "When did you last eat?"

Wind Blossom tried to sit up, to push him out of her way. "No time, I must do my rounds—"

He pushed her firmly back into the chair. "You will sit with your head between your knees. You will drink and you will eat. Then maybe I will let you up."

"Pierre! I have to go, people are dying," she protested, but her movements were feeble.

"They will not get better if you keel over, too," Pierre said. "Emily spoke to me after you left. How many are sick? How many doctors are there?"

Wind Blossom shook her head. "I don't know."

"What, do you not confer with each other?"

"Of course," Wind Blossom said, trying again to sit up. This time Pierre let her. "But I must have been late for the last meeting and I guess no one could wait around—"

"When was the last meeting?"

"Yesterday evening," Wind Blossom said. "I think."

"Drink this," Pierre said, handing her a glass of *klah*. "How many were at the last meeting, the one before?"

"Maybe ten," Wind Blossom replied. "But I think some were too busy tending the sick to come."

"Emily said that they've buried fifteen hundred already. How many sick are there?"

Wind Blossom shook her head. "I can only guess. Maybe twice that number."

"Eat this," he said, handing her a breadroll. "Are you saying that we have one doctor for every three hundred sick people?"

She nodded. "Now you see why I must get going."

"You must rest!" Pierre said, raising his hands in a restraining motion. "Eat, drink, and we'll see. What does Paul—oh! He is sick, too. So who is in charge now?"

"I think maybe I am," Wind Blossom said in a small voice. "Pol Nietro died two days ago, I think, and Bay Harkenon I last saw sick in bed herself. The dragonriders are all safe."

"That's a mercy," Pierre said with feeling. "Finish that roll, please."

Realizing that she was going nowhere until she satisfied

the towering Pierre—of course, anyone towered over her—
Wind Blossom tried to cram down the proffered roll.

"Non, s'il vous plaît!" Pierre said. "I spent more time
making that food than you are spending eating it!"

In the end, she had two rolls and another drink—not
water, some sort of fruit juice—before Pierre let her go.

The last time she returned, Pierre met her at the door.

"She is dead," he told her woodenly. "Her heart stopped
beating a few minutes ago. She told me not to try resuscitat-
ing her." He rubbed his eyes, wiping away tears. "I was just
coming to look for you. Where should I put her body?"

Numbed, Wind Blossom slipped past him into the room.
She took one look at Emily and sat down in the chair beside
her, head bowed.

After a moment, she spoke. "When I first saw her, she was
the most beautiful person I had ever seen. She would light up
the room, lift the spirits of everyone who met her. She did
not allow even the threat of total annihilation to upset her.

"When the Nathi were bombing Tau Ceti day and night,
it was Governor Boll who pulled everyone together. She
worked tirelessly, always there, always ready—"

"I had heard," Pierre interrupted, "but never like this."

"I was young, still a girl," Wind Blossom continued. "My
mother was often away, unavailable. When I did see her, it
was for my lessons—and her scoldings." She sighed. "Governor Boll always found the time to say something encouraging to me. Even when cities were being obliterated, she
would still find the time to talk to a young girl."

"I did not know," Pierre said.

"I did not tell anyone," Wind Blossom confessed. "My
mother would have been furious, and I was too embarrassed
to tell Governor Boll myself."

Pierre nodded. "But now she is not here. And we are left
to do her work."

"Yes," Wind Blossom agreed, rising from her seat. "Can
you carry the body?"

"I think so," he said. "Where should I take it?"

"There's a makeshift morgue over at the College," she told him.

Pierre looked thoughtfully down at Emily's body. "I can manage. And then what?"

Wind Blossom shook her head. "The lab technicians, both first and second team, have been overcome. I suppose I should see what I can do there first. But I still have to make my rounds, there are patients—"

Pierre held up a hand. "No one can be in two places at once; not even Emily could do that. Which is more important?"

"Both."

"Who can help?"

"If there are some nurses or interns, they can tend the sick, but I don't think anyone else knows how to operate the lab equipment."

"Then you have your answer," Pierre said.

"I don't know if there are enough interns," she said.

"There will have to be," Pierre said after a moment's thought. "If you are the only one left to handle the lab equipment, then the others will have to make do."

And so it was decided. With Wind Blossom in the lab, Pierre found himself first blocking anyone from disturbing her and then later increasingly taking charge of the whole medical organization, starting with providing food and rest for the medical staff and their supporters, and then moving on to organizing the quarantine of the sickest and the burial of those beyond aid.

At the end of the second day, Wind Blossom had isolated the disease: As she had feared, it was a crossover of Pernese bacteria into Terran bacteria. The poor lab teams, following their medical training to look for the most likely causes, had been looking for either a flavivirus like Ebola, or a combination of viral and secondary bacterial infections. Instead, they had themselves become victims of the object of their search.

They had had the right symptoms but the wrong culprit. The colonists of Pern had no natural protection against the hybrid bacteria. Wind Blossom, following her training as an ecologist, isolated the mutation, sequenced its genetic core, and developed a vaccine and a course of treatment.

The pitifully few remaining medical personnel were innoculated first, then their assistants, and finally the population at large, and the epidemic was broken.

But not without cost. Among those lost were most of the children under four years of age, almost all expectant or new mothers, nine out of every ten medics at Fort Hold—and Emily Boll.

In private conversations first with Pierre and then with the recovered Paul Benden, it had been decided that it was better to ascribe the epidemic to a "mysterious" illness rather than a crossover infection—at least until Wind Blossom could train enough medical personnel to combat any future crossovers. Because the vaccine had been introduced along with a course of treatment, it was easy to convince most people that the treatments were only palliative and that only those with natural immunities had survived, leaving the survivors unconcerned about future recurrences.

Before she passed away, Emily had written a note to be given to Sorka. Sorka had never shown the note to Wind Blossom, but shortly after she received it, Sorka had asked Wind Blossom to visit her.

Their first meeting had been awkward.

Over time, their professional relationship deepened into respect and, finally, into friendship.

When Wind Blossom's first and only child was born, she named her Emorra—combining Emily and Sorka—and had asked Sorka and Pierre to be godparents. Both had enthusiastically agreed.

"How's your daughter?" Sorka asked, guessing at Wind Blossom's thoughts.

Wind Blossom sighed. "She has not learned wisdom."

Sorka squeezed Wind Blossom's hand weakly. "I'm sure she'll get it."

"But not from me," Wind Blossom said.

"M'hall, leave us," Sorka said. M'hall gave her a rebellious look but she forestalled his arguments, saying quietly, "I'll call you back in good time, luv."

Clearly still uncomfortable, M'hall withdrew. Sorka's gaze rested on the doorway for a moment, to assure herself that he wasn't coming back. She turned her attention to Wind Blossom. "So, tell me."

Years of familiarity enabled Wind Blossom to take the open-ended question at its value. "We are doing all right," she said.

Sorka gave her a sour look. "Wind Blossom, I'm dying, not stupid. I heard about your short-term memory."

Wind Blossom managed to keep her surprise from her face, but Sorka detected it in her body language. The first Weyrwoman allowed herself a satisfied chuckle. "What are the implications?"

Wind Blossom sighed. "I'm concerned because we have not had enough time to transfer our practical knowledge—things that have to be learned by doing rather than merely studying—from our eldest to our newer generation."

"So we'll lose some knowledge," Sorka observed. "It's happened on colony worlds before and they survived."

Wind Blossom inclined her head in a nod. "True. But always at a cost: The knowledge had to be relearned, usually through trial and error at a later date. And sometimes the lack of that knowledge hit the affected colony world with a major setback."

"This could happen here?"

"Yes. We are particularly vulnerable because of the population loss we suffered in the Fever Year and subsequent epidemics."

Sorka grimaced. "I knew that and we've discussed this before."

Wind Blossom allowed herself a rare smile. "But now we are discussing it for the last time, my lady."

Sorka snorted in derision at Wind Blossom's use of the title. "Not you, too!"

"I figured that if I am being so honored, you would deserve no less!"

Sorka allowed her free hand to primp at her hair and smiled. "Well, it's not as though us distinguished ladies are not entitled."

"Quite," Wind Blossom agreed with a grin of her own. "But it disturbs me because it shows that people are beginning to adopt a caste system."

"And how does that affect the Charter?" Sorka mused.

"Sociologically, I can see why this 'elevation,' this endowing of the old lord and lady titles, makes sense in our young population," Wind Blossom said.

Sorka waved her free hand dismissively. "We've had this conversation before."

"I hadn't forgotten," Wind Blossom said. "But it bears repeating. The youngsters needed to relinquish a lot of control to the older colonists simply because we older people had learned the skills needed to surive. And survival on Pern is still touch and go—as those young people who do not heed their elders discover with the forfeit of their lives."

Sorka pulled her hand free of Wind Blossom's and used both hands to make an emphatic "hurry up" gesture.

"I can't hurry up, Sorka, I'm thinking out loud," Wind Blossom said. She paused, striving to recover her train of thought.

"So Pern's going to have a bunch of lords and ladies in the form of Weyrleaders, Weyrwomen, and the men and women who run the holds," Sorka supplied when Wind Blossom's silence stretched.

The sound of boots striding loudly up to the entrance of Sorka's quarters distracted them. Sorka's bronze fire-lizard, Duke, looked up from his resting place at the foot of her bed, looked back to Sorka for a moment, and lowered his head again, unperturbed.

"M'hall!" Torene shouted. "Why didn't you tell me? What's going on? Don't you think I wanted to pay my respects?"

M'hall's voice was a murmur as he strove to placate his outraged mate.

"Have you looked at the casualty reports recently?" Wind Blossom asked Sorka once they both determined that they were not going to be immediately interrupted.

"I have," Sorka's voice was pained.

"I am sorry. My mother had predicted those numbers when she first calculated the mating cycle," Wind Blossom said. "But with such a short life span fighting Thread, and with the difficulties of the holders in providing sufficient food for the colonists, maintaining a sufficient margin to support such luxuries as education and research is quite problematic."

Sorka nodded and gestured for the older woman to continue.

"So our society will ossify and stratify at least until the end of this Pass."

"And then?"

Wind Blossom shook her head. "Then population pressures will force an expansion of the Holder population and the creation of new Holds across this continent. The lack of Thread should allow the dragonriders several generations in which to increase their numbers and recover from this first Pass; the dragonriders in the next Pass should be much more able to handle the onslaught. There will be pressure in both the Weyrs and the Holds to consolidate what they have and to build conservatively. Any skills not directly needed in expansion or retention will atrophy."

"That's already happening."

"By the next Pass the skills needed to maintain our older, noncritical equipment will have been lost."

"Maybe before then," Sorka agreed.

Wind Blossom nodded. "Our descendants should survive anyway."

"Unless the wrong skills are lost," Sorka noted.

"That is my worry, yes," Wind Blossom agreed.

"You are an Eridani Adept, so you would worry about the ecology," Sorka noted. She closed her eyes and took a deep breath. "You're worried about the dragons, aren't you?"

"At some point there will be crossover infections from the fire-lizards to the dragons," Wind Blossom said.

"There are the grubs and the watch-whers—what about them?"

"Tubberman's grubs were well-designed," Wind Blossom

said. "They are a distinct species derived from other native species. This gives them both the native protection and the native susceptibilities. Given that there are other similar species, there will be a high degree of crossover, as Purman demonstrated with his vine grubs. That actually provides a certain degree of protection because there are multiple species for a particular disease to assault. Any successful defense by one of the species will rapidly be spread to the other species. Also, because we plan to plant the grubs throughout the Northern Continent—and they have already been distributed throughout the Southern Continent—there is a strong likelihood that any severe parasitic assault on the grubs will devolve into a symbiosis before all of the species has been eradicated."

"Just like the Europeans and the Black Death," Sorka observed.

"Yes, rather like that," Wind Blossom agreed.

"If we're spread across the Northern Continent that won't be a major problem, will it?"

"I hope not," Wind Blossom agreed. "The effect of another epidemic should dissipate with the added distance between settlements."

"So the weak point in all this is the dragons, right?" Sorka said.

Wind Blossom shook her head. "It is difficult to point to just one. The dragons or the watch-whers appear to be the most susceptible. We have thousands or millions of grubs but only hundreds of dragons and fewer watch-whers."

"Are the two genetically so similar that one disease might destroy them both?"

Wind Blossom pursed her lips. "I strived to avoid that. In fact, I engineered so many changes . . . which might be one of the reasons that we had so many infertile watch-wher eggs."

Sorka's eyes gleamed. "*One* reason."

Wind Blossom returned her stare with a blank look.

"I am curious about the other reasons," Sorka said. "I am

now convinced that some of those failures were planned to make you look less skilled than you are."

Wind Blossom said nothing.

"Your mother was trained by the Eridani," Sorka said. "You were trained by her, weren't you?"

Wind Blossom shook her head. "There are some questions I should not answer even for you, Sorka."

A wheezing cough shook Sorka's body and M'hall glanced inside, Torene hovering worriedly behind him.

Sorka waved them back out as the cough passed.

"If you cannot answer my questions, I won't hinder you with them," she said after taking a sip of water from the glass Wind Blossom proffered her.

Wind Blossom winced. "I do not want to burden you."

Sorka smiled. "And I was trying to lighten your load. A burden shared, as it were."

Wind Blossom spent a moment in thought. "I do not know everything. I was not told myself."

"But you made guesses," Sorka observed. "I have made guesses, too. Let me share some with you.

"I think it odd that such heroic figures as Admiral Benden and Governor Boll should willingly take themselves into oblivion just after the Nathi War when their skills were still very clearly needed."

Wind Blossom nodded. "Yes, I had wondered about that."

"And the Eridani?"

"When the Eridani agree to husband a new ecosystem they assign three bloodlines," Wind Blossom said. "It is a major undertaking. There has only been one time that I know of where the Eridani have been willing to make such an assignment without having thorough knowledge of the ecosystem in question."

"Here?" Sorka asked.

Wind Blossom nodded.

"Three bloodlines?"

"To avoid mistakes and provide redundancy," Wind Blossom said. Sorka's face paled and Wind Blossom reached for her hand, placing her finger over her wrist to take the Weyrwoman's pulse. "Your pulse is failing, Sorka. Let me call the others."

"Wait!" Sorka's voice was nearly a whisper. "What can I do to help you?"

Wind Blossom was silent for a moment. "Go quietly and peacefully, dear friend."

Sorka smiled. "What can I do to help Pern? Do you want to perform an autopsy?"

Wind Blossom's eyes widened in horror. "No."

"But I heard that you need cadavers."

Wind Blossom shook her head. "Not yours."

She turned to the doorway and gestured to M'hall and the others to enter.

Sorka glared at her but was so quickly surrounded by her offspring and relatives that she could do no more.

"Her pulse is dropping," Wind Blossom explained to Torene. "I do not know how much longer she has."

"Nice of you to let us in," Torene returned tartly.

"My request, Torene," Sorka said. "I had to talk with my friend."

Torene looked chagrined but did not apologize.

Tall men surrounded the Weyrwoman and she greeted each with a smile. "M'hall. L'can. Seamus. P'drig."

The men gave way to the women, Sorka's daughters. "Orla. Wee Sorka."

The last was an elegant woman in her early thirties. Sean had insisted on naming their last-born Sorka because, as he'd said, "She looks just like you, love."

"Wee" Sorka leaned over from the far side of the bed to give her namesake a strong hug. Sorka hugged her back.

"I'll miss you most of all, I think, my wee one," she told her youngest.

"I'll miss you too, Ma," the younger Sorka replied, tears streaming unchecked down her face.

Sorka turned from her to grasp M'hall's hand. "My strong one." M'hall gave her hand a gentle squeeze.

Sorka looked at Torene. "Take good care of him for me."

Torene ducked her head, her cheeks wet with tears. "I will, Ma, you may depend upon it."

Sorka let go of M'hall's hand and sought out L'can's. "My silent one," she said. L'can squeezed her hand, rubbing the tears from his face with the other.

"We could bring you down to the Cavern, to Faranth, Ma," P'drig said.

Sorka smiled, letting go of L'can's hand and grabbing his. "No. She knows my heart in this. I will leave my body behind here, in your company and Wind Blossom's keeping."

There was a concerted gasp and heads swiveled toward Wind Blossom.

"Your father and I have given everything we can for you and Pern," Sorka told them. "This poor body is but the least I can leave."

"You don't need to do this," Wind Blossom said.

Sorka waved her objections aside. "I have heard about the pressing needs for cadavers—"

"And I have told you that I do not want yours, Sorka," Wind Blossom interrupted, her face wrought with emotion.

"We must do what is best for Pern," Sorka said. "It is my last request, Wind Blossom, that you perform an autopsy to investigate the early dementia you've recently noticed. Use my body for whatever medical purposes you see fit. I'd heard that you had wanted to practice for Tieran's surgery—"

"Mother!" The word was torn from M'hall's throat.

Wind Blossom shook her head. "I do not want to do this."

"The boy deserves a new face," Sorka said. "I have thought about this for a fortnight now. In my bedside table you will find my will, with specific references on these matters."

Sorka looked around the room, catching the eyes of everyone in turn. "My loved ones, I will not deny you every protection I can think of. Soon I will no longer need my body. Let the people of Pern find a last use for it. Please, follow my will on this." She turned her gaze to her eldest. "M'hall, in this I appoint you my executor."

"Mother . . . Ma . . ." M'hall broke down.

Torene wrapped comforting arms around Sorka. She gave Wind Blossom a sour look, then looked at Sorka. "My lady, it shall be as you wish. I pledge my word as your daughter-in-law, and as Benden's Weyrwoman. It shall be."

"Thank you," Sorka said softly. She gave a deep sigh and turned back to the others. "Now, let me look at you all. Tell me how you are."

The conversation wandered on from son to daughter and back again. Sorka managed to get them to laugh once, and someone brought up refreshments. Gradually the talk wore down and Sorka ordered them to leave her, all but M'hall and Wind Blossom.

"I want you to stay with me, Wind Blossom," Sorka said, feebly patting her bed. "You and M'hall, here."

It was late. The two sat silently beside Sorka's bed while the first queen rider of Pern sank slowly into sleep. M'hall went around the room covering all the glows save one. Every now and then Wind Blossom would check Sorka's pulse by pressing gently on her wrist.

As dawn neared and its gray light began to fill the room, Sorka gave a faint gasp. Wind Blossom looked up just as Faranth's despairing wail broke the silence, amplified by Duke's higher but equally piteous wail, and was immediately silenced itself as the first Impressed fire-lizard of Pern and the first queen dragon of Pern went *between*. Their stilled voices were replaced by the keening of all the dragons at Fort Weyr.

M'hall rushed to Sorka's side, but Wind Blossom already knew from the lack of a pulse that the first Weyrwoman had joined her husband. Wind Blossom stirred herself, ignoring the complaints of her joints, and knelt beside M'hall.

"Let me tend to her for a moment, and then you may come back," she offered.

M'hall looked at her through tear-soaked eyes and nodded slowly.

She guided the bereft rider out of the room and into the arms of his wife and weyrmate.

"Just give me a few minutes," she said to Torene.

Fort's Headwoman had delivered clean bedsheets and toiletries earlier in the evening. Wind Blossom, ignoring the tears rolling down her face, made one final inspection of Sorka's body, and then gently made the body presentable, as she had done for Emily Boll and her own mother before her.

Satisfied that she had done all she could to make things easier on Sorka's children, Wind Blossom left the room and let them enter.

M'hall was the first to his mother's side. L'can, P'drig, and Seamus stood at the end of her bed, while her daughters, Orla and Sorka, closed in on the side.

D'mal and Nara, Fort's Weyrleader and Weyrwoman, arrived to pay their respects, but Wind Blossom asked them to wait for Sorka's family to complete theirs.

"Please ask Torene to let us know when there is a good time," Nara said. Wind Blossom nodded. A while later one of the weyrfolk came with a chair and a basket of fruit for Wind Blossom, courtesy of the Weyrwoman. Gratefully, Wind Blossom sat down before the door and ate daintily from the selection.

Sorka's children drifted out in ones and twos over the next half hour.

When Torene came out, Wind Blossom relayed Nara's request. Torene glanced back into the room at M'hall.

"I'll give him a few more minutes," she said. "I'm going down to the caverns for some lunch—" She glanced at the early morning light and remembered that Benden was six time zones ahead of Fort. "—er, breakfast."

Wind Blossom waited outside until she heard M'hall's voice from in the room. Thinking, in her wearied state, that he might be asking for her, she stepped through into the room—and stopped.

M'hall stood beside his mother's bed, holding her dead hand in his. Tears streamed down his face and onto the bed.

"What will I do now, Ma?" M'hall repeated.

Wind Blossom could see the small boy inside the grown man struggle with the awful loss of his mother and last parent.

She knew that M'hall was groping with the awful realization that he no longer had some higher authority to turn to, no one to confide in, no one to seek praise from, or to ask, "Do you love me?" without fearing the answer.

M'hall turned at the sound of her footsteps and Wind Blossom cast her eyes to the ground, not wanting to meet his.

"What—" M'hall swallowed, and continued more strongly, "What did you do?" He did not need to say "when your mother died."

Wind Blossom reflected on the question. Then she looked up and answered him honestly: "My mother never loved me. When she died it was my obligation to assume her dishonor, and she savored passing it on to me."

Wind Blossom gestured to Sorka. "She showed me some of her love. I felt like the desert in a cloudburst," she continued softly. Her voice hardened. "For my mother, I could never be good enough."

M'hall nodded and wiped his eyes. "She was a great lady."

"Yes."

"She gave everything for this planet," M'hall said. He looked down at the still, lifeless body. "I think I understand her last request now."

"I don't," Wind Blossom said. "I would prefer to leave her undisturbed and keep the memory of her body as it was alive, not as it is dead."

M'hall shot her a penetrating look. "I had not thought of it that way. Wind Blossom, will you honor my mother Sorka's last request?"

"M'hall, I do not want to."

"My father always taught me that I had to honor a lady, particularly my mother." He shook his head. "I cannot gainsay her."

Outside the room they heard the sound of footsteps and Torene's voice: "M'hall, are you all right?"

"In here," M'hall answered. "Yes."

Torene, D'mal, and Nara entered. Wind Blossom moved closer to M'hall to make room.

"We wanted to pay our respects," D'mal told M'hall.

"I learned so much from her," Nara added. "She was like a mother to me."

Beside her, Wind Blossom felt M'hall flinch as her words reinforced his sense of loss. He said nothing.

With an inquiring glance at M'hall, Nara approached the side of the bed, bent over, and gave Sorka's cheek one last kiss. D'mal gently drew his Weyrwoman out of the room, their grief and sympathy evident on their faces.

M'hall leaned forward and gently stroked Sorka's cheek one last time. Then he straightened, his features showing his grief being subdued by his self-mastery. He looked at Wind Blossom, his face a leader's mask.

"I must honor my mother's last request. Is there anything more you need to do before we can depart?"

"Yes."

"Then we will wait outside until you are done," M'hall answered, gesturing for Torene to precede him.

Gingerly, Wind Blossom completed shrouding Sorka's body. When M'hall returned, he started at the sight of the body all covered in white cloth. Recovering his composure, he gently lifted it cradled between his arms.

"Brianth awaits us outside," he said to Wind Blossom, gesturing that she precede him.

Outside Sorka's quarters, a group of Fort riders gathered to pay their respects. Once M'hall had wearily hauled himself up on Brianth's neck, two of the riders lifted Sorka's shrouded body up to him. He placed it before him on his dragon's neck. Then the riders helped Wind Blossom up behind M'hall.

"Are you ready?" M'hall called over his shoulder as Brianth beat effortlessly into the air. "I assume time is of the essence."

"It is," Wind Blossom agreed. The cold of *between* answered her.

Proteomics: The study of proteins, typically those created by genetic codes, and how they work.
— *Glossary of terms,* Elementary Biological
Systems, 18th Edition

Chapter Eight

Fort Hold, First Pass, Year 50, AL 58

WIND BLOSSOM WAS surprised by the length of time they remained *between.* When the cold of *between* ended, it was abruptly replaced by a different chill. It was still night and rain was falling, lashing into them as Brianth dived around the Drum Tower toward the College.

"What happened?" Wind Blossom shouted over the noise of the wind.

"I took us back to last night, when I picked you up," M'hall replied.

"You timed it?" Wind Blossom asked, her tone disapproving.

"I wasn't thinking carefully enough and gave Brianth these coordinates," he added ingenuously, concealing that he knew that he had already been here. "Here, let me help you down."

Wind Blossom grabbed his hand and scrambled with a distinct lack of dignity down Brianth's side. Just as she belatedly realized that she was far too short to jump to the ground without hurting herself, hands reached up to grab her.

It was Tieran. Wind Blossom schooled her pleasure at seeing him into a more neutral expression, saying, "Get help. The body must go to the cold room."

"Body?" Tieran repeated. Before Wind Blossom could

give him an explanation, a group of people rushed out from
the College and grabbed the shrouded body from M'hall.
Wind Blossom followed the group in and was inside the College, heading to the surgery, before a second boom announced
the arrival of another dragon. Wind Blossom paused but
realized that she was too tired and too stressed to concern
herself with the second arrival. As she started forward again
toward the surgery, a wave of fatigue swept through her and
she wavered on her feet.

"Mother?" Emorra had turned at the sound of the second
arriving dragon and had seen her mother falter. "Janir! Janir
come quick, Wind Blossom has collapsed!"

M'hall shivered more from grief than from the cold of *between* as he lowered his mother's body down to the waiting
arms gathered below Brianth. He let out a sob as the group
carried her body out of sight.

A boom heralded the arrival of his own younger self, timing it so as to bring Wind Blossom to his still-living mother.

"No!" M'hall yelled, tears coursing warmly down his
cheeks. "Don't do it!"

He knew it was pointless, that he couldn't create a time
paradox, but his grief was too great. If he didn't go, then
maybe Sorka would still be alive, he thought wishfully.

"Would you make a time paradox?" his younger self
asked, eyes wide with horror.

M'hall tried to answer but couldn't. Finally, he jumped
back onto his dragon and cried, "Go then! Don't say I didn't
warn you!"

Brianth gave one powerful leap and beat the air once with
his wings before taking them *between,* to Benden Weyr and
the comfort of Torene.

Wind Blossom found herself lying down on one of the infirmary's beds with a blanket laid over her. A hand on her
chest resisted her immediate effort to rise. Wind Blossom
looked up and connected the hand to Emorra.

"I must get up—I have work to do," she said, modulating

her tone from one of outraged impatience to calmly clinical as she realized that she was too weak to bring off the former.

Quirking an eyebrow at her, Emorra reached to the bedside table and picked up a small steaming cup. Wind Blossom inhaled the fragrant odor of *klah* and suppressed a brief flash of regret that the tea plant had been lost in the mad dash to the Northern Continent.

"Drink this," Emorra said, deftly slipping her other arm supportively under her mother's back to help her sit up. "Janir's coming."

"You shouldn't have disturbed him," Wind Blossom replied unconvincingly. She sipped from the proffered cup. The *klah* was warm, not hot, but she could feel it rejuvenate her. She took the cup from Emorra's hand, drained the contents, and pressed the cup back into her daughter's still outstretched hand in one quick, surprising move. "There, all better."

"Mother! You still need to rest. Your collapse shocked everyone."

"Nonsense," Wind Blossom said. "The sudden change from day to night triggered an attack of lethargy. I'm recovered," she lied assuredly, swinging her legs to the side of the bed opposite Emorra, "and I have work to do."

Wind Blossom encountered Janir entering the room just as she was leaving. "Where has Sorka's body been placed?"

"In the cold room," Janir replied. "But it can't stay there much longer."

"Have it prepped for autopsy, then," Wind Blossom said, striding past him and causing him to turn around and match her stride. "I'll be in the main surgery."

"At this hour? Do you think that wise?"

"I have to work before rigor sets in, Janir," Wind Blossom answered. "Can you do it?"

"Yes, but—"

"Fine. Five minutes?" Wind Blossom turned toward the surgery, leaving Janir speechless.

Wind Blossom roused the night-duty student to get her hot water with which to scrub. She forced herself to clean her hands and arms methodically, going the full five minutes customary for surgery on the living. As she did, she called forth one of the Eridani focusing mantras. She pulled her training around her like a cloak.

When she turned from the wash basin, Sorka's body had already been placed on the operating table. Janir, and to Wind Blossom's surprise, Emorra, were waiting for her. Janir was close to the operating table; Emorra had positioned herself deferentially at a distance, declaring her observer status.

"I can do this," Janir offered, indicating the tray of biopsy equipment that he'd laid out.

Wind Blossom looked the gear over, picked up the most delicate of probes, and shook her head. "No."

Deftly she performed her cerebral biopsy, content that only a magnifying glass could reveal her handiwork. She handed the sample to Janir. "Have that analyzed, please. I'm interested in any deviations in chemistry and cell structure, particularly any signs of advanced geriatric degradation."

Janir took the sample reluctantly. "But—"

Wind Blossom shook her head. "I—I, Janir, I must honor her last request." Emorra glanced between Janir and Wind Blossom but the outcome was foregone: With a slight nod of his head, Janir took the sample and left the room for the lab.

Wind Blossom turned to one of the surgical chests that lined the walls and selected a standard set of scalpels and clamps. She placed the set on the operating tray in place of the biopsy set she'd used earlier.

She moved to the right side of Sorka's head and grasped a scalpel. For a long time she stood there, poised to re-create the gash on Sorka's body that a watch-wher had inflicted on young Tieran.

Slowly, as though on their own, tears began to leak out of her eyes, first on the left side and then the right, creating long rivulets that dripped down her cheeks and off her jaw. Her hand spasmed and she flung the scalpel away. "I cannot, I cannot, I cannot!"

Emorra crossed the distance between them with long strides, paused hesitantly, then laid a tentative hand on her mother's shoulder. As though released, Wind Blossom turned to her daughter with an inarticulate cry and buried her head against her.

"I cannot do it, Emorra, I cannot," she whispered into the hollow of Emorra's shoulder. "I dishonor our family, but I cannot do it."

Emorra patted her mother gently in a way that she herself had never been patted and—she realized with a start—that Wind Blossom had never been patted by *her* mother, Kitti Ping.

"Hush, it's all right. Of course you can't. No one has a right to expect it of you," she found herself saying. The words served double duty, reassuring not only her mother but Emorra herself.

Wind Blossom pushed back and looked into her daughter's eyes. "But it was her last request!"

"It was only a request, mother," Emorra answered. "Sorka only wished to ease your burdens, not add to them. Take it in the spirit it was given—"

A harsh sound broke through her words. Drumbeats, loud, fast, staccato.

Wind Blossom stood back and cocked her head, listening intently.

Emergency! Emergency! Emergency! The rules were emphatic—each repeat of an emergency gave increased urgency to the call. One more repeat and the drummer would be reporting a Pern-wide emergency.

Emergency! Medical alert. Wind flower—there was no code for "blossom"—*bring medical bag immediately!*

"It's Tieran!" Emorra said.

Janir dove through the door in the same instant. "What's all that drumming about?" he demanded.

"Janir, get my bag and meet me at the Drum Tower," Wind Blossom ordered, bundling past him through the door.

"The Drum Tower? Wind Blossom, it's pouring in buckets outside—you'll drown!"

"Just do it, Janir," Emorra said, following hard on Wind Blossom's heels. "Tieran just sent a planet-wide emergency."

Janir caught up with them halfway to the Drum Tower. As he passed them, Wind Blossom yelled, "Stay back! Give me my bag and stay back."

"We can't have both of you get infected," Emorra explained as Janir looked questioningly at her.

With a decisive nod, Janir heaved to and crouched, lungs heaving in the downpour.

When did the boy get taller than me? Wind Blossom found herself wondering as she drew near the Drum Tower and Tieran, who was standing at the foot of the stairs. High above in the tower itself, she could make out the shape of another person peering down anxiously, all glows exposed to light up the scene. She nodded approvingly to herself—Tieran had remembered his quarantine protocols.

Tieran cupped something in his hands protectively. Beside him, on the ground, was the crumpled form of a fire-lizard.

"They fell from the sky," he shouted down to them. "I couldn't catch them both."

It was quite dead. From its little mouth flowed some ugly green spittle.

"You were lucky to catch either on a night like this," Emorra shouted back encouragingly.

Wind Blossom flung an outstretched arm in Emorra's direction. "Stay where you are! This area is in quarantine."

Emorra stopped, examined the situation for a moment, then stepped boldly forward, grabbing her mother's outstretched arm.

"Silly girl! Why did you do that?" Wind Blossom hissed at her only child.

"You'll need help," Emorra answered firmly.

"But not at the loss of my only child," Wind Blossom answered sadly. "Not with him in danger, too. Pern can't lose both of you."

Emorra arched an eyebrow. "One day you must explain that," she said. "But not now. What can I do?"

Tieran heard them and looked relieved when he saw Wind Blossom's medical bag.

"This one's still alive," he said, indicating the fire-lizard in his arms. "He needs antibiotics."

"How can you know?" Wind Blossom demanded, stepping forward and kneeling down to examine the dead fire-lizard on the ground. She prodded it gently, got out a spatula from her medical bag, and gingerly sampled some of the green fluid leaking from the fire-lizard's mouth.

"Get me a specimen bag," she ordered Emorra curtly. When Emorra complied, Wind Blossom put the spatula in the bag.

"He's wheezing—he's got an infection," Tieran said. "He needs antibiotics."

"Which one?" Wind Blossom asked. "How can you know the right sort of antibiotic? What dosage level?"

Tieran gritted his teeth. "There is only one and you know it. The general-spectrum antibiotic. Maximum dosage for his body mass."

"There isn't that much of the general antibiotic left, Tieran," Wind Blossom said, voice barely carrying over the wind and the rain. "If we use it and it's not enough, the fire-lizard will die. And even if it lives, that antibiotic was being saved for your surgery."

Tieran remained silent, focused on an internal debate.

When he spoke again, it was with a harsh certainty. "It's the only chance he has, Wind Blossom."

Jump,
Cup air,
Bound into the sky.
A wink
Between; beyond the eye.

Chapter Nine

Benden Weyr, Second Interval, AL 507

TWO DRAGONS BURST into existence under the low clouds near Bay Head. One was gold, the other, bronze.

"I can't believe we're doing this," Tullea grumbled to her dragon. She looked around and found B'nik's Caranth sidling up on their right side. Her eyes darted to the seashore and the nearby rain-soaked fields. "I can't understand why I let B'nik talk us into this."

Because you love him, Minith replied with a hint of questioning in her tone.

Tullea laughed and patted her beautiful gold dragon's neck. *And* you *wanted some exercise,* she said, smiling despite herself.

"She'll rise to mate soon," B'nik had told her calmly not a sevenday before. His eyes were clouded with an unasked question. Tullea knew the question but perversely decided to keep the answer to herself. Oh, she was pretty sure which dragon Minith would mate with, but she felt a sneaky thrill at the notion of keeping B'nik on tenterhooks. Besides, she thought to herself, it's really the dragons' choice.

"A well-fed, well-worked dragon will fly farther and lay more eggs," B'nik had reminded her this morning when he'd asked if she wanted to go searching. "And we can drill on reference points."

Tullea grabbed at the chance. Minith, at a little over three Turns old, had just matured enough to be flown and to go *between*. After three Turns of constant feeding, oiling, and loving, Tullea was more than ready to enjoy the fruits of her labors.

Besides, she admitted to herself, she *loved* to fly.

So do I, Minith agreed, once again reading Tullea's private thoughts.

But the weather is awful, Tullea thought sourly to her dragon.

I don't mind it, Minith said.

Tullea snorted. *Of course not! You think the cold of* between *is just fine!*

The cold of between *is cold,* Minith replied, with a hint of reproof in her tone.

"Well, this is worse," Tullea growled aloud, looking toward B'nik.

The bronze dragonrider was waving excitedly and pointing to the ground below. Tullea looked but saw nothing—no, there was a bunch of rags on the beach. B'nik's Caranth pinwheeled tightly downward on one wing tip, and Minith, with no urging from Tullea, happily followed. As they got closer, Tullea noticed that the rags had legs and arms sticking out from them.

Perhaps they had found J'trel's stray after all. Good, Tullea thought to herself, then we can go home!

"B'nik and Tullea have found someone," K'tan said as he entered Harper Kindan's quarters.

"J'trel's stray?" Kindan asked, rising from his stool and gently hanging up the guitar he'd been playing. "Come on, Valla," he called to the bronze fire-lizard dozing on his bed. The little bronze stirred, stretched, and leaped into the air, hovering near Kindan's right shoulder.

K'tan shrugged. "They should be here now."

The two walked out of Kindan's quarters and out to the

Weyr Bowl. The sun had broken through the morning mist that had settled in the Bowl, but the air still held a chill.

Above them two dragons burst into view and spiraled down. Gold Minith landed first, followed by bronze Caranth.

Valla took one look at Minith, gave a surprised squawk, and disappeared. Tullea wasn't fond of fire-lizards.

K'tan gestured to Kindan, and the two jogged toward the bronze dragon. Kindan could see that B'nik was holding someone in front of him.

"She's very cold," the bronze rider called out as he lowered the woman down to them.

"Where are her fire-lizards?" Kindan asked as he and K'tan took hold of the unconscious body.

"We saw no sign of them."

Lorana woke, warm. And dry. A small, warm lump nestled against her back and she felt blankets wrapped around her. She smiled lazily and turned to face the fire-lizard lump, wondering if it was Garth or Grenn—

With a shock she saw that it was neither—and then she remembered.

The little bronze took one look at her expression and leaped into flight and *between* out of sight.

Lorana sighed, eyes bleary with tears that did not fall. She had sent Garth and Grenn away. She had been certain she was about to die and she had wanted to save them.

And now she was alive and they were—? She closed her eyes and focused her mind, questing for them, looking for them.

A fire-lizard's squawk distracted her, followed immediately by a dragon's bellow.

"You're awake," a voice called from beyond the doorway. A man strode into the room. He looked to be a few years older than Lorana, and was dressed in harper's blue. The bronze fire-lizard hovered over his shoulder. The man had keen blue eyes and jet black hair. He was taller than Lorana and rangy, his body hinting at a wiry strength.

"Valla?" the man addressed the fire-lizard. The bronze

chattered back at him in obvious agitation. "Valla, she needs food. Go tell Kiyary our guest is awake. Valla, will you go?"

The fire-lizard gave Lorana one more concerned look and chirped a warning before vanishing *between*.

"Fire-lizards are not the best messengers," the man observed dryly. He looked down at her. "I'm Kindan."

As she began to sit up, Kindan put out a restraining hand. "Don't try to get up—you're too weak."

Lorana was already in motion, but she stopped as soon as she discovered the truth in his words: She felt as weak as a leaf.

A noise outside the room heralded the arrival of another person—a middle-aged man with the lean, muscular look of a rider. His brown hair had only a few strands of silver in it, and his brown eyes were kind.

"I've brought food," he announced, setting the tray he was carrying on the bedside table. He picked up a pot and poured some of its contents into a cup. "Though I suggest this herbal, first. A starved stomach needs to learn to eat all over again."

With a wordless gesture, Kindan helped Lorana sit up, rearranging pillows underneath her.

"I'm K'tan," the man said as he handed the cup to her. "The Weyr healer." He shook his head sadly. "You required much of my art these last six days."

"Thank you," Lorana told him gratefully. "I'm Lorana."

The healer and the harper exchanged looks, and Lorana got the impression that they had just silently agreed to shelve some question they had.

"Let me help you," Kindan said, sitting carefully on her bedside and handing her the cup of tea.

Gratefully, Lorana sipped the tea. The liquid was just lightly warmed, and her throat welcomed its soothing presence.

K'tan regarded her carefully as she drank. After a moment she pushed the cup away.

"Thank you," she said to Kindan. To the healer she said, "This is very good."

K'tan inclined his head in acknowledgment.

Suddenly Valla appeared, chittering. The fire-lizard took in the somber scene and closed his mouth instantly, giving Kindan such a regretful look that Lorana smiled.

"Is he always such a character?" Lorana asked, her eyes twinkling.

"He's usually much worse," Kindan agreed. "I think he's on his best behavior because—"

"I was on death's door," Lorana said, guessing what he hadn't said.

"You'll get better now," K'tan declared firmly. "If you can finish the tea, there's some broth here you might try."

"And then I'll fall asleep," Lorana surmised.

"You've been this ill before," K'tan guessed.

"The Plague." She remembered how hard she and her father had fought to save her mother, brother, and sister. And how, after battling for a fortnight, they'd lost first her sister, Sanna, then her brother, Lennel, and finally her mother.

After the fever had taken her mother, she and her father had cried in each other's arms. Neither she nor Sannel had wanted to live. And then she'd caught the Plague herself and her nightmares intensified to fill her waking days. The only pleasant thing had been her father's face peering down at her as he gently wiped her forehead or held her up and spooned down broth. She had wanted to go, to join her mother and siblings, but she couldn't—the thought of leaving him behind was too much. And the fever had passed, and she'd recovered.

She sensed a motion or a change in posture from Kindan and looked at him carefully. His face had many smile lines on it, but it was carefully schooled; she could see the pain he was hiding and she knew that this man had seen people—many people—die.

"Will I live?" she asked him quietly.

Her memory came back to her in a rush: the storm, Colfet, her plunge overboard, her blind thrust at the fire-lizards . . .

"Has anyone found Colfet?" she asked suddenly, trying once more to sit up. Kindan held up a restraining hand but she struggled against it. "He was all alone on the launch and his arm was broken."

Kindan gave her a startled look, followed immediately by careful scrutiny. Beyond him, Lorana felt K'tan tense with worry.

"The dragonriders found nothing," K'tan told her softly.

"Please ask them to keep searching," Lorana implored.

"I shall talk with the Weyrleader," K'tan promised.

Lorana turned her eyes to Kindan. "My fire-lizards? Did they get to safety?"

Kindan shook his head. "There's been no word of them."

Lorana slumped back into the bed.

"Here, try some more tea," Kindan told her softly, raising the cup once more to her lips. When she'd finished the cup he asked her, "Do you want to try some broth, too?"

Behind him, K'tan shifted, his tension easing. "I'll be going," the healer told them. He glanced at Lorana. "I'll check in on you later."

He gestured toward Kindan. "You're in good hands."

Lorana woke, tired but alert. The room was dark. The only light came faintly from a glow in the farther room. Something had startled her into wakefulness. The lump at her back—Valla—was a warm and comforting presence.

Suddenly the fire-lizard tensed up, and in a rapid motion sneezed, loudly and violently.

Do dragons get coughs often? Lorana's own words echoed in her memory.

The fire-lizard sneezed again.

"Kindan?" Lorana called.

"Kindan," she shouted, her sense of urgency heightened, "there's something wrong with Valla!"

She heard his startled movement from the room beyond as he roused himself out of bed. Valla needed the healer, Lorana decided. She felt about with her mind amongst the sleeping dragons in the Weyr, found the right one, and said, *Kindan has need of the healer.*

* * *

"He seems hot, nearly feverish," K'tan said minutes later as he examined the fire-lizard. Kindan had uncovered every glow he could find and the room was bright with light for the healer's examination.

K'tan shook his head. "I've never seen the like—not in fire-lizards."

"Did *your* fire-lizards cough, Lorana?" Kindan asked her, his eyes full of concern and worry as he stroked his fire-lizard. A wave of sadness washed over Lorana: She had tried several times to reach the minds of her fire-lizards, without success.

"No, but J'trel's Talith did," she replied.

Kindan and K'tan exchanged worried looks.

After a moment, K'tan said to Kindan, "I don't know what to do."

"My father used to make a brew for herdbeasts," Lorana suggested, then made a face. "I don't know if it would work for fire-lizards, though."

"It might be worth a try," K'tan said with a shrug.

"Do you remember the ingredients?" Kindan asked. Lorana nodded.

Kindan trotted off to the outer room and rummaged about for stylus and paper, which he brought back to Lorana. She wrote quickly, in her fair hand. K'tan leaned over, scanning the list as she wrote.

"We have these ingredients," he said when she finished. He took the list from her and headed for the door. "I shall have a brew presently."

Kindan turned to watch the healer leave, gauging how soon he could hope for his return. When he turned back to Valla and Lorana, he was surprised to see her hunched over the paper, stylus drawing furiously.

"This is Colfet," Lorana said as she finished the drawing. She handed it up to him. "I thought perhaps it might help in his search."

"I had forgotten that you drew," Kindan admitted. "When we heard from Ista Weyr, they mentioned the drawings you'd done for Lord Carel at Lemos."

Lorana blushed slightly and feebly waved the compliment aside. "They weren't that good."

She shifted her attention again, rapidly making a new sketch. "What I really wanted to do was *this*."

She showed the new drawing to Kindan. Two small six-legged creatures were on the page.

He raised an eyebrow inquiringly at her.

"I was hoping to draw every animal I could find on Pern, to understand their differences and similarities."

Kindan bent again to the drawings. "I recognize this one," he said, pointing. "I've seen it around in fields here." He pointed to the other one, shaking his head. "But—where did you find that?"

"Igen seashore," Lorana replied. She gestured at the differences and gave him a condensed version of the same observation she'd given J'trel nearly a month before.

"I'm impressed," Kindan said. He looked at the drawing again and then back at her. "Do you draw in colors?"

"Colors?" Lorana repeated in surprise. "I could never afford colors."

K'tan returned at that moment, bustling into the room quickly.

"Here we are!" he called, placing a tray with a steaming brew in Kindan's hands. "Have your little one try this."

It took all of Kindan's coaxing to get the first drop of the brew into the fire-lizard's mouth. Then Valla snorted indignantly and, with a red-eyed glare, blinked *between*.

"I don't think he liked it," K'tan observed dryly.

"It doesn't taste *that* bad," Lorana said defensively. "I tried a drop myself!"

"The trick now is to get him back," Kindan said with a sigh.

"So he can finish the medicine," K'tan added.

Kindan twitched a frown. "I had better go after him."

"I could stay with Lorana," K'tan offered.

"No," Lorana said. "I'm fine. If I need anything, I'll tell Drith."

K'tan's eyes widened, and Kindan turned to her in surprise.

"You spoke to Drith?" the healer asked. "He told me I was needed—that was *you*?"

Lorana nodded.

"I'd better go," Kindan repeated, clearly torn.

"Go, find your fire-lizard," K'tan said, passing the mug of brew to him. "See if you can convince him to try some more."

Kindan took the mug and trotted away.

As Kindan's footsteps faded away, K'tan looked back to Lorana and chose his next words carefully. "Can you speak to *any* dragon?"

"I think so," Lorana said. "I could talk with Talith."

"There's a Hatching soon," K'tan began. "And a queen egg—"

"J'trel thought I should be a Weyrwoman," Lorana said, shaking her head. "I don't know if I'd be any good," she admitted. "But I'd like to see a Hatching."

K'tan gave her a searching look and then nodded.

"Right now, you need your sleep." He gestured for her to lie back down. "I'll turn the glows down on the way out."

After K'tan left, Lorana tried to get back to sleep. She couldn't. She kept mulling over the events in her life. She felt sorry for Kindan and his sick fire-lizard. She felt responsible.

She knew, from her work with her father, how some herdbeasts would get sick and pass the sickness on to others. She knew from bitter experience that people could also pass sickness from one to another.

Her father had taught her that the best cure for sickness among herdbeasts was isolating the whole herd if one became ill.

"Even the healthy ones?" young Lorana had asked in amazement.

Her father had nodded. "They might be healthy today and

sick tomorrow. That's why the quarantine. We keep the sick
from the healthy."

"And if they don't get sick?"

"Well, we leave the herd isolated long enough to be sure
no more beasts are getting ill," he'd told her.

When the first incidents of Plague had been reported, and
worried rumors were flying thick amongst holders and crafters,
Sannel had said confidently, "This is a human illness. It may
affect the herdbeasts, but it won't affect the dragons or fire-
lizards."

Lorana knew that had something to do with the differences between native organisms and those transplanted from
Earth. Could it be, though, that humans or herdbeasts could
carry an illness that would affect fire-lizards?

She tried to shake the worrying thoughts away, tried to
find sleep, but she couldn't. To distract herself, she tried
searching once more for Garth and Grenn. The effort left her
sweating; her failure left her crying.

Her tears were still wet on her cheeks when she caught
sight of a light above, toward the entrance to her room. It was
multifaceted, like a fire-lizard's eye.

"Garth?" she called out. "Grenn?"

No answer. The light in the room was growing, and Lorana saw another glittering jewel in the room beyond.

The shapes were wrong for fire-lizard eyes. She frowned
in concentration. Slowly the light grew and she realized that
the faceted lights were always brighter than the light in the
rest of the room.

She turned on her side, propped herself up on an elbow,
and pushed herself upright in the bed, legs dangling over the
floor.

She felt light-headed but not quite faint. The room threatened to twist drunkenly away from her, but she forced herself
to concentrate on the faceted light and find the horizon above
her.

Lips tightened in determination, she pushed herself to her
feet.

She was shaky.

I should be resting, she told herself. But the lights tempted her.

Her first step was awkward and ungainly, but she found her feet and slowly walked toward the door.

Standing in the doorway, she could see the next room clearly. In the ceiling were more of the bright jewels. Lines of light stretched from jewel to jewel. One line of light seemed to be coming toward the jewel in her doorway from the jewel in the center of the room.

She gasped in amazement.

The jewels were some sort of glass, she realized, placed to mirror light into the rooms. The whole effect was beautiful.

She followed the line of light from her ceiling jewel to the one in the center of the room, pivoting around to see all the rays reflected from it to still more jewels.

Wind Rider had had something like these jewels to bring light from the deck down to the lower deck, but that glass had been fogged and green. The glass in these jewels practically shone with glistening clarity.

Tottering slightly, Lorana turned back to her own room to retrieve the paper and stylus Kindan had left behind for her.

Quickly she drew a sketch of the bejeweled ceiling. When she was done, she walked into the hallway, intent on following the line of jewels to their outside source. The hallway was anticlimactic, as the jewels and light path disappeared into the ceiling above.

Still, she followed the line of white light above her until she came out into the great Weyr Bowl and the warm morning light.

"Oh!" she gasped, looking up into the sky. "Oh!" Her eyes locked on the scene above her, she fell to her knees, laid the paper on them, and, fingers flying, tried to capture the images she was seeing.

The sky was full of dragons and fire-lizards cavorting like clouds of light brought to life in the early morning softness. Blue, green, bronze, brown, and gold. The fire-lizards flitted like swarms of dutiful attendants around the soaring drag-

ons, who took in the attentions of their smaller cousins with
the pleasure of elders for infants.

The chitters of the fire-lizards and bugles of the dragons
were reflected in her head by the deep mental voices of the
dragons and the flighty feelings of the fire-lizards—and Lorana thought that never had she seen a more beautiful dawn
chorus or had a more enjoyable moment in her life.

The moment was shattered, horribly, in an instant, as from
somewhere in the swarm, Lorana heard an unmistakable
cough. It was echoed, moments later, by another.

Dragons don't get sick. J'trel's words resounded horribly
in Lorana's mind.

It seemed that as Lorana's strength grew, Valla's strength
ebbed. In a sevenday, Lorana was nearly back to her full
health, while the little fire-lizard had become listless and
nearly lifeless.

Lorana did everything she could to help Kindan and his
fire-lizard. She and K'tan conferred often on herbal remedies, and K'tan even visited the Healer Hall at Fort Weyr in
search of more suggestions, but nothing seemed to help.

At K'tan's request, Lorana remained sequestered in her
room, even though she was much mended.

"We don't want you to wear yourself out and relapse,"
K'tan had said with a wag of his finger.

But Lorana, recalling her father's words about quarantine,
suspected that was not his only reason for the injunction.

A hoarse, wracking cough woke her in the middle of the
night. Sounds came from the large room outside her quarters. A shadow approached her.

"I brought you some colored pencils," Kindan called out.
"I was hoping you'd draw . . ."

Lorana sat up, found the glowbasket, and quickly turned
it. The glow did not light the room brightly, but it was
enough to see Kindan's worried face and the limp fire-lizard
he cradled in one arm.

He extended a bundle of colored pencils to her with his other arm.

"I'd be happy to draw Valla, Kindan," Lorana told him.

"It's not that—" Kindan began, but just then Valla coughed a long, rasping cough and spat out a gob of green, slimy mucus. Kindan made a face and pointed at the mucus. "It's *that*."

Lorana peered at the discharge for a moment and then took Kindan's bundle, picked up her new sketchbook—a gift from K'tan—from the bedside table beside, and drew rapidly.

"I've seen that sort of discharge from sick herdbeasts," she said as she finished her sketch and held it up to Kindan.

"Did they survive?" Kindan asked, looking down fondly at his fire-lizard.

Lorana quirked her lips. "Some of them."

"K'tan's still asleep and I'd hate to wake him. He was up all hours last night with a sick child," Kindan said after a moment. He gestured to her drawing. "I can show him this drawing when he wakes. In the meantime, could you make some more of that herbal for Valla?"

"K'tan wants me to stay here," Lorana protested.

"It's just a short trip to the Kitchen Cavern and no one's there—I checked," Kindan said, his eyes pleading with her. "We'll be back in no time."

Reluctantly Lorana nodded, unable to tell him that no herdbeast needing a second dose of herbal had survived.

They walked out into the Weyr Bowl. Lorana looked up at the dim rows of lights that stretched up from the basin of the Bowl to its rim.

"Are those dragons?" she asked Kindan.

"Mostly they're glows," Kindan told her. "You can just make them out during the day, but at night . . ."

He gestured and led her into another large cavern.

"This is the Living Cavern," Kindan told her, gesturing around at the trestle tables laid out in neat, long rows. One wall glowed with banked fires. He led her toward the brightest fire.

"This is the night hearth," he explained. "If ever you're hungry, you'll find something—including *klah*—here."

He gestured to a sideboard. "The cooks usually leave some bread and butter here, as well as fruit."

"Where do they store the herbs?" she asked.

Kindan gave her a puzzled look as he tried to remember, then brightened, pointing to a large cupboard at the far end of the cavern. "I believe the spices are there. Do you need any special herbs?"

"If the cooks keep the usual supply, I should be fine," Lorana said, heading across the room. She opened the doors and took a deep lungful of the tantalizing smells that came from the stored herbs. With the help of a glow Kindan held up for her, she quickly collected the herbs she required and walked back to the night hearth. In a few short minutes, she had the herbs simmering in a pot of water over the open flames.

"Not much longer," she said. Kindan nodded and gestured to the nearest chairs.

"Oh, let me!" Lorana said when she saw him trying to seat himself while not disturbing Valla. She pulled the chair at the head of the table out for him and pushed it back in a bit as he sat.

"Thank you."

Lorana sat herself nearby, angled so she could watch the fire.

An awkward, slightly sleepy silence, descended between them. Lorana found herself concentrating on the wheezy sound of Valla's breathing and dividing her gaze between the sick fire-lizard and his owner.

"I've never seen him like this," Kindan said after a long while, shaking his head sadly. "I've seen others, though."

"Fire-lizards?" Lorana asked in surprise.

"People," Kindan replied, eyes bleak.

"All my family, except my father, died in the Plague," Lorana said, shuddering at the memory.

Kindan gave her an encouraging look and Lorana found

herself recounting how the illness had taken her family, how the holders had been afraid that with their wandering ways, they might have brought the Plague with them, how—

"I was at the Harper Hall, to start," Kindan said when Lorana broke off with a sob. He explained how he had been sent to Fort Hold in disgrace after being accused of starting a fire in the Archives room. How he had worked with the healer at Fort as the first few Plague victims fell ill and then, as more and more succumbed, how the healer himself had taken ill and died, leaving Kindan alone, at just fourteen Turns, to carry on as best he could.

"You must have been very brave," Lorana said in awe.

"I was very tired," Kindan said with a shake of his head. "I was too tired to be brave."

"Very brave," Lorana insisted.

"They needed me," he said simply, his voice full of emotion. "I couldn't leave them."

"What about your family?" Lorana asked, trying to change the subject to something less painful for the harper.

"I have a sister still alive," he told her. "My father and all my brothers are dead." He grimaced. "Most died in a cave-in; the last died of the Plague."

"I'm sorry."

"My story's not that different from many others," Kindan replied with a shrug. "And better than some."

Not sure what else to say, Lorana went to check the herbal brew. Satisfied, she poured some into a tall glass.

"We'll have to let that cool," she said. She sniffed it. "It smells right."

"You can tell by smell?" Kindan asked, eyebrows raised.

"No," Lorana admitted. "I can only tell if something's not right—like if I left out an ingredient."

"I should have asked you for the ingredients, then I could have made it myself," Kindan apologized.

"With a sick fire-lizard in your arms?" Lorana asked, shaking her head. "Anyway, I'm happy to help."

"Well, thanks again," Kindan said. Valla snorted and turned.

Lorana leaned forward and held a hand just above the fire-lizard's head, careful not to touch it.

"I can feel the heat from here," she said.

Valla coughed green phlegm, which coated Lorana's hand before she could pull it away.

"I'm sorry," Kindan said.

"Don't apologize," Lorana said, rising to her feet. "I'll just wash it off. Perhaps I can find a small measuring spoon while I'm up."

"They're over there," Kindan said, pointing.

"You certainly know your way around a kitchen," Lorana answered with a grin.

"Only this one," Kindan agreed. "And mostly I know where to find the medicinals for a late night of harpering—headaches from the wine, sore throat from singing."

Lorana washed her hands, then chose a small measuring spoon and brought it back to where Kindan sat. She poured some of the herbal tea into the spoon and gestured to Kindan. With Kindan holding Valla still, Lorana managed to pry the fire-lizard's mouth open and coax him to swallow the dose.

"And now we wait," Kindan guessed. He looked over to Lorana. "You should go get your rest—it'll be dawn soon."

Lorana nodded, stifling a yawn, and left.

Back in her room, she found herself looking up at the ceiling once more, watching as the brilliant light jewels started to glow with light from the early morning sun.

Inspired, she rose again, found her sketchbook and the colored pencils Kindan had brought, and strode out into the Bowl.

Just as before, the Bowl slowly filled with fire-lizards and dragons, rousing and going to the lake at the far end to wash and drink, or *between* to the Feeding Grounds outside the Weyr. She sketched quickly, filling page after page with the brilliant colors of the dragons and fire-lizards frolicking in the warm morning sun. She stopped when she ran out of paper and, eager to show her work, rushed to the Kitchen Cavern.

She found Kindan just where she'd left him. He looked up at her, and his bleak expression told all she needed to know.

"He's gone," the harper said in a choked voice.

"How is he taking it?" M'tal asked K'tan later that morning when the Weyr healer gave him the news of the loss of Valla.

"As well as any," K'tan replied, shaking his head. "He's survived the loss of a watch-wher, and he lived through the Plague."

"Which is more than some of us can say," M'tal acknowledged ruefully, for he still felt guilty over his decision to close the Weyr when news of the Plague first reached them.

"It was the only choice we could make," K'tan told the Weyrleader firmly.

"Which does not make it any less painful."

K'tan nodded. "We helped as much as we could when the Plague was over."

M'tal grunted and made a throwaway gesture, signaling an end to the topic.

"We have another hard choice," K'tan told the Weyrleader after a moment of silence.

M'tal nodded in understanding. "Do we know if Valla's death was from contagion?"

"Other fire-lizards are coughing," K'tan said.

M'tal froze for a long moment. His question, when he asked it, was dire. "Can the dragons catch this sickness?"

"I don't know," K'tan admitted.

"And we can't afford to take the risk," M'tal surmised. He locked eyes with the healer who pursed his lips and nodded reluctantly. "Are you proposing that we ban the fire-lizards from the Weyr?"

K'tan's nod was nearly imperceptible.

"You must leave," K'tan said to her.

Lorana looked up from her drawing of the fire-lizards, eyes stricken. Behind him she could see Kindan, his eyes burning with hate.

"You killed the fire-lizards," Kindan snarled at her. "You brought the sickness."

"You must leave," K'tan repeated.

Yes, I must leave, Lorana thought to herself. This is my fault. I must go into quarantine. Until . . . until . . .

Lorana woke with a start, sweating. She looked around, trying to place herself. It was late, dark. She had been dreaming.

It had been nearly four days since M'tal had ordered the fire-lizards from Benden Weyr. Lorana had recovered her strength, but she had remained in the infirmary, scared of being seen by the weyrfolk, particularly those who'd had fire-lizards.

She gathered her gear together and found a carisak to stuff them into. She left the colored pencils and her drawings behind—perhaps they would make payment for all that the weyrfolk had done for her.

Slowly she crept out of the infirmary and toward the Weyr Bowl. Inside, she was numb. She felt nothing.

Except, maybe, hungry. No, definitely hungry. In fact, Lorana was painfully hungry. She could feel it in her belly, she could feel it in a hunger headache pounding in her head. She couldn't understand how she could feel so hungry so suddenly.

Her ears caught a faint humming. Her nose picked up the scent of food cooking, and her stomach rumbled.

Don't worry, you'll get fed, Lorana told her stomach.

But I'm so hungry, her stomach protested. Lorana was momentarily surprised; she couldn't remember her stomach ever answering her. She pushed the issue aside, allowing that it could be the product of many things—her exhaustion, her exposure, her weakness.

As she neared the end of the corridor, the sound of humming grew louder, and the smell of roasting meat stronger. Her stomach knotted in anticipation. Then, when she reached the torchlit Weyr Bowl, comprehension burst upon her like a wave.

A Hatching! In the Hatching Grounds across the Bowl,

dragons were hatching, and new riders were Impressing—and around them all, the adult dragons were humming encouragement.

For a moment, Lorana considered heading toward the sound. To see a Hatching! What a glorious thing!

But, no, she had to get away before anyone found her. Before they knew—

But I'm hungry! her stomach complained.

I'll feed you, honest, Lorana responded, wondering exactly when her stomach had become so demanding, and also wondering when she'd become so good at placating it.

She heard a murmur of voices growing louder, coming from the Hatching Grounds.

"I've never heard of such a thing!" someone said, his voice carrying loudly across to her. It sounded like Kindan.

"Hasn't a hatchling ever left the Grounds before?" a female voice asked.

Ahead, the darkness split off into three shadows. Two were human shaped, and they seemed to be following something. A hatchling!

What's a hatchling doing here? Lorana wondered. She shrank against the wall, trying to remain unseen, but the hatchling turned toward her.

I said I was hungry!

Lorana stopped dead, frozen in shock and fear, her breathing shallow, her eyes wide. It could not be. The dragonet couldn't be talking to her—it had to be her stomach.

Please, my wing hurts. The pitiful voice in her head was accompanied by a painful mewling that Lorana's ears heard.

Her instincts took over. She could never let an animal suffer. She rushed to the waddling dragonet and quickly untangled its baby clawed feet from its left wing tip.

"There, better?" Lorana asked out loud, oblivious to the crowd gathering around her, concentrating solely on this marvelous young gold dragon who had asked her for help.

Much, thank you, the dragonet replied, butting her head against Lorana's side. *I am Arith.*

And in that instant Lorana recognized the impossible. She had Impressed.

Lorana's sense of shock was overwhelmed by her nurturing instincts. She wobbled but did not fall down. Instead, she crouched beside Arith's head and began to gently rub, then scratch, the dragonet's eye ridges.

"Please," she said, looking up at the crowd for the first time, "Arith is very hungry. Can you get her something to eat?"

"Certainly," someone replied instantly. A figure broke from the crowd and hastened away toward the source of the distant succulent smells.

"Best get Lorana something, as well," Kindan added, in a rich, well-modulated tone that carried the length of Benden's great Bowl.

"Here," a voice much closer to her—a woman's voice—said, "Put this on." Lorana felt a warm jacket being draped over her. "You must be as frozen as you are hungry."

Lorana looked up to see a woman about six or seven Turns older than herself with blond hair and piercing blue eyes. A red-haired man stood beside her, looking protective. Lorana couldn't see that the woman needed it, she had rarely seen such a self-possessed person in her life.

"For a moment I thought maybe she was coming for me," the woman said with a chuckle. "I'm so glad it was you. *Two* would be impossible."

A sound, not quite a dragon sound, burst in the sky above them, and a small, ungainly, ugly gold shape descended toward them. It was a watch-wher, and when it alit deftly on the floor of the Bowl, it trotted over to the woman.

The gold watch-wher snuffed at Arith, who returned the gesture full of curiosity; then, with a satisfied *chirp,* the watch-wher sidled over to place her head under the blond woman's hand.

"I know you!" Lorana exclaimed. "You're Nuella."

"I told you your fame has traveled far and wide," Kindan said, bowing toward Nuella.

"This is Weyrleader M'tal," Kindan continued, gesturing to a silver-haired, wiry older man beside him.

"My lord—" Lorana was abashed to have been in the Weyr all this time without meeting him.

M'tal cut her off with a wave of his hand. "M'tal, please," he said. "Or Weyrleader, if you must. You are one of us now, Lorana."

Tears burst from her, running unchecked down her face. Arith looked at her worriedly.

Are you hurt? the dragonet asked, ready to both comfort and defend her mate.

It's all right, it's all right. I'm just so happy, Lorana assured her. And she was. M'tal's words had been just what she'd needed to hear. She had a home. She was Lorana, rider of gold Arith, dragonrider of Benden Weyr.

"I could not be happier," she said aloud.

Lorana found herself ensconced in the last empty Weyrwoman's weyr, her scant things moved without her asking, her stomach—and Arith's—filled beyond bulging, and all the while she was lost in the magic of gold Arith's whirling eyes.

Her dragon's eyes.

All the pain, the loss, everything that had gone before in Lorana's life was redeemed, erased, made nothing in the warmth of Arith's love.

It was as natural as breathing to Lorana that she'd pull her bedclothes over to her hatchling's lair and fall asleep, curled up tight around *her* dragon.

Kindan's rich voice woke her the next morning. "There's a warm pool just the other side of your sleeping quarters. I'm afraid you'll need it."

Lorana stretched—and winced. The hard stone of Arith's lair might be comfortable to the dragon, but it had left a lot to be desired by her weyrmate. Her muscles ached and threatened to cramp as she gently disengaged herself from the still-sleeping dragonet.

"I brought you some *klah*," Kindan added, extending a mug toward her as she rose.

"Would you happen to know where a robe is?" Lorana asked, feeling awkward in her nightdress.

Kindan pulled something off his other shoulder and tossed it to her. He turned away to give her privacy while she robed herself. "She'll sleep for several more hours, judging by her stomach," he told her.

"And she'll wake ravenous," Lorana added.

"Ten of the eggs still lie on the Hatching Grounds," Kindan said suddenly. "Ten out of thirty-two."

Lorana turned suddenly to Arith, reassuring herself that the dragon was all right, still here—still hers.

"That's not normal?" she asked, turning back to him with an apologetic look.

Kindan shook his head. "Not at all," he answered. "Oh, sometimes one or two are stillborn, but Salina's Breth has never had a stillborn egg in any of her clutches."

"What of the other Weyrs?" Lorana asked, her curiosity blending with her growing sense of unease.

"M'tal has spoken with C'rion," Kindan said, "the Weyrleader of Ista." He continued, "C'rion's queen has just laid a new clutch, so it will be some time before we find out more from there."

"And the other Weyrs?" Lorana asked.

Kindan shrugged. "We are only beginning to think of the questions we want to ask," he admitted. "That's why I wanted to talk with you."

"Me?" Lorana asked, trying to keep a note of panic out of her voice. What if she *was* the cause?

"K'tan and I would like you to work with us," Kindan told her. "Your drawings alone would be a great help."

"My drawings?" Lorana asked in surprise.

"Yes," Kindan agreed. He held up the drawing she'd made of the green sputum Valla had coughed up. "K'tan said we dare not keep samples of the actual infection, but with your drawings we can compare differences, and track changes in the sick.

"Which is not to say that your understanding of herd-beasts won't also be a great help," he added.

"Dragons aren't herdbeasts," Lorana protested.

"No," Kindan agreed with a nod. "They're not. But you'd be surprised at how similar illnesses can be between man, beast, and dragon."

Behind Lorana, Arith stirred in her slumber. Kindan noticed.

"I didn't mean to disturb her," he said. "In fact, I should leave you to yourself. I'm sure you'll want to wash up."

Lorana forced herself to relax. "Yes, the ground was harder than I'd thought," she said.

"Have your dragon bespeak Drith, K'tan's dragon," Kindan said as he made to leave.

Lorana nodded. "Is there a good time?"

He chuckled. "I suspect that your time will be more constrained than ours," he said, gesturing toward the sleeping hatchling. "Whenever you're ready and your dragon is asleep."

"Which won't be much longer," Lorana said as Arith shifted position again.

"No it won't," Kindan said, agreeably shaking his head. "I've kept you too long, I'm sorry. It's just—"

"I understand," Lorana replied.

Kindan made a half-bow and departed.

Arith awoke faint with hunger. Again. It had been three sevendays since she'd hatched. In all those sevendays, Arith had eaten scraps brought by the Weyrlingmaster. Lorana had been amazed at the dragonet's appetite, which rapidly grew from one large bucket, to two, then three, and finally five.

Arith's sleep was as erratic as any newborn's, which slowed Lorana's own recovery from her exposure and exhaustion. It was all Lorana could do to keep Arith fed, feed herself, and keep up with the constant oiling necessary to keep the dragonet's growing skin from cracking. She would wake up bleary-eyed and go back to bed bleary-eyed, never quite sure what hour of the day it was.

Fortunately, Arith's newborn growth spurt was finally smoothing out and her sleep pattern normalizing.

"She's growing very fast," P'gul, the Weyrlingmaster, had exclaimed the last time he had come to check on her. "She'll be ready for the Feeding Grounds soon."

He shook his head in amazement. "Catch her own food, too, I don't doubt."

Now, as Lorana guided the increasingly irritable dragonet out of their quarters on the lowest level of the Weyr, she realized that she did not know where the Feeding Grounds were. She stopped in confusion and stood in the great Bowl of the Weyr, looking around desperately.

"Are you going to wait until she dies from hunger, or were you perhaps hoping that her keening would disturb the whole Weyr?" a voice from behind her demanded caustically.

Lorana spun around to come face-to-face with a woman not all that much older than herself. The woman's face had a pinched look, as if she had been caught in a perpetual sneer. Her blue eyes were pallid and her lips were pursed tight in a thin line. Blond hair was pulled together behind her neck.

"I don't know where the Feeding Grounds are," Lorana said apologetically.

"Peh! Some Weyrwoman you'll make!" the other returned. "Didn't bother to listen to the orientation, did you? Too high and mighty. Expect the rest of us to look after you, do you?"

"No, I—"

"It's not as though we all don't have our own dragons to look after—" At this point a large queen burst into air above them, hovering near the other woman.

Arith took one fearful look up at the full-grown queen, gave a wistful chirp, was answered by an encouraging bellow, and promptly disappeared herself.

In a moment, Lorana could feel Arith's pleasure as she made her first kill, and she saw an image of the Feeding Grounds in her mind's eye. She looked up at the large queen, certain that she was the source of Arith's inspiration, and said with relief, "Thank you."

My pleasure, the queen responded, settling gently on the ground beside her rider. *Your little one was quite agitated.*

I'm sorry, Lorana apologized. *I hadn't expected to Impress her.* She got a feeling of amused tolerance from the queen. *I'm Lorana.*

I know, the queen responded. *I am Minith.*

"You talk to other dragons?" Minith's rider asked, shocked.

"Oh, yes," Lorana said, forgetting that this was not a common trait among the weyrfolk. The look on the other rider's face quickly disabused her. Trying to be civil—after all, the queen *had* helped Arith to the Feeding Grounds—Lorana stretched out her hand and said, "I'm Lorana."

The other eyed her hand dubiously but did not take it. "Tullea, Weyrwoman second," she said, still looking like she'd just bitten into a bitter fruit. "Salina asked me to check on you," she added in a tone that made it clear what she thought of that imposition.

"That was very kind of Salina," Lorana replied, desperately trying to place the name but failing. She knew she'd heard it before, but she was too groggy to dredge up the memory.

"You don't know who she is, do you?" Tullea asked accusingly.

"Her Breth is Arith's dam," Lorana temporized, feeling overwhelmed by the other woman's manner.

"Salina is the *senior* Weyrwoman," Tullea snapped. "Don't you know anything?" She didn't give Lorana time to respond before continuing, "Well, obviously you don't. I can't see what sort of help you'll ever be. Perhaps it would be best if—"

Minith erupted in a loud disapproving roar, cutting Tullea off. Tullea looked up at her dragon, her eyes softening somewhat.

"Now look what you've done, you've upset her."

"I'm sorry," Lorana muttered. Silently, she said to Minith, *My apologies, gold dragon.*

Minith gave Lorana a pert nod, eyes whirling red-green.

Lorana turned her attention to Arith, partly out of desperation. *Are you all done?*

One more, please! the dragonet pleaded.

Lorana couldn't help smiling. "Very well, silly," she said aloud.

"If your dragon gorges, don't come to me!" Tullea said, climbing up to Minith's neck. "I've better things to deal with."

With a great bound of her hind legs, Minith leaped into the air and beat her way up out of the Bowl. Once clear she blinked out of existence *between*.

Lorana watched the maneuver with her eyes wide. The adult queen was so graceful and her movements so beautiful.

Soon I'll be able to do that, Lorana marveled to herself, her thoughts going back to her splendid Arith. She had discovered with her fire-lizards that they knew how to go *between* from the moment they were born. Training them to come back, to go where she wanted, had taken many months of hard work. She knew from the Teaching Ballads that Arith had the same innate talent—in fact, she had just demonstrated it by going *between* to the Feeding Grounds—but it would take careful training over several Turns for Lorana to be able to ride her precious gold *between* to places of her own choosing.

Still, she entertained visions of rising into the air, blinking into the cold *between* and out again—anywhere on Pern.

Her heart gave a lurch as she realized the vistas her new-found freedom offered. She reached out with her mind to *her* dragon and made her presence tenderly felt. A rebounding wave of affection swept back to her from Arith. Lorana's vision suddenly misted as her eyes brimmed with joyful tears.

A moment later, she felt Arith quench her thirst with the hot blood of a herdbeast, felt her dragonet rend the flesh of the small beast, and felt her swallow without so much as a bite.

Chew! Lorana told her sternly.

I'm hungry, Arith complained. Lorana could feel the little gold's hunger, lessened by the two other herdbeasts she had consumed.

Greedy guts! Lorana thought back. She felt Arith's amusement and self-satisfaction. *That's your last one.*

Lorana felt Arith tense up in nascent disobedience.

I mean *it,* she warned the dragonet with the same fierce intensity she'd used to her fire-lizards. Biting back a pang of grief over their loss, she sent a second firm order to Arith.

All right, Arith allowed.

A burst of cold above Lorana heralded the hatchling's return through *between.*

Arith landed quickly, stumbled just a bit, and immediately proceeded to stroll nonchalantly up to Lorana with a very obvious I-meant-to-do-that swagger. Lorana laughed at her, reaching down indulgently to scratch the dragonet's eye ridges.

Ah, that's better, Arith sighed.

"They're not really supposed to go *between* until they're much older," a voice said beside her. It was K'tan.

Lorana smiled fondly at her little queen and stood up to face the Weyr healer.

"It's all right, I knew where she was," Lorana said.

"Even *between*?" he asked, eyebrows arched in surprise.

Still smarting from her encounter with Tullea, Lorana bit back her immediate irritated response and settled for, "Well . . . yes."

"Impressive," K'tan remarked.

"Kindan told me that you needed to talk with me several sevendays ago," Lorana said hastily, "but I'm afraid with Arith—"

K'tan held up a hand, shaking his head. "No need to apologize." He turned toward Arith, then turned back inquiringly to Lorana. "May I look at her?"

Lorana nodded.

K'tan's inspection was swift and gentle. He ran his hands from her head down her neck, to her forelegs, across her distended belly, and on to her withers and tail.

"She's making her own kills already?" he asked, his face showing surprise.

"That's not normal?" Lorana asked in response. "The fire-lizards usually need several sevendays of hand-feeding, but I thought dragons—"

"Dragons are not so different," he said. He stood up, backed away from the young queen, and shook his head admiringly.

"She's beautifully proportioned," he announced at last, adding with a grin, "barring her stomach."

Lorana felt herself grinning back in relief. She arched her neck to scan the weyrs around the Bowl, spotted one brown head looking down at them, and waved at the dragon she knew was Drith. Drith twitched, startled that she had recognized him, and nodded back at her.

"He's quite a beauty," Lorana said.

K'tan, who had followed her gaze, laughed. "Indeed he is," he agreed, his voice full of fondness for his dragon. Then he changed the subject back: "You say you knew where she was?"

Lorana nodded.

"How do you do that?"

Lorana thought for a moment, then shrugged apologetically. "I don't know how; I just do," she said.

"There she is!"

Lorana looked up. A tall, graceful, older woman was striding quickly toward them, accompanied by M'tal, the Weyrleader.

"Is it true that you can talk to any dragon?" M'tal asked when they arrived.

Lorana nodded. "Yes, Weyrleader."

"Excellent!" M'tal said.

"What is it like?" the woman asked. Lorana realized that this was Salina herself, Breth's rider and Benden's Weyrwoman.

"I don't know how to explain it," she began slowly. "I could talk to my fire-lizards of course—" She made a sad face at their mention, but continued on. "—so I guess I just didn't know I wasn't supposed to be able to talk to all dragons."

Salina nodded encouragingly. Lorana groped for words,

and found them. "It's like being in a room full of your best friends."

Her eyes lit as she peered up at all the weyrs above and the dragons looking back down at her.

"Sometimes I hear individual conversations, sometimes I don't," she said. "I don't pry," she added hastily, "and would never eavesdrop. But most of the time the dragons talk amongst themselves, you know."

"They do?" Salina's eyes widened in surprise. She glanced up to where her Breth lay. "Well, I suppose I'd never thought about it, but they *do* have a lot of time on their hands."

"At least until Thread falls," M'tal said. He asked Lorana, "Can you talk to watch-whers, too?"

"Watch-whers?" Lorana repeated. She shrugged. "I don't know, I've never tried."

"Hmm," M'tal murmured thoughtfully.

"If she can talk to all dragons, I would be surprised if she couldn't talk to all watch-whers, too," K'tan put in.

" 'A room full of your best friends,' " Salina repeated, mulling over Lorana's words. "Why are they your best friends?"

"Maybe they aren't," Lorana admitted with a frown. "But they seem like it. They're all so nice and courteous and always asking about me and Arith."

"Well, that's to be expected—you're a queen rider now," Salina said, with a touch of tartness in her tone.

Lorana flushed. "It's not quite like when my Garth rose to mate," she said, her thoughts racing along lines similar to Salina's.

"Garth?" M'tal asked.

"I had two fire-lizards," Lorana explained. "Garth was my queen."

"Oh," M'tal responded, his tone both enlightened and relieved. "So you've been through a mating flight."

Lorana nodded empathically. "Yes, definitely *through*," she agreed, her eyes flashing with amusement.

"It's a bit more intense when a queen dragon mates," Salina cautioned. M'tal grabbed at her possessively and pulled her close to him. Salina smiled and curled against him, wrapping an arm around his waist.

"So I've been told," Lorana said. The dragons had just filled her in, and she couldn't help but smile.

"The dragons told you?" M'tal asked.

"Well, not told, as it were, but more showed," Lorana admitted.

"When?" M'tal asked incredulously.

"Just now," Lorana answered.

"Showed?" K'tan asked.

Lorana frowned thoughtfully. "Sort of like a flurry of images and emotions," she reported. She caught the alarmed look that passed between Weyrleader and Weyrwoman and quickly added, "All very dragonish."

M'tal and Salina looked relieved, and Lorana guessed that they'd entertained the notion that the dragons might have conveyed intimate details.

I'm sleepy, Arith interjected.

"Of course you are, you just gorged yourself," Lorana replied. "Why don't you go lie down?"

All right, Arith agreed, tottering off toward their quarters. *Why don't you go eat?*

"I will," Lorana said. "I promise."

"What?" M'tal and Salina both asked.

"Eat," Lorana said. She raised a hand apologetically. "I'm sorry, but I'm just up."

"May we accompany you?" K'tan asked, gesturing toward the Lower Caverns.

"I don't know where I'm going, actually," Lorana admitted. "I've only been to the night hearth."

Salina's brow creased thoughtfully. "Why didn't you ask the dragons?"

Lorana looked surprised. "I hadn't thought of that."

"Actually," K'tan admitted, "I pretty much descended upon the poor girl just after Tullea finished with her."

M'tal sighed and exchanged a concerned look with Salina.

"Did you have words with Tullea?" the Weyrwoman asked,

pushing herself out of her cuddle with M'tal and starting across the Bowl.

"Well . . . yes," Lorana admitted as she and the others followed Salina.

M'tal pursed his lips tightly before saying, "Tullea seems to—"

"Have problems dealing with people recently," Salina finished.

M'tal arched an eyebrow in disagreement. "Recently being the past three Turns," he corrected.

"You mean she's like that with everyone?" Lorana blurted and then clapped a hand to her mouth in surprise. The other three laughed.

"I'm afraid so," M'tal said when he'd recovered, eyes still dancing with amusement.

"You shouldn't feel singled out," K'tan added.

"I'm sure she'll settle down when Thread comes," Salina said.

"Or her dragon rises," M'tal added.

"*Preferably* when her dragon rises," K'tan murmured.

"Her dragon hasn't risen yet?" Lorana asked, feeling the beginnings of some sympathy for Tullea.

K'tan leaned in close to Lorana, to murmur, "We're *hoping* that a mating flight will calm her nerves."

"Or something," Salina added, arching an eyebrow at K'tan.

"Ah, you found her!" Kindan called from a table as they entered the Living Cavern. "Are you hungry, Lorana?" he asked, then shook his head at himself. "Of course you are, I can see it from here! Sit, sit! I'll arrange for food."

Kindan eyed the group of women preparing food in the cavern and shouted out, "Kiyary! Could we have food for five—including one with a new hatchling?"

A young brunette in the group looked up, caught sight of Kindan, and waved acknowledgment. In short order Lorana found herself replete, filled with succulent fruits, hearty porridge, and warm *klah*. The others politely kept up conversation all around her while she wolfed down her food with all the abandon she had so abhorred in her dragonet.

Salina must have caught her mood, for she said, soothingly, "It's common for new riders to find themselves eating more—the appetites of their dragons can be overwhelming."

"Not to mention the work," K'tan added with a laugh. When he caught the confused look on Lorana's face, he added, "You oiled your fire-lizards, right?"

"Yes," she replied, around a bite of food and still a bit dazed. Then comprehension dawned, and her eyes widened. "Oh! Oh, she is already quite a bit larger than my two."

"Oiling a dragon is a large part of what we dragonriders do," K'tan admitted, eyes twinkling.

"But if you've had two fire-lizards, then you probably won't find *one* dragon all that difficult," Kindan said reassuringly.

"At least not to start," K'tan corrected. He gestured to Lorana's plate. "Eat up, you'll need your strength."

"I think I've had enough, already." Lorana covered her mouth to stifle a yawn.

"And after you eat, you sleep," Kindan said. "When you're not eating, or sleeping—" The others joined in. "—you're oiling."

"Dragons and fire-lizards aren't the same," M'tal said, directing his comment to Salina.

Lorana's eyes narrowed as she detected an undercurrent in the conversation. She realized that it had been there all along but she'd been too hungry and too distracted to notice it. In fact, now that she had recovered from her encounter with Tullea, Lorana became aware of a shadow of dread in the Weyr's atmosphere.

She looked entreatingly at K'tan, but the Weyr healer had ducked his head in thought. She turned her attention to Kindan. He caught her glance and imperceptibly tilted his head toward Salina.

Something was wrong with the Weyrwoman? Lorana wondered. Salina looked pensive, withdrawn, but otherwise healthy. Lorana gave Kindan a slight shake of her head to say "I don't understand."

Just then she heard a loud cough and a snort, which echoed around the Weyr. Salina started, looked out toward the Bowl, and then lowered her head slowly, leaning against M'tal.

"It may not be the same thing," M'tal said, grabbing her hand consolingly. "It may not be the same thing at all."

Lorana felt her stomach wrench in fear. She did not have to ask which dragon had coughed, nor did she need to hear Breth's apologetic, *Sorry.*

"Repeat that herbal recipe for me," K'tan asked her urgently. All too willingly, Lorana complied.

Salina lifted her head from M'tal's shoulder and smiled wanly at Lorana.

"We shouldn't keep you, dear," she told her. She gestured toward the weyrs. "Go, get some rest. Your Arith will be awake again soon enough."

"I will not tolerate shirkers," Weyrleader D'gan growled at the blue rider in front of him. Telgar's Weyrleader was dressed ready to ride. Above him in the distance were arrayed the wings of Telgar Weyr—all except one. D'gan's face was twisted in a scowl.

"But Jalith is—"

"Shirking!" D'gan shouted back, towering over the shorter blue rider in his rage. He spared a contemptuous glare for the blue's Wingleader, who wilted visibly. Jalith and M'rit were oldsters who had been at Telgar Weyr when D'gan had first arrived. "They are testing my authority as Weyrleader."

D'gan remembered the derision he and the riders from Igen Weyr had received when they had first arrived at Telgar Weyr. It was not their fault that Igen had fallen on such hard times, nor that their dying queen had failed to lay a gold egg.

"I honestly don't think so," K'rem, Telgar's Weyr healer, said as soothingly as he could. "Jalith is aspirating the same ooze that the fire-lizards—"

"Don't tell me!" D'gan roared again. "I don't care." He

jabbed a finger upward, pointing to the sky. "Thread is coming. I won't have any shirkers. 'Dragonmen must fly when Thread is in the sky.' "

It had taken hard work—more work, D'gan was certain, than old Telgar riders would have required—for D'gan to win respect at his new Weyr, and finally to win the senior queen and become Weyrleader. Since then he'd shown them, every day, what sort of riders came from *Igen* Weyr.

"I know my duty," D'gan growled. "And all the riders in *my* Weyr will do *theirs*."

"Thread is not in the sky today," K'rem protested. "Perhaps if we let Jalith rest . . ."

"No!" Veins stood out in the side of D'gan's neck. "Not today, not tomorrow, not any day. All my wings will fly with all their dragons. We will *train* to fight Thread. There will be no shirkers." He pointed at the wilting blue rider. "Mount your dragon, join your wing."

The blue rider blanched.

"Maybe if I could give Jalith something—" K'rem suggested.

D'gan cut him off. "You may do anything you like, Healer—*after* we fly our pattern." He took two quick strides toward his bronze, leapt onto the great neck, and drove his dragon skyward.

The next several sevendays were a blur of feeding and oiling Arith, occasionally catching food for herself and snatches of sleep where she could. Lorana naturally assumed that young dragons were awake at all hours—just like young children—so it was not until K'tan explained that she realized there was anything out of the ordinary.

"Normally things wouldn't be this disrupted," the Weyr Healer told her as he met her on her way to the Food Cavern, "except for Breth's problems. When the queen doesn't sleep, the Weyr doesn't sleep."

"Does Arith wake the others, too?" Lorana asked, worriedly.

K'tan shook his head. "Only a little," he assured her. "All

the bronzes and most of the browns are attuned to the Senior Queen, so . . ."

Lorana nodded in understanding.

"And then there are the fire-lizards," Kindan chimed in from behind them.

Lorana whirled, and Kindan gave her an apologetic wave, all the while smiling most unapologetically.

" 'A harper's best instrument is his ears,' " K'tan said, quoting the old saying.

Kindan shook his head, grinning and pointing to his forehead. "Ears are second, brains are first."

"Then mouth is third," K'tan said with a snort.

"Of course," Kindan agreed, grinning. His mood sobered. "As I was saying, the fire-lizards."

"What about them?" Lorana asked.

"We're trying to understand how they got sick and how long before . . ." Kindan's voice trailed off.

"They die?" Lorana finished. Kindan nodded, lips drawn tight.

They reached the Cavern and sat near the fire. Kindan waved cheerfully to Kiyary, who smiled back and brought over a plate of cheese and a pitcher of *klah*. Mugs and plates were already laid out on the table in anticipation of the midday meal. Kindan grabbed a roll out of the basket in the center of the table, tore it open, and deftly spread it with the soft cheese. With a raised eyebrow, he tilted the basket toward Lorana, who grabbed a roll with a nod of thanks, and then Kindan repeated the performance with K'tan.

For a moment the three were silent, intent on preparing and eating their rolls. Kindan finished his first, then reached for the pitcher of *klah* and filled his glass and the glasses of the other two. He drank deeply before continuing. "If we can understand how the illness progresses in fire-lizards, then maybe we can gain some understanding about how the illness will affect dragons."

"I can't help you," Lorana told them, shaking her head sadly. "I don't know quite when my two got sick—I'm not even sure if they did."

"And you sent your two *between*?" K'tan asked, eyes narrowed in thought.

"Valla went *between,* too," Kindan added.

"To die?" K'tan wondered.

"Valla was hot and feverish," Lorana said.

"Maybe the cold of *between* is too much for them when they're sick," K'tan suggested.

"Or they got disoriented," Kindan said.

"Lost *between*?" Lorana shuddered. Then she thought for a moment. "So the first thing to do would be to prevent a sick fire-lizard—"

"Or dragon," Kindan interjected.

"—or dragon," she continued, "from going *between.*"

"But that doesn't answer whether the disease itself is deadly," K'tan objected.

"True," Kindan agreed with a shrug.

"On the other hand," K'tan noted, "we'll *never* know if the disease itself is fatal if we can't keep a fire-lizard from going *between.*"

"Or a dragon," Kindan added darkly.

"I hope," K'tan said fervently, "that it doesn't come to that."

"Someone's coming," Lorana said suddenly, eyes wide.

The other two looked around. "Where?"

"Between," she said. She looked pained. "The dragon is unhappy; so is the rider."

"You can feel them?" K'tan asked.

Lorana nodded. "They're *very* distressed."

Outside came the sound of a dragon popping out of *between.* The watch dragon bugled a challenge.

Nidanth and C'rion from Ista, was the response Lorana heard from the arriving dragon.

"Come on," K'tan called as he started out toward the Bowl.

A wave of emotion swept Lorana off her feet. Kindan grabbed her before she could fall.

Dragons keened mournfully. *Kamenth of Ista is no more,*

Gaminth reported. Then the noise redoubled. *Jalith of Tel-gar has gone* between, Salina's queen, Breth, added.

"Here, lean on me," Kindan told Lorana. She pushed away from him. The pain of the dragons' loss tore her heart.

"No! I must get up—Arith will be worried."

"Then let me help you," Kindan repeated firmly.

Lorana forced herself to recognize his logic and, with an angry sigh, wrapped her arms around him. "Be quick," she told him.

In the Bowl, a bronze dragon was just landing. The rider looked shaken. Other riders, no less shaken than he, were gathering about him. Lorana recognized M'tal and Salina. Tullea was clinging unnaturally to B'nik.

K'tan was beside the bronze rider, supporting him while the bronze dragon curved its head down close beside, eyes whirling in distress.

"I'd heard you had some cure," C'rion, Weyrleader of Ista Weyr, said hoarsely to K'tan.

A loud, gurgling cough from high above startled them all.

"Breth, no!" Salina shouted as her queen leaped off her ledge and into the air. "No! Stop!"

Lorana took a hasty breath, looked up just as the queen went *between,* and closed her eyes. In her mind she leapt after the queen, calling, *Breth, come back! Come back!*

She bent her will to holding onto the queen, but Breth was stronger. Slowly, Lorana felt the queen draw away from her, farther *between* than Lorana had ever been before. In a frightened instant, she lost the queen, and then felt herself become lost.

Arith! She called out desperately in her mind, groping to find her way back. She heard no answer. Frantically, she thrashed, lost in an aloneness more vast than *between.* Then, at the edge of her being, she felt some "other." She grabbed at it, was rebuffed by it, and felt no more.

All life functions are the product of the interaction between thermodynamics and chemistry.
—*Introduction*, Elementary Biological Systems, 18th Edition

Chapter Ten

Fort Hold, First Pass, Year 50, AL 58

WIND BLOSSOM WOKE with a start. There was danger. Danger to dragons. *No,* she told herself, pushing herself upright on her cot with one arm, *I was dreaming.* She dropped her feet off the bed and sat up, her bare feet resting on the cold wooden slats that lined the tent floor. Her body complained more fiercely than usual; she was still aching from the cold and the rain.

I'm just extrapolating from the fire-lizard to the dragons, she told herself. Which is logical.

She thought back over the past several weeks.

The fight to save Tieran's precious fire-lizard had taken over seventeen days, even with the last of the antibiotics.

The infection was so severe that Wind Blossom was tempted to destroy the specimen of green ooze she'd collected for fear of infecting others with it. As it was, she ordered the dead fire-lizard's carcass dissolved in boiling nitric acid—and she seriously considered ordering the same for the living fire-lizard.

In the end she'd destroyed neither the surviving fire-lizard nor the specimen. Under the microscope, she'd managed to identify a vast array of antibodies in the green sputum. Unfortunately, she hadn't been able to go much further than that. If the technicians had still been alive to operate the equipment, she could have dried samples sufficiently to put them under an electron microscope, if there'd been one still working.

Better yet, if even more advanced technology were still available, and they'd managed to complete their microbial survey, Wind Blossom could have employed computerized micro-arrays to assay the genetic material of the microbes found in the sputum and search for one matching previously known infectious bacteria with similar characteristics. But the sad truth was that the first Threadfall had occurred at Landing long before they had acquired an understanding of Pernese ecosystems.

As it was, Wind Blossom got more useful information by observing the living fire-lizard's response to the general-purpose antibiotic.

It took more than four days, using a maximum body-weight dose, for the fire-lizard's lungs to stop showing signs of distress. She continued the antibiotic until it ran out—still not certain that she'd managed to knock out all of the infection.

She had only a vague idea of what had caused the fire-lizard's infection. Repeated but guarded requests for any signs of unusual behaviors in fire-lizards had turned up nothing. Unbelievably, it seemed that only these two fire-lizards had acquired the new illness.

While she was busy coordinating the establishment of their quarantine—including the acquisition of this tent from Lord Mendin, who was much put out when later informed that the tent and everything in it would have to be burned once the quarantine was lifted—Janir and Emorra had been busy answering questions from the four corners of Pern. A prime concern was controlling the curiosity of uninfected fire-lizards. They had to be directed to come to either the College or Fort Hold—not the Drum Tower.

The Drum Tower's watch—after the tower itself had been disinfected thoroughly with hot ammonia—had been strengthened to provide continuous coverage of the place set aside for the tent, which housed Wind Blossom, Emorra, Tieran, Kassa, and their fire-lizard patient.

Rain beat down upon the tent. The interior was dimly lit by glows. Through the flap at the front of the tent, Wind Blossom could see that it was getting lighter outside, and she guessed dawn would come in a few more hours.

Tieran was sleeping oddly, one arm gently draped over a bulge in his blanket—the fire-lizard.

Kassa, who had the current watch, gave Wind Blossom a nod, then returned to her brooding by the stove. In their time together, Wind Blossom had come to respect the young woman and to understand that Kassa had been willing to look beyond Tieran's disfigurement to the young man beneath the surface.

Emorra started in her sleep, and her eyes opened. Catching sight of her upright mother, she wearily sat up in her own cot.

"Are you all right, Mother?"

Wind Blossom waved a hand dismissively. "I'm fine," she said. "The fire-lizard is probably also fine." She gestured toward the lump in Tieran's blanket.

"Then why are you up?" Emorra asked, a touch acerbically.

Kassa turned from her place at the fire to follow their conversation attentively.

"I had a dream," Wind Blossom confessed. "A nightmare, really."

Kassa looked up at Wind Blossom expectantly.

"Dragons?" Emorra asked, her body going tense.

"Something wrong with dragons?" Kassa repeated. "I dreamed that, too."

When the others looked at her, she shrugged. "Daydreamed, really. I was awake, staring into the fire."

"It—the dream—felt odd, it startled me awake," Emorra confessed.

Wind Blossom sighed. "It was nothing," she decided. "We are all worried, especially now that the little brown seems to have recovered. It's natural."

Emorra gave her a skeptical look.

"I've never had a dream like this before," Kassa said. "My dreams aren't as vivid as this."

"It's probably just nerves," Emorra said. "We are not sleeping in our usual quarters."

"Maybe," Kassa allowed.

"I, for one, will rest easier when we discover the owner of the fire-lizards," Emorra said.

Early on, Wind Blossom, Emorra, and Tieran had examined the brown fire-lizard and noted with admiration the carefully reset break in its wing. It was obvious from that alone that these two fire-lizards belonged to someone. Tieran insisted on keeping the brightly decorated bead harness that the fire-lizard had worn, convinced that it was vital to identifying the owner.

The harness had been sterilized in boiling water for over thirty minutes and would be sterilized once more before Wind Blossom ended the quarantine.

"Go back to sleep, Mother," Emorra said, lying back down on her bed. "It's not yet dawn and the weather looks no better than yesterday."

In consultation with Janir, Emorra, and Mendin, Wind Blossom had decided that the quarantine could end when the fire-lizard showed no signs of illness for more than a week, and when the weather was good enough to burn their encampment. She hoped it would be a warm day, because the final decontamination treatment promised to be a chilly affair.

Wind Blossom had informed the others in quarantine of it the week before, so they had had plenty of time to get over their shock. She had arranged with Janir to get them a mild acid solution. When they were ready for the final decontamination, they would strip, remove all body hair, leave the tent, and scrub each other with the acid solution.

The acid would instantly turn the oils of their skin into soap and kill any germs on their bodies. It would be a very chilling process, and Emorra had argued against that treatment for her mother, but Wind Blossom had been adamant.

"So we're all going to be standing around out there naked as the day we were born?" Kassa had squawked.

"What about the fire-lizard?" Tieran asked.

"You'll have to explain to him that we'll need to do the same thing to him, too," Wind Blossom said.

"If you tell him that he'll get an extra treat after we're done, and especially oiled as well, maybe he'll stand for it," Emorra suggested.

Tieran looked dubious. There had been too many times when he'd been afraid that the fire-lizard would take off *between* never to be seen again. He had spent many sleepless nights worrying about that until the fire-lizard's fever had broken.

Tieran had woken that morning to a head softly rubbing against his cheek and a plaintive *cheep*. Small green eyes whirled. As Tieran stared in amazement, his heart beat faster and faster with the hope that this fire-lizard would stay with *him*. And so the little brown had.

Now Wind Blossom regarded her daughter thoughtfully, considering whether she would take her advice and go back to sleep. Just as she had made up her mind and was ready to lie back down, Emorra's eyes opened again and she said, "What would happen if the dragons *did* get infected?"

Wind Blossom gestured for her to continue, noticing that Tieran had awakened and, like Kassa, was listening intently.

"Threadfall's over; the dragons don't have to fight," Emorra said. "If the infection is just in the lungs . . ."

"Are you suggesting that the shock of *between* killed the queen fire-lizard?" Wind Blossom asked.

Emorra frowned. "If so, would going *between* kill infected dragons?"

"So the dragons would be unharmed as long as they could be prevented from going *between*?"

"If the infection itself isn't deadly," Emorra agreed. "And hopefully the dragons would build up an immunity."

"True, but the immunity would not be expressed in the germ plasm," Wind Blossom countered.

"Meaning what?" Kassa asked, her brow creased in irritation. She had done her best to try to follow their various discussions for the past sevenday, but it was difficult for someone not trained in medicine.

"She means the next generation of dragons would be just as likely to catch this infection," Emorra explained. "Assuming, of course, that it ever mutates sufficiently to infect dragons instead of fire-lizards."

"No," Wind Blossom said, shaking her head. "There is little doubt that an organism that attacks fire-lizards will also attack dragons and watch-whers."

"But the dragons are so much bigger!" Kassa objected.

"There is something to that," Wind Blossom conceded with a nod of her head.

"Do you mean that there would have to be many more of the organisms—"

"Bacteria," Wind Blossom corrected.

"Why bacteria?" Emorra wondered.

"Because the infection in the fire-lizard was suppressed with an antibiotic," Wind Blossom replied with a look of exasperation. "If it were viral, the antibiotic would not have worked."

"Of course," Emorra said, and grimaced, feeling like an especially dim pupil in front of an acerbic teacher. "I'm tired, Mother. My mind's not working at its best."

"Obviously," Wind Blossom agreed tartly. She looked at Kassa. "Your point about size was a good one. It is quite likely that there would have to be more bacteria on a dragon before the infection manifested itself."

"And that gives the dragon's immune system more time to build antibodies," Emorra pointed out. "So maybe this infection wouldn't affect dragons or watch-whers."

"Perhaps," Wind Blossom allowed. "But would you risk all of Pern on a possibility?"

Kassa worked on the question. The answer left her horrified. "Are you saying that if the dragons got infected, they could all die—and leave Pern defenseless against Thread?"

"We hope it won't come to that," Emorra said fervently.

"But that is why we must know more about this fire-lizard and its owner," Wind Blossom declared.

"Why not look at its harness," Tieran suggested sleepily. The others all jumped.

"I didn't meant to disturb you," Wind Blossom apologized.

"Fine," Tieran replied grumpily, "then stop talking and let me get back to sleep." He turned over and then turned back again, looking at Wind Blossom. "I thought I heard you say that the fire-lizard's illness was bacterial."

"I did."

Tieran gave her a surprised look. "I can't see why you say that. What if the bacteria infection was only opportunistic?"

Wind Blossom's eyes widened as she considered his question. "That is certainly a possibility," she admitted.

"You were the one who told me to know what you're talking about before you open your mouth," he observed grumpily, rolling back in his bed again.

Kassa regarded Wind Blossom with wide eyes, waiting for the older woman to flay the young man with her tongue. She was disappointed. Wind Blossom raised an eyebrow at Tieran, shrugged, and lay back down on her cot.

Emorra and Kassa exchanged amazed looks and then Emorra, too, closed her eyes.

Presently, it was quiet once more in the tent. In her memory, the whole conversation began to assume an unreal air as Kassa waited for dawn to properly wake them all.

"Food's here!"

Moira's shout woke them several hours later. Tieran and the fire-lizard were the first out of the tent.

"How are you today, Tieran?" Moira asked.

She had volunteered to bring their food every day since the quarantine had started, rain or shine—and it was mostly rain. Tieran was very grateful for her dedication.

"What's the news?" he asked, carefully taking the basket of food from where Moira had left it and carrying it toward the tent.

"The weather is supposed to break in three days," Moira said. "Maybe if Wind Blossom says—"

"If the fire-lizard is still well, that would be a good time," Wind Blossom said, slipping out of the tent. "Please tell Janir."

"I will," Moira replied with a bob of her head. "Janir sends his apologies and says that he'll be along later in the day."

"Janir is always busy," Wind Blossom said. Tieran gave her a look, not quite certain how to take her statement. "Please tell him he must make a stockpile of nitric acid—"

Moira looked confused.

"My mother means HNO_3," Emorra said, stepping out of the tent to stand beside Wind Blossom. She looked at her mother. "Why should he do that?"

"Precaution," Wind Blossom said. She looked back to Moira. "Tell him to get at least thirty barrels."

"Thirty barrels," Moira repeated with a nod.

"Quickly," Wind Blossom added.

"Very well, I'll tell him," Moira answered. She turned to leave. "I must get back to the College, to start the next meal."

"Someone wake Kassa," Emorra said, "or Tieran will eat her breakfast, too."

Janir came by that afternoon, stopping a good ten paces upwind of the tent. Tieran was on watch and called to the others.

It was raining, a cold, steady drizzle. Emorra carried an umbrella to cover their group; Janir protected himself with an umbrella of his own.

"Moira said that you wanted thirty barrels of nitric acid, is that right?" Janir began.

"Yes," Wind Blossom answered simply.

"Why?" Janir asked. "I thought burning the tent and its contents would sterilize the area enough."

"Not for the tent, for emergencies," Wind Blossom corrected.

"For other fire-lizards," Emorra said.

"Or dragons," Wind Blossom added. "Have we heard any news?"

"About other fire-lizards getting sick?" Janir asked. At Wind Blossom's nod he replied, "No."

"It's hard to believe that this infection is an isolated incident," Wind Blossom said.

"Maybe we were lucky," Emorra suggested.

"How much luck can we have?" Wind Blossom asked. "Do you want to bet on luck when one of the fire-lizards is dead and all our antibiotics are gone?"

"Has anyone asked which Holds are beading their fire-lizards?" Tieran wondered suddenly, holding up the bead harness that the fire-lizard had worn. The little brown saw it and gave a chirp of recognition.

"We'll get it back on you soon enough, little one," Tieran told him apologetically. The fire-lizard made a small noise and rubbed his head affectionately against Tieran's hand.

Janir shook his head. "We've heard nothing so far."

"It's been nearly three weeks," Emorra said with a touch of heat in her voice. "How long can it take?"

"The holders aren't being as responsive as we'd like," Janir confessed. Wind Blossom quirked an eyebrow.

"There's some feeling that this is a bit of a tempest in a teapot," he explained. "There have been no reports of holders even considering putting bead harnesses on the fire-lizards. There just aren't all that many of them, and everyone pretty much recognizes each fire-lizard."

"Then where did he come from?" Wind Blossom demanded. "Are there others like him? Other sick fire-lizards?"

"Wouldn't they all have died or recovered from the infection by now?" Janir asked her.

"What if the infection can be passed to dragons?" Emorra demanded. "What then?"

Janir raised his hands. "No dragon has gotten sick like this—"

"Before now," Wind Blossom interrupted him, "I have never seen a fire-lizard sick like this. Ever."

"But he recovered, didn't he?" Janir protested. "I'm sorry,

Wind Blossom, but you know the backlash we got from Mendin over what will happen to his best festival tent—"

"Not important," Wind Blossom cut him off. "We must find out where this fire-lizard came from. We must know more about this infection. We must know how it spreads, what its symptoms are, and how fatal it is."

"Right now you have a baseline of fifty percent mortality," Janir pointed out.

"And this one survived only with the last of the anti-biotics," Emorra added. "We don't know if a fire-lizard could survive unaided."

Wind Blossom raised her hands and said, "We know how hard the human population was hit by the Fever Year forty-two years ago. Can you imagine what would happen to the dragons if half of them died?"

Janir's face slowly drained of all color.

Bronze for golds,
Brown, blue, for greens,
So do the dragons
Follow their queens.

Chapter Eleven

Telgar Weyr, End of Second Interval, AL 507

"AND YOU'RE SURE, D'nal, that the watch dragon has her orders right this time?" D'gan sneered. They were up high at the top of Telgar Weyr, where the watch dragon was posted.

"Yes, I'm sure," D'nal, the object of Weyrleader D'gan's derision, replied. "No more fire-lizards will come into the Bowl."

"No!" D'gan shouted. "No more fire-lizards are to come *anywhere* near the Weyr!"

D'nal nodded, his fists clenched tightly to his side. D'gan stared at him, jaw clenched, until the shorter rider took a backward step involuntarily.

"How will the holders communicate with us if they can't send their fire-lizards?" L'rat, leader of the second wing at Telgar, asked.

D'gan raised an eyebrow at L'rat's question and saw the other dip his eyes, unwilling to match D'gan's look. He snorted. "They'll light beacons and raise the call flags," he replied. "The useless flitters were no good with messages anyway."

"No one really knows, D'gan, if the fire-lizards brought the illness," K'rem, the healer, said.

"Well, then, we'll find out, won't we?" D'gan returned sourly.

Fifteen. Fifteen dragons had died in the past sevenday,

three of them so sick that they could not even go *between* but expired in their weyrs.

"They were useful for communicating with the Masterhealer," K'rem added.

D'gan vetoed the idea with a shake of his head. "The Masterhealer concerns himself with people, not dragons."

"We should tell the other Weyrs—" L'rat began.

"We will tell them *nothing*!" D'gan roared. He turned away, facing east, away from the Weyr Bowl behind him, away from his Wingleaders, his face into the wind.

"But surely they will have the same problems," D'nal said.

"Listen, all of you," D'gan said angrily, whirling around, jabbing a finger at each of them. "Telgar Weyr will take care of itself," he declared, pointing at D'nal. He turned to L'rat, saying, "I will not have that addled M'tal or that cretin C'rion making fun of us, telling us what to do.

"Remember how they chided when we brought the two Weyrs together? How jealous they were that they hadn't thought to absorb poor Igen when our last queen died? How envious they were once we started winning the Games, Turn after Turn?

"We are the largest Weyr, the strongest Weyr, the best-trained Weyr," he said, emphasizing each point by slapping a clenched fist into the palm of his other hand. "We will be the best at fighting Thread," he declared. He turned eastward toward Benden Weyr, then south toward Ista Weyr. "And then *they* will come asking us for advice."

To the healer he said, "If you can figure out a way to defeat this illness, *then* we'll have something to talk to the other Weyrs about."

K'rem pursed his lips tightly. L'rat and D'nal exchanged troubled looks.

"K'rem, have you isolated the sick dragons?" D'gan asked.

"There are thirty dragons that are very sick," K'rem said with a shake of his head. "I don't think they should be moved. Another dozen or so are only showing the first signs of a cough—"

"Move them! Move them all," D'gan commanded. "I told you that already—why did you delay?"

"Do you want to lose more dragons?" K'rem asked. When D'gan's brows stormed together he continued quickly, "If we move them, they may die. Do you want their deaths on your hands?"

"Do you?" D'gan replied. The healer dropped his gaze and D'gan snorted. "I didn't think so. Move the sick ones!"

"You will have to break up the wings," D'nal pointed out.

"Then do it," D'gan said. He looked at K'rem. "Isn't this the way the herders isolate sick beasts and save their herds?"

"But these are *dragons,* D'gan," L'rat protested. "We don't know how they are getting sick, how the illness spreads."

"And we won't begin to find out until we isolate the sick ones," D'gan responded with a pointed look at K'rem.

Reluctantly, K'rem nodded. "If we isolate them, who will look after them?" he asked. "My Darth is not ill."

"Hmm. Good point," D'gan agreed. He bent his head to his hand in thought. Finally he looked up, decisive. "Have some of the weyrfolk help them."

He gestured to the others.

"Let's go to the Star Stones and see how much time we have before the Fall starts," he said in a suddenly cheerful voice. "Things will sort themselves out when Thread comes, you'll see."

M'tal stood back from his observation at the Star Stones of Benden Weyr, grim-faced.

"The Eye Rock has bracketed the Red Star," he told K'tan and Kindan, gesturing for them to look for themselves.

Kindan told the Weyr healer to go first. K'tan stepped forward and looked through the Eye Rock, aligning his view with the Finger Rock beyond. There, just above the Finger Rock, as the Records had warned, was the Red Star.

They were all warmly bundled against the morning chill, M'tal and K'tan in their riding gear, and even Kindan in a thick wher-hide jacket. M'tal's Gaminth and K'tan's Drith lounged on a ledge near the plateau that held the Star Stones, unperturbed by the chill in the air. As the sun rose farther into the sky, Kindan could see patches of fog along the coastline to the east. He turned around, looking down into the darkened Bowl far below. When his eyes adjusted to the gloom, he found he could spot a fog-diffused glow at the entrance to the Kitchen Cavern, but nothing more.

"How much time do we have before the first Threadfall?" he asked, turning back to the other two. He had been invited to the morning gathering by the Weyrleader himself.

M'tal shook his head. His face was gaunt with fatigue. "Less than a month, I'd guess."

"We'll be flying wing light," K'tan said, stepping back from the Star Stones. His breath fogged in the chilly air.

Another three dragons had started coughing just that morning, bringing the total to eighteen. Twelve had died in the fortnight since Breth had gone *between* forever. Counting those hatchlings old enough, there had been over 370 fighting dragons at Benden Weyr. Now there were fewer than 340 fit to fly against Thread.

"It's worse at Ista," Kindan said. C'rion had had a brief chance to commiserate with M'tal and Salina and exchange notes with K'tan on the illness. Neither learned anything new, and C'rion had returned to his Weyr as soon as he was able.

Before C'rion left, a messenger from Fort Weyr had arrived. His news arrived before he did: The dragons keened for another four dead. C'rion, M'tal, K'tan, Kindan, and Lorana—invited for her ability to talk to *any* dragon—had gathered in the Council Room for a hasty conference. They agreed that the Weyrs should close themselves to outsiders, should banish fire-lizards, and should communicate by telepathy as much as possible. When it was revealed that Lorana could hear all the dragons, C'rion had suggested that all communications go through her, as it would be quicker than passing messages from rider to dragon and dragon back to rider.

Kindan had been doubtful. "I don't know," he'd said. "It seems that Lorana not only hears dragons but *feels* them, too."

C'rion was stunned. "Even when they die?" he asked gently. Lorana nodded.

Memories of the death of the queen, and of all the dragons after her, came at her like physical blows.

"I have Arith," she said, looking toward the Bowl and their quarters, a wan smile on her lips. "We comfort each other."

"I'm glad of that," C'rion had said feelingly. "This must be a very hard time for you."

"I think it's harder for others," Lorana had replied. "I still have my dragon."

Something jarred Kindan back from his wool-gathering to the cold morning air and the ominous view through the Star Stones. "Shouldn't Tullea be here?" he asked M'tal.

M'tal pursed his lips. "She decided that she needed her rest," he said. It was obvious that he was torn between disapproval and sympathy. Kindan could understand that—the toll on all of them had been great.

"What about the other bronze riders?"

"B'nik said that he would trust my observation," M'tal responded. "The others agreed."

With the death of Breth, Tullea's Minith was the senior queen at Benden Weyr. When she rose to mate, the leadership of the Weyr would pass to the rider of the bronze she chose. Everyone expected it would be B'nik, even though Tullea had already found the time to tease several of the other riders. M'tal had pointedly not risen to any of her taunts, preferring to spend all his spare time consoling Salina.

In fact, that was where Lorana was at the moment—with Salina. Kindan thought he knew, through his bond with the watch-wher Kisk and later through the bond he had had with his fire-lizard, some of the great pain Salina and all the other newly dragonless must be feeling. The harpers' laments captured that pain—a pain greater than the loss of a loved one, greater than that of a parent losing a child. The pain was all that and the tearing of a limb—half a heart, half a soul, and more.

Some never recovered. They refused to eat, refused comfort, and simply wasted away. Others managed to find solace from loved ones and rebuilt their lives. But Kindan had never heard of a dragonrider remaining in the Weyr after losing a dragon.

K'tan and M'tal gave a start and headed toward their dragons.

"Lorana has asked us to return," K'tan explained. "Arith is hungry and Lorana needs to watch her."

"I'll stay here a bit more, if that's all right," Kindan said.

"It's a long walk down," K'tan cautioned. "Ten dragon-lengths or more."

"That's all right," Kindan said, waving them away. "I can use the exercise."

"If you're sure," M'tal said.

"I'm sure," Kindan said. M'tal mounted his dragon and waved farewell to Kindan, and then the two glided away, back down to the Weyr Bowl.

"You'll find me in the Records Room," K'tan said from his perch on Drith's neck.

Drith leapt into the air and glided down to the Bowl below. After they had receded from view, Kindan turned back toward the rising sun. It was just over the horizon and its brilliance obscured his view eastward. Looking southward away from the sun, Kindan could make out the Tunnel Road and the plateau lake as the mountains fell away from high Benden Weyr to the plains below.

Kindan was a miner's child, so to him, Benden Weyr was a special marvel, one that the dragonriders and weyrfolk who had grown up there took for granted. But for him, with his trained eye, the Weyr was an engineering miracle. He turned around, northward, toward the artfully constructed reservoir even higher than the Star Stones. Over its sluices came a constant stream of water, guided into channels that spilled northward and southward into the rock of the Weyr. The streams ran centrally through the Weyr, servicing each of the nine different levels of individual weyrs—living quarters— carved into the walls of the Weyr before falling down to the next level and down again until the waste stream finally plunged deep into a huge septic dome way beneath a lush field far below and south of the Weyr itself.

The weyrs on each level all adjoined a long corridor toward the outside edge of the Weyr. The corridors were punctuated by wide flights of stairs leading down to the Bowl. Each weyr, or those that were finished—there were many partially made weyrs still unused and unfurnished—had a bedroom, a meeting room, and a lavatory for the rider, and a large cavernous weyr proper for a dragon. The walls of the finished weyrs were usually whitewashed with lime, although several had been treated with dyes in marvelous shades of blue, green, bronze, gold; some occupants had even opted for accents of purple, pink, and tan.

Kindan could always tell newer stonework from the original—while there was clear craftsmanship in every bit of rock carving done in the Weyr, the new work was never as smooth or as clean as the original. The stairs leading from the top level of the Weyr up to the Standing Stones were a case in point. Instead of a handrail of smooth-melted rock, a rope had been bolted at intervals into the wall. The stairs themselves were nearly perfect, but Kindan's legs noted a subtle unevenness as he descended to the Weyr.

Kindan wondered if the original settlers, who had created the dragons from the fire-lizards, could have come up with a cure for whatever was killing both fire-lizard and dragon alike. The problem seemed more than the people of his time could handle, given the skills available at the end of the Second Interval and the start of the Third Pass. How would the original settlers have felt if they realized that their great weapon against Thread would be annihilated scarcely five hundred Turns later, all their amazing craftsmanship and effort undone by disease and Thread, and the Weyrs left as lifeless, empty shells, ghostly monuments to a failed past?

Kindan made his way to the First Stairs, those on the south nearest the Hatching Grounds, climbed down to the Second Level, turned right, and entered the second opening, into the Records Room.

"Find anything?" he asked as he spied K'tan. The Weyr

healer was propped against one side of the opening to the Bowl below, an old parchment angled toward it to get more light. Kindan realized that the healer's head was on his chest and his eyes closed at the same moment that his words startled the dozing man into wakefulness.

"Huh? Ah, Kindan," K'tan said, shaking himself and gesturing with the parchment to the light outside. "I was trying to get more light and must have dozed off."

"I'm not surprised," Kindan replied. "You haven't slept in a sevenday and you practically live here. Does your dragon know you still exist?"

K'tan gave him a sour look at the gibe. "Drith, at least, has manners."

Kindan saw the pitcher of *klah* on the table in the center of the room, felt the side of it—cold—and shook his head.

"At the very least you should be drinking warm *klah*," he rebuked the healer.

"It was warm," K'tan replied absently, placing another Record on one stack and pulling a new one in front of him.

"When? Yesterday?" Kindan grabbed the tray with the pitcher and carried it and the half-empty mugs back down the corridor to the service shaft. He placed the tray in the down shaft, rang the service bell, and shouted, "*Klah* and snacks for two!"

A moment later he heard Kiyary's muffled voice drift back up to him: "On the way, Kindan! I've sent extra, just in case."

Kindan waited until a fresh tray arrived on the up shaft, grabbed it, and shouted down, "Thank you!"

Back in the Records Room, he poured a fresh mug of *klah* and handed it to K'tan, who had moved from the window to a chair but was still nodding off.

"Thanks," K'tan said. He took a sip from the mug, eyes widening as he tasted the fresh, hot *klah*, and said again with more enthusiasm, "Thanks!"

"Did you find anything?" Kindan asked after pouring himself a mug and choosing a snack.

"Nothing," the healer said, frowning. He reached for a snack. For a moment the two chewed in silence.

"I did notice that the holders seem to get sick much more often than weyrfolk," K'tan said at last.

Kindan cocked his head at him encouragingly, still chewing.

"Yes," K'tan went on. "I made notes. It seems that there's some sort of illness among the holders and crafters once every twenty Turns."

"Well, we're good for another four or five Turns at least, what with the Plague behind us," Kindan commented.

"It didn't affect the dragonfolk," K'tan said.

"You dragonfolk are a hearty lot," Kindan agreed. "I wonder if it's the thin air—"

He cut himself off, as his words sunk in. K'tan's eyebrows furrowed thoughtfully.

"Are you thinking that if thin air is good for riders, thinner air might be better for dragons?" the healer asked.

"Or worse for whatever ails them," Kindan suggested. He mulled the idea over and then shrugged it off. "Well, it's a thought."

"Worth keeping," K'tan replied, finding a stylus and making a note on his slate.

"If thin air is good, what about *between*?" Kindan mused.

K'tan shook his head. "The illness seems to disorient the dragons—they would never come back from *between*."

Kindan frowned and gestured to the Records. "You've seen nothing about dragon illnesses?"

"I've only gone back fifty Turns, Kindan," K'tan said. "There might be something more."

"At the Harper Hall, I found that Records over fifty Turns were very hard to read."

"And they're probably better kept there than these here," K'tan said with a wave toward a stack of Records.

"Wouldn't it make sense, then, to check the Records at the Harper Hall?" Lorana asked from the doorway, startling the other two.

"I'm sorry," she added, "but I heard you from the Weyrwoman's quarters."

"Were we too loud?" K'tan asked.

"No," Lorana answered. "Not loud enough to wake Salina, at least." She smiled.

Kindan gestured to the table. "Come in, there's hot *klah* and fresh snacks."

"Did you hear much of our deliberations?" K'tan asked, adding, when Lorana nodded, "And do you have any other insights?"

Lorana entered the room and took a seat at the table. Kindan passed her a mug, which she cradled in her hands, enjoying the warmth.

"I thought Kindan's idea about thin air might make some sense," she said, sipping her *klah*. "Also, cold kills germs, too."

"So if we could get our sick dragons to cold high places—"

"Without killing them," Kindan interjected.

"—without killing them," K'tan agreed, accepting Kindan's amendment with a nod, "then perhaps . . ."

Lorana shrugged. "It depends on the infection."

"We don't know enough about this infection," Kindan swore.

Kindan and Lorana sighed in dejected agreement.

"But what about the fire-lizards?" Lorana asked. "Have they ever gotten sick?"

"Not according to those Records," K'tan said with a wave of his hand.

"Maybe we're looking in the wrong Records," Kindan suggested. "Maybe we should be looking at the Harper Hall—"

"Or Fort Weyr," Lorana interjected. When the other two responded with questioning looks, she explained, "Isn't Fort Weyr the oldest? Wouldn't the oldest Records of dragons—and fire-lizards—be there?"

K'tan and Kindan exchanged looks.

"She's right, you know," Kindan said.

"Mmph," K'tan agreed. "But the Weyrs are closed to anyone but their own now."

Kindan pushed his mug away and reached for a Record. "Maybe we'll find our answers here," he said dubiously.

* * *

The next day, M'tal dispatched watch riders to every Hold, major and minor, with orders to report any signs of Thread. P'gul, the Weyrlingmaster, had the weyrlings bag more sacks of firestone.

"With any luck, the weather will hold either too wet or too cold for the first Threadfalls," M'tal told the watch riders. "Keep an eye out for drowned Thread or black dust, and let us know immediately."

"We have Threadfall charts that should tell us when the next Threadfall will occur once we've charted the first," Kindan added. "But at the beginning of a Pass, Thread often falls out of pattern."

"So watch out for it," M'tal concluded. "Report in to me or Lorana if you notice anything out of the ordinary."

"And if you see fire-lizards, stay clear of them," K'tan warned. "But let us know of any sightings, too," he continued. His voice dropped as he added, "We're not sure if there are any fire-lizards left."

"Good flying!" M'tal called, making the arm gesture to disperse the watch riders. Eighteen riders and their dragons rose high above the Bowl and then blinked out, *between,* to their destinations.

Gaminth, M'tal said to his dragon, *warn the watch-whers.*

It is done, Gaminth reported. A few moments later the bronze dragon added, *Lorana wonders if you will introduce her to the watch-whers.*

M'tal picked Lorana out of the crowd and made his way over to her. "That's a good idea," he told her. "But I'm not sure if there's time."

"Could someone else train me?" Lorana asked. "From what Kindan has told me, it seems like it would be a good idea if the watch-whers knew me."

M'tal rubbed a hand wearily across his forehead. "It would be a good idea," he agreed. "But—"

"Perhaps Nuella would teach her," Kindan suggested, stepping closer to join the conversation.

"Nuella is at Plains Hold," M'tal said. "How are you proposing she teach Lorana?"

"She could come here," Kindan said.

M'tal shook his head. "We don't know if watch-whers can catch this illness; I don't think it's fair to ask her to risk it."

"A good point," Kindan conceded. "But watch-whers have been around fire-lizards as much as the dragons have, and I've not heard of any watch-wher getting sick."

"Could they be immune?" Lorana wondered. The idea surprised her—everyone knew that watch-whers and dragons were related.

K'tan had zeroed in on the group and joined it just in time to hear the last exchange between Kindan and Lorana. "If the watch-whers are immune, could they fight Thread?" he asked.

Kindan considered the idea for only a moment before shaking his head. "Watch-whers are nocturnal, and Thread falls during the day."

"It sometimes falls at night, as well," K'tan disagreed. Something about his comment troubled Lorana, but she couldn't determine what.

M'tal's next comment drove the thought from her mind. "Watch-whers might well be immune, but that might not stop them from *carrying* the illness. Bringing a watch-wher here might bring more illness, too."

Kindan nodded in agreement. "I hadn't thought of that." He turned to M'tal. "You're right, Weyrleader, this doesn't seem to be a good time."

"A pity," K'tan murmured.

M'tal's brows creased in thought. "Perhaps we can use Nuella after all." The others looked at him questioningly. "She met Lorana at the Hatching, so perhaps she and Nuella could share images with the other watch-whers," M'tal said. He shrugged. "It wouldn't mean that Lorana could contact individual watch-whers, but *they* might be able to contact her."

"That's a great idea," Kindan exclaimed. "We'll get right on it." He grabbed Lorana by the arm. "Come on, Lorana, let's get out of this crowd."

M'tal waved them away with a look that was nearly cheerful. "That's one more thing off of my mind," he said to K'tan.

"It is, Weyrleader," K'tan agreed dubiously.

M'tal shot him a look.

"It's another thing on Lorana's mind," K'tan explained.

"Is she overworked?"

"We're all overworked," K'tan said. "You more than most, particularly with Breth gone. But there's a mating flight soon, and Tullea rides the senior queen."

M'tal gave the healer an encouraging gesture.

"And I worry," K'tan continued, "that Tullea might not appreciate having Lorana's abilities become so necessary to the success of the Weyr."

M'tal's lips thinned as he slowly nodded in agreement. "She hasn't been the same since High Reaches closed their Weyr, three Turns ago."

"Perhaps she had a lover there," K'tan mused.

M'tal snorted. "If she did, I'd never heard of it." He shook his head. "From what I've heard, they still take their tithes, but that's all."

K'tan cocked his head at the Weyrleader. "Do you suppose they guessed about the illness?"

M'tal frowned thoughtfully, then shook his head. "I can't see how," he said. "D'vin and Sonia were always a bit odd, maybe they just got . . . odder."

K'tan shrugged in turn. "Well, I need to get back to the Records," he said, turning toward the First Stairs.

"Speaking of overwork," M'tal quipped. The Weyr healer flashed a smile over his shoulder, and the Weyrleader waved him away genially.

"And there are no fire-lizards left at all?" Masterharper Zist asked Harper Jofri. The harper nodded.

"I'd heard that the Weyrs have banned them," said Bemin, Lord Holder of Fort Hold. "But I don't think any were left by then."

He had lost his marvelous brown Jokester. After the Plague had carried off his wife and his sons, the loss of his fire-lizard had been easier to bear, if still painful, but his real distress had come in comforting his young only surviving child, Fiona, on her loss of her gold fire-lizard, Fire.

"I've heard some people say that the dragonriders were jealous and bothered by the fire-lizards," Nonala, the Harper Hall's voice craftmaster added.

"I think it's mostly grumbling," Jofri said. "When people are upset and worried, some like to complain."

"Nonetheless, it is a very real concern," Bemin said. The others looked at him. "Holders and crafters pay their tithes to the Weyrs and wonder what they get for it."

He drew another breath to continue, but the Masterharper suddenly raised his hand and the others cocked their heads, listening.

"Dragons? Dead?" Nonala gasped as the drum message rolled in.

"Ista, Benden, Telgar," Jofri added in a whisper.

"Benden's queen," Zist said, with a pained look on his face.

Bemin looked from one to the other as they spoke. It was a moment before he could find his voice. But when he did, it was to declare with the heartfelt pain of a father who has lost children, of a husband who has lost a wife, of someone who knew something of the pain the bereft riders must be feeling, and—last of all—as the Lord Holder of Pern's oldest Hold. "Whatever I can do, or my Hold, you—or the Weyrs—have only to ask."

At lunch the next day, Kindan bounded into the Records Room to tell Lorana breathlessly, "Fort Weyr has reported black dust!"

Lorana was up on her Records enough to realize that black dust was what happened when the weather was too cold and Thread froze on the way to the ground.

"When?" she asked.

"M'tal says that K'lior's watch riders noticed it just around dinnertime—that would make it around lunchtime here," Kindan said. "M'tal says we can expect Thread to fall from the shoreline over the Weyr and on to Bitra nine days from now."

Lorana stifled a groan and buried herself back in her Records.

The morning bustle was louder than usual nine days later as the Weyr waited for its first Threadfall. Lorana had just managed to get Salina back into a fellis-laced, troubled sleep when the alert came: *Thread falls! Thread falls at the shoreline!*

The alert woke Arith out of a fretful sleep and Lorana spent precious moments calming her beloved dragon before she could race down the stairs to help.

"Go back to your rest," M'tal said when he saw her. "Tullea will handle this."

Lorana's eyes widened in surprise at the suggestion, for Tullea was nowhere to be seen. She waited until a disheveled B'nik appeared beside an even more disheveled Tullea, whose mouth smirked at the expressions of the other dragonriders. As their faces remain fixed in disapproval, Tullea's smirk changed to a pout.

"We were just getting to bed," she said defensively.

"Thread falls at Upper Bitra," M'tal told her. He looked past her to B'nik, "Is your wing ready?"

J'tol, B'nik's wingsecond, appeared beside him. "Just ready now, Weyrleader," the sturdy brown rider said, his gaze focused directly between the elder M'tal and the younger B'nik, as if casting doubt on whom the title should be conferred.

M'tal chose to ignore the taunt. "Good, good," he said, moving toward Gaminth as the bronze glided to a landing beside him. "We'll form up at the Star Stones and go *between* on my coordinates."

K'tan says that there are thirty-one dragons with the illness, Lorana heard Drith say to Gaminth. *And they are spread throughout the wings.*

Tell him that it can't be helped, we'll sort it out later, was the reply Gaminth relayed from M'tal.

Kindan, who had started laying out the healer's medical supplies, saw Lorana wince and approached her. "What is it?"

"The sick dragons are flying, too," she reported dully.

Far above them, over Benden's Bowl, wings formed into Flights, and Flights arrayed themselves in attack formation. And then, in one instant, three hundred and fifty-eight dragons disappeared—*between.*

For over twenty Turns M'tal had led Benden Weyr. In all that time, he had had just one thought: to prepare for Thread. This day—now—was the culmination of all he had worked toward.

It was a disaster.

Three dragons failed to come out of *between.* Their loss cast an immediate pall on the fight.

Worse, it threw off the organization of the wings.

The teamwork that M'tal had drilled his riders so assiduously in maintaining fell apart before the first of the Thread arrived. Ruefully, M'tal reflected that he had not considered training his dragonriders in sustaining losses.

M'tal's own wing had lost blue Carianth and his rider, G'niall.

"Close up!" he shouted. "Gaminth, tell them to close up."

M'tal cast a glance ahead and up, toward where Thread should be falling momentarily, and then another at the dragons in his wing as they re-formed without the blue. M'tal had had the Weyr arrayed in a line of multiple V formations. Now, with Carianth gone, the V of his wing was shorter on the left than on the right.

"Thread!" M'tal heard W'ren cry from behind him. He turned, following W'ren's arm, and saw them—up high, silvery, shimmery wisps floating in the morning sun. Gaminth let out a bellow, echoed triumphantly in challenge by all the dragons of Benden Weyr, and craned his neck back to M'tal for a mouthful of firestone. M'tal found that he already had some in his hands, not remembering when he pulled it out of his firestone sack, and fed it to the bronze without thinking.

That much of the training worked, he thought with bitter satisfaction.

As one, the dragons and riders of Benden Weyr rose to meet the incoming Thread. In unison, the dragons belched their fiery breath into the sky. Gouts of flame met clumps of silvery Thread, and the Thread wilted, charred, and fell harmlessly to the ground below.

The ease of the destruction of the Thread elated M'tal and all the riders. The dragons roared and charged to assault the next wave of Thread.

And then everything unraveled. The first cry of a Thread-scored dragon seared M'tal's ears like a hot poker, thankfully cut off as the dragon went *between* where the freezing cold would destroy the Thread.

Then another dragon went *between,* and another—and that one did not return.

M'tal issued sharp orders to his Wingleaders to regroup, but try as they might, the increasing casualties meant that they never quite recovered from the initial disorder.

The battle against Thread turned more dangerous, desperate. Worse, Gaminth informed him that many of the dragons going *between* and not returning to the Fall had not returned to the Weyr, either.

The pain of that additional loss weighed heavily on the remaining riders. Those riding ill dragons responded by doing their best to avoid going *between*—often with worse results. Four, then five dragons were Threaded at once and went *between* so terribly Thread-scored that M'tal *knew* nothing could be done to save them.

And then it was over. The Thread tapered off until there were no more in the sky.

M'tal, struggling to create a tally of dead, injured, and able dragons, found himself trembling with relief, rage, sorrow, and overexertion.

Have L'tor send out sweepriders, order K'tan back to the Weyr, and let's go home, M'tal said to his dragon.

He *knew* that Thread had got through their flight and had burrowed into the grounds of Upper Bitra, where great stands of trees grew up toward the snow line on the mountains. He wished that Salina's Breth was still alive. With two queens—and no danger from strange illnesses—they could have a small queen's wing battling any missed clumps of Thread before they reached the ground. The queens, with their greater wingspan, could easily handle flying low to the ground for the length of a Fall. But Breth's death meant that it was not to be and, because of it, the number of burrows would be higher than normal. It was too dangerous to risk Benden's remaining adult queen dragon flying alone, let alone the distraction it would give the other dragons.

M'tal took a deep breath, surveyed the area one last time, then put the image of Benden's Star Stones firmly in his mind and gave Gaminth the word to go home.

Mikkala, the headwoman at Benden Weyr, a stout, bustling woman who said little and kept her eyes open, tutted in disapproval of Kindan's work.

"Never met a man who's not happy the minute he's done the least bit of work," she said, sending a hard look toward the harper, who raised his hands in mock defense. Her look softened and she shook her head wryly. "Other people will be needing to find these bandages, not just you and the healer!"

"If you're complaining about a man's work, then you'll need to ask Lorana," Kindan told her.

So Lorana found herself in charge of laying out the medicine and bandages in preparation for injured riders and dragons.

Kiyary was detailed to help, and Lorana found herself so engrossed in setting up first-aid trays and assigning tasks to the weyrlings that she didn't have time to notice that Kindan had disappeared.

She *heard* the reports from Gaminth of the three dragons that failed to come *between* from the Weyr to Upper Bitra. She chided herself for not noticing their loss sooner, only to realize that she had felt a momentary worsening of the general pall that hung over her and everyone else in the Weyr, but had put it down to mere nerves.

It was only when Lorana had everything in order and sought to feed Arith that she noticed that the Weyr harper was nowhere in sight. She dismissed the issue in favor of ensuring that Arith was well fed and well oiled. She smiled proprietarily as she realized that her queen was nearly as big as some of the fully-grown smaller green dragons. Still, it would be years before Arith was ready to fly—or to mate, a thought that caused Lorana some vague discomfort.

In the meantime Arith was just as comforting, loving, considerate, confounding, wretched, ill-tempered, and fractious as any youngster could and should be. All of which meant that Lorana was glad to be able to see her marvelous friend happily ensconced on her freshly built bed of warm sand, curling up for a good after-food and after-grooming nap.

Lorana had just decided that Arith was fully asleep when she *heard* the piteous cries of dragons being Thread-scored in the Fall at Upper Bitra. Their pain came to her thankfully dulled, like the remnant soreness of a wound not quite healed.

Arith picked up her unease and an echo of the pain she felt through their link and looked over at her, eyes blinking sleepily.

"I'm sorry," Lorana cried aloud. "I can't help it. Try to sleep, little one."

There is no need to apologize, Arith said. *I am glad that you can hear the other dragons. It is a gift.*

"A gift?" Lorana repeated.

Yes, the queen replied. *You hear us the way we hear each other. It's special. I like that.*

Lorana hadn't considered her ability in that light. She winced as she *heard* another dragon bellow in great pain and go *between*—and then she winced in greater pain when the dragon did not return. She tried to find it *between,* could feel herself going—

Don't! Arith cried. *Don't leave me.*

Lorana opened her eyes and thrust her arm against the wall for support.

I didn't mean to, she apologized. *I was trying to get Minerth.*

Minerth is gone, Arith said firmly. *You cannot save her.*

Lorana found herself comforted by Arith's assurance, but deep down she felt that she almost *could* have brought Minerth and C'len back from wherever they had gone *between.* But both had been scored by Thread, Minerth fatally so.

Salina comes down with the harper, Arith told her. *You should go meet them.*

"Are you keeping watch on Salina?" Lorana asked, surprised.

Yes, Arith said, *She was the rider of my mother. And she is very sad. I would like to cheer her up.*

"I'll see what I can do," Lorana said, standing upright once more. "If you get some sleep."

I'll try, the queen promised.

Lorana spotted the harper and Weyrwoman easily as she made her way across the Bowl toward the aid station. Kindan was talking animatedly, and Salina—well, Salina looked like one of the dead.

Lorana joined them, adding whatever cheerful comments she could until she managed to get close to Kindan's ear while Mikkala was offering Salina some special sweets. "I don't think this is the best thing for her," she whispered.

"I can't leave her by herself," Kindan responded in equally hushed tones. "So many don't survive the loss of their dragon, you know."

Lorana pursed her lips thoughtfully. "Maybe—maybe it would be a mercy," she said carefully.

"But not the best for Benden, not now," Kindan replied. "Think of what would happen to M'tal. And the Weyr."

Lorana shuddered. "I hadn't thought of that," she confessed.

Around the Weyr, hatchlings bugled fearfully. Lorana and Kindan looked up in time to see a badly scored dragon plummeting down toward them.

Get away! Lorana shouted. The hatchlings veered away

from the falling dragon bare moments before it landed—
hard—on the floor of the Bowl.

"Get some numbweed!" Lorana shouted over her shoulder
as she ran toward the wounded dragon and rider.

The beast was horribly injured—she could see that immediately. Both wings were in tatters, scored repeatedly by
Thread. Ichor oozed from hundreds of sharp wounds.

It's all right, it's all right, Lorana called soothingly to the
dragon.

Kindan leaped up and grabbed the rider, throwing him
over his shoulder and carrying him to a clear spot not far
from his dragon. Gently, he laid the rider out on the ground.
Lorana rushed over to him and knelt on the opposite side of
the injured man. Kindan felt the rider's neck for a pulse and
then looked up at Lorana, his eyes bleak.

With an anguished bellow, the dragon rose clumsily to its
legs and jumped into the air—gone *between.*

Lorana rose and spotted Salina approaching in the distance. The Weyrwoman took one look at Lorana and her
hand went to her mouth in sorrow.

Another dragon bugled in the sky above them, falling,
with just barely more control than the first dragon.

The next several hours were a horrid blur of scored dragons and riders, hasty bandages, numbweed, fellis juice, and,
all too often, the forlorn keen of a dragon going *between* on
the death of its rider.

Lorana only vaguely noticed when M'tal and the rest of
the Weyr returned. When M'tal asked, "Where's Tullea?" she
could only shake her head and turn back to the injury she
was working on. Only later, much later, did it occur to Lorana that Tullea should have been helping tend the injured.

Once, Lorana found herself grabbed by K'tan. "Wash
your hands," he told her. She noticed that her hands were
covered in blood from the rider she had been tending. "Blood
shouldn't mix," the Weyr healer warned.

Lorana's hand flew to her face but she stopped it just in
time, eyes wide. "I'm sorry," she said. "I didn't wash when I
went from Jolinth to Lisalth."

K'tan shook his head and gave her a pat. "Dragon ichor isn't the same. You can mix it any time," he assured her. "It's just human blood that can cause problems. People have different blood, and mixing it can cause fevers."

"I'll remember," Lorana promised, washing her hands in a bucket that one of the weyrlings had brought over at K'tan's beckoning.

Some time later, as Lorana rose from bandaging another dragon's wing tip, she swayed and the world wheeled around her. Hands reached out and steadied her, and she found herself looking up into a face.

It was Kindan. "When did you last eat?" he asked her.

Lorana tried to remember but couldn't. She feebly shook her head.

"Come on," Kindan said decisively. When Lorana tried to resist, he added, "K'tan's back; he can handle things for a while."

"Eat!" K'tan agreed loudly from where he was working on a wounded dragonrider.

"We'll send you something, too!" Kindan promised as he led Lorana toward the caverns.

"I have to get back as soon as I can," Lorana said.

"No," Kindan replied firmly. "You need to rest. You've done enough, more than enough, for one day."

"But—but there's a fracture to set on Aliarth," Lorana protested.

"K'tan will see to it," Kindan said. "Or it will wait until I'm sure you're up for it." He shook his head in amazement. "You've been working for ten hours!"

"So have you," she retorted.

Kindan was taken aback. "Well, so I have!" he agreed. "It's a wonder I'm not fainting of hunger myself."

They were scarcely seated before they were served a hot bowl of thick soup and a mug of mulled wine. Fresh-baked bread with butter was set beside the soup.

"There's more where that came from," their server told them with a broad smile. Kindan recognized her as Tilara.

"Thank you," he replied, gesturing for Lorana to eat.

"There's no need," Tilara responded. She looked at Lorana and told her, "I saw the way you stitched up Jolinth's wing." She gave Lorana an admiring look. "I never would have believed it possible, but it looks like he'll fly again."

Kindan remembered her as one of the women sweet on K'lar, Jolinth's rider.

"Is K'lar resting, now?" he asked.

Tilara smiled wickedly and hefted a large pitcher she'd been holding in her other hand. "He is now. I doused his wine with fellis juice."

"Rest is what he'll need," Lorana agreed. K'lar had been scored, a nasty sear from forehead to cheek which fortunately required only a clean bandage and some numbweed for the pain.

"Ah, look at me!" Tilara protested. "Here you're supposed to be eating and I'm jawing away at you." She turned away, then called over her shoulder, "Eat up, because I'll be bringing seconds shortly. *And* dessert."

Lorana found that she was far hungrier—and thirstier—than she'd realized. The soup bowl was empty before she realized, and she reached for the bread and butter, only to have Kindan catch her hand.

"Allow me," he said, passing her the platter.

Lorana nodded her thanks and proceeded to pile butter on bread. Tilara was back and had refilled their bowls before they noticed.

"Would you be ready for something heartier after the soup?" she asked. "There's a nice bit of spiced wherry just about ready. And tubers, and fresh peas."

"That would suit me very well," Kindan said. He quirked an eyebrow at Lorana, who caught his look and nodded, her mouth full.

"Food for two!" a voice called from nearby. Lorana recognized it as Tullea. She looked over. The queen rider looked fresh and rested. Beside her, B'nik made shushing motions.

"You there!" Tullea shouted at Tilara, ignoring B'nik's gestures. "Did you hear me?"

"I'm busy," Tilara responded. She added in a voice that

only Kindan and Lorana could hear, "I'm helping those who helped the Weyr."

She took herself off, oblivious to Tullea's shouts. Tullea rose from her seat and was about to go after Tilara when M'tal entered.

"Tullea, I was looking for you," the Weyrleader called. Tullea turned to him, face still red with anger, but before she made any response, B'nik placed a hand on her arm, soothingly. None of the scene escaped M'tal's eyes, tired though he was.

"What are the casualty figures?" he asked Tullea as he closed the distance.

"What?"

M'tal rephrased his question. "How many riders and dragons are too injured to fly in the next Fall, and how long will it take for them to recover?"

"I don't know," Tullea snapped. She thrust a hand toward Lorana. "Ask her."

W'ren, M'tal's wing-second, entered the Cavern and placed himself beside his Weyrleader.

"I am asking you," M'tal said. "With the loss of Breth, you have become the Weyrwoman of Benden. It's your duty to keep track of the injured."

Tullea recoiled from M'tal's words and then, as the full import dawned on her, her eyes gleamed and she gave him a wicked smile.

"That's right, I am, aren't I?" she said with unconcealed glee. She gave B'nik a knowing look and then returned her gaze to the Weyrleader. "And when Minith rises, who knows who'll be Weyrleader then?

"Mind your manners, M'tal, you wouldn't want to upset your queen, would you?" Tullea purred.

M'tal gave her a hard, penetrating look. "Your duty is to the Weyr, Weyrwoman."

"I'll do my duty," Tullea snapped, "when my queen mates. As for now, ask her." She cocked her head toward Lorana.

"Tullea," B'nik said pleadingly. Tullea looked down at him and merely shook her head.

"And there'll be changes in the Caverns, too," she said in a louder voice before she sat back down. "I'm tired, B'nik—get us some food."

The bronze rider looked between the Weyrleader and Tullea, sighed, and gave the Weyrleader an apologetic look as he rose and headed over to the hearth.

K'tan entered the Cavern, caught sight of M'tal, and lengthened his stride to approach the Weyrleader.

"Weyrleader," K'tan said with a nod of his head.

"How bad is it?" M'tal asked. He had some idea from the fighting itself and from the field of injured dragons and riders spread across the floor of the Bowl.

The Weyrleader had not even tried to hide his tears as he went from rider to dragon, consoling, cheering, doing what he could to comfort and show that he shared their pain—and more. He felt responsible for each and every Thread score. Worse, he *knew* that his order that the coughing dragons fly Threadfall had immensely increased the losses.

"Forty-five are known to have gone *between*," K'tan said. "Another twenty-three are badly injured and will need at least a month before they can fly again. Another thirty-seven have more minor injuries and should be able to fly in the next sevenday."

M'tal slumped as though he'd been hit in the chest. Nearly a third of the Weyr's strength had been lost in the first Threadfall. Behind him, W'ren gasped in surprise.

I must think, M'tal told himself. He looked around the Cavern and spotted Kindan and Lorana.

"Let's join them," he said, gesturing the others toward them.

Kindan spotted them first. He took in M'tal's grim expression and waved them to seats nearby. Lorana looked up from her soup as the others sat down. Guiltily, she put her spoon in her bowl, waiting for the others to be served.

"No, no, eat, Lorana," M'tal said. "Someone will come with food soon enough."

"I'll see to it myself," Kindan said, rising to his feet.

"He's a good lad," W'ren commented as they watched

Kindan approach one of the Cavern women and strike up an animated conversation.

"It's a wonder he never Impressed," K'tan said.

"Or a blessing," M'tal added. The pain in his voice was obvious to all.

"Come on, M'tal, it's not all that bad," W'ren protested. "We took losses, sure, but the Records show that every Weyr takes losses in its first Fall."

"One-third of the Weyr?" M'tal's response was full of pain and self-directed anger. He waved a hand toward the Bowl outside. "Did you not see them? They're littered all across the Bowl."

"Not anymore," K'tan responded firmly. When M'tal shot him a look, he explained, "They're resting in their weyrs, now, Weyrleader."

"Food for three or five?" a pleasant voice interrupted. Lorana recognized Tilara, back again, laden with food. Kindan bore a huge tray behind her, like a beast of burden.

"Set it for five, Tilara," Kindan begged. "I couldn't carry this food back again."

"That's because you're just a lazy harper," Tilara retorted, but there was no sting in her voice. Quickly, she laid out plates, bowls, and mugs. Then she directed Kindan in the proper placement of the platters of food, pitchers of *klah,* and baskets of bread. She gave the table one long, satisfied look, then said to Kindan, "If you've ever a mind to change professions, you'd do well here in the Caverns."

"Why, thank you, Tilara," Kindan replied with a slight bow. "But I think I've found my craft."

Tilara laughed and patted him gently on the arm before heading back to her cooking.

"Is that spiced wherry?" K'tan asked, looking longingly at a platter piled high with steaming meats.

"It is indeed, good dragonrider," Kindan said. He speared several slices and deftly transferred them to the Weyr healer's plate. He turned to M'tal. "And for you, Weyrleader?"

"I'm not hungry," M'tal protested.

"You'll eat," a voice said from behind them. It was a woman's voice, firm. "You'll eat and you'll like it, old man."

"Salina?" M'tal cried, rising from his chair and turning around.

The look they exchanged was so full of emotion that Lorana found herself looking away, fearful of intruding on their privacy. Her gaze brought her eyes to Kindan, who had also looked away.

M'tal guided Salina to the chair beside him, which W'ren had vacated as soon as he'd seen Salina arrive.

"Kindan, serve him some of that wherry," Salina ordered. When Kindan stabbed three slices, Salina shook her head. "Make it five, and see if you can find some raw meat."

A faint smile crossed M'tal's lips as he and his mate shared a private joke.

W'ren gestured to Salina with the pitcher of *klah*. "May I serve you, my lady?"

"Wait until I get this old flame stoked," Salina told him. All the dragonriders grinned. Satisfied that M'tal's dinner was laid out to her order, she told him, "Eat."

Salina sat back in her chair and simply watched M'tal until, with a long-suffering sigh, he started to carve up his meat and chew it.

"Slowly," Salina told him. M'tal nodded affably and, with great exaggeration, ponderously chewed his meal.

Salina ignored the over-response. "Better."

"*Klah,* my lady?" W'ren repeated his offer. Salina accepted with a grateful nod.

"And some soup, to start," she said. Kindan and Lorana found themselves colliding in their haste to fill the Weyrwoman's bowl. With a graceful gesture, Kindan let Lorana have the honor.

"Please join me," Salina said after she'd been served, "if you're still hungry."

"I don't think K'tan has yet eaten, my lady," Kindan said before the Weyr healer could make any objections.

Salina glared at him balefully until K'tan filled his own

soup bowl, then she turned her attention to W'ren, who reddened and filled his plate with the still-hot spiced wherry.

Satisfied, Salina filled her spoon again and brought it toward her lips. Before she sipped the soup, she said to Lorana, "How bad was it?"

"Forty-five dragons went *between*," Lorana told her.

The Weyrwoman shuddered, forced herself to finish her mouthful. With her other hand, she gestured for Lorana to tell her the rest.

"Twenty-three with serious injuries, and thirty-seven with minor injuries that will heal in two sevendays or less."

Salina nodded, placing her spoon back in her bowl. "How many were left dragonless?"

"Four," K'tan told her, his face tight with pain.

"And they're being tended?"

"They are in the care of weyrmates or weyrfolk," K'tan assured her. "With their loved ones whenever possible."

"Good," Salina said. She looked at Lorana. "The dragons that went *between*—did you feel it?"

"Yes," Lorana replied, her throat tight with pain.

Salina reached out and grabbed Lorana's hand. "I'm sorry, that's quite a load to bear," she said.

"We're tough, my lady," Lorana said, "Arith and I."

"That's good, for these are tough times," Salina responded. She looked at the Weyr healer. "What are we going to do about it?"

"I'll go back to the Records Room. There *has* to be something there," K'tan replied, rising from the table.

"Sit, sit," Salina ordered, gesturing him back into his chair. "You've fought Thread, tended the ill . . . you must be exhausted."

K'tan met her eyes and nodded frankly.

"You'd miss more than you'd see," the Weyrwoman continued. She looked at M'tal. "When is the next Threadfall?"

"For our Weyr?" M'tal asked.

Salina nodded.

"Not for another three days. But I don't know how the

other Weyrs will do. Telgar Weyr fought Thread over Igen Weyr today, as well. I wonder how they fared."

"I—" Lorana began. The others glanced at her. "I think they did badly," she said. Her eyes gleamed with tears. "There were *many* dragons who went *between*."

"And you felt them *all*?" Salina asked in a voice filled with awe. Lorana nodded.

"My poor dear," the Weyrwoman replied, reaching for Lorana's hand once again. "And to think I grieved for one."

"I—I don't think I feel their loss as strongly as I would the loss of my own dragon," Lorana protested.

"And I hope that never happens," K'tan told her fervently. All the others nodded.

"But even so, the loss of so many dragons," Salina said, then stopped. "How many dragons, do you know?"

"I don't," Lorana confessed. "Maybe a hundred."

"A hundred," W'ren exclaimed.

"Maybe more," Lorana added.

"At the beginning of this Pass, to lose a hundred dragons," K'tan murmured, shaking his head.

"There were less than three thousand dragons on all Pern," M'tal said, speaking for the first time. "If a hundred are lost every Threadfall . . ."

With a roar of anger, D'gan slammed his hand against the table in the Council Room. "How many did you say?"

"Fifty-four are severely wounded and will take six months or more to heal, eighty-three are lightly wounded and may be able to fly in the next three months," V'gin repeated.

"And we lost seventy," D'gan added, his anger spent in that one loud outburst. It had been a rotten Fall. The Weyr had been arrayed perfectly, but the air currents over old Igen Weyr had always been difficult and they roiled the Thread up and down unpredictably. Once the wings had taken their first losses, D'gan's brilliant array of dragons had flown apart and things had only gotten worse.

This was supposed to be his triumph, his first Threadfall, his chance to show everyone who had doubted, after all the success in the Games, after all his tireless efforts, that he, D'gan of Igen Weyr, was the proper Weyrleader of Telgar.

He remembered the sad day when Morene had died and the last queen of Igen had gone *between*. He remembered how V'lon had grown old, his face seamed with age, practically overnight. How Telgar, Benden, Ista, and Fort had begged off providing Igen with a replacement queen. How in the end, D'gan's suggestion that Igen ride with Telgar was grudgingly accepted. But on that day, over twenty Turns ago, D'gan had vowed that he'd show them all, that he'd prove to the doubters that Igen riders were the best. He'd vowed to become Telgar's Weyrleader, to fly their queen and show the rest of Pern his mettle.

And he had. He'd worked tirelessly, still was working tirelessly. But on the way, perhaps after the first mating flight, or even before, D'gan had found that his aspirations had changed. He was more than just a displaced rider finding a home in a new Weyr, he was a Telgar rider and he was a Weyrleader. He would show them—M'tal, C'rion, that young boy, K'lior, all of them—what a *true* Weyrleader was like.

It had been *his* Weyr that had won all the Games. *His* Weyr had the most dragons, *his* Weyr had the most queens, and *his* Weyr was responsible for the most territory on Pern.

And now this. He turned to V'gin. "How many dragons will I have to fight the next Fall?" he asked, knowing the answer.

"There are fifteen more dragons showing signs of the fever—"

"They'll fly the Fall," D'gan interjected.

V'gin grimaced. "We don't know how much the sickness contributed to our losses, D'gan."

"Exactly," D'gan said, "we don't know. So they'll fly. 'Dragonmen must fly, when Thread is in the sky.' So, Weyr healer, how many dragons will fly with me over Telgar Weyr and Hold in six days' time?"

V'gin sighed. "If you include the fifteen sick dragons—"

"And any others that get sick in the meantime," D'gan said pointedly.

V'gin accepted the correction with a shrug. "Counting them, you'll have three hundred and thirty-eight fighting dragons and two queens."

"The queens will stay behind," D'gan said. "A proper queen's wing is three or more." His tone failed to hide how much it galled him that Garoth had not been able to provide the Weyr with another queen dragon. Well, perhaps on the next mating flight, he thought to himself.

"I think you're right," Lina, Telgar's Weyrwoman, agreed. She was older than D'gan, and he often wondered how much of her affections were for him, D'gan, and how much for Telgar's Weyrleader, even though they had sired a child between them.

"D'lin did well today," D'gan commented. The youngster was really too young to be hauling firestone, but he had insisted and T'rin, the Weyrlingmaster, had allowed him. Still, it had been a surprise to recognize his own son throwing a sack of firestone as Thread fell all around them.

Lina smiled, although her eyes were still weary. "I'm glad to hear that," she said. "He so wants to live up to your example, you know."

Unconsciously, D'gan felt stung by the comment, even though he knew it had been kindly meant. He was determined to set a standard no other could attain.

C'rion stopped, pulling his back straight and forcing a pleasant expression onto his face before he stepped out onto Ista Weyr's Bowl. All above him, from one side of the Bowl to the other, the Weyr was full of the sounds of dragons coughing, snorting, and sneezing.

Directly above him, he heard a dragonrider call out, "Valorth! Valorth, no!"

A dragon dived out from its weyr and winked *between,* leaving behind T'lerin—no, C'rion grimaced, Telerin; the honorific contraction for a dragonrider lasted as long as his dragon. C'rion turned to head toward the ex-dragonrider, to console him as he had consoled so many others in the past three sevendays.

"I'll do it," a voice behind him said. C'rion whirled, swaying slightly from fatigue, as he caught sight of J'lantir.

Wearily, C'rion nodded. "Get Giren," he said, "he'll know what to do."

J'lantir shook his head. "I don't think that's a good idea, just now. T'lerin spent too much time comforting Giren when Kamenth went *between*."

C'rion gave him a blank look.

"T'ler—Telerin might blame Giren," J'lantir explained.

"Then G'trial—I mean, Gatrial—" The look on J'lantir's face stopped him.

"I'm sorry," J'lantir said, tears welling up in his eyes. "I was coming to tell you—"

C'rion bowed his head and nodded. He had feared that the Weyr healer would not survive the loss of his dragon, especially after experiencing all the pain and suffering of watching over thirty other dragons succumb.

"It was fellis juice, laced with wine and something else, I couldn't identify," J'lantir said. "Dalia said she'll look after him."

C'rion shook his head, biting his lips. "No, no, I'll do it, it's my duty."

J'lantir touched his shoulder gently. "You've too many duties, Weyrleader. Thread is falling—"

"The Weyr must be led," C'rion finished, swallowing hard. "How many have we lost so far?"

"Thirty-six," a new voice answered. Dalia joined them. "I've got weyrfolk looking after Telerin," she said. "We've got another thirty or more that don't look well."

"Thread falls nine days from now," C'rion responded.

Dalia smiled grimly, walked wearily up to him and hugged him. "You'll do all right," she told him.

"For every action, there is an equal and opposite reaction."
This is as true in ecosystems as it is in physics. Any new
species will incite a reaction from the ecosystem.
— Fundamental Principles of Ecosystem Design,
11th Edition

Chapter Twelve

Fort Hold, End of First Pass, Year 50, AL 58

M'HALL LEANED BACK on Brianth and gazed up into the
darkening sky. Nothing. Some stars had started twinkling
and the Red Star, which had been invisible for months in
daylight, was definitely fading in intensity.

Torene wants to know if that's it, Brianth relayed, adding
an echoing rumble of his own.

*We haven't seen any more signs of Thread for the past
hour,* M'hall replied. *I think that's it. Have Torene assign a
watch rider and tell the rest to go back to the Weyr.*

Torene wants to know if you're coming, too, Brianth said.

M'hall pursed his lips in thought. *Might as well,* between
won't get any warmer while I'm waiting.

It was hard to imagine that Thread would not return. That
he would not be called upon to fight them day after day, again
and again. That finally, he and all his surviving dragonriders
could rest.

Rest, M'hall thought with a snort of amusement, I wonder
what that's like. He patted his hardworking bronze partner on
the neck and thought, *Come on, Brianth, let's go home.*

Brianth had obligingly dropped M'hall off near the Caverns before retiring to his weyr. M'hall waited for his Wing-

leaders to assemble, patting them on the back or exchanging words as they arrived. Ghosts of lost riders ringed them: M'hall could bring up many faces, scarred or young, bitter or thrilled, that were no longer seen in the Weyr.

I wonder how Father would have handled this, he mused. Or Mother.

"So that's the last of it, M'hall?" G'len called out.

"As far as I can tell," M'hall replied. "And right on schedule."

"Well that's something to be grateful for," young M'san said.

"Wine all around!" a voice bellowed from the background. M'hall roared in hearty agreement. The cold of *between* filled the air as another dragon returned. Without looking, M'hall knew it was Torene and Alaranth.

"Mugs tonight," Torene declared. "You'll all just break the glasses."

They waited patiently while the wine was passed around. Soon the Cavern was filled to overflowing with riders and weyrfolk.

"I didn't know we had this many mugs," Torene remarked in surprise.

"I didn't realize we had this many people," M'hall returned with a smile. He looked out at the people of Benden Weyr, survivors of the First Pass of the Red Star, and bellowed in a voice so loud that the dragons roared, "To absent friends!"

"Absent friends!" The shouted response shook the very rocks of the Weyr.

"Come down and join the celebration," Emorra called to the drummers on the tower.

"We can't, we're on duty."

"Suit yourselves, then," she called back to them. She was drunk and she knew it. She hadn't been drunk in—she couldn't remember how long. She must have been drunk once before, or she wouldn't have recognized it now.

She turned back to the College, watching her feet to keep from stumbling. Then she glanced over her shoulder at the tower behind her, realizing that the voice that had answered her wasn't Tieran's. Where was he? She hadn't seen him for a while. Emorra pursed her lips, wondering exactly why she cared.

The celebrants in the courtyard of the College had dispersed, some going back to their rooms and others settling down for quieter revelries right there. Emorra startled when her ears picked out Tieran's voice. He was in one of the classrooms. She headed toward it.

Partway there, Emorra paused. She heard a woman's voice talking to him. Well, maybe I should leave them alone, she thought sadly to herself. The voice spoke again, passionately, and Emorra recognized it.

She charged into the room, yelling, "Just what do you think you're doing? You're old enough to be his *grand*mother!"

Her agitation took her all the way into the room. Tieran was seated at one of the tables. No one was seated in his lap. No one was muttering sweet nothings into his ear.

Instead, Wind Blossom was in front of the chalkboard, scribbling genetic coding sequences on it. Of course, Emorra thought to herself with slowly dawning comprehension, I've never heard her use that tone *unless* she was talking genetics.

Tieran and Wind Blossom were startled by her bold entrance. Wind Blossom recovered more quickly, giving her daughter an inscrutable—even to Emorra—look. Tieran just looked puzzled. The brown fire-lizard had leapt into the air, but did not go *between*.

"I was explaining the sequencing differences between the dragons and the fire-lizards," Wind Blossom told her daughter calmly. After a pause, she added with only the slightest hint of a purr in her voice, "Were you enjoying the end of Pass festivities?"

Emorra thought that over before responding. "I'm drunk," she declared.

"So I had gathered," Wind Blossom said frostily.

"What's it like?" Tieran asked, eyes wide with interest. "I've never been drunk," he admitted. Hastily he added, "Yet."

"I think it'll hurt in the morning," Emorra admitted, her face still red. *Why in the world would I* ever *have thought that my mother and Tieran were . . . ardent about anything,* Emorra berated herself. "Why worry about the sequencing?" she asked, trying to sound normal.

"We're looking for common immune system limitations," Tieran explained.

Emorra blinked, thinking. "The infection?"

"I was hoping we could prove that it couldn't cross to dragons," Tieran said.

Emorra cocked her head, questioningly.

"We are still working on it," Wind Blossom added pointedly.

"It's the end of the Pass—haven't you got anything better to do?" Emorra blurted. "Alcohol blunts inhibitions and slows reasoning," she remembered as her brain processed the words her mouth had just uttered.

"Like what?" Wind Blossom asked.

"Like—like . . . well, *you're* too old!" Emorra said. Clasping her hand to her head in frustration at her own stupidity, she turned around and stomped away.

"Alcohol reduces sexual function," Emorra recalled with infuriating clarity as she strode away. *Hmmph!*

"It was bacterial in nature," Wind Blossom repeated. "The general spectrum antibiotic knocked it out."

"Didn't you teach me not to jump to conclusions?" Janir asked. "Isn't it also possible that the bacterial infection was a secondary infection that took advantage of the compromised immune system, just like Tieran said?"

"So you're arguing that we only knocked out the secondary infection, giving the fire-lizard's immune system a chance to handle the primary infection," Emorra suggested.

They were gathered in one of the classrooms at Wind Blossom's invitation.

"Exactly," Janir agreed.

"Wind Blossom and I agree that it really can't be proved either way," Tieran said, with an apologetic look toward the old geneticist. "But what *can* be proved is that the antibiotics saved Grenn's life." The little brown fire-lizard gave Tieran an approving chirp.

"Grenn?" Janir asked.

"That's what he's named the fire-lizard," Wind Blossom explained, waving a hand toward Tieran.

"No, that's the name that was on his bead harness," Tieran corrected. "It's the name he was given by his original owner."

Emorra's eyes narrowed. "Do you have that harness?"

Tieran nodded. He drew it out of the pouch he had hanging over his shoulder. "Right here."

"May I see it?" she asked, extending a hand. Tieran handed it over, not without misgivings. He didn't know if he was more afraid that Emorra would be immediately able to identify Grenn's owner by the beads, or that she wouldn't. Emorra was studying the beadwork carefully.

"This symbol here—do you see it?" she asked, holding the harness up to the others. "What do you make of it?"

"There's the caduceus of Aesculapius," Janir said. "The standard symbol for medicine—"

"Or a doctor," Emorra interjected. She peered more closely at the beadwork. "But what's beneath it?"

"It looks like some sort of animal," Tieran suggested tentatively.

"But it's hard to tell," Janir complained.

Emorra looked at them all. "I just received a message from Igen, detailing a plan to begin a beadworks," she told them. "To my knowledge, there were no beads brought over from Landing, nor any that landed with the original settlers."

She fingered the small beads sewn into the fire-lizard's harness.

"These beads should not exist."

* * *

"Really, Mother," Emorra said, "you and that boy!"

"He is not a boy," Wind Blossom countered. "He is nineteen!"

Emorra tossed the correction off with a wave of her hand. "Are you so desperate to make amends with him that you'd deprive someone else of their fire-lizard?" she sniffed. "That's beneath you, you know."

"Emorra, it's been two months since the fire-lizard appeared," Wind Blossom replied. "I would have thought that if anyone was missing a fire-lizard, we would have heard of it at the College by now.

"You can't deny that the fire-lizard was sick with an illness we haven't seen before," she continued.

Emorra grimaced. The fire-lizard *had* been ill. Both fire-lizards had been ill. Clearly they had caught the disease somewhere. If they could get it, so could other fire-lizards. If the fire-lizards could get it, then perhaps the dragons. Possibly the day of planet-wide disaster she had been fearing was just around the corner. Although, it could be that the disease was rare, or propagated slowly, or its method of transmission . . .

"Were you asking people if they'd lost one or two fire-lizards?" she asked abruptly.

"Tieran's drum message asked if anyone was missing a gold or brown fire-lizard," Wind Blossom answered.

"Did you mention the illness?" Emorra asked, trying to recall the drum messages that had been sent while they were in quarantine.

"Not in connection with the fire-lizards," Wind Blossom said. "But we had to have a reason for the quarantine. It's a wonder that more people haven't been asking, putting two and two together. In fact, I'm rather surprised that—"

The sound of a dragon arriving cut her short.

"I would have expected him sooner," Wind Blossom said, glancing out the window to confirm the arrival of M'hall from Benden Weyr.

"Maybe he had better things to do," Emorra said waspishly.

"Maybe he didn't wish to infect his dragon," Wind Blossom returned imperturbably. She started out to greet the bronze rider, then turned back to ask Emorra, "Did you want to come along?"

Emorra shook her head. "No, I've got a class to teach."

Wind Blossom met M'hall just inside the archway of the College.

"I was hoping to meet you," M'hall said as he caught sight of her.

"And *I* had been expecting you," Wind Blossom answered with a courteous nod. She gestured toward the kitchen. "Shall we see if Moira has anything for a Weyrleader fresh from *between*?"

M'hall smiled. "Yes, please!"

Moira did, indeed, have a fresh pot of *klah* and some scones still warm from the oven. "There's butter, too," she said. "Alandro's gone to fetch it."

"Many thanks!" M'hall replied, taking the tray and finding a quiet alcove. Once seated, he poured for both of them and waited until Alandro arrived with the butter. They each had a hot buttered scone. That done, M'hall got right to it: "Tell me about these fire-lizards and your medical emergency."

Wind Blossom repeated the events as best she could. When she was done, M'hall leaned back slowly on his bench and sighed. Then he straightened again, buttered another scone, and ate in thoughtful silence.

"And the beadwork? No one on Pern now could have made it?" he asked at last.

"So Emorra informs me," Wind Blossom said. She waved a hand in a throwaway gesture. "Of course, beads are such tiny things that they may have come across from Landing uninventoried."

M'hall snorted. "Not from what I've heard of Joel Lilienkamp! Rumor has it that he hand-counted each *nail* that he came across. I can't see how he'd miss beads."

"But it *is* possible," Wind Blossom reiterated without conviction.

M'hall nodded in understanding. "It's particularly possible for those to whom the other explanation is too incredible."

"Or uncomfortable," Wind Blossom added.

"And not too many people know about all the capabilities of fire-lizards," M'hall said. In a lower voice, he added, "Or dragons."

After a moment of silent reflection, he continued. "So, if they came from the future, what then?"

Wind Blossom shrugged. "Perhaps it was a minor outbreak, and these two were the only ones who succumbed to it."

"That's the best-case scenario," M'hall agreed. His voice hardened. "What about the worst-case?"

Wind Blossom pursed her lips tightly before responding. "In the worst case, the disease could be transmitted to others."

"Including the dragons?"

Wind Blossom nodded.

"What about the watch-whers?" M'hall pressed.

"Those, too, in the worst case," Wind Blossom agreed solemnly. "Although I would have greater hopes for them."

"Why?" M'hall asked.

"I made an effort to differentiate them somewhat more from the original genome than we did with the dragons," she answered.

"I always knew that dragons were fire-lizards writ large," M'hall said. "What were watch-whers, then?"

"Dragons 'writ' differently," Wind Blossom told him.

"Could you differentiate the dragons from the 'original genome,' too?" M'hall asked.

"Perhaps," Wind Blossom responded. "But whether it would be enough, I don't know."

"Why not work on a cure for all three—fire-lizards, dragons, and watch-whers?"

"Because if I did that," Wind Blossom responded, "then, judging by those two fire-lizards, I failed."

M'hall stroked his chin thoughtfully. "How long do you

think it would be before someone comes up with those beads and uses them to make harnesses?"

"Do you mean, how far in the future do I think those fire-lizards came from?" Wind Blossom asked.

M'hall nodded.

Wind Blossom shrugged. "I have no idea."

"But sooner in the future rather than later," M'hall suggested. "I can't see fire-lizards jumping far *between* times."

"They were sick, disoriented," Wind Blossom pointed out. "I know too little of the breed to say whether they'd jump farther or shorter in such circumstances."

"Well, they must have been here before: To return here they must have had a good visual image of the place."

"Perhaps," Wind Blossom said. At M'hall's probing look, she expounded, "I recall that fire-lizards can sometimes locate a person they know in an unfamiliar setting."

M'hall nodded. "Yes, I've heard that, too. But usually they go where they've been before, looking for someone they already know. Given that they were sick—"

Wind Blossom raised an eyebrow reproachfully. M'hall caught the look and laughed.

"Very well," he said, "I'll leave the diagnosing to you. Are you saying they might have gone back in time to a familiar person?"

"I was saying that I don't know," Wind Blossom responded.

M'hall nodded and resumed a thoughtful expression. After a moment he stirred. "Is there anything you can do? Is this talk just conjectural?"

"Perhaps I can do something," Wind Blossom said. "I would need to know more about the problem."

"And there's no way to do that," M'hall said. "Not unless another fire-lizard or"—his voice dropped—"a dragon falls out of the sky."

"I have considered that, yes," Wind Blossom replied.

M'hall gave her a startled look. "Is that why you ordered all that agenothree?"

"Do you mean nitric acid, HNO_3?" Wind Blossom asked primly.

The redheaded dragonrider blushed. "Yes, I do," he said, looking chagrinned. "When you're flying Threadfall, you tend to slur words, so it becomes agenothree."

"Mmm," Wind Blossom murmured noncommittally.

"You're teasing me!" M'hall exclaimed suddenly with a startled laugh. "I don't believe it! You're actually teasing me."

Wind Blossom lowered her eyes shamefully for a moment and then raised them again to meet his. "It is very rude of me, I know," she said sheepishly.

"I never even *knew* you had a sense of humor."

"My mother would berate me for it," Wind Blossom agreed. "However, it has kept me company in trying times. I had hoped to keep it under control but apparently it got away from me again."

"Oh, you enjoyed that all right," M'hall said, wagging a finger at her. "Don't deny it, you enjoyed it."

Wind Blossom nodded. "I do not deny it."

M'hall sobered suddenly. "You say that your humor surfaces in trying times? Are these trying times?"

"Every day is a trying time," Wind Blossom answered evasively. M'hall pinned her with his gaze and the old lady accepted his chiding with a nod of her head.

"We have embarked on a great experiment in ecological engineering," she explained. "Every ecosystem is resilient and conservative in nature. It will always try to maintain the status quo. Adding dragons, watch-whers, Tubberman's grubs, and, most importantly, all our Terran ecosystem has altered the status quo. It is inevitable that there will be repercussions."

"And it's your job to guard against those repercussions," M'hall said firmly.

"It's my job for this generation," Wind Blossom corrected. "I am eighty-one years old, M'hall. I might possibly live to see ninety, but certainly not one hundred."

"Did you ever determine the cause of the early dementia?" M'hall asked choosing his words carefully.

"No," Wind Blossom replied softly. "The emergency with the fire-lizard came before I could complete my analysis."

M'hall shifted uncomfortably.

Wind Blossom noted his unease. "Janir and I have talked about this," she told him. "We agree that my short-term memory is fading, but my long-term memory, particularly of events in my youth, remains strong."

"Is there anything we can do?" M'hall asked softly, relieved that Wind Blossom had answered the question he could not bring himself to ask.

"Janir knows to keep an eye on me," Wind Blossom said. "And now, so do you."

"And Emorra?"

"I have not told her myself, but I believe she has made her own diagnosis," Wind Blossom said after a moment. She looked the dragonrider squarely in the eyes. "You know how difficult it is to lose a parent."

M'hall nodded swiftly in agreement.

"Janir and I have agreed that whatever is reducing mental capacity in the elderly will probably not be a factor in the future," Wind Blossom continued.

M'hall thought that over for a moment. He could think of no one still alive near Wind Blossom's age. His own mother had been only seventy when she died, and his father, Sean, had been sixty-two. He did not need Wind Blossom to tell him that the harder life on Pern would mean reduced life expectancies.

He sought a new subject. "What happens after you, Wind Blossom?"

"In the Eridani Way there should be others for the succeeding generations."

"Do you mean Emorra and Tieran?" M'hall asked. "That smacks of slavery, to expect them to continue blindly in the tradition."

"It is more of a genetic destiny," Wind Blossom said. The

look in her eyes made M'hall realize that she herself was an example of that "genetic destiny." "The Eridani Way involves a discipline transcending generations and millennia, a dedication to the good of the ecosystem."

"I can appreciate their goals, but I don't like their methods," M'hall replied.

Wind Blossom nodded. "Neither do I," she agreed. "And I have better reason than most to appreciate their goals and question their methods. In fact, if we were in contact with the EEC, I'd have some comments to make to the Eridani Council itself."

M'hall's eyebrows rose as he considered the image of this tiny old lady berating the prestigious Eridani Council. He imagined the Eridani Council would soon see the error of its ways.

"What would your comments be?" he asked, his eyes dancing humorously.

"I would say that I consider it a mistake to engage an aristocracy in maintaining ecologies—that it should be something that is the inheritance of every sentient being living in the ecosystem," Wind Blossom told him.

"I see," M'hall said. "And how would you implement that here, on Pern?"

Wind Blossom shook her head. "I don't know," she replied. "With an adequate technology base and a larger population, there would be time to teach everyone. But this is a world built on agriculture—we don't have the tools required to do delicate genetic testing. There are not enough people and not enough food for our expanding population."

"It would seem that here," M'hall said, waving his hand around to indicate the College, "would be the place to retain that knowledge."

"We're already losing that knowledge," Wind Blossom said. "Shortly we'll be unable to perform any invasive surgery. We haven't got the equipment to monitor the effect of an anesthetic on a person, let alone the people trained to administer it."

"What about genetics?"

"Genetics is even worse," Wind Blossom said. "Fortunately the base population is pretty healthy, but there will be mutations—there are about six to seven hundred mutations in every newborn—and some of those will be malevolent.

"We could teach something about basic genetics, plant breeding and so on, but nothing about genome manipulation—how to detect and repair defective genes."

M'hall grimaced. "So do you see no hope?"

"I didn't say that. There's a chance that at some future date—perhaps a thousand years or more—our society will advance to the point where it will be possible to recover what was lost at Landing and reestablish contact with the *Yokohama* or the other ships in orbit. When that happens, all the knowledge we had will be made available to our descendants," she said. "What they do with it will be up to them, of course."

"So you're worried about the short-term only?"

Wind Blossom shook her head. "My *training* leaves me worried about our world."

M'hall nodded sympathetically. "I share your worries, you know," he told her. He rose and stretched. "I must get back to my Weyr."

Wind Blossom nodded understandingly.

"There is less to do now, but more than I'd realized," he added with a rueful grin. "Still, if anything else happens to fall out of the sky—let me know. And if you come up with any ideas on how to solve these problems you worry about, let me know and I'll do all I can to help."

"Thank you, M'hall, that's all I could hope for," Wind Blossom answered.

As they walked back out through the courtyard to where Brianth was waiting, M'hall looked down at the dimunitive old-timer and said conversationally, "You know, Wind Blossom, you need a break from all this."

He wagged a finger in response to her shocked expression. "Some time off will do you a world of good. If you want to go someplace, like a warm seaside cottage, you send word and I'll get you there."

Wind Blossom opened her mouth to protest, but her expression changed before she could utter a response. A thoughtful gleam entered her eyes.

"Why thank you, M'hall. I think I will."

Dragon, turn
Dragon, climb
Dragonrider, watch for sign
Firestone, chew
Dragon, flame
Char the Thread, make it tame.

Chapter Thirteen

Benden Weyr, Third Pass, 4th day, AL 508

"TODAY WE'LL DRILL with mixed wings," M'tal announced the next morning. It had been a long, hard night for the entire Weyr. The evening and early hours of the morning had been punctuated with the sorrowful cries of injured riders and dragons. Two more dragons had gone *between* before dawn.

M'tal had called the Wingleaders together at first light.

"Not only do we need the training," M'tal told the group, "but it will keep us focused on our duties."

"What about the sick dragons, M'tal?" someone called from the back.

"They won't fly, J'ken," M'tal said, recognizing the speaker's voice. "I learned my lesson yesterday. We'll let them rest."

There was a murmur of agreement and some muttering about being a day late.

M'tal raised a hand for silence. "Yesterday none of us had fought Thread before," he said. "Today we know better. In two days, we'll be able to handle any losses in our flights. It's vital that we practice today and tomorrow as hard as we can to handle losses during Threadfall.

"I've asked Lorana and Kindan to call out dragons as 'casualties' from time to time, so that we can really learn how to cope," he told them. He saw the other riders looking at each other, nodding as they digested the idea and found they liked it.

"But what about the sickness, M'tal?" J'ken called from the back of the group. "I lost two good riders yesterday because they were too sick to fly. What if more get sick?"

"Lorana and Kindan will also be in the Records Room searching for any hints they can find," M'tal assured them. "I've sent word to Masterharper Zist to search the Records at the Harper Hall, too."

"Do they keep dragon Records at the Harper Hall?" J'tol, B'nik's wingsecond asked, frowning.

"We'll find out soon enough," M'tal said.

"Sounds like Kindan and Lorana are working too hard," L'tor muttered. He looked up at M'tal. "Let's hope they aren't so tired that they miss something vital."

"Could we get someone else to help?" J'tol wondered.

"Traditionally, it's been the duty of the Weyrwoman to examine the Records," J'ken noted.

M'tal raised a hand placatingly. "I'm afraid that Salina is still recovering from her loss," he told the group regretfully. "I'm sure—"

"I wasn't talking about her, M'tal," J'ken interjected. "I was talking about Tullea."

He shot a glance at B'nik's wingsecond. "What about it, J'tol? Where's Tullea? And where's B'nik for that matter? Late again?"

"B'nik is setting up a surprise for us," M'tal assured the others. "I asked him to."

"What about Tullea?" J'ken persisted. From the grumbling of the group, it was obvious that he was not the only rider who was displeased by their new Weyrwoman's behavior.

"What matters now, dragonriders," M'tal called in a voice pitched to carry over the grumbling, "is that Thread falls in two more days' time and we need practice. To your dragons!"

The first two hours of practice were dismal. B'nik's surprise was that half his wing was aloft with the ropes used for practice in the Games. They popped in and out of *between* well above the riders, and threw down handfuls of the ropes, to simulate clumps of Thread.

After two hours, J'tol took the other half of B'nik's wing high aloft to throw ropes, while B'nik and the others practiced flaming it along with the rest of the Weyr.

Slowly, with many false starts and restarts, the dragonriders began to learn to become more flexible in their formations, to quickly regroup when a dragon became a casualty. And both the dragons and their riders grew more confident and adept.

When the dragonriders returned to the Weyr for a lunchtime break, M'tal felt cautiously confident that they would be ready for the next Threadfall.

"How far back do you think we should go?" Kindan asked, wheezing as some dust from the latest pile of Records flew into his face. "Some of these are disintegrating."

"Shouldn't we get them copied, then?" Lorana asked, carefully leafing through another pile of musty records.

"Spoken like someone who never spent days copying old Records," Kindan responded. "Do you know how boring it is, day in, day out, copying musty old Records?"

Lorana allowed herself a slight smile. "I imagine there would be a lot to be learned," she said.

Kindan shook his head. "No, not really," he said. "Most of the Records are repetitious. There are only so many ways you can record crop yields and rainfall. Occasionally there's a note of a wedding or a birth but—honestly—you'd think whoever wrote those Records was numb! Not a single joke, no songs, nothing but dull, dry facts, Record after Record."

"Well, it's dull, dry facts we're after," Lorana responded. "No joke or song is going to help us here."

Kindan paused mid-search and looked up at Lorana. She looked back at him quizzically until he shook his head and gave her a dismissive hand gesture. "Nothing," he told her. "I thought I remembered a song . . . but it was nothing."

Lorana glanced over at the sandglass they'd brought up with them. "Ooops, our time's up! Name another dragon," she told him.

"Mmm, Ganth," Kindan said. "T'mac's brown. That'll leave J'ken without a wingsecond."

Lorana raised her eyebrows in appreciation of the choice. "Very well," she said, and gave the order to Ganth. She smiled as the brown dragon thanked her and asked if he could take a swim in the lake.

I think that's up to your rider, don't you? she replied.

Lorana looked back down at her stack of Records and then threw her hands up in disgust. "You know, we're going at this the wrong way," she said.

"I've been saying that for hours," Kindan agreed. He looked over at her. "What is your plan?"

"Well, I was thinking that anything that happened to the dragons recently, we'd remember," she said. "So why work our way back through the Records? Why not start with the oldest Records and work forward?"

"The oldest Records!" Kindan groaned. "Queen rider, you certainly know how to darken a day."

Lorana started to protest but Kindan raised a hand, silencing her.

"I didn't say you weren't right," he told her. "I just dread the prospect." He stood up and went back to the stacks of Records, searching. "You know, I'm going to have to move the newer stacks first."

"I'll order more *klah,* then," Lorana suggested.

Kindan turned back to her with a grin. "Ah ha! This is just a plot to take a break."

Lorana laughed and went to the shaft to order more food.

By the time they broke for the evening meal, Lorana's good humor had frayed.

"Musty old, *useless* Records!" she swore.

Kindan gave her a shocked look.

"I'm sorry I ever suggested we start with the oldest ones," she apologized, stifling a sneeze. "My nose is running and my eyes are watering with all this dust. The writing's barely legible and I've probably missed something important because it's buried in a mass of gibberish!"

"Maybe I can help."

Lorana looked over to see Salina standing in the doorway.

"You should be feeding your dragon, anyway," Salina said.

"After you've done that, you can feed yourself," Kindan added. "You haven't had anything since you took a break to help K'tan with that injured wing tip—if you call that a break."

"But there's so much to do!" Lorana protested, waving a hand toward the high stacks of unread Records.

Salina entered the room and sat at the table. Catching Lorana's eyes, she jerked her head toward the door.

"I'll do it while you do your other chores," Salina said. "I've heard someone say that this is the Weyrwoman's job, anyway."

Kindan couldn't bring himself to point out that the Weyrwoman being referred to was Tullea, not Salina.

"Ask Mikkala to send up some fresh glows, please," Salina told Lorana as she was leaving. She looked over at Kindan. "Now, Harper, what should we be looking for?"

Two days later, with Threadfall due over lower Benden and Upper Nerat, M'tal grimaced. Three of the severely wounded dragons had gone *between*. And there were eight more feverish dragons. He would be leading only one hundred and ninety-six dragons—slightly more than two flights of dragons—against Thread over Nerat.

We will fight smarter this time, M'tal thought confidently.

He knew from the Records of the Second Pass that the Weyr had successfully fought Thread with less than one full flight—three wings of dragons. He also knew that the casualties in those Threadfalls had been much higher than when more of the Weyr's strength was available.

Well, it can't be helped, he told himself. *Gaminth, give the order to go* between *to Nerat Tip.*

* * *

With the lush green of lower Benden below them and clear skies above, M'tal surveyed the arrayed wings approvingly as they awaited the coming of Thread. He had three wings arranged as one flight flying high, with a second flight behind and lower. The sixteen spare dragons were arranged in a "short wing," trailing behind the lower flight but ready to fill in any gaps either as individual dragons or as a full wing.

M'tal squinted, scanning the sky above him for signs of Thread. Wouldn't it just be too much if Thread failed to fall? he mused sourly.

A dragon's roar alerted him. There! Faintly, like a blur on the sky above, he saw it. As one, the dragons of Benden turned to their riders for firestone; as one the riders fed them the flame-bearing rock; and as one the dragons chewed the rock, digesting it deep in their second stomachs.

As one, the Weyr rose to flame Thread.

And then, behind him, dragons bugled a strange challenge. M'tal turned in surprise to find the source of their bafflement.

"What is she doing?" M'tal bellowed in outrage.

Far below and behind him, he spied the large wings of Benden's only mature queen dragon.

Thread! Gaminth warned—but it was too late. A stream of fire seared across M'tal's cheek and onto his chest before the nothing of *between* brought blessed relief from the agony of Threadscore.

M'tal clawed off the frozen Thread and then they were back in daylight again.

Gaminth, tell her to return to the Weyr! M'tal ordered.

Minith says that Tullea says it is her "duty" to be here at Threadfall, Gaminth informed him.

M'tal's rage grew as he watched the flying formations behind him dissolve and grow unmanaged, with some bronzes striving to protect their queen.

Order the "short wing" to protect her, M'tal said. *And have the rest of the wings re-form.*

His orders had little effect on the chaos behind him. Grimly, M'tal wondered if it had been a wise idea to put his wing in the forefront. It had seemed a good choice to lead from the front, but he hadn't counted on not being able to handle the confusion behind him—he hadn't expected *this* sort of confusion!

Tell Minith that I order her back to the Weyr, M'tal said to his dragon. *She is too near her mating flight to risk Threadscore now.*

Minith says to tell you that Tullea is only doing her duty, Gaminth relayed apologetically.

"Talk to Lorana!" M'tal shouted out loud. "Have *her* explain it to Minith."

Behind him, M'tal could hear dragons shrieking in pain as Thread struck them. It didn't have to be this way, he thought furiously to himself. Damn the girl! I'll wring her neck myself when we get back.

She is gone, Gaminth reported. *The wings are re-forming. It will be all right.*

Tullea jumped off her dragon as soon as she landed at Benden Weyr and launched herself toward Lorana, shrieking at the top of her lungs, "How dare you! How dare you call my dragon back!"

Lorana was tending an injured rider and had no time to rise to her feet before the other queen rider was upon her. Kindan raced over to her side, but it was Arith, awakened by the raw emotion of Tullea's assault, who arrived first, appearing from *between* with a cold burst of air.

The little queen hissed at Tullea, who found herself skidding to a halt. Behind her, Minith rumbled a warning at Arith, but Arith only hissed at her, too.

"Tullea, what is this?" Salina demanded as she appeared, breathless, having run all the way across the Bowl. "What is going on?"

"M'tal had me order Minith back to the Weyr," Lorana explained, her bandaging done. The wounded dragon's grateful rider rose with her and stood beside her. Lorana motioned Arith aside. "I'm sorry Tullea, but M'tal explained that if Minith were injured, she might not mate."

Tullea's eyes widened as the words sunk home. "I was doing my duty," she said dully. "I'm supposed to take on the duties of the Weyrwoman."

"When there is only one mature queen," Salina told her, "those duties do not include flying against Thread."

Tullea nodded, but her gaze turned back to Lorana. "You had no right," she told her hotly, "to order my queen about."

"It was M'tal's orders," Lorana protested.

"M'tal!" Tullea snapped and started to say more, but a hiss from both Salina behind her and the dragonrider beside Lorana forestalled her from saying more. She glared at the rider, who did not flinch, and then at Lorana. "You will not tell my dragon what to do, girl."

"I have more patients to attend," Lorana said, ignoring the comment. "Arith, it's all right. Go back to your weyr, dear."

"This isn't over," Tullea growled at Lorana's back.

"If you're interested in a Weyrwoman's duties, Tullea, now is a good time to start," Salina said from behind her. "There is numbweed ready and those who need it."

Tullea's hands clenched at her sides and she turned sharply to glare at Salina, but the old Weyrwoman merely gestured toward the Lower Caverns.

"I can't say I think much of your teaching," a voice growled in Kindan's ear later that evening as he sat at one of the dining tables in the Food Cavern.

Startled, Kindan looked up to see K'tan looking down at him, grim-faced. Kindan gave him a quizzical look.

"You are responsible for teaching dragonriders their manners, are you not?" K'tan asked.

"Mmm, that might be more a function of the Weyrlingmaster than the harper," Kindan returned, his eyes twinkling. "I take it you heard of the exchange today between Tullea and—"

"Just about everybody," K'tan returned. A puzzled look crossed his face. "She's the only person I've ever heard of who got *less* sociable after she Impressed."

"That was—what?—three Turns back, now?" Kindan mused.

K'tan nodded. "She's weyrbred. She was quite the charmer even before she Impressed. I had an occasion—"

Kindan snorted. "I would have thought you had better taste!"

K'tan glared down at him. "As I said, she was more sociable back then," he said.

"There, you see, it's not my fault," Kindan said with a smile.

K'tan laughed and sat down beside him. "I know, lad, I was just ribbing you." He let out a long, tired sigh. "You did good work today," he said. "You've the makings of a good healer. Perhaps you learned from Master Zist—"

"Master*harper* Zist, if you please," Kindan corrected. "We harpers are rather touchy about rank."

K'tan snorted. "Very well, *Journeyman* Kindan." He lowered his voice so that it would travel only to Kindan's ears. "Not that I haven't heard that you'd been tapped for Master."

"This doesn't seem like a good time to leave the Weyr," Kindan replied.

K'tan clapped him on the shoulder. "Good on you, lad," he said. "And you're right, this isn't a good time to leave the Weyr." His voice dropped. "There might not be a Weyr left on your return."

Kindan raised an eyebrow. "The losses today weren't that bad, were they?"

K'tan shook his head. "No, thank goodness. We lost four, though—more than we would have if it hadn't been for *her*."

There was no need for him to explain who he meant.

"Another fifteen severely wounded and twenty-two with minor injuries," the Weyr healer went on.

"How's M'tal taking it?" Kindan asked, careful to keep his voice low.

K'tan gave him a measuring look. "Badly. Worse than he should, I think."

"What about the other Weyrs—how have they done?" Kindan asked.

K'tan shook his head. "I haven't heard."

"I would have thought you would have been in touch with the other healers," Kindan remarked.

"I've only met G'trial of Ista," K'tan replied. "But none of the others."

"And what does G'trial say?"

K'tan's face grew closed. "His dragon went *between* two days back," he said, waving aside Kindan's attempts at commiseration, "but I'd heard that there were more sick dragons at Ista than at Benden."

"Ista has to fight Thread three more times in the next nine days," Kindan remarked. *That* much he had learned from the Records.

"It's going to be tough, then," K'tan said. "What about us?"

Kindan smiled. "We're getting a break. We've got nineteen days before Thread falls over Upper Bitra."

K'tan shook his head. "None of the injured we've got will be ready by then."

L'tor approached them. "K'tan, when you've got a moment, M'tal would like to talk with you."

K'tan rose. "I'm ready now."

Kindan rose with him. "I've got to get back to the Records."

"It'd be better if you could find out about the other Weyrs," K'tan said. The Weyrs operated autonomously and some, such as D'gan's Telgar and D'vin's High Reaches, were unwilling to discuss their internal affairs with outsiders.

A thoughtful look crept into Kindan's eyes. He nodded his head decisively. "I'll do that," he said.

"How?"

"Do you suppose M'tal would be willing to spare K'tan long enough for him to give me a lift?" Kindan asked L'tor. "I feel a need to practice some drumming."

The Weyr drum was up on the watch heights. When he was up here during the day, Kindan never tired of the view. As it was, in the evening it was cold, and a steady wind leached all heat from him. Still, if he peered carefully and held steady enough, Kindan could make out the fire-pits of Bitra Hold to the west and maybe, or maybe it was his imagination, a faint glow from Benden Hold to the south. Kindan adjusted his drum to point more toward Bitra.

He took his sticks and pounded out "Attention." Then he waited. Several seconds later, and closer than he'd imagined, he heard a drummer respond with "Proceed." Kindan grinned. Clearly some minor hold that he hadn't noticed before had recently gotten a drummer. Excellent.

He leaned into the beat to rap out his message, hoping that he had phrased it with sufficient nonchalance that it wouldn't alarm the relayers but would still yield its true meaning to Masterharper Zist, the intended recipient.

The message sent, he listened carefully to the drummer repeating it back, and on to the next drummer in the station. With any luck, sometime in the next day or so, Masterharper Zist would get the message.

Which meant, Kindan realized with a groan, that there had to be someone up here listening for the answer for the next several days.

"I'll get one of the weyrlings," he said to himself, glad that there was no one else to notice his chagrin.

L'tor directed K'tan to the Council Room. As they entered, K'tan noticed that the only other rider present was B'nik, who looked rather uncomfortable.

Get used to it, lad, K'tan thought. If you want to lead, it's going to get harder.

He made a face, annoyed with himself for thinking so sourly of B'nik. He had known the rider since before he'd Impressed, and the truth was that B'nik was a steady, careful rider and a good leader. It was only B'nik's continued association with Tullea that marred K'tan's opinion of him.

"Glad you're here," M'tal said as he caught sight of them entering the room. He gestured to a pitcher. "There's warm *klah* if you need it."

K'tan silently shook his head and found a seat.

"Did Kindan have any news?" M'tal asked.

K'tan shook his head. "He asked to be dropped up to the watch heights to drum a message to the Masterharper."

B'nik frowned. "What for?"

K'tan shrugged. "I don't know, to be honest," he said. "We were talking about the losses of the other Weyrs before L'tor found us, so . . ."

"I'd heard that he had thought of asking the Masterharper if there were any Records of illness kept at the Harper Hall," L'tor suggested.

"He could have done both," M'tal said. He looked at the others seated around the table. "We could use all the information we can get," he admitted. He held up a slate. "I've been looking at our strength, trying to get an estimate of how we'll fare.

"We started this Pass with over three hundred and seventy fighting dragons," he said. "After two Falls, we're down to two hundred and fifteen."

"I thought it was more than that," B'nik said. "Are you counting the coughing ones?"

M'tal shook his head. "No, I'm counting them as sick," he said, "and I wish I'd kept them back from the first Fall. I think we lost most of our dragons because they were so muddled they got lost *between*."

"You can't blame yourself for that, M'tal," K'tan said heatedly. "Dragons don't get sick, no one knew—"

"Well, they're sick now," M'tal cut in. "And until they're better, I'm not letting sick ones fly with us."

B'nik frowned. "But the losses—"

M'tal held up a hand. "They were worse when the sick ones flew with us."

"The last Fall was a short one—you can't really compare the two," K'tan said.

"Even allowing for the length of the Fall," M'tal corrected, "the losses were much higher when the sick ones flew.

"The real question is, how many more will get sick and how soon?" M'tal asked, looking pointedly at K'tan.

K'tan shook his head. "I can't say. Lorana, Kindan, and I have been going through the Records and so far haven't found anything like this. We've got nothing to compare it with: Dragons—and fire-lizards—haven't gotten sick before."

M'tal gave the Weyr healer a long look, then sighed deeply. "In nineteen days, we fly against Thread over Bitra. I need some idea of how many dragons will be flying," he said slowly. He looked at B'nik. "If things go well, I'd like you to lead that Fall."

The others in the room startled. M'tal raised a hand to quell their impending speech. "It's customary for the Weyrleader to ask other Wingleaders to lead a Fall," he said. "It's good practice, too. No one can ever say when a Weyrleader might be injured or lost *between*.

"And," he added, "there's a very good likelihood that Caranth will fly Minith when she rises. It will make the transition easier all around if you've had some experience leading a Fall beforehand."

B'nik spluttered for several moments before regaining his speech. "M'tal—I'm honored," he said finally.

"Don't be," M'tal said firmly. "You're a good rider. You're good enough to know it, too. I'd be asking you to lead a Fall soon enough even if"—he paused, taking a deep breath—"even if Salina were still Weyrwoman."

M'tal looked back to K'tan. "That's why I want to know what you think our strength will be. It will be hard enough for B'nik to lead a Fall the first time, even with everything under control. It wouldn't be fair to ask him to lead one without giving him some idea of the number of dragons he'll be leading."

K'tan nodded in understanding, then closed his eyes in thought. When he looked up moments later, his face was clouded. "The trouble is, I can't really give you a decent guess, M'tal," he said. "We don't know how many dragons were lost *between* because they had the sickness but didn't tell us or didn't realize it themselves."

Before anyone could comment, he continued, "All the same, if you look at the first sicknesses and losses, we've lost

seventy-three dragons—not all of them to the sickness—but
it's the worst number." He waited for M'tal to nod. "That's
seventy-three out of three hundred and eighty-five fighting
dragons, or about one in five who've either been lost or gotten sick in the past three sevendays. So I'd say that you could
possibly expect the same ratio in the next three sevendays."
He raised a cautioning hand. "It might get worse, it might get
better. But, let's say that another forty-three dragons will not
be able to fly the next Fall."

M'tal nodded, though his face was pale. He looked at
B'nik. "That would leave you with about one hundred and
seventy dragons," he said. "Can you do it?"

B'nik was just as pale as the Weyrleader. "Forty-three
more dragons," he echoed, aghast. He shuddered, then forced
himself to answer M'tal. "I'll do my best."

"That's all anyone can do," M'tal said with a satisfied nod.
He stood up and turned to leave. "I'll make the announce-
ment tomorrow morning. After that, I want to leave the training to you."

B'nik nodded. "I think I'll continue with the exercises you
had us doing before the last Fall," he said after a moment.
Then he grinned. "I don't suppose your wing would mind
slinging 'Thread,' would it?"

"I don't suppose," M'tal agreed with a grin and a nod.
"Now, if you'll excuse me, it's been a long day"—he covered
his mouth to stifle a yawn—"and I'm in need of some rest."

A voice called him urgently from sleep: "Master Zist, Master Zist!"

Masterharper Zist raised his head wearily from his pillow
and blearily looked up. He made out the shape of the watch
drummer, Terilar, silhouetted by the glows from the Hall.

"What time is it?" he asked, confused. Too much wine, he
thought.

"It is three hours past midnight," Terilar replied.

No, not enough sleep, Zist thought, correcting his previ-
ous assessment.

He sat up and rubbed his hair back.

"It's a message from Harper Kindan," Terilar said. "He asks if you would trade him news about the Weyrs."

The Masterharper of Pern looked up sharply at the drummer, who seemed nonplussed by his sudden keen look.

Zist rose, turning the glow over beside his bed. "Have someone rouse Master Jofri, Master Verilan, and Master Kelsa," Zist ordered. "And please ask someone to bring us up some *klah,* if there's any still hot."

"Very well," Terilar said, dashing away.

"So, Kindan wants to trade, does he?" Zist muttered to himself, mostly to hear a voice in the middle of the night. Masterharper Zist appreciated his ex-apprentice's choice of words. It was clear from Terilar's look that the drummer hadn't taken any deeper meaning from Kindan's message, just as it was clear to Zist that if Kindan "wanted to trade," he didn't know what was going on with the other Weyrs himself. And that meant that the Weyrleaders were being more close-mouthed than he had thought.

"You woke us up in the middle of the night to tell us that Kindan wants to trade?" Kelsa demanded as the rest of the harpers gathered in the Masterharper's office. Her words ended abruptly in a great yawn. She glared at the Masterharper, gripped her mug of *klah* tightly, and took a long drink.

"I've got classes to teach in the morning, you know," she added.

"This *is* morning," Verilan added with a yawn of his own. He frowned thoughtfully at the Masterharper. "And you wouldn't have woken us without a reason," he added, "which means that Journeyman Kindan's message has more meaning to you than I'm getting from it." He narrowed his eyes. "Which is what you wanted to know—whether others could discern that message."

"Well, I can't," Kelsa said. She glanced at Jofri. "You taught the lad, I suppose you know."

"I do," Jofri agreed, nodding. He looked at the Master-harper for permission, and explained, "Kindan's message makes it plain that he doesn't know what's going on with the other Weyrs, at least not in detail."

Verilan nodded slowly, as comprehension dawned. "The Weyrs aren't talking to each other," he surmised.

"But they can relay messages telepathically from dragon to dragon!" Kelsa protested.

"It's not the same as a face-to-face meeting," Jofri told her. "You'd have to know exactly what you want to ask."

"And the questions could easily be misinterpreted," Verilan said. When Kelsa looked at him inquiringly, he expanded, "Such as how many dragons did you lose, which some Weyrleaders might take to be criticism of their abilities."

"Exactly," Master Zist said. "So it's up to us to find out more."

"Very well, but what do *I* or Verilan have to do with that?" Kelsa demanded.

"I'm supposed to tell Master Zist what I've found in the Archives about sick dragons or fire-lizards," Verilan predicted. Master Zist nodded in agreement. The Master Archivist made a face. "Sadly, I don't have anything to report. We've searched back over two hundred Turns and have found no records of illnesses in either fire-lizards or dragons."

"How about watch-whers?" Master Zist asked.

"We checked for all the related species," Verilan replied, shaking his head. "And we've found nothing. I have hopes that we can go all the way back to the Records from the Crossing—most of them are in better shape, I'm sad to relate, than those from later times."

"More grist for the mill," Kelsa said with a laugh. "Turns of work for your lads, then."

The Master Archivist shook his head. "They'd much rather be copying your songs than dusty old Records that mean nothing to them."

"I suspect that in the days to come, your apprentices—and all the students at our Hall—will find their interest in preserving our old Records increasing," Master Zist said.

Verilan nodded in agreement. "These times do make us appreciate the need to preserve our history."

"So we know why *him*," Kelsa persisted, "but why did you have to wake me?"

Master Zist looked at her as if the reason was obvious.

"Because he needs you to figure out a song our Weyr harpers can answer discreetly," Verilan told her. "So that we can find out how the Weyrs are doing."

"That's assuming that the Weyr harpers haven't succumbed themselves," Jofri pointed out.

"Them, or their dragons?" Kelsa asked.

"It amounts to the same thing," Master Zist replied. He added, with an apologetic shrug toward the Master Archivist, "And while our good Archivist here may have found nothing, I also felt that your expertise in the area of song might possibly aid us."

Kelsa responded with a raised eyebrow.

"Master Verilan's apprentices may well have concentrated their efforts on written Records," the Masterharper explained. "But I want you, Kelsa, to search your memory, and your library, for any songs concerning lost fire-lizards or dragons." It was his turn to shrug. "Who knows? Perhaps there, in our older songs, we might find a clue."

M'tal had scarcely got in bed when shouts from outside his quarters disturbed him. Salina murmured in her sleep and moved away from the noise.

The shouts grew louder as they came closer, and M'tal could make out the words and the speaker.

"M'tal! What do you think you're doing?" Tullea shouted as she strode through the entrance into his quarters, thrusting aside the sleeping curtain that he had drawn closed just moments before and allowing the dim light of the hall glows to enter the room.

The shouts could be heard in the Records Room next door. Kindan and Lorana both looked up, jolted out of their reading.

"What's going on?" Lorana wondered.

"I don't know," Kindan answered, rising from his chair, "but it sounds like trouble."

Lorana frowned, then stood up and followed him to the doorway. He gestured with a hand behind his back, telling her to stay put, as he craned his head around the corner and cocked an ear to listen.

Tullea glared at the Weyrleader from the doorway, demanding an answer.

"I was planning on getting a good night's rest," the Weyrleader responded irritably. "What have you in mind?"

Tullea stopped, thrust her hands onto her hips, and glared at him, momentarily at a loss for words.

"You know what I mean," she continued after a moment, her volume rising. "You're trying to kill B'nik! Don't think you can wriggle out of it."

Salina had lost her battle for sleep and sat up blearily. "Tullea? What is it? What's wrong with B'nik? Who's trying to kill him?"

Tullea pointed a finger accusingly at M'tal. "He is!" she shouted. "And I'm sure you're in on it, too. Or do you mean to tell me that you didn't know your precious Weyrleader has ordered B'nik to lead the next Fall?"

Salina furrowed her brow and glanced at M'tal. She rubbed her eyes, bringing herself more alert.

"Next Fall? B'nik?" she repeated, digesting the news. M'tal nodded in confirmation. Salina looked up at Tullea and said, "I think that's a good idea, don't you?"

"What?" Tullea cried in disgust. "If he isn't trying to get B'nik killed, he's trying to discredit him in front of the whole Weyr." She turned her attention back to M'tal. "You're supposed to lead the Weyr, Weyrleader. *You* fly the Fall, do your duty."

M'tal took a steadying breath.

"It *is* my duty to prepare the Weyr to fight Thread," he agreed. "It is my duty to ensure the dragonriders are trained, ready, and able to meet that threat."

Tullea nodded, a satisfied gleam in her eyes.

M'tal continued, "It is my duty to ensure that our Wingleaders are able to do their jobs. And it is my duty to train those Wingleaders to fight Thread in any and all positions expected of them—including leading a Fall themselves."

Tullea's nostrils flared angrily. "You will not make B'nik lead the Fall!" she shouted. "You're trying to get him killed so that your dragon will fly Minith!" She drew herself up to her full height. "Well, it's not going to happen! I'll not let it happen, no matter what!" Her eyes darted to Salina. "And you! You're part of this, I can tell. Well, you're not the Senior Weyrwoman anymore. I want you out of my quarters immediately."

Kindan swore. "That's it!" he snarled, darting out of the room. Lorana, who had not heard as clearly what had been said, followed close behind.

Salina glanced at M'tal, who touched her shoulder gently.

"Salina's things were moved into my quarters before the last Threadfall, Tullea," M'tal said, tamping down his temper. "Mikkala and a crew of weyrfolk have given it a good cleaning and were just waiting for it to finish airing before they offered it to you."

Tullea huffed at the news. "Why wasn't I informed earlier?"

"I've been busy with the injured dragons and riders, Tullea," Salina said in a soft voice. "And I thought that you might not want to move in so soon after"—her voice caught—"after Breth's death."

"No one knows how the illness spreads," Kindan broke in from behind Tullea.

The Weyrwoman whirled. "You! What are you doing here? This is a private conversation."

"Private conversations are not normally conducted by shouting," Kindan responded. "We heard you all the way in the Records Room."

"We?" Tullea looked behind him and spotted Lorana. Her eyes narrowed. "What are you doing here?" she snapped at Lorana. "Spying?"

"Hardly," Lorana said. "I was coming to see if anyone needed help."

Salina grabbed at the statement. "Perhaps some *klah* and a bite of food." She glanced at Tullea. "Or maybe some wine."

"Good idea," Kindan agreed quickly, turning to Lorana and adding in an undertone, "Laced with fellis juice."

"I'll see what I can find," Lorana answered, with a wink for Kindan.

Tullea watched her disappear with a sour look on her face. "That girl takes far too much on herself," she proclaimed. "When I am Weyrwoman, I'll order her to tend to her dragon."

"I'm sure she'll be delighted to oblige," M'tal purred. "When you're Weyrwoman—perhaps you'd care to start now and take over the search through the Records?"

Tullea jerked as the barb went home. "Don't try to distract me," she barked. "I ordered you not to let B'nik lead the next Fall."

As Lorana raced down the steps, still grappling with the bizarre events above her, she ran straight into B'nik.

"Have you seen Tullea?"

"She's up with M'tal," Lorana answered.

B'nik groaned. "She's not the one who's been shouting, is she?"

Lorana could only nod. The rider swore, then gave her an apologetic shrug.

"She's accused him of trying to get you killed," Lorana said.

"I *told* her not to!" B'nik growled, starting up the steps. He stopped to look back at her. "Where are you going?"

"Down to get some food and drinks," she said.

"Make sure to put some fellis juice in her wine," he told her, shaking his head sadly. "When she gets worked up like this, it's about the only thing that calms her."

Lorana frowned. "This has happened before? Is she all right?"

"Yes. No. I don't know," B'nik said in rapid response. Another shout prompted him to start back up the stairs. "I'd better get going."

When Lorana returned with a tray, B'nik deftly took the

wineglass and handed it to Tullea, who had grown quieter but no less determined.

"I don't care," she said. "You shouldn't fly this Fall."

"It's my duty, Tullea," B'nik said. "Besides," he added with a grin, "I *want* to do it." He grabbed a mug from the tray Lorana had set down and poured himself some *klah*.

"I know you do," Tullea snapped. She took a sip of her wine. "It's just that, if anything were to happen to you, particularly before Minith rises, I—" She broke off.

B'nik hastily passed his mug to Kindan and wrapped his arms around Tullea, drawing her into a tight embrace. The move caught her off guard and she tipped her glass, spilling some of the wine onto his tunic.

"I'm sorry," she said. She looked at the others, her eyes moist with emotion. "I'm sorry," she repeated.

"It's all right, come on," B'nik said soothingly, leading her from the room. "It's late—you'll feel better in the morning."

There was an uncomfortable pause as the others listened to their steps as they walked down the hall back to their weyr.

"Stress does strange things to people," Salina murmured when their steps had faded away.

"She wasn't like this before," M'tal muttered, looking puzzled.

"She said she's always tired, always edgy," Salina commented. She looked at Kindan. "Could it be something in her diet?"

Kindan shrugged. "K'tan would know best." He cocked his head toward Lorana, adding, "But Lorana might have some thoughts."

Lorana was still digesting the events of the evening. She shook her head. "My father bred herdbeasts," she said. "Sometimes they would go off their feed for no reason. We could never explain it."

"Well, Tullea's been 'off her feed' for the past three Turns now," Kindan commented sardonically.

"I think she's just scared," Salina said sympathetically. "And who can blame her? These are very worrying times."

Kindan recognized the end of the conversation and picked up the tray.

"We need to get back to our work," he said to the others, gesturing for Lorana to precede him.

"No, you need to get to sleep," M'tal corrected. "I can't have you two acting like Tullea."

Out of earshot, Kindan turned back to Lorana and said quietly, "Could it be that the dragons are off their feed?"

Lorana looked at him questioningly.

"Could they be missing some nutrient we aren't aware of? Something that would make them susceptible to this illness?"

Lorana shook her head. She started to speak, but it turned into a wide yawn before she could answer.

"M'tal is right," Kindan declared. "You do need your sleep."

He placed the tray on the return shaft to the Lower Caverns, turned back to her with a grin, and raised his elbow invitingly. "May I escort you back to your weyr, my lady?"

Lorana smiled in return, placing a hand on the proffered elbow, and getting into "my lady" character. "Why certainly. Lead on!"

"I think I've got something," Lorana said as they pored over Records the next day.

Kindan looked up from his Records and gave her an encouraging look.

"This is the third reference I've seen to Fort Weyr."

"I've seen about the same," Kindan said.

"I think that when the Weyrleaders get really stumped, they go to Fort Weyr and check the Records there," Lorana declared.

"That would make sense," Kindan agreed. "And Fort Weyr's close enough to the Harper Hall that they could draft some of the archivists to maintain copies in good condition."

"Didn't you say you used to do copying at the Harper Hall?" Lorana asked. When Kindan nodded, she continued, "Do you remember copying Fort Weyr Records?"

"No," Kindan admitted. "But that doesn't mean it wasn't done Turns before."

"I think it's worth investigating," Lorana said.

Lorana sprang up from her seat, gave herself an almighty stretch, and said, "Anything to get away from these musty old Records."

Kindan looked at her quizzically. "Are you accusing me of that sentiment, or admitting it yourself?"

"Both," Lorana answered, laughing.

"B'nik."

A voice in his ear and gentle shaking roused the dragonrider. He turned over, coming face-to-face with Tullea, her eyes worried.

"I—" she began, voice low and full of apology.

"Shh," B'nik said, raising his fingers to her lips in a gesture of understanding. Tullea's face crumpled and she crushed herself against him.

"I'm sorry," she muttered into his shoulder. "I'm so sorry."

"It's all right, love, it's all right," B'nik told her, stroking her graceful neck and clasping her tight to him.

Tullea tensed and pulled back. "But it's *not* all right," she protested, her eyes shiny with tears and her nose running. She shook her head helplessly. "I don't understand, B'nik—"

B'nik tried to shush her again but she dodged his fingers.

"I never used to be like this," Tullea continued. "I feel pulled apart, dizzy; I can't concentrate. I feel out of control all the time, B'nik. And it's been like this for *Turns*."

B'nik nodded sympathetically.

"I want *me* back," Tullea cried. "I want to be who I was, not angry all the time."

She looked into his warm eyes and told him her deepest fear: "And if I lose you, I don't think I'll ever be able to do that."

M'tal wasn't in his quarters, nor in the Kitchen Cavern. As they wandered across the Bowl, they found K'tan first and decided to try the idea on him.

"Two more dragons have started coughing this morning," he told them as they approached. "That makes seven more since the last Fall."

"Nearly two a day," Kindan observed. "How long from the start of the cough until . . ."

"Death?" K'tan finished. He shook his head. "Two, maybe three sevendays."

Lorana eyed the walls of the Bowl above them, picking out each individual weyr. She spotted one dragon lolling with its neck extended out over the ledge of its weyr, saw it sneeze and send a cloud of green ooze spraying down and out across the Bowl. She pointed at it.

"It may not be the way it starts to spread," she said to the others, "but do we know if the latest sick are close by or under those already infected?"

K'tan gasped in surprise. "I hadn't thought of that before."

"I hadn't either," Lorana admitted.

Kindan raised his hands. "Nor I."

K'tan stroked his chin thoughtfully. "But if you're right, then we need to isolate the sick ones on the lowest levels."

Lorana shook her head. "That won't work," she said. When the other two looked at her in surprise, she explained, "Because the riders still have to walk across the Bowl—and the dragons wash in the lake."

"They could be getting it from the waters of the lake, then, couldn't they?" Kindan said, with an apologetic look at Lorana for countering her theory.

Lorana's shoulders slumped.

"They could. For that matter, they all eat the same food. The contagion could be spread through the herdbeasts."

"There's a map of the weyrs in the Weyrleader's quarters, I believe," K'tan said. "Given that any of these theories could be right, wouldn't it make sense to see if we spot the pattern Lorana suggested?"

"It might," Lorana agreed. "But if the weyrs aren't grouped by wings, it probably won't."

K'tan gave her a questioning look.

"The dragons could infect each other while they're training," she explained sadly.

Kindan groaned. "So we're no nearer than we were."

K'tan shook his head. "No, I think there's some progress—we have a number of good ideas we can follow." He looked at Lorana. "When your father dealt with sick herdbeasts, what did he do?"

Lorana started to marshal the list of actions in her mind. Seeing that she was preparing a lengthy response, he interrupted her with an upraised palm.

"I mean, what did he do first?"

"He tried to isolate the sick from the healthy," she said immediately. And then, as she registered the import of the words, she groaned. "Why didn't we think of this earlier?"

"Because we've been too near the problem," K'tan answered swiftly. "We've been too busy dealing with Thread and the day-to-day battle with the sickness." He shook his head sadly. "M'tal's off training."

"Not anymore," Lorana declared. "I just called Gaminth back."

Kindan whistled in surprise at her forwardness.

"Now *that's* acting like a Weyrwoman," K'tan said approvingly.

"You were right to call me back," M'tal said to Lorana when they had explained their purpose. "Fighting this illness is just as important as fighting Thread."

They were gathered in the Council Room. At M'tal's invitation, Salina had joined them. Kindan gave M'tal and Salina a quick review of their thinking.

Salina pointed to a slate chart and said, "Here're the assignments for the riders." She looked it over and sighed. "I'm afraid it's not very up-to-date."

She laid it on the table and the others looked it over. It was arranged by levels, with quarters numbered from the Weyrleader's weyr.

K'tan found some colored chalks. He circled in red all

those weyrs occupied by dragons that had gone *between,* and in yellow all those who were coughing.

Lorana pursed her lips unhappily. "That tells us how things are now," she said. "What we want to know is the progression of the sickness."

"Mm." K'tan agreed. He went back and started putting numbers beside each illness. Salina's Breth was, sadly, number one.

"But there were others sick before Breth," Salina noted.

K'tan grunted agreement, dusted off some numbers and corrected them. They peered at the final arrangement.

"I don't see a pattern," Kindan said.

"Well, there wouldn't be," M'tal said after a long moment's silence. "If the sickness is airborne and carried in the dragons' sneezes, then the sickness would sink down into the Bowl. Because every dragon comes down to the Bowl at some point, they would breathe in the infected air."

"Although some dragons sleep lower down and would be exposed to the infected air more," K'tan commented.

M'tal accepted this point with a shrug.

"If the disease was spread by water, then every dragon would have an equal chance of catching it," Kindan observed. He pointed to the distribution of the sick dragons. "The upper levels are less infected than the lower ones, so perhaps it *is* an airborne sickness."

"You can't rule out something in their food, either," Salina countered.

Kindan nodded.

M'tal looked up at Lorana. "Gaminth said you had a plan. What was it?"

Lorana paused before answering. "I noticed repeated references to Fort Weyr. It seems that every time the Weyrleader encounters something extraordinary, there's a trip made to Fort—"

"No," M'tal said shaking his head. "I can guess what you're thinking and we can't risk it. No one knows how the sickness spreads and we don't want to spread—"

"But the fact that more dragons have gotten sick since we

imposed the quarantine indicates that however the sickness was first acquired, it's being spread by our own dragons now," K'tan interjected.

"Maybe our dragons can't get sicker," M'tal said, "but we can't say whether Fort Weyr's dragons could." He shook his head. "It's a risk I don't want to take. And I can't ask K'lior to take it, especially as he's fighting his first Fall tomorrow."

"Perhaps after?" Lorana suggested forlornly.

M'tal drew a loud, thoughtful breath. He let it out again in a sigh, shaking his head. "No."

Kindan started to speak, but Lorana grabbed his arm, shaking her head. "Very well," she said. "We'll do what we can."

"Have you heard from Masterharper Zist?" M'tal asked Kindan.

Kindan shook his head. "Not yet. I've got a weyrling up on the watch heights listening for the drums."

"Perhaps he'll have good news for us," M'tal said wearily. He looked at the others. "Well, if that's all, I think I'll get back to B'nik's training flight."

"It's time to do our rounds, anyway," K'tan said, rising from his seat. He gestured to Lorana. "Coming?"

Lorana roused herself from her musings over the chart. "What? Oh, yes! I want to see Denorith's wing."

Thread falls
Dragons rise
Dragonriders scan the skies
Dragons flame, Thread dies.

Chapter Fourteen

"WAKE UP! Come on, K'lior, get up—it's time to fight Thread," Cisca called from across the room, full of irrepressible enthusiasm.

K'lior rolled over and up. In truth, he hadn't slept and even though he had gone to bed very early in the morning, he had found himself faking sleep so as not to upset Cisca.

"You were faking last night," she said as she came across the room and kissed him.

K'lior groaned. "I didn't want to worry you."

"I couldn't sleep either," she admitted. "But it's time: Thread falls over lower Nabol and upper Ruatha in less than two hours." She gestured toward the bathing room. "Get a good bath, start the day right."

K'lior smiled. If there was any mantra to Cisca's high energy life, it was "get a good bath." It was about the only time he could get her to slow down. Well, one of the only times, he corrected himself with a wicked grin.

"I heard that!" Cisca called from the bathing room.

"I didn't say anything," K'lior returned mildly.

Cisca reentered the room, grabbed his hand, and tugged him playfully toward the waiting bath. "I heard it anyway," she said.

Wisely, K'lior said nothing. As he eased into the bath, he

opened his mouth to ask for some breakfast but Cisca hushed him with a raised finger.

"I've already sent down for some *klah* and scones," she informed him. "Eat light up here, so that you can eat a hearty breakfast with the riders."

K'lior nodded: That had been his plan. He once again blessed his luck that his Rineth had managed to catch Melirth when she rose. He had been so afraid that one of the older, wiser dragons—and his rider—would have managed to outmaneuver the young bronze on his first mating flight. He and Cisca had already formed a strong attachment before her gold rose for the first time, and while he understood and accepted the ways of the Weyr, he was honest enough to admit that he did not want any other dragonman entwined with her.

"I know that look," Cisca said, returning with a tray. She put it down beside the bathing pool and sat herself beside it. "You're worrying about me again."

K'lior could never understand how his thoughts could be so transparent, no matter how hard he worked to keep his face expressionless.

"Afraid I might let another ride Melirth, eh?" she teased, punching him lightly on his exposed shoulder. "Well," she said consideringly, "I will, too, if you don't behave."

"I'll do my best," he promised somberly.

Cisca flicked water at him, grinning. "That's the spirit! Now finish bathing so we can get downstairs and make a suitable appearance."

"There are two hundred and twenty-two fighting dragons, excluding the three queens, and they will *all* fly!" D'gan shouted at V'gin and Lina. For the third time since the last Fall, they had asked him to keep the sick dragons behind. Now he took a breath and let his anger ride out with a deep sigh.

"We have only two hundred and twenty-two fighting dragons," he repeated, ignoring the startled looks on the faces of the other dragonriders milling about the Lower Caverns.

They should be used to his shouting by now, he reflected. They should know that his roar was always worse than his flame.

"I know that, D'gan," Lina said soothingly. "Which is why I still think it might be best if the sick ones don't fly."

D'gan shook his head. "They fly. Every dragon that can go *between* will fly against Thread." He looked pointedly at Norik, the Weyr harper, who had stood beside the other two to lend support. "Isn't that the duty as written in the Teaching Songs?"

"It is, but the—"

"No buts!" D'gan replied hotly, his anger coming back. "Harper, I heard no 'buts' in the Teaching Songs. It doesn't say 'Dragonmen must fly when they feel like it.' It says, 'Dragonmen must fly when Thread is in the sky.' "

Norik bit his lip and heaved a deep sigh.

"Very well," D'gan said, confident that this repeated revolt had been snuffed out. "Lina, order the wings to assemble above the Star Stones." He raised his voice to be heard by the massed riders. "We ride against Thread over Telgar!"

As the riders mounted their dragons, D'gan turned back to Lina. "You'll want to assemble the queen's wing to come along on my command."

Lina opened her mouth to try once more to dissuade him, but the set look on D'gan's face quelled her. She closed her mouth again and nodded mutely.

Her Garoth was one of the dragons that had most recently started sneezing.

"You will be careful, won't you, old man?" Dalia asked as she and C'rion glided down to the Bowl below them. She had chided C'rion for his decision to relocate the queens and senior Wingleaders to the highest weyrs—it ensured that all their meals were either in the Kitchen or cold—but she couldn't fault his logic. If the sickness was spread from dragon to dragon, and that certainly seemed so, then the dragons' sneezing was the surest way it spread. So moving the fit dragons to the highest part of the Weyr—above the sneezers—seemed a good precaution.

"I'll be careful," C'rion promised. Not, he reflected, that being careful was enough these days.

The sickness had more than decimated the Weyr. When he had seen the Red Star bracket the Eye Rock at Fort Weyr, he could count on three hundred and thirty-three fighting dragons. Now he would be taking only one hundred and seventy-six to fight Thread at South Nerat.

Fortunately, the path of the Thread would only graze South Nerat in this Fall, and C'rion hoped that his new tactics—and the short Fall—would give the Weyr the thrill of success without the numbing pain of lost dragons.

"You'll keep an eye on things around here?" C'rion asked.

Dalia grimaced. "I'd rather be going with you," she admitted. "You still haven't convinced me that your tactics can make up for missing the queens' wing."

C'rion shrugged. "But I can't have our queens flying underneath any sick dragons."

"I thought the sick dragons were staying behind?" Dalia asked, brows raised.

"The ones we *know* about," C'rion corrected. "Oh, the Wingleaders and the riders themselves understand the risks, but that's not to say that a dragon who feels fine right now won't be coughing and sneezing when we arrive over South Nerat."

Dalia nodded. He was right—the onset of the symptoms was that quick. Why, it had seemed like only minutes had passed between Carth's first sneeze and the moment Gatrial's anguished cry was echoed by the keening of the Weyr's dragons at yet another loss.

In the three days since the last Fall, they had lost twenty-seven dragons to the sickness. Dalia shut her eyes against the painful memory.

It will be all right, Bidenth soothed her. Dalia nodded to herself. A new healer would be sent from the Harper Hall. It might be awhile, because no one would risk sending a dragon to the Harper Hall, so the poor lad would have to travel over land and sea when the sky was Thread free. In the meantime, they would make do.

"Good morning, my lady!" a young woman called cheerfully up from the Bowl below.

Dalia smothered her retort, instead alighting swiftly from Bidenth and striding over to the smiling holder girl.

"Jassi," she said with a touch of acerbity, "*please* just call me by my name."

Jassi dipped a curtsy and bowed her head. "I'm sorry my—Dalia—that takes some getting used to."

Dalia shook her head but couldn't help smiling at the holder girl. Jassi had arrived in response to C'rion's pleading request for anyone who knew anything about Healing.

"I've really only dealt with the cuts and scrapes we got at my father's inn," Jassi had confessed immediately upon arrival. She ticked off the injuries she'd tended on her fingers. "The odd broken bone, deep puncture, a collapsed lung once, and—"

Dalia had hugged her. "Please, just see what you can do," she had begged. "If it doesn't work out, no harm done."

"I'll try, my lady," Jassi had replied, very much on her best manners.

She had nearly bolted when their first charge proved to be a dragon, but Dalia had calmed her down and introduced her to the dragon, who was reeling in pain from a badly scored wing.

After the first day, Dalia couldn't imagine being without Jassi. The girl had recovered from her initial awkwardness and slipped easily into the role of authority so completely that Dalia suspected the girl had been a major force in the now-closed inn. Jassi had confessed that she felt claustrophobic in the tight society and narrow corridors of Ista Hold.

Now, after nearly a sevenday at the Weyr, Jassi had found herself thoroughly at home and, except for a tendency to address all the dragonriders as "my lord" or "my lady," had completely adjusted to Weyr life. In fact, Dalia had decided to coax Jassi onto the Hatching Grounds the next time there was a queen egg.

The girl's cheerfulness was irrepressible, even in the worst of times. Dalia's eyes watered at the memories of all the hands she had seen Jassi hold while a rider lost a dragon to the sickness.

"It's much worse for them," Jassi had explained when Dalia had carefully steered one of their conversations to the topic. "So I try to keep a good face on and do what I can."

And that, Dalia supposed, was all that could be expected of anyone in these terrible times. To do what they could.

High over the west branch of the Telgar river, two hundred and thirty-one dragons burst into the sky, perfectly arrayed in a three-layer arrow formation.

"Right, we're here, where's Thread?" P'dor shouted from his position behind K'lior. K'lior smiled at his wing-second's jauntiness. He looked up, then looked around.

The sight of his Weyr arrayed behind him made him swell with pride. All the training was going to pay off, he was sure. He looked at the skies behind him. Thread. His bronze dragon, Rineth, bugled as he sensed K'lior's thrill of alarm.

"Where's Telgar?" he wondered aloud. To Rineth he said, *Have the lower flight remain here and order the other two flights to turn around to face Thread.*

In an awkward flurry the Weyr rearranged itself. Rineth turned back to K'lior for firestone, and then suddenly there was Thread, raining down on them and no one from Telgar in sight.

It was time to fly.

Time to flame.

Time to fight.

Thread would be over Nerat for less than an hour, C'rion reminded himself as he and Nidanth emerged into the morning sunlight. He glanced around, satisfied that the wings were organizing themselves quickly. It was an awkward Fall to fight, just grazing Nerat before sheering back out to sea. So, while it was a short flight, it had its own unique perils. Thread had been falling on the sea for some time already, and the pattern of the Fall had been established—except that the morning breeze had already started, with great thermals roiling the Thread and clumping it unpredictably.

C'rion was glad that it was a short Fall. He considered rearranging the Weyr's dragons to fight from the shore, rather than pick up the Fall as it came in from the sea and follow it.

There! He could see them, flecks of white against the high clouds. He ordered Nidanth to spread the news. The bronze complied, then turned his massive head back for firestone. C'rion fed it to him, all the while scanning the skies above him, trying to time when to climb up to fight the falling Thread.

J'lantir, arrayed in the wing behind him, saw the menacing clump of Thread as it whirled down and streamed onto C'rion and Nidanth from behind. Before he could even shout a warning, Thread had scoured C'rion's back bare and had torn great gaps in Nidanth's inner wings and back. The pair vanished *between*. J'lantir counted slowly to himself, his eyes scanning the skies around him.

When he reached five, he swallowed hard and said to Lolanth, *Tell Pineth to have M'kir take their wing to the rear. Tell the rest of our wing to close up to the front.*

Tears streamed down J'lantir's face as Lolanth relayed the orders and sped up to bring the wing forward to the Thread. And then there was Thread to fight, to flame, to char from the skies.

Grimly, J'lantir did his duty for his Weyr and planet.

Kindan was worried when he didn't see Lorana come to dinner. They had worked all day together, part of the time in the Records Room, and part of the time helping K'tan tend to the injured dragons and riders—as well as the sick dragons.

Lorana had been cheerful in the early morning, but as the day wore on, and dragons from Fort, Telgar, and Ista Weyrs were lost fighting Thread, her face took on a sickly pallor. Kindan could see her wince visibly with each new loss.

"I'm all right," she had told him when he'd asked her about it.

Shortly before the evening meal, M'tal came searching for her in the Records Room.

"I just heard from Lolanth," he began, his eyes troubled.

"I heard," Lorana said in a flat voice.

"Did you—" M'tal cut himself short. "I was wondering if perhaps you'd felt Nidanth's passing."

Lorana shook her head sadly. "There were so many," she said hoarsely, her voice barely audible. "Less than the first Fall, but still so many."

M'tal nodded slowly. "C'rion was right, then, to pity you."

Lorana met his eyes. "I'll survive," she said firmly. "It's hard, but I have Arith to comfort me."

"If there's anything you need," M'tal said, "or anything I or Salina can do to help . . ."

"Thank you," Lorana said, forcing a smile. "We'll manage, Arith and I."

But now, as Kindan's eyes scanned the crowded tables, he wondered. With a sigh, he left and headed up to the Records Room. Perhaps she had decided to eat there instead.

He was halfway up the steps when Arith called, *Lorana needs the harper.*

The dragon's message made him jump, but as soon as he recovered, he was running down the stairs and across the Bowl to Lorana's quarters.

Kindan slowed as he neared Lorana's rooms, halting just before the door, catching his breath and listening. Through the curtain, he heard the soft sounds of sobbing.

"Lorana?" he called. "May I come in?"

"Yes."

Kindan pushed the curtain aside. He noticed that the tapestries were covered with drawings pinned to them. They were drawings of dragons and riders. Some he recognized as dragons from the Weyr—all dragons lost to Thread or the sickness. He guessed the other dragons were those lost from other Weyrs, although he couldn't imagine how Lorana knew enough to draw them. As he peered closer, he saw that she didn't—the characteristic features of a dragon's face, the shape of its eye ridges, the spacing of the snout, the shape and number of teeth were all left as nebulous, shadowy hints. But he could plainly see their riding harness, the faces of their grief-stricken riders—and Kindan was struck by the amount of pain that he saw in those faces, pain that he knew Lorana must have felt directly.

He noticed the light reflected off Arith's whirling eyes as the dragon looked in worriedly from her lair toward her rider.

As his eyes adjusted to the gloom, he saw Lorana lying in her bed. He went over and sat on the edge. She was lying on her stomach, face in her pillow, her upper arms and back uncovered. For a moment he sat there, silent. He started to put a hand on her shoulder, paused, and pulled it back.

"Do you have any lotion?" he asked.

"What?" Lorana turned over to face him. In the dim light, Kindan could see her blotchy face and the streaks where tears had washed down her face. He had seen people like this before, worn out with pain, bodies tight with grief and sorrow.

"Lotion," Kindan repeated. "Or scented oil?"

"There's some oil by the bath," she answered, sounding quizzical.

Kindan went to the bathing room, found the oil and returned. He placed it close to the bed.

He took some oil into his hands and rubbed it until it was warm. Then he leaned forward and gently began to massage the tight muscles of her neck.

"Turn over, I need to do your hands," he ordered her softly. He could sense her puzzled look. "You can't have done all those drawings without cramping your hands," he explained. "Turn over."

He gathered more lotion and, gently grasping her left hand in his right, he stroked over it with the oil, teasing out the kinks in her fingers and working the tight muscle at the base of her thumb. Slowly he worked up her arm, relieving tension in the forearm, biceps, and shoulder.

Lorana let out a deep sigh of contentment.

Kindan allowed himself a small smile, then returned to his work. He worked her other shoulder and arm.

He spent a great deal of time working the kinks out of the arch of her foot and her heel, knowing how much tension got wound into the balls of the feet. He repeated his efforts on the other leg.

At last Kindan let out a deep breath and looked down at Lorana, lying relaxed beneath him. Quietly he stood up and tiptoed out of the room.

In the morning, Lorana awoke suddenly with a burning passion, fierce and nearly frightening in its intensity.

Kindan ducked his head in, eyes snapping with emotion. "Tullea's Minith has blooded her kills."

"She will mate soon," Lorana said, stretching her senses and feeling the young queen's passion. She looked up at Kindan, her eyes warm but also challenging. "Stay with me?"

Kindan gave her a surprised, half-hoping look. Lorana sat up in her bed and patted it.

"I've never been near a dragon's mating flight," she explained.

Kindan moved to her and, at her beckoning, sat on the bed beside her.

"The emotions from dragons mating are very strong," he said, his voice low.

At that moment, Lorana gasped as she felt Minith being caught in her mating flight and—

When she could speak again, she leaned up and captured Kindan's mouth with hers, kissing him deeply.

Kindan responded by clutching her more tightly, returning her kiss as ardently as she had given it. Like dragons entwined, they drew together, burning with a passion born on dragonwings.

Afterward, they broke apart, still touching each other loosely. Lorana looked at him as he lay beside her and traced the line of his jaw lovingly. Kindan turned his head, caught her hand, kissed it, and released it again, all with a gentle smile.

"Who was it?" he asked, referring to the mating flight.

"B'nik's Caranth flew her," Lorana told him immediately. She had known the dragon's touch instantly.

Kindan sighed and Lorana heard a world of unspoken thoughts in that sigh. Things would change at Benden Weyr. She reached for his hand, grabbed it, brought it to her lips, and kissed it.

Such a union of disparates, K'tan thought to himself as he watched Lorana and Kindan enter the Main Cavern later that evening, not too far from Tullea and B'nik. M'tal and Salina were already seated.

Tullea walked with the obvious soreness of a woman recovering from her dragon's mating. B'nik looked equally uncomfortable.

Lorana, on the other hand, moved *through* her pain, a smile close to her lips, her hand entwined in Kindan's, projecting the sense that the pain served a purpose that she accepted and welcomed.

She and the harper made a good pair, he reflected, and he was glad that some were happy with the day's events.

The same could not be said from the looks of Tullea and B'nik. They had been lovers, and passionately so, for many Turns, so K'tan would have expected Minith's mating to be a great pleasure to them. But from Tullea's red-rimmed eyes and the way she winced as she strode, he got the impression that it had not been so.

The mating flight had taken place early in the morning, just after Minith awoke. K'tan could not remember how many bronze riders had gathered around Tullea as the enraged queen started blooding her kills. He remembered B'nik screaming at Tullea not to let her gorge, and Tullea looking back at him with a smirk in her eyes. Whether it was from Tullea's contrariness or her inability to control her dragon, Minith managed to eat two whole herdbeasts before a bellow from Caranth and more loud shouts from B'nik got her under control. She blooded only two more kills before leaping into the air, chased by the lusty bronzes.

The mating flight had not been that long. Indeed, all the

bronzes were still flying strongly when Minith dove into them and was snared by Caranth. K'tan sighed, shaking his head at the memory. A short mating flight, gorging on her food—those spoke of a small clutch and more problems for the Weyr with a Weyrwoman who would not control her dragon.

M'tal and Salina rose as they caught sight of Tullea and B'nik. The new Weyrwoman noticed their movement but deliberately turned toward a different table. Obviously not accepting the affront, M'tal gestured to Salina and they walked over to the table Tullea had chosen.

"Congratulations Weyrwoman, Weyrleader on your mating flight," M'tal began the traditional greeting. "May your hatchlings be many."

Tullea glowered at him. B'nik looked pained at that part of the traditional salutation but nodded politely to M'tal and Salina.

"I want you out of B'nik's quarters by tomorrow," Tullea told M'tal. "The Weyrleader needs to be close to the Records Room." She glanced at Kindan and Lorana, who had stopped in their tracks. "Lorana, you and Kindan will conduct your research elsewhere."

It was an obvious taunt. Lorana deflected it with a polite nod. "If you wish, we could continue our research in my quarters."

Tullea sniffed. "I don't care where, as long as it's not in the Records Room." A new thought entered her mind and she turned to M'tal, a sly smile on her face. "As Weyrwoman, it is my duty to arrange assignment of quarters," she declared. "I think, Wingleader M'tal, that your wing would be best up on the highest level. You may move there immediately. B'nik's wing will occupy the quarters yours vacates."

M'tal accepted the order with a nod and a smile. "Thank you, Weyrwoman," he said. "I have heard it said that the higher levels are more likely to be free of the sickness."

Tullea's eyes widened in shock, then narrowed again as she decided he was toying with her.

"Weyrleader, your wing may begin moving tomorrow," she told B'nik with a purr.

B'nik looked nonplussed. He told M'tal, "My men won't be ready by then. Please ask yours to move at their convenience."

"Yes, Weyrleader," M'tal replied. He gestured to Salina and they departed, leaving Tullea no happier than she had been.

The night air was broken by the sound of a dragon coughing. Startled looks went around the Cavern as they tried to identify the dragon, only to change to looks of anguish as everyone realized that yet another dragon had fallen ill. B'nik bent his head toward Tullea, engaging her in a rapid conversation.

M'tal's wing had moved to the upper levels before noon the next day, although they were left with a lot of cleaning still to do.

"It's our due for having it so easy in the training," he teased them. They responded in kind, but there was a marked strain in their humor.

Lorana and Kindan decided to move their research to the harper's quarters, as they were on the Lower Caverns and closer to the Records Room than Lorana's rooms. They took only as many Records as they felt they could sort through in a sevenday. The smaller piles gave them a false sense that the task would be easier.

K'tan stopped in to check on them late in the afternoon.

"I went to the Weyrwomen's quarters first, thinking you'd be there," he told them as he ducked inside the doorway. He glanced around Kindan's cozy rooms and nodded approvingly. "This makes more sense."

"Well, it's really harper's work anyway," Kindan said by way of agreement. "How are the sick ones doing?"

K'tan grimaced, shaking his head. "Worse. And more of them," he replied.

Kindan turned back to the piles of Records. "Then I guess we'd better get to work."

"We won't find anything here," Lorana protested, jumping out of her seat in frustration. "We need to go to Fort."

K'tan looked at her questioningly.

"That's where the oldest Records are," she explained. "And that's where every Weyrleader has gone when they couldn't find an answer in their own Records."

"M'tal said that you can't go," Kindan told her reprovingly.

"M'tal's not the Weyrleader anymore," Lorana shot back rebelliously.

"Well, Arith's too young to take you," Kindan continued. "So how were you planning on getting there?"

"I could take you." Startled, they turned to see B'nik standing in the doorway. "I need to see K'lior, anyway."

"But—the sickness," Kindan protested.

"They have it at Fort, as well," B'nik said. "K'lior's agreed." He turned his attention to Lorana. "When would you be ready to go?"

"I'd like to come also," Kindan said.

B'nik shook his head. "I need you and K'tan to stay here, caring for the sick and injured."

Lorana pulled out a slate and stylus. "When can we go?"

"Whenever you're ready," he replied. "I believe that Tullea and Minith are still sleeping," he added disingenuously.

"Very well, then," Lorana responded pertly. She glanced back at the others and then to the new Weyrleader. "Arith still sleeps, but she'll be hungry in another hour or two."

B'nik nodded thoughtfully. "Then we'll be certain to return before she needs to feed, no matter how long we're gone," he told her.

"Is it such a wise idea to time it, Weyrleader, just after the mating flight?" K'tan asked solicitously. He knew how tiring going *between* times was on both rider and dragon—and the mating flight had been no less exhausting.

"Caranth is up for it," B'nik declared. "And I may need the practice," he added ambiguously. He gestured to Lorana. "Weyrwoman?"

As they were heading out of sight, Kindan turned to

K'tan. "Do you think you could hold things down without me?"

K'tan thought it over and shrugged. "Some of the weyr-folk will help, I'm sure."

"Thanks," Kindan said, racing after the others.

"B'nik!" Kindan called when he caught sight of the new Weyrleader. B'nik paused, turning back to watch Kindan as he raced up to them.

"I think it'd be a good idea if I stopped in at the Harper Hall. Could Caranth carry another?" Kindan asked.

"I hadn't thought of that," B'nik said, after a moment's consideration. "I'd planned to bring the Masterharper up to date on our affairs—you could fill him in for me. That will save time."

He nodded toward the Bowl. "Come along, by all means. Caranth can carry three."

Lorana craned her neck over B'nik's shoulders as they spiraled down into Fort Weyr's Bowl. The watch dragon's bugle had already challenged them, and Lorana had heard Caranth's response and the watch dragon's wary greeting.

Kindan had been left at the Harper Hall, where B'nik had been congratulated and had exchanged brief pleasantries with Masterharper Zist.

"We're expected," B'nik relayed unnecessarily but politely to Lorana. The Weyrleader's attitude during the whole trip puzzled and pleased Lorana, who had been used to his silent obsequiousness with Tullea. The man was displaying depths she had not seen before.

Caranth alighted lightly and then, after dropping off rider and passenger, took to the air again to seek a place on the Weyr heights.

"Fort Weyr sees the sun six hours after we do at Benden," B'nik commented as he examined the early morning sun rising over them.

"Won't we still have to time it on our return?" Lorana asked.

"Indeed we will," B'nik told her. "Have you ever gone *between* times?"

"Once with J'trel," she told him.

"Were you very tired afterward?"

Lorana nodded.

"That is the price of going *between* times," B'nik said. "If it weren't for our pressing need, I'd never risk it." He looked as if he were ready to say more but decided against it. Instead, he scanned the area and noticed a group approaching them. "Ah, here we are."

The man in the center of the group was younger than B'nik, handsome and wiry. His long hair was tied at the back of his neck, a style uncommon among dragonriders, but the hair was such a honey-gold and so wavy that Lorana could well imagine the attraction it would hold for some women. Her eye moved to the woman beside him. Cisca was even taller than her Weyrleader, a brown-eyed, brown-haired beauty with a strong, cheerful face. She was much more buxom than Lorana, but she carried herself proudly, her stride neither apologetic nor flaunting.

"Weyrleader B'nik, welcome to Fort Weyr!" K'lior called as he approached the group. Cisca added a welcoming smile of her own.

"Thank you," B'nik replied. "I wish I were coming at a more pleasant time . . ."

"As do we all," Cisca agreed, her lovely features creasing into a frown. "How bad is it at Benden?"

B'nik looked at Lorana.

"There are twenty sick dragons at the Weyr," Lorana told them. "Three times that number have already gone *between*."

K'lior and Cisca exchanged looks. The Weyrwoman spoke. "We have nearly sixty sick dragons and have lost over forty."

"I'll be lucky to have five wings able to fight when Thread comes again," K'lior admitted.

B'nik nodded. "We still have seven wings of able dragons," he said. He saw K'lior's look of distress and hastily added, "But I don't know how long that will last—and we started with more dragons than you."

"What can we do to help?" Cisca asked, looking at Lorana. She frowned. "Are you Tullea?"

"This is Lorana, rider of Arith. Minith rose yesterday," B'nik said.

"Congratulations!" K'lior said, his face brightening.

"A good flight?" Cisca added, catching K'lior's hand in hers proprietarily.

B'nik found himself grinning at their obvious affection. "Unexpected," he admitted. "I had not expected to be Weyr-leader today."

"Well, I can see you've already settled into the role," Cisca pronounced approvingly.

B'nik's grin broadened.

"I can get nothing from High Reaches Weyr," Master-harper Zist said to Kindan as he completed his summary.

Kindan quirked an eyebrow. "Is there any reason?"

"The only message I got from G'relly was cryptic," Zist admitted. "The message was 'wait.' "

"That doesn't seem too cryptic," Kindan commented.

"Not at the time," Zist agreed. "But it's been nearly a fortnight since then and I've heard nothing further."

Kindan frowned. "What do we know from the other Weyrs, then?"

Masterharper Zist gestured to the Masterhealer.

Masterhealer Perigar sighed. "I cannot—my specialty is humans," he temporized.

"Surely a disease is a disease no matter whether it affects animals or humans?" Voice craftmaster Nonala asked in exasperation.

"Even if it were so," Perigar responded, "I don't have enough information to begin to guess—"

"I do," Verilan, the Master Archivist, interrupted gruffly. The others all turned to him. "I don't know anything about disease, but I can read and cipher."

He pushed a slate across the table. "There are the numbers

of dragons sick in all the Weyrs we know of," he said, tapping one line of numbers.

"And there are the numbers of dragons lost *between* to this illness." He tapped another column, then pointed to a third. "And there's the number of injured from each Fall."

"What's this tell us?" Masterharper Zist asked.

"The sickness has accelerated the losses of dragons," Verilan said. He raised a hand as the others started to protest the obviousness of his statement.

"This sickness has accelerated it so much that the Weyrs are losing half their fighting strength each time they fight Thread." He raised his hand higher to forestall further protests.

"I know, I know, the numbers are not exact. But the pattern is there," he pronounced. He gave a deep sigh and continued. "And, given that a Weyr needs at least one Flight—three full wings—of dragons to fly successfully against Thread . . ." He shook his head. "Given that, the Weyrs will be incapable of fighting Thread after the next two Falls."

"What?" The others were out of their chairs, grabbing at the slate, trying to examine it.

Kindan sat back first, then Masterharper Zist. They ignored the others and the shouting. They had each seen enough of Verilan's calculations to know that the Master Archivist was right.

Soon—in the next two Falls or less—there would not be enough dragons to protect Pern from Thread.

"Any luck?" B'nik asked cheerfully, sliding a platter of cheeses in Lorana's direction. She and Cisca looked up from the stacks of Records they had placed in front of them. Lorana shook her head mutely and Cisca looked back down quickly to her reading.

"When did you last eat?" B'nik asked. Lorana's face took on a puzzled look and before she could respond, he grinned.

"I thought so," he said. "It's the first question I ask Tullea, too." He tapped the platter. "Eat. Now. That's an order from your Weyrleader."

Lorana quirked her lips, dropped her Record, and dragged a plate in front of her. B'nik started to pile some cheese and crackers on it for her. With a gesture, he inquired if Fort's Weyrwoman wanted any.

"I think I'd better check on K'lior," Cisca said. She rose quickly but turned back to tell Lorana, "I'll be back."

"Thanks," Lorana told her.

"This," Cisca gestured to the Records spread in front of them, "is for all of us."

"Tell me what to look for," B'nik said as Lorana spread soft cheese on her cracker, feeling guilty to be eating while the Weyrleader was working.

"Anything that might be useful," she told him. "Mention of illness, Records of other Weyrleaders consulting the Records, that sort of thing."

B'nik nodded but his face showed confusion. Lorana shrugged. "We really don't know what we're looking for," she told him. "Dragons *don't* get sick."

"Except now."

They continued their work silently. Sometime later, K'lior and Cisca joined them, wordlessly pulling more stacks of Records and seating themselves at Fort Weyr's Records Room table.

It got darker. Glows were brought by the Fort Weyr Headwoman.

Finally, B'nik pushed himself back from his work, sitting upright. Lorana looked at him, expecting him to call it a day—and she was quite ready to end another fruitless search.

But as he drew breath to speak, Cisca, who had been tearing through the Records so fast Lorana wondered how she could read them, sat upright with a gasp of surprise.

"I think I've got something," she told the others. She had a puzzled expression on her face. She tapped a section on the Record she was examining.

"This Record says that there was a special place built just at the beginning of the First Interval." Cisca immediately had their undivided attention. "There was much argument about it but finally M'hall"—she nodded at B'nik's surprised expression—"prevailed and it was built at—"

"Benden Weyr," B'nik finished.

". . . So we have found nothing, in our Records or those of the Healercraft, to alter this conclusion?" Masterharper Zist asked, recapping the end of several hours' worth of intense research and debating.

"I have found nothing in the Archives," Master Archivist Verilan admitted. He cast a glance around the room, adding, "And I stand by my projections."

Perigar shook his head ruefully at the Archivist and threw up his hands in resignation. Masterharper Zist cocked an eyebrow at him, awaiting an answer.

"As I've said before, I'm not an animal healer. Perhaps the Masterherdsman might give a different answer, but my craft knows nothing that will help the dragons," the Masterhealer said finally.

The others all sat back from the table, either throwing up their hands or shaking their heads sadly. Except Kelsa. Zist gave her an inquiring look.

"I hesitate to bring this up," she said. "It's only a snippet."

"Anything," Kindan said desperately.

"I found part of a song, an ancient song," she said. "It has a sour melody—even if it is haunting—which is doubtless why no one sings it these days, and I've only found a verse or two . . ." She cast a meaningful glance at Kindan. "It was poorly copied . . ."

Kindan gasped in horror and recognition. Then he drew a breath and sang:

"A thousand voices keen at night,
A thousand voices wail,
A thousand voices cry in fright,
A thousand voices fail."

"But that hasn't happened," Verilan protested. "There have been no thousand voices—"

Kindan held up a hand for silence, closing his eyes in concentration. He continued:

"You followed them, young healer lass,
Till they could not be seen;
A thousand dragons made their loss
A bridge 'tween you and me."

Outside, a dragon appeared from *between* unnoticed as Kindan continued:

"And in the cold and darkest night,
A single voice is heard,
A single voice both clear and bright,
It says a single word."

He paused, then opened his eyes, shaking his head. "That's all I can remember."

"Has there been a healer lass come to Benden Weyr?" Perigar asked of everyone, looking particularly to Kindan.

"Lorana," Kindan said instantly, certain of his conviction.

"But she's not a healer," Perigar protested. His continued protests were halted by Masterharper Zist's upraised hand. The Masterharper tilted his head toward the corridor outside. Steps were running toward them.

A figure burst through the doorway.

"Kindan, come quick! Arith is sick," Lorana cried through her tears.

Ecosystems are constantly changing, adapting to new life-forms, while simultaneously life-forms are adapting to the ecosystem. To engineer a change to an ecosystem is to commit to a lifetime of monitoring.
— *Glossary of terms*, Ecosystems:
From -ome to Planet, 24th Edition

Chapter Fifteen

Tillek Hold, First Interval, AL 58

"I WOULDN'T QUITE CALL Tillek *warm* this time of year," M'hall shouted over his shoulder to Wind Blossom as they spiraled down toward the northern Hold.

"It will do for my purposes," she replied calmly, although she was enjoying her ride on dragonback too much to let anything like a mere chill in the air, or a foggy day, disturb her.

M'hall's Brianth was wise and experienced—as was Benden's Weyrleader himself. All the same, the descent through the foggy air was unnerving for both of them. M'hall was just about to give up and order Brianth *between* to safety when they broke through the cloud cover and saw land beneath—far too close for M'hall's comfort.

Brianth immediately shifted from a spiral to a hover, allowing his rider to direct him toward a safe landing spot.

The fog was so dense that it wasn't until M'hall and Wind Blossom were through the gates of Tillek Hold that anyone noticed them.

"At least it's not cold," M'hall admitted as they waved at the startled guards. "Da said old Ireland—on Earth where he lived as a boy—could get like this, in the summer, with a fog coming in off the shore."

He craned his neck up behind him and let out a whistle as a gap in the fog showed the mountains in the distance.

"It is a beautiful view, isn't it?" a voice called cheerfully to them.

A shadow in the fog resolved into a figure, which grew clearer as they approached. It was a man. He was bearded and wore a heavy-knit sweater. He had seaman's hands and the swaggering walk that came from months spent at sea.

"Malon of Tillek at your service," he said, extending a hand first to Wind Blossom and then to M'hall. "Your fire-lizard messenger told me you were coming, but I wasn't sure in this fog."

M'hall recalled from L'can that Malon had taken over the running of Tillek Hold just recently, after Jim Tillek's successor had passed on. The man was about M'hall's own height, big-boned, brown-haired and brown-eyed, with a pleasant gentleness in his eyes.

"Pleased to meet you," M'hall said.

"I think the pleasure is ours," Malon responded, gesturing toward the Great Hall. "We've got a hearty fish stew waiting and a warm spot for Wind Blossom for her stay." He peered down at the diminutive old lady, his curiosity obvious. "Although why you would prefer our shores to the warmer ones of Southern Boll . . ."

"You have a spot picked out for me on the beach?" Wind Blossom asked. "No prying eyes?"

Malon nodded, his expression perplexed. "We do, and a shelter for all occasions."

"I asked for some other things—were you able to provide them?" Wind Blossom continued.

"With pleasure," Malon said, white teeth flashing bright against the brown beard. "Although I will confess that you've got many people scratching their heads in wonder."

"An old lady's folly," Wind Blossom said. She jerked her hand at the Benden Weyrleader. "M'hall said I needed a rest." She gestured around at the fog. "This will be restful, I think."

"You are welcome to whatever we can provide you, Wind Blossom," Malon told her. He shook his head, adding, "Although I don't quite know what you'll want with a bell, a coil of rope, and some planking."

"It is a science experiment," Wind Blossom told him. M'hall shot her a penetrating look but she waved it aside. "I wish to see how far sound will travel over foggy water."

A clattering sound behind them caused Wind Blossom to turn around. A watch-wher approached eagerly, only to be hauled short with a hiss of pain by a stout chain attached to its neck with a collar.

"What is this?" Wind Blossom asked, her voice going dangerously soft.

"One of yours, I think," Malon said, waving a hand affectionately toward the watch-wher.

Wind Blossom turned to Tillek's leader and looked up at him with a dangerous intensity. "Why is it chained?"

"Oh, Tilsk here was always getting into mischief," Malon said dismissively. "It's for its own good."

"Watch-whers are 'he' or 'she,' " Wind Blossom corrected sternly. "This one is a green; that makes her a 'she.' "

"I'm sorry, *she* was getting into trouble," Malon said. "I apologize if chaining her up distresses you."

"More than distress," Wind Blossom said. She glanced up at M'hall. "This is bad."

"The Pass is over," M'hall protested. "There is no danger. And, you must admit, an uncontrolled watch-wher can be a menace."

"A watch-wher needs training, just like a fire-lizard," Wind Blossom corrected. "Or a dragon," she said with added emphasis, glaring up at M'hall until the Weyrleader nodded in agreement.

"What if we start chaining up dragons?" she asked, nodding in satisfaction when both Malon and M'hall recoiled in horror. She looked back up at Malon. "It is the same thing, to chain a watch-wher."

She glanced again at M'hall. "And when Thread comes again, what if the watch-whers are still chained? You know their purpose."

"Lady Wind Blossom, I meant no disrespect," Malon told her emphatically. "I know you are attached to your creation—"

"It's not that, Malon," M'hall interrupted. "Wind Blossom is right. The watch-whers serve a greater purpose."

"They fly at night," Wind Blossom explained, "when the dragons sleep."

A look of dawning comprehension flowed across Malon's face. "That was why we chained her in the first place," he said with a groan. "She went missing one night!"

Wind Blossom nodded. "Eating Thread," she said, her eyes showing delight. "Good."

"If I had known . . . I'll release her at once!"

"No," Wind Blossom raised a hand. "Pick someone to work with her, like a fire-lizard. Train her, earn her respect, *then* let her free."

"They are like fire-lizards then?" Malon asked, brows raised. "If so, she's too old to bond . . ."

"Apparently they are not quite like fire-lizards *or* dragons," M'hall told him.

"More independent," Wind Blossom agreed. "Able to take care of themselves, if they must."

"Fortunately, Thread usually freezes at night so their skills are rarely needed," M'hall added. Wind Blossom nodded approvingly.

"I see," Malon said. "So I should probably keep this news to myself and not alarm the Hold."

"That has been our consensus so far, yes," Wind Blossom agreed.

M'hall raised an eyebrow questioningly, but Wind Blossom gave him a nearly imperceptible shake of her head and he changed the topic.

"I'm glad we could clear that up," he said. Then he shivered theatrically. "Did you say something about a stew?"

Malon was only too happy to follow the change of topic and lead them into his Hold.

Over the next several days the weather cleared and the sun came out—and then for the rest of the week the weather turned foul. Either way, it did not alter Wind Blossom's routine. She was up with first light and out at her shelter.

She spent her evenings with Malon and the other fishermen, happily relating what little she knew of marine biology and gladly hearing what they had been taught through the cruel lessons of the sea. The oldsters were content to gather around her; many remembered her from the Fever Year, and some even from the Crossing.

Malon soon guessed Wind Blossom's reason for coming to Tillek Hold.

"I don't think they'll come," he told her after she returned to the Hold on the third evening. He sounded wistful. "I've seen them in the warmer waters, but I think it's too cold up here for them."

Wind Blossom smiled at him. "Could you give me a supply of fish? Or fish leavings?"

Malon shook his head admiringly. "You don't give up, do you?"

"I have had years to learn patience," she replied.

"You would do better in a boat, you know," Malon said after a moment's reflection.

"I am not a sailor," Wind Blossom confessed.

"I could get someone to take you," he offered.

Wind Blossom shook her head. "Thank you, but that would be . . . unwise."

"I see you have a secret you are reluctant to share," Malon observed.

Wind Blossom shook her head. "I have a secret I am sworn to keep," she corrected.

Malon nodded slowly, taking no offense. "Well, do please let me know if you think of anything else I can do to help."

"And the fish?" Wind Blossom reminded him.

"Of course."

* * *

The eerie light of glows in one of the classrooms caught Emorra's attention as she made her way to the kitchen late one night. She paused outside the room. She heard voices. Cautiously she opened the door and peered inside.

Inside, Tieran was standing at the blackboard, which was covered in various block diagrams and chemical formulas. She recognized the one he was working on as a decision tree. "What are you doing?" she asked.

"What are *you* doing?" he responded.

She raised the tray she was carrying. "I'm returning my dishes."

"I'm working late," he told her.

She walked into the room and put her tray down on one of the student desks. She came up to the blackboard and examined Tieran's work.

"Is this a diagnostic flowchart?" she asked.

Tieran nodded.

"For what purpose?"

"I'm trying to figure out what could have made the fire-lizards sick," he told her.

She looked at his chart. "I see you've got bacterial and viral, but why the Terran and Pernese? And why not dietary?"

"If it's a disease caused by poor nutrition, then it's self-limiting, isn't it?" Tieran said.

"It is if the missing nutrient can be found," she agreed. "Like vitamin C to prevent scurvy." She narrowed her eyes as she followed the flowchart to the next branch. "What's this about a microscope?"

"If it's bacterial, you could see the bacteria with a microscope," Tieran explained. "If you can't, then it's viral."

"But that's ignoring the fact that secondary infections could be either bacterial *or* viral," Emorra observed.

"I'm not trying to make this harder," Tieran protested, "I'm trying to make it easier."

Emorra's lips quirked upward. "If it was easy," she began, and Tieran joined her in the finish, "then anyone could do it."

They exchanged grins. Then Emorra shook her head. "I don't know why you're bothering," she told him. "I mean it's obvious that Mother's given up."

Tieran cocked his head at her.

"She's on a vacation, isn't she?" Emorra asked.

"Is she?" Tieran asked.

Emorra dismissed the issue with a shake of her head. She looked back at the flowchart, intending to leave Tieran to his own devices, when a sudden thought struck her.

"You know," she said musingly, "you're going about this all wrong."

"I'll take any help I can get," Tieran responded feelingly.

"The question isn't what initial vector started the illness," she said slowly, testing out the idea as she said it, "but what was the cause of death."

"It seemed to be some sort of extreme upper respiratory infection or complications therefrom," Tieran said.

Emorra nodded in agreement. "So, what would be required to survive a severe upper respiratory infection?"

"Lots of antibiotics," Tieran replied instantly.

"That's a short-term solution," Emorra observed.

"Well . . ." Tieran paused, pursing his lips in thought. "The long-term solution is the antibodies built by the immune system." He frowned. "But, obviously, the immune system didn't recognize the infection quickly enough and was overwhelmed."

"So we need to keep the immune system from being overwhelmed," Emorra said.

"How?" Tieran asked miserably.

"The sea giveth, and the sea taketh away," Wind Blossom thought wryly. She bundled up her collection from the shore, checking each item carefully as she placed it in her carisak.

In the distance, out on the ocean, she could just make out the group of fins heading away from her. In her mind, she ticked off each of the missing items from her inventory. Some things "lost" in Crossing were now returned.

Her gait as she negotiated her way back to the Hold was steady, purposeful.

When M'hall came to collect her, he insisted upon helping her with her carisak. After she was firmly mounted on Brianth's neck, he handed the carisak to her before hoisting himself up.

"Your sak is heavier, I noticed," he commented as he found his seat. "The Eridani like doing things in threes, don't they?"

Wind Blossom chuckled. "Yes, they do."

"I believe that Admiral Benden would have praised their dedication to backup systems and redundancy."

"If he had known," Wind Blossom told him, "I'm sure he would have agreed."

At M'hall's command, Brianth leapt lightly into the air and, with strong beats, soared high up into the sky before going *between*.

Bursting once more into existence over the College, M'hall had Brianth commence a lazy spiral toward the landing site.

"So, I take it your vacation was fruitful?" he inquired pleasantly.

"I have found some answers to some of my questions," Wind Blossom agreed. "I must go back there sometime."

M'hall raised his eyebrows in surprise. "To get more buried treasure?"

"No," Wind Blossom responded, shaking her head. "To return it."

They were met by Emorra and Tieran.

"Hello, Mother," Emorra said to her. "Did you have a good vacation?"

"Yes, thank you," Wind Blossom replied, wincing inwardly at the formality of her own tone. Emorra's face took on a strained look. Trying to smooth things over, Wind Blossom added, "But I missed you."

"We've been busy while you were away," Tieran told her. Emorra glowered at him.

"I shall be delighted to hear about it," Wind Blossom replied.

"What are all these things?" Tieran exclaimed in awe when Wind Blossom met him and Emorra in one of the laboratories the next day.

Janir poked his head in curiously. His eyes widened in amazement and he crowded up behind Tieran to get a better view.

"Where did you get these?" he asked excitedly as he started visually cataloging the items. "Are the power packs full?"

He reached forward, longing to touch one of the precious instruments, only to have Wind Blossom bat his hand away. He withdrew with all the alacrity of her onetime student and exchanged rueful looks with Tieran.

"She's fast," Tieran muttered to Pern's head physician.

"She always was," Janir returned. He looked down at the elderly woman. "Wind Blossom, these are invaluable to us. Where did you get them?"

Wind Blossom shook her head. "I cannot say." She looked up, shaking a finger at him. "And don't you think to borrow them, Janir." As Janir raised his arms in protest, she added, "Remember what happened the last time."

Janir opened his mouth to object, but Wind Blossom just shook her finger at him again, and with a sigh, he dropped his head resignedly.

Wind Blossom pointed to one of the instruments. "This is a code viewer and sequencer."

"What's it tuned to?" Janir asked.

"Pernese genetic code," Wind Blossom told him. "It was one of the first units we adjusted."

"What's it do?" Tieran asked.

"It can read genetic material and sequence it," Wind Blossom explained. "It can also produce new genetic sequences or alter existing ones."

"But reading genetic material isn't good enough, is it?"

Emorra asked. "I mean, you have to know what you're reading, what it means."

"You need a map," Janir added in agreement.

Wind Blossom pointed to another, smaller device. "This is a mapper," she said. "When we built the dragons, we had a fully integrated unit, which in turn was integrated with AIVAS and the *Yokohama*."

Tieran looked confused.

"AIVAS—Artificial Intelligence Visual Audio System," Emorra translated. "A smart computer."

"Much more," Janir corrected. "And the *Yokohama* was the largest of the ships that brought our ancestors to Pern."

"I've seen them," Tieran said excitedly. "The astronomy students brought a telescope up to the Drum Tower just before dawn one morning." He shivered at the memory of the three huge starships hovering in orbit above the planet. "The students call them the Dawn Sisters."

Janir turned back to Wind Blossom. "What are you hoping to do with this equipment?" When she didn't answer, he persisted, "I thought you'd said that if the fire-lizards came from the future, then obviously your solution had failed?"

Wind Blossom nodded. "I am thinking," she told him. "There must be a solution that works."

"Wouldn't it just make more sense to leave the equipment for those that need it?" Tieran wondered.

"It would," Wind Blossom agreed, "if they could learn how to use the equipment in time."

Firestone, dry
Dragons fly.
Firestone, wet
Riders die.

Chapter Sixteen

Benden Weyr, Third Pass, 6th Day, Later, AL 508

KINDAN'S STOMACH LURCHED as Caranth began a sharp descent the moment they came out from *between* over Benden Weyr. Their drop was so steep that Kindan was pitched forward, hard, against Lorana when Caranth suddenly stretched his wings to cup air and slow them for a landing. Even so, the dragon hit the ground with a jolt.

Lorana was off and rushing toward her weyr before either B'nik or Kindan could move. Kindan followed quickly, with B'nik not far behind.

K'tan was waiting for them in Lorana's quarters. Arith's eyes were whirling, and when she saw her rider she gave a happy chirp—which ended in an unmistakable sneeze.

I'm all right, Arith told Lorana over and over as Lorana wrapped her arms around the young dragon's head. *I'm all right.*

No you're not, Lorana chided her gently. *But you will be, I promise. We'll find something. We found something at Fort Weyr.*

She looked up at K'tan. "We found something at Fort Weyr," she said. Kindan raised his eyebrows in surprise—in their haste to get back to the Weyr, they had not even spoken.

"What?" K'tan asked.

"The Records at Fort say that something was built here, at

Benden Weyr, just at the start of the First Interval," B'nik explained. He looked keenly at K'tan. "Some special rooms. Do you know of any such rooms?"

K'tan frowned and shook his head. "There've been some cave-ins; perhaps the rooms are buried," he told them.

"If they're buried, we'll dig them up again," B'nik declared fiercely.

K'tan looked at Lorana. "It could only be a cough . . ."

"Dragons don't get coughs," Lorana corrected him in a flat, dead voice.

"It's only started," B'nik said. "She's young—she could fight it off."

I don't feel too bad, Arith added comfortingly with a soft croon.

K'tan motioned for Lorana to come to him. She followed and he brought her out of her rooms and into the corridor.

"I know this is hard," he told her softly. "But you have to understand that your attitude and strength are the best hopes for Arith right now."

A hand crept up on her shoulder and she turned to see Kindan standing behind her. "He's right," the harper said.

Lorana took a deep breath. "I know," she told them. She squared her shoulders. Kindan tightened his grip reassuringly before dropping his hand back to his side. She turned and went back to Arith.

"I haven't been giving you enough attention," she told the young dragon.

You have been doing your work, Arith said staunchly. *And you always come when I need you.*

Lorana knelt down once more and wrapped her arms around her dragon's neck.

"I love you," she said out loud.

I know, Arith responded, firm in her knowledge and wondrously grateful. She nudged Lorana with her head. *Go! I'll be all right.*

Lorana pulled back from Arith and looked up into her whirling faceted eyes. "Are you sure?"

You can't find these rooms while you're here, can you?

"I'll check on you every hour," Lorana promised aloud.

Check on me when I ask, Arith responded.

"You are stubborn," Lorana chided her dragon.

"I can't imagine where she learned it," B'nik remarked teasingly. He stretched out his hand to her. "If you would, Weyrwoman, I believe you can help us in this search."

Lorana smiled, although her eyes still held a lingering fear, and took the Weyrleader's hand.

"We are as ready as we'll ever be," J'lantir told Dalia as the rest of Ista Weyr's Wingleaders filed out of the Council Room.

"You did an excellent job, J'lantir," Dalia agreed. "C'rion would have been proud."

Only three days had passed since the Weyrleader's death. Dalia had known, of course, the instant that C'rion and Nidanth had been lost. She was still in mourning, but she was Weyrwoman—she would not let down C'rion's men, nor destroy his legacy.

She had appointed J'lantir as interim Weyrleader. The response of the other Wingleaders had been unanimous support.

J'lantir had swallowed his personal misgivings and had drilled the remaining dragonriders as well as he could in the short time between the Threadfall at South Nerat and today.

"I wish the weather were better," Dalia told him.

"Or worse," J'lantir responded. "Then we'd have more time to train."

"Yes, a cold snap or torrential downpour would be best," Dalia agreed.

"We must fly the Thread we were given," J'lantir said resignedly.

The dragonrider who had been sent ahead to abandoned Igen Weyr reported that the weather was gusty, with scattered clouds at fifteen hundred meters.

A lousy height, J'lantir thought to himself as he made his way down to the Weyr's great Bowl. Dragons could fly up to just over three thousand meters in the daylight—as high as a man could fly and not pass out from lack of oxygen.

With clear skies, dragons could fight Thread all the way down to five hundred meters or less. But with the scattered clouds it would be imperative to flame the Thread before they entered the clouds or risk missing clumps as they fell through.

Some of those clumps of Thread would drown in the water of the clouds but, as the clouds were scattered, it was just as likely that some would survive the descent and burrow into the arid plains around Igen Weyr or—worse—into the lush green shoreline of the Igen coast.

J'lantir climbed onto Lolanth, grabbed and secured the firestone sacks handed up by one of the weyrfolk, and surveyed his wing. The other five wings were already airborne above him—all flying wing light.

One hundred and twenty-four dragons and their riders would face Thread today, less than half of the number that had first flown over Keroon on their first Fall. At least there were enough dragons to be certain that they would get most of the Thread that fell.

J'lantir nodded his thanks to the youngling who handed up his last bag of firestone, made sure that it was securely fastened beside him, and, with one final glance at his riders, gave the arm-pumping gesture to fly.

Dalia looked on from the Bowl below as the dragonriders of Ista Weyr arrayed themselves over the Star Stones and then winked out of sight *between* to fight Thread. She fought the impulse to bite her lips or cross her arms, knowing that the rest of the Weyr was watching her.

Some riders would not come back this time, just as C'rion had not come back the last time, Dalia knew. She and C'rion—her throat suddenly had a lump in it—had known that these days would come since they first Impressed their dragons.

They had pored over the Records together when C'rion's Nidanth had first flown Bidenth and he had become Weyr-leader. They knew that dragons and their riders would be injured fighting Thread. They knew that dragons and their riders would *die* fighting Thread. That was the way it had to be, that was the price paid for riding a dragon, that was the price that had to be paid to keep Pern from being utterly destroyed by Thread.

Dalia turned away, looking down from the Star Stones to those around her. Her eyes picked out Jassi coming toward her.

"I've got the fellis juice up from the store rooms," Jassi reported. "And we've got enough numbweed on hand."

"And the sick dragons?"

Jassi grimaced, looking down. "Two are getting worse," she answered. Then she raised her head and added cheerfully, "But the others seem all right."

Dalia nodded brusquely. "Very well," she said. "It will be hours before the Fall is over—let's see what we can do about dinner."

"That's handled," Jassi said. "But I wasn't sure about which weyrlings should be sent to bring more firestone during the Fall."

Dalia changed direction, heading to the weyrling barracks. V'rel, the Weyrlingmaster, had insisted on flying Threadfall, and neither she nor J'lantir could turn down an able dragon and rider, particularly as V'rel and Piyolth were several Turns their junior. "Let's go see, shall we?"

One hundred and twenty-three dragons joined the watch dragon over Igen Weyr.

"Lousy weather," J'lantir shouted to B'lon, his wing-second.

"If only it'd get worse," B'lon agreed. The clouds below them were as reported—scattered and thin. Above them the sky was obscured by wispy high cirrus clouds. B'lon pointed to them. "Is there any chance that the air's too cold above and the Thread will freeze?"

J'lantir followed his gaze. "It could be," he said. "But we shouldn't count on it."

A noise from behind them caught their attention.

M'kir has sighted Thread, Lolanth reported, at the same time turning his head back to J'lantir, jaws wide and ready for firestone. J'lantir opened a sack and began feeding the stones to Lolanth.

Tell the others, J'lantir responded. He gazed up at the skies, picking out the thin Thread among the wispy clouds above them. This is going to be a mess, he thought.

K'tan caught up with Kindan as evening began. They had seen each other earlier in the day while tending to the injured dragons and working with B'nik in plotting which parts of the Weyr to explore for the Oldtimer Rooms. Since then, Kindan had been off checking out the highest places in the Weyr. Now he looked anything but elated.

"Any luck?" K'tan asked him without any hope.

Kindan shook his head. "No," he said. "You?"

"I've spent more time tending the sick than looking," K'tan told him. He leaned closer to the harper. "I just wanted to remind you that Ista is about to fly Thread."

Kindan's confusion showed in his expression.

K'tan nodded toward Lorana's quarters. "You might want to be there for her," he said softly.

"Yes," Kindan agreed quickly. "You're right." He started to head off, his stride increasing. Back over his shoulder he called, "Thank you."

He was halfway across the Bowl when B'nik hailed him.

"Ista should be fighting Threadfall over Igen soon," the Weyrleader called warningly. Kindan smiled and waved acknowledgment, pointing toward Lorana's quarters. B'nik nodded.

Kindan found Lorana in Arith's room, curled up next to her dragon. The room was gloomy, the setting sun cut off by the lip of the Bowl. Arith stirred fitfully as Kindan entered the room, but Lorana's eyes were already wide open, staring blankly into space. She looked up at Kindan.

"She's resting," she reported. "Her breathing seems easier."

Kindan nodded.

"I just ate a while ago," Lorana added, as though that were the reason for Kindan's appearance. Her tone was acerbic as she continued, "Mikkala checked up on me in the last hour."

Kindan took in her words and tone with a quickly suppressed grimace. If anyone knew the deathwatch drill for a rider and a sick dragon, it would be Lorana. She had held the hands of the distraught riders, had uttered all the comforting words she could imagine, and had held the riders in her arms as they collapsed with grief and despair when their dragons went *between* forever.

"Thread falls over Igen Weyr soon," Kindan told her bluntly. "Ista will be fighting it."

Lorana took a deep breath and let it out slowly. She tilted her head up to look into Kindan's eyes. "Thank you," she told him.

"Should I turn on the glows?" he asked, jerking his head toward the nearest glow basket.

"More light would help," Lorana agreed. As Kindan busied himself with the task, she followed him around the room with her eyes, partly to distract herself and partly because he was such a pleasant distraction.

He turned back to her when he was done. "May I stay?"

Lorana met his gaze with a bittersweet look and patted the ground beside her. "I was hoping you would," she told him. "The ground's hard, but you don't notice it after a while."

Kindan sat beside her, unsure whether to lean against Arith as she was doing, or to offer himself as a support for Lorana, or to lean himself against her.

She sensed his unease and turned her back to him, stretching her neck from side to side to get out the kinks. She reached behind her and said to him, "Could you?"

Kindan stifled a laugh and began to gently massage her tense shoulder blades and upper back. He took his time and was thorough.

Partway through, Lorana gasped and Arith jerked awake, eyes opening quickly. The little queen keened softly beside her rider, and Kindan didn't need to see Lorana's face to know that she was crying with the pain of dragons forever lost.

In the end, Kindan couldn't say who was more distraught: Lorana, Arith, or himself. Through the course of the evening—the length of the Fall as it traveled from Igen Weyr southwest, over the Ista Strait and onto the southern tip of Ista Island—Lorana shuddered as though beaten down by a miner's hammer, and Arith keened, sometimes so often that it almost seemed as if the small dragon was chanting. The pain and anguish that both rider and dragon were suffering hurt Kindan even more because he did not feel it except through them and could not anticipate the next loss.

All through the long Fall he stayed by them, gently massaging Lorana's tense back, softly patting Arith's hide. Kiyary or Mikkala must have come to check on them several times, for Kindan remembered nodding thankfully to them at various points in the night and resisting the same wine he tried to force unsuccessfully on Lorana.

In the end, Kindan had started to count when either Lorana or Arith gasped or shuddered with the pain of dragons and riders far away. He stopped when he reached seventy. Ista Weyr had some one hundred and twenty dragons or more able to fight Thread; if seventy were injured or lost, it was just as Verilan had said: Ista would not be able to fight another Threadfall. Two Falls like that and Benden Weyr would not be able to fight Thread either.

And then Thread would fall—unchecked—and leech all the life from the land. And even if the Holders survived, locked in their Holds, how long would it be before they starved in a lifeless and barren land?

J'lantir surveyed the surviving Wingleaders as they gathered in the Council Room at Ista Weyr.

"You shouldn't be here," he said to M'kir, barring the brown rider as he tried to enter. M'kir's left arm was in a sling, his shoulder heavily bandaged where Thread had gouged it, the left side of his head bandaged to hide the gaping hole that had once held a fierce blue eye.

M'kir opened his mouth to protest but stopped as J'lantir swayed in the doorway.

"You need to get some rest," the brown rider told his Weyrleader, sliding past him.

J'lantir turned to face the others in the room. S'maj was the only Wingleader left besides himself. B'lon was favoring his left leg, wrapped in a bandage placed over his now-useless flying pants—a long thin line of blood showed where Thread had eaten through it and into his leg, but the score was not deep; B'lon's Lareth had been able to take them quickly *between,* where the Thread had frozen, shriveled, and cracked off.

A sound from behind him caused J'lantir to swivel his head. His eyes went unfocused for a bit as the movement caused the world to wobble.

You must rest too, Lolanth chided him. J'lantir knew his dragon was right, just as he knew he had to ignore the advice.

Dalia entered, smoothing her features as she surveyed the occupants of the room.

"How bad is it?" M'kir asked her urgently.

"It's bad," B'lon predicted.

"Perhaps we should let our Weyrwoman tell us," J'lantir said with a tone of reproval in his voice. He inclined his head toward her—a mistake, his stomach informed him. *I'll feed you later,* J'lantir growled back at his stomach.

Dalia raised an eyebrow at J'lantir, clearly recognizing that he was suffering, but stopped herself from commenting as she caught the pleading look on his face.

"Fourteen dragons went *between,*" she told the others. "Twenty were severely injured, and it will be more than three months before they will fly again."

A groan went around the table.

"Another thirty-one have lesser injuries but will need at least several weeks to recuperate." She took a breath before finishing. "And we've identified another eleven sick dragons."

"So how many dragons will be able to fly Thread over Ista Hold in three days' time?" J'lantir asked, dreading the answer.

"Forty-eight," Dalia answered, unable to keep the pain out of her voice.

Kindan woke the next morning to Arith's coughing. It took him a moment to realize that he was leaning against her back and that Lorana was sleeping in his lap. Arith turned her head to give Kindan an apologetic look.

"Think nothing of it," he responded with a courteous nod of his head. At that moment Arith sneezed, covering him with green mist.

Lorana twitched and sat upright, blinking the morning into focus.

"Shh, it's all right," Kindan said soothingly.

Lorana focused on his face. "She sneezed again, didn't she? You're all covered in green."

Arith gave an apologetic *bleek*.

"So are you," Kindan told Lorana. Then he frowned consideringly. "Well, maybe not quite as much."

Are you hungry? Lorana asked Arith.

Thirsty, Arith replied after a moment's reflection.

"Arith's thirsty," Lorana announced, standing up. Kindan followed her action.

"We'd best clean up before we go anywhere," he said, peeling off his stained tunic. "Or people will think that *we're* sick."

Lorana gave no reaction to his attempt at humor. With a polite nod to the humans, Arith stood up, stretched, took a few quick steps to the ledge of her lair, and blithely jumped off it, gliding surely toward the lake in the Weyr Bowl.

"You know," Kindan said, gesturing fondly after the departing gold, "I've never seen a dragon so young act so self-assured."

Lorana's lips twisted up in the ghost of a smile. "She *is* agile, isn't she?"

They met Arith again as she splashed about on the shoreline of the lake.

"Well," someone behind them drawled, "now that you two have deigned to join the rest of us, perhaps you'd care to look for these special rooms I've heard so much about."

They turned to see Tullea leaning indolently against Minith's foreleg. B'nik stood beside her.

"Arith was sick," Lorana explained, turning back to catch sight of the young queen as she splashed back to the shore.

"All the more reason to search, then," Tullea responded. "Unless you two are more inclined to *cavorting*?" She cast a disdainful look at Kindan's bare chest. "And get some clothes on."

With that, Tullea turned away from them and headed back to her weyr, B'nik following, stony-faced.

"I'll go on," Kindan said to Lorana. "I've got to get a clean shirt from my room anyway."

Passing by the Kitchen Cavern on the way to his room, Kindan was hailed by Kiyary.

"Tullea giving out to you, was she?" Kiyary asked, smiling evilly. "I can see why, too—your bare chest is enough to make a dragon swoon."

Kindan, who knew full well that most dragonriders were, of necessity, more muscled than he, took Kiyary's mocking in the well-intentioned manner it was delivered. "It's all that hard work with my guitar," he said, grinning.

"And those drums up on the heights don't hurt either," Kiyary responded, giving him a more thorough appraisal than when she'd been teasing him. "Come to think of it, maybe Tullea has a point."

Kindan snorted and headed off with a backward wave over his shoulder. In his room, he pulled out a fresh shirt and hastily donned it. He paused, as he was tucking it in his pants, to look over the map of the Weyr he'd drawn in chalk on a slate board. He'd marked the map with X's to show where they'd searched already. He pursed his lips sourly; he couldn't see an unmarked spot.

He spun around at a noise from the doorway behind him. It was B'nik. Kindan lifted up the map and showed it to the Weyrleader.

"I can't think of anywhere else to look," he said.

B'nik entered the room and peered closely at the map. "Perhaps the Records at Fort were wrong," he said after a long moment.

Kindan shook his head. "If they are, then we have no hope."

"I can't see what could be so special in those rooms," B'nik said. "Nor why they were built here at Benden."

"Fort would have made more sense," Kindan agreed abstractedly. Something in the Weyrleader's comment nagged at the edge of his consciousness.

"I came to tell you that K'tan says the new riding harnesses have arrived," B'nik said, obviously not at all clear why the information was important to the harper.

"They have?" Kindan answered excitedly, looking toward the door. He caught B'nik's questioning look and explained, "Salina had me order Lorana's riding brightware a while back, and now there's leather to attach it to."

B'nik smiled. "I can see how that'd cheer her up," he agreed. "What sort of design did you get?"

Kindan searched around in a drawer and pulled out a small sack. He opened it, searched for a moment, then pulled out one of the smaller pieces of brightware and handed it to B'nik.

"Silver, is it?" B'nik asked as he took the proffered piece and examined it. It was a small circular piece, meant to be attached over one of the standard steel buckles on the riding leathers. That way, as the leathers and metalwork wore out, it could be removed and placed on a replacement riding harness.

"I can make out the Benden Weyr symbol, but what sort of symbol is this?" B'nik asked, pointing at one of the images. "That's a healer mark! And—there's an animal beside it."

"Salina made me order them soon after Lorana Impressed," Kindan said. "So I used what I'd learned about Lorana. Apparently, that's about the same as the mark she used for her fire-lizard's harness."

"She had fire-lizards?" B'nik asked, looking up from the silver brightwork.

"Two," Kindan told him. "They were lost at sea in a storm."

B'nik digested this information with discomfort. "Her fire-lizards weren't sick, were they?"

"I believe they were," Kindan responded. "She doesn't talk about them much."

B'nik acknowledged Kindan's reply with a grunt, absently fingering the brightwork with his thumb. With a start, he pulled himself out of his musings and handed the silver circle back to Kindan.

"I'm sure she'll be pleased at the thought," he said. "Why don't you get the leathers for her and present the whole array?"

"Thank you," Kindan said. "I'll do that."

"When you're done, come find me and we'll talk some more," B'nik told him as he turned to leave.

"Very well, Weyrleader," Kindan said. "Where will you be?"

"Practicing," B'nik called back over his shoulder. "You might ask Lorana if Arith would talk to Caranth when you need me."

"Thank you, I will."

Does this mean we'll ride together soon? Arith asked excitedly as Kindan and K'tan helped Lorana put on the flying gear.

"She wants to know when I'll ride her," Lorana said out loud.

"It will be many months yet," K'tan said with a shake of his head. "Arith's bigger than all the other hatchlings of her clutch—she's the queen so you'd expect her to be—but she's still got a lot of growth before she's ready to carry even your light weight."

Arith made a plaintive sound and Lorana laughed. "Never you mind. First you need to get used to wearing the riding gear," she said out loud.

"Indeed she does," K'tan agreed emphatically. "In fact, if she gets used to it soon enough she might try flying with it some."

Could I? Arith asked wistfully. *Now? I could go eat.*

"She wants to eat with it on," Lorana told the others.

"The riding harness will need to be oiled first," K'tan said, shaking his head again. "It would be better, young queen, if you waited until you'd had the harness on for a day or two, so we know that we've got it adjusted right."

Arith blew a dejected sigh through her nose, which turned into an open-mouthed cough.

Sorry.

Kindan and K'tan exchanged concerned looks.

"Maybe this was a bad idea," Kindan said.

"No," Lorana responded emphatically. Beside her, Arith made a similar noise, though quieter, for fear of exacerbating her cough. "And I love the brightwork, Kindan. It's very well done."

"A friend of mine," Kindan told her.

"Well, please thank her for me."

"Him," Kindan corrected with a grin. "But I'll pass the thanks on."

"How's the search going?" she asked, feeling awkward and wanting to change the topic. Seeing the worried looks exchanged by the other two, she regretted the question instantly. "Not well?"

"No," Kindan said. "I can't think of anywhere else to look."

"That's because you're not weyrbred," K'tan said, clapping the harper on the back. "Why don't we talk about it while we check on the injured?"

"Arith, I'd like to go with them. Will you stay here?" Lorana asked her dragon out loud, so that the others could hear. "Should we take your harness off so you can lie down?"

No, the queen replied, shaking her head so firmly that

her body swayed in counterpoint. *And I won't get it dirty, I promise.*

Lorana laughed and hugged Arith's neck. *Let me know if it itches, or if you need me.*

Of course.

I won't be long, Lorana promised.

Take your time, Arith replied, *I'll call you if I need you.*

Lorana turned to Kindan and K'tan. "I'll come with you."

Lorana appeared distracted while the three of them checked on the injured dragons. Several times K'tan had to repeat a question or a request to her before she responded. Kindan noticed that she kept looking around the Weyr, particularly whenever a dragon sneezed or coughed.

Their work took them through the morning and still they'd only checked on half of the ninety-two injured dragons.

"I think we should group all the sick dragons," Kindan said as they walked to the next weyr.

"We've been over this," K'tan said. "How would you do it?"

"Just together, at least," Kindan said. "Probably on the lowest level."

"Why not a high field?" Lorana asked. "It would be colder up there—it might prevent the spread of the sickness."

"Or it might speed it up," K'tan countered. "If the cold makes it harder on the dragons' resistance."

"But aren't dragons pretty much inured to cold?" Kindan asked. "I mean, they go *between*."

"But only for short periods of time," Lorana admitted.

"But they do fly where the air is cold," K'tan mused. "They don't seem to mind the cold as much as we do."

"Exactly," Kindan said. "But if you have the sick dragons up high where it's cold—and I presume you mean a landing outside of the Weyr—then what about the riders? And how will we get food and supplies to them?"

Lorana threw up her hands in capitulation.

"Let's bring it up to B'nik," K'tan suggested. "It's his decision."

B'nik listened to them carefully when they approached him at lunchtime. Tullea was with him.

"If I understand you, then," the Weyrleader said, "the correct quarantine method depends on how the sickness is transmitted."

"Yes, that's right," K'tan agreed.

"But we don't know how it spreads," B'nik continued, "so you want to try all three precautions—is that right?"

"At least with the sick dragons," K'tan said.

"But you can't say if a dragon that seems healthy hasn't already got the sickness," Tullea remarked.

"No," Lorana agreed. "We can't."

"So we might end up with the whole Weyr up in high fields," Tullea interjected sourly. "What a *great* idea."

"It's the best we can come up with," Kindan said with a shrug.

Frowning, Tullea opened her mouth to retort, but B'nik raised an open hand, silencing her.

"What about those rooms?" he asked. "Wouldn't it be better to find them?"

"What is supposed to be in these rooms, anyway?" Tullea demanded.

"We don't know," Lorana told her. "But the Records specifically stated that they were built here at Benden."

"So you don't know where they are or why they were built—and yet you want to spend precious time searching for them?" Tullea gestured to the rest of the Weyr. "And let our dragons die while you search?

"Weyrleader, I think this is some old tale that will waste the time of our healer and harper," Tullea said formally to B'nik. "As Weyrwoman, I can see no point in it. Why not have Lorana conduct the search on her own?"

"But her dragon is sick," Kindan protested.

"All the more reason for her to be diligent, then." Tullea pressed a hand to her head, as though to ease pain. "And Harper, you've been too long from your duties. I could use a good song, and I'm sure the weyrlings need more instruction."

"Lorana has been helping me tend the injured dragons as well as the sick," K'tan protested.

"Well, perhaps *I* can assist you," Tullea replied sweetly. "It *is* one of my duties, after all."

"It's settled then," B'nik said, standing hastily. "Lorana will search for the missing rooms, and K'tan and Tullea will tend the sick and injured dragons, releasing Harper Kindan to his teaching duties."

"Well, Lorana, I'm sure you'll want to feed your dragon before you begin your search," Tullea said dismissively, grabbing Kindan's arm and pulling him away. "Tell me, Harper, what new songs will you sing for us tonight? I'm sure the Weyr needs cheering."

"I was wondering how long it would be before she started in."

Lorana turned to see Salina standing beside her.

"I'm sorry that I haven't come to see you," the ex-Weyrwoman apologized.

"You've been busy," Lorana excused her.

"No, I've been afraid," Salina corrected. She gave Lorana a frank look. "I'd heard about your Arith, and I . . ."

"It's all right," Lorana said, patting Salina on the shoulder. "I understand."

"Well *I* don't. You did everything you could when Breth was ill," Salina said. She gestured with a hand. "Walk with me, please?"

Lorana nodded and fell in beside Salina as they walked out into the Bowl. Salina turned to the entrance to the Hatching Grounds.

"I've always loved this place," she said. "Since I first Impressed—and before—I've been in love with Benden Weyr, its high walls, morning mists, brilliant sunsets, but most of all, I've loved the Hatching Grounds."

They were at the entrance, looking in.

"There's something marvelous about them," Salina breathed. "Right now it's so quiet in here, waiting, but soon Minith will clutch and this cavern will be filled with her hissing and challenging anyone who comes near her eggs. And then—there'll be the Hatching."

She gestured to the heights surrounding them. "Dragons—mostly bronzes—will stand up there, keening welcome to their newest offspring. And the Weyr, all of us, will be made alive again with each Impression, reliving all the joy"—her voice dropped—"and the pain of our bond with our own dragon."

She grabbed Lorana's hand and patted it gently. "And one day, your Arith will be here, guarding her hatchlings."

Lorana shook her head. Salina cocked her head questioningly.

"I don't know," Lorana said.

"I heard Tullea's set you a task," Salina said, changing the topic with another pat of Lorana's hand. "What is it?"

Lorana explained about the Records they'd found at Fort Weyr.

"Rooms?" Salina said musingly. "Special rooms, eh? And not mentioned in our own Records?

"Perhaps the Records were lost—" Salina dropped Lorana's hand and raised one of her own for silence, head bowed as she thought.

"Perhaps they aren't mentioned in our Records because they were considered obvious, like the Kitchen Cavern or the Bowl itself," she said, looking up again. "If everyone knew about them, then there was no reason for special mention, was there?"

Lorana gave her a dubious look.

"And now no one can find the rooms," Salina continued, musing out loud. "So if someone were to build rooms that everyone knew about and were obvious and they become lost—how would that happen?"

"I don't kn—"

"A cave-in!" Salina exclaimed.

Lorana's look of doubt changed to one of excitement. "But where?"

"I know where the rooms are," Salina told her, starting down into the Hatching Grounds. "Follow me."

"Wait a minute," Lorana called. "Shouldn't we get glows?"

"And probably some help, too," Salina agreed, her enthusiasm only slightly quenched by her common sense. "If I'm right, the rooms are buried behind a rock slide."

"We should get Kindan," M'tal said as soon as Salina outlined her theory to him that evening.

Salina shook her head. "Tullea wants Kindan to sing tonight. I think she wants to separate Kindan and Lorana."

M'tal snorted, shaking his head. "Is she trying to make B'nik jealous, or Lorana angry?"

"I can't imagine Lorana getting angry," Salina said. "Unless it was over something involving her dragon."

"Righteous anger, then," M'tal agreed. "And perhaps not just for her dragon. She seems to have good priorities."

"She does," Salina agreed emphatically. "It may help her survive—"

M'tal cocked an eyebrow at her.

"—if she loses her dragon," Salina finished softly.

"None who have gotten sick have recovered," M'tal said softly by way of agreement. "But this can't go on. Our ancestors were smart enough to make the dragons from fire-lizards; I can't believe that they weren't smart enough to anticipate a sickness like this."

"If they could predict it, and they could make dragons from fire-lizards, why didn't they make it so the dragons wouldn't get sick?" Salina asked.

M'tal shook his head. "I don't know. Perhaps we'll find the answer when we get into those rooms."

"So why wait for Kindan?"

"Kindan's miner bred," M'tal reminded her. "If there's a cave-in, he's the right one to handle it."

"And if he can't?"

"Then he's the right one to get help," M'tal replied, miming a miner holding a pick in two hands. Salina smiled and gestured toward the door of their new, lofty weyr.

"It's not such a bad idea of Tullea's to have Kindan sing

tonight," Salina said as they started down the many flights of stairs to the Bowl.

"Mmm?"

"Well, he's got quite a good voice, and we could use the cheering."

"Let's hope, then, that Kindan's in a cheering mood," M'tal returned. Neither of them mentioned on the long descent from their weyr that M'tal's Gaminth could have flown them to the Bowl in a moment: M'tal because he was sure that Salina was still quietly grieving her loss; and Salina because he was right.

As they crossed the Bowl to the Kitchen Cavern, they could hear Kindan's voice lead off in the opening chorus of "The Morning Dragon Song," subtly altered:

"Through early morning light I see,
A distant dragon come to me.
Her skin is gold, her eyes are green;
She's the loveliest queen I've ever seen."

"He *must* have changed that for Lorana," Salina remarked. "That song normally refers to a bronze dragon."

"But I wouldn't be at all surprised if Tullea thinks it's for her," M'tal said.

Several big fires had been built in braziers outside of the Kitchen Cavern, and the long tables had been pulled out into the cold night air. Torches lined a way through the tables.

The harper and his helpers were set up on one table placed against the wall of the Weyr Bowl itself. The sounds of Kindan's guitar and voice echoed eerily off the walls of the Bowl. All around them, M'tal could see gleaming pairs of dragon eyes peering down from the heights above.

By the time M'tal and Salina found seats, Kindan had finished his revised version of "The Morning Dragon Song."

"This is a different song, now," Kindan said, his voice carrying over the murmurs and chatting of the dragonriders and weyrfolk.

"Not all of it's remembered, but perhaps its time has

come." He modulated his guitar chords into a dissonant, melancholy sound.

> *"A thousand voices keen at night,*
> *A thousand voices wail,*
> *A thousand voices cry in fright,*
> *A thousand voices fail."*

The murmuring of the crowd grew silent as Kindan continued:

> *"You followed them, young healer lass,*
> *Till they could not be seen;*
> *A thousand dragons made their loss*
> *A bridge 'tween you and me."*

M'tal and Salina exchanged worried glances and watched as B'nik and Tullea huddled together in an exchange that could almost be heard over Kindan's voice as the harper continued:

> *"And in the cold and darkest night,*
> *A single voice is heard,*
> *A single voice both clear and bright,*
> *It says a single word."*

Salina bent to whisper something in M'tal's ear, but he gripped her arm tightly and gestured at Kindan. The harper's look was intent, as one who was desperately trying to remember something. His face brightened and he continued:

> *"That word is what you now must say*
> *To—"*

Lorana suddenly leapt up from her seat and raced away across the Bowl. M'tal had a fleeting glimpse of her distraught look as she passed him, but before he could react to that, Tullea shouted out: "Enough! That's quite enough! Harper Kindan, I do not want to hear that song ever again."

"But I do, Weyrwoman," Kindan replied firmly. There was a gasp from the crowd. Everyone knew that Kindan could be outspoken, but speaking against the Weyrwoman was an affront to the honor of every dragonrider.

"Tullea is right, Harper," B'nik said loudly, rising beside his Weyrwoman. "That is not a song for this Weyr."

Kindan looked ready to argue the point. M'tal cleared his throat loudly, catching Kindan's eyes and shook his head slowly. For a moment the young harper looked ready to pursue his rebellion. Slowly the color drained from his face and he calmed down.

"Weyrleader, Weyrwoman," he said with a half-bow from his chair, "my apologies. The song has me perplexed," he explained. "But I will respect your *orders*"—he laid a slight emphasis on that word—"and return to more traditional lays."

"Very well then," Tullea replied. She waved a hand at him imperiously. "Continue, Harper."

Kindan gave her another half-bow, signalled to his accompanists, and stood to sing in a strong, martial voice:

"Drummer, beat, and piper, blow,
Harper, strike, and soldier, go.
Free the flame and sear the grasses
Till the dawning Red Star passes."

"Go see to Lorana," M'tal said to Salina as soon as he was sure that the situation was back under control.

Salina found Lorana in Arith's weyr, her arms wrapped around her dragon's head.

"He means me, doesn't he?" Lorana asked as Salina entered. She didn't look up at the ex-Weyrwoman. Her voice was choked with tears.

"I don't know," Salina answered honestly. "But I hope he does."

"You hope?" Lorana asked incredulously, turning to face the Weyrwoman. "How can you?"

"Because that song—if it has anything to do with what's happening to us—"

"How can it? When was it written?" Lorana demanded. "It's probably just some old harper song written by someone who'd drunk too much."

"It could be," Salina admitted honestly. "And, now that you mention it, that makes the most sense."

"So why did he sing it?" Lorana cried angrily.

"You think it was about you?" Salina asked.

"Don't you?"

"I don't know," Salina told her. "You're not a healer, we know that."

Lorana shook her head angrily, fingering one of the silver pieces of brightwork on Arith's harness.

"Do you see this?" she asked, pulling the piece off and waving it at Salina. "Do you see how it's marked? A healer's mark."

Salina gasped, startled.

"Exactly!" Lorana cried, turning back to replace the brightwork on Arith's riding harness. "And everyone will know that, too. So what will they think, Salina?"

"What do you imagine?"

Lorana took a steadying breath and wiped the tears off her cheeks. "I think that the riders will believe that I brought this sickness here with me," she said slowly.

Salina felt as if she'd been struck in the stomach. She slumped down to her knees as the full impact of Lorana's words struck home.

If Lorana *had* brought the sickness, then it was her fault that Breth had died. For a moment Salina felt anger rise up in her and she knew that her face showed it, even without seeing Lorana's stricken reaction. It would be so much easier, such a relief, if she could blame *someone* for her loss. But then her brain overcame her emotions, and Salina realized that Lorana stood to lose her own dragon, too, long before her time.

"My fire-lizards," Lorana continued, unable to control herself, "I think they got sick. And—" She stopped, eyes going wide with astonished fear. "J'trel and Talith—they went *between* forever." She gulped down her tears. "I was so sure that it was me. I was going to leave, but then I Impressed Arith. I couldn't leave her—I didn't know what to do."

"You're right," Salina said, "you couldn't leave her. And as you're Weyrwoman, once you'd Impressed, I would never consider asking you to leave the Weyr. We will solve this problem together."

"Of all the stupid, ill-considered, blockheaded, unthinking—"

"Don't stop," K'tan told Kindan as the harper poured out a litany of self-contempt. "You forgot fardling."

"—fardling, moronic, imbecilic—" Kindan paused, groping for more words.

K'tan shook his head sadly. "A harper at a loss for words when they're so desperately needed."

"Why did you do it?" M'tal asked, joining the other two.

Kindan let out a deep sigh, shaking his head ruefully. "It just came to me," he said. "Stupid, stupid, stupid!" He punctuated each word by banging his head with his hand.

"How's Lorana?" K'tan asked M'tal. "I noticed you sent Salina after her."

"I have no way of knowing," M'tal answered with a grimace.

"You could ask Arith," Kindan suggested hopefully.

"I don't think so," M'tal answered frostily. Kindan grimaced and dropped his head.

"I suppose I could talk to Lorana," he said.

"No." M'tal's voice was firm.

"You've caused enough trouble," K'tan agreed.

"I don't know how I'll make up for it," Kindan said, giving M'tal a look that begged for advice.

"I don't know if you'll be able to," M'tal told him grimly.

"But there is one thing that would be a good start." At Kindan's hopeful look, he continued, "Salina says that she thinks the Oldtimer Rooms are hidden behind a rock fall near the Hatching Grounds."

"You mean? . . ." K'tan started, his eyes taking on a far-away look.

M'tal nodded. "That rock slide back by the way we used to come to look at the eggs back when we were candidates."

"It seemed dangerous, even when I was young," K'tan said. "I never went too close."

Kindan braced to the challenge. "Well, let's grab some glows and have a look, shall we?"

"Tonight?" K'tan asked, taken aback.

"What better time?" Kindan replied. "While Tullea's occupied."

"Should we wait for Salina?" K'tan asked.

M'tal shook his head. "No, I think we might be in for a very long wait."

Kindan groaned.

In the end, M'tal and K'tan talked him out of acting immediately, reasoning that the job was properly one for miners, and that Kindan would best be employed in engaging some. So with B'nik's blessing, M'tal, K'tan, and Kindan left at first light the next morning.

It took only moments after their arrival at Mine Natalon for Dalor to agree to come to Benden with miners. K'tan and Kindan returned to Benden to make preparations while M'tal arranged transport. Kindan had just finished alerting Mikkala that there would be extra mouths to feed when he heard a shout.

"Kindan! Is it you?" the red-haired woman cried joyfully as she crossed the Bowl along with the other arrivals. "It's been ages!"

Kindan gave the woman a startled look and then recognition dawned: It was Renna. Memories of his youth at Camp Natalon came back to him. This woman was the youngster Kindan had set to keeping the watch when he'd been put in charge of his watch-wher, Kisk, over ten Turns ago. Renna had grown taller and broader, but she still bore the easygoing intelligence he had seen so long ago.

Renna ran up to him and Kindan closed the remaining distance to be met by a tight hug and a peck on the cheek, both of which he returned fully.

"You're looking great," Renna said, pushing him away to look him up and down. "Life at the Weyr agrees with you?"

Kindan nodded, then broke into a grin. "I remember ages back when Nuella said, 'I know who he's sweet on.' "

Renna blushed and laughed as Dalor, Head Miner at Mine Natalon, clumped up beside them. He shook Kindan's hand, then clapped him firmly on the back.

"Thank you for coming," Kindan told Dalor.

"For a chance to see a Weyr close up, it's I who should be thanking you," Dalor responded with a snort. He took in the sight of the great Bowl with a whistle. "Not to mention a chance to do some clean mining." Hastily, he added, "Not that coal hasn't been good to us, nor that we don't need it. But it—"

"—gets everywhere!" Renna joined him in chorus. She turned to him and kissed his cheek.

"But you clean up nice, love," she said. Dalor blushed and looked down at the ground, smiling.

Three other miners drew up beside him, waiting for orders.

"I'll show you the spot," Kindan said, leading the way toward the Hatching Grounds.

As he had planned, Kindan gave them a quick tour of the Grounds and a chance to recover from the impressive view before leading them down the corridor toward the cave-in. They were followed by a group of weyrfolk, mostly young boys, who were just as interested in the miners as the miners were in them. Kindan sent some of the youngsters back to the Bowl to haul down the miners' gear.

"You're right when you say this is Oldtimer work," Dalor commented, running his hands appreciatively along the smooth walls. He took a closer look at the rock. "It looks like they melted their way through."

"That's what I thought," Kindan agreed.

"Ah, but they weren't so smart, were they?" Dalor went on, pausing to glance carefully at a part of the smooth wall.

Kindan looked at him questioningly.

"Look here," Dalor said, pointing. "You can see where the rock faces are formed. They must have hoped that the two layers would never slip over each other, or they must not have realized what they were dealing with."

"Slip?" M'tal, who had been following along, asked.

"Aye, my lord," Dalor said with a nod. "There are two different layers here, see?" He pointed to the spot where the different colors were close to each other. "You can tell by the color. The layers can slip over each other, which happens when there's an earth shake."

M'tal examined the spot with renewed interest.

"Can you get through to the other side?" Kindan asked.

"Well, we don't know how far it is, do we?" Dalor replied.

"It can't be too far," M'tal said. "This section can only go so far before it comes out the far side of the Bowl."

"There's that," Dalor agreed, nodding. "That'd be about five or six meters, right?"

M'tal frowned in thought. "About," he said. "Maybe a bit more, maybe a bit less."

"Might not take so long, Dalor," another miner said. "If the rock gave at the layers, there'd only be a meter or two falling from the roof."

"I hadn't thought of that, Regellan," Dalor said. In an aside to Kindan, he added, "It turns out our Regellan here is quite the thinker. I brought him along in part to see what he would learn from looking over the Weyr."

"He's welcome to look all he wants," Kindan told him. He remembered Regellan as one of the new apprentices assigned to Mine Natalon just before he'd left for the Harper Hall.

Dalor smiled. "I was hoping you'd say that," he replied.

Then he gestured at the cave-in. "We'll get this sorted out first."

Having said that, Dalor immediately began organizing the men for digging. He politely waved away M'tal and Kindan— "You've no miner's hats; we'll call you when we're done"— and swiftly got his crew started on the work.

Kindan led Renna and M'tal back to his quarters. While Renna looked around appreciatively at Kindan's musical instruments, Kindan explained to M'tal, "A good crew can mine about a meter of rock a shift."

"I'd say they'll be faster with that loose rock," Renna put in.

Kindan made a face and waggled his hand. "It might be harder, and they'll have to do some shoring."

Renna nodded. "That's so, but I don't think Dalor plans to be here too long."

"It was good of him to come," M'tal said.

"We're happy to help the dragonriders," Renna said in a tone that made it clear to the other two that the decision to help out was as much hers as Dalor's. Kindan and M'tal shared a fond smile for Renna's spirit, no different from their memories of her as a youngster, back when Kindan had first met the Weyrleader over ten Turns earlier at Camp Natalon. Ignoring it, Renna asked Kindan, "You say you hope to find some Oldtimer Rooms beyond the rubble? And somehow what's in them will cure the dragons of their sickness?"

"That's our hope," M'tal answered. Kindan nodded fervently.

It took the miners until lunchtime the next day to break through the cave-in.

"It's remarkably clean," Dalor said admiringly as he ran his hand along the smooth walls. "Only the ceiling above gave way."

"Your men did a great job," M'tal commented approvingly.

"Thank you, Weyrleader," Dalor replied, then blushed when M'tal cleared his throat and jerked his head toward B'nik.

"I'm sure that Wingleader M'tal is appreciative," Tullea said bitingly, "as am I, the *Weyrwoman*."

B'nik chose to smooth things over. "Indeed, a remarkable job, Miner Dalor," he said.

Tullea marched past the others and up through the newly cleared corridor, a glow held in her hand. Suddenly, she stopped, scanning one side of the corridor intently.

"This looks like a door," she exclaimed. She hunkered down, peering to either side of it. "What's this?" she asked, seeing a square plate to the left of the door. She pressed it just as Dalor, who had been watching her actions with growing alarm, shouted, "Don't touch it!"

Too late.

With a rumbling groan, the wall began to slide open and light flooded in from the other side.

Dalor raced to Tullea and pulled her back away from the door. Even as he did, she slumped toward the floor so that B'nik had to catch her other side to prevent her from falling.

"What is it?" B'nik asked as they hastily withdrew toward the Hatching Ground.

"Bad air," Kindan said, looking intently at Tullea. "She's breathing, and not in any distress."

Gently the miner and Weyrleader laid Tullea on the ground, and Kindan examined her more carefully.

"Yes, I'd say that the air was stale," he declared finally. He looked up to B'nik. "She'll be all right. Just let her breathe and wake up slowly."

Kindan frowned thoughtfully and asked Dalor, "How long do you think before the air will be replaced?"

"I'd give it an hour, at least," Dalor said. "And then I'd move cautiously." He glanced around the Hatching Grounds as though searching for something. "I don't suppose you have any watch-whers?"

Kindan shook his head. "Nor fire-lizards."

"I'd heard they'd been banished," Dalor said, his tone carefully neutral.

Kindan shook his head sadly. "I think most of them died

before that anyway." He composed himself and straightened up. "Let's get Tullea to softer ground," he suggested.

The moment her eyes fluttered open again, Tullea protested loudly and demanded to go see the Oldtimer Rooms. To Kindan, she sounded as if she wanted revenge on the rooms for causing her embarrassment. But B'nik was firm and insisted that someone else go in first once the rooms finished airing.

"I'll go," Kindan volunteered when they reassembled in the Hatching Grounds.

"I will go," Regellan declared, shaking his head. "I've no family," he added by way of explanation.

"I'm not so sure that Melena would agree," Dalor said with a grin. "But you've earned the right."

He glanced at B'nik and Tullea. "If that's all right with you, Weyrleader?"

"Absolutely," B'nik replied.

In the end, Regellan was fine. He peered inside the open corridor, blinked several times, purposefully drew great, deep breaths, and then walked through the doorway and out of sight. The rest of the party waited tensely outside until he returned again, his eyes wide.

"The room is full of the most amazing things," he declared, beckoning them inside.

Tullea elbowed her way past the others and raced to be second into the rooms. She paused just past the threshold, not so much for fear of bad air but in amazement at what she saw. Most of the far wall was covered from floor to ceiling with a drawing of several ladderlike columns composed of weird interconnected varicolored rods and balls.

"Look at this!" Regellan called out, pointing to the drawing, as the others flooded into the room.

Tullea glanced at the wall drawing, made a hasty scan of the room, and then headed unerringly for something glittering on an open shelf at the other end of the room.

Kindan entered the room and stared wide-eyed at the drawing. Then a flash of movement in his peripheral vision caught his attention and he turned just in time to see Tullea pocket a small, silvery object. Before he could move to intervene, she was picking something else up from the counter.

"What are these?" she asked, holding up a crystal clear glass vial. She shook it, examining the powder-like substance inside, then casually placed it back on the counter and picked up another.

There were four vials in all, Kindan noticed. The countertop bore not only dust-free spots where the vials had been placed. Each clear spot was centered over a colored mark: red, green, blue, and yellow.

His eyes widened as Tullea negligently put the fourth vial back on the countertop, well away from any of the colored marks.

"Do you remember which vial went where?" he asked her shortly, trying to see if he could guess the original position of the last vial she had picked up.

"No," Tullea replied with a shrug.

"I think it's important," Kindan told her. B'nik came up beside him and frowned at the misplaced vials.

"I'm sure you'll figure it all out," Tullea replied with a dismissive wave of her hand, turning to explore a set of cabinets. After some fiddling, she discovered that they were magnetically locked and spent several moments opening and closing them before she noticed what was inside.

"I wonder what *this* is," she said, reaching in to pull the object out.

B'nik caught K'tan's and Kindan's horrified looks and quickly intervened. "I think we should leave this for our harper and healer to examine," he said. "They can report when they've had a chance to inventory everything."

"And I think I should get Miner Dalor and his good crew back to their homes before dark," M'tal added. Dalor and the other miners looked both eager to be going and disappointed not to be staying to learn more about the mysterious room.

"We've kept you from your work too long," B'nik agreed.

Dalor waved this aside. "We're glad to help," he said. "Didn't you say there was another rock slide up above?"

"There is," Kindan agreed. "But I think we'll find enough here to keep us occupied for a while."

"We'll be glad to help again," Renna said. Dalor nodded firmly in agreement.

"When we're ready, we'll be happy to have you back," B'nik said. "You've been a great help."

M'tal's Gaminth and K'tan's Drith were waiting in the Bowl as they emerged from the Hatching Grounds. Kindan helped the miners climb up on the dragons' backs.

"I'll get started while you're gone," he told K'tan when all the miners were settled a-dragonback.

"I'll expect you to be done by the time I get back," K'tan called down. Kindan grinned and tossed the dragonrider a sloppy salute.

With a leap and a few great sweeps of their wings, the two dragons were airborne and then gone *between.*

"There's got to be something more," Kindan said to K'tan hours later.

"Why do you say that?"

"Because, aside from those four glass vials and whatever's in them," Kindan replied, "there isn't anything there."

"There are these," K'tan said, pulling open a drawer and pointing at some long, thin clear objects with strange handles on the top. "They *have* to be syringes for injections."

"Injections?"

K'tan nodded. "Sometimes the herders use syringes when there's a particularly nasty spread of infection going around. They take the blood from one of the recovered herdbeasts and inject it into the others, spreading the immunity."

Kindan gave the healer a dubious look.

"Lorana would know about it," K'tan added. He looked at the vial. "I suspect that this is supposed to be liquefied and injected."

"Liquefied?"

"Probably with sterile water," K'tan said.

"For what purpose?" Kindan asked.

"I don't know. I'd be a whole lot happier if there was a

sign that said this was the cure we were looking for," K'tan agreed.

"Do you see any sign?" Kindan asked, pivoting to look all around the room.

"The marks on the walls," K'tan pointed out, gesturing.

"Which don't serve any purpose that I can make out," Kindan said, making a sour face.

"What about that song of yours—doesn't it offer any suggestions?"

Kindan shook his head, his jaw clenched. "I can't remember any more of it." He slammed his fist onto the countertop in anger. Then he tapped his head. "It's in here, I know it is, but I can't remember it—even just after the fire in the Archives, I couldn't remember—and *I'm* the last one who read that dratted song."

"Certainly the last one left alive," K'tan agreed grimly. He had heard the story from both Kindan and M'tal, although their accounts differed: a playfight in the Harper Hall's Archives had caused a fire that had burned countless old Records to ashes. He remembered hearing how Kindan had been banished to Fort Hold until his fate was decided, how the Plague had interrupted everything, how Kindan's efforts had saved the survivors of Fort Hold, and how the grateful Lord Holder had seen to Kindan's reinstatement in the Harper Hall.

K'tan's expression grew grim. "If we don't find a cure soon . . ."

Dejectedly, Kindan turned toward the exit. "I have to report to B'nik."

It was Arith's coughing that drove Lorana down to the newly opened Oldtimer Room. She waited until her dragon was sleeping as well as could be expected, waited until she felt hopeful that Arith might not have another coughing episode—which meant that she didn't leave until late in the night.

Softly she made her way across the Bowl and into the Hatching Ground. She searched in the dim light until she found the new opening, visible by the faint light coming from it. Her steps grew surer as she got closer and the light from the room grew brighter. She paused for a moment at the doorway, stifling a gasp of wonder at the drawing on the other side of the room, and then entered.

Salina and Kiyary had both given her good descriptions of the room, but she needed to see with her own eyes. Kindan was sitting behind the tabletop that held the four vials. When she entered the room, he started, wiping the fatigue from his eyes.

"I must have dozed off," he muttered when he saw her. He straightened up and asked, "How is Arith?"

"Her cough is getting worse," Lorana said, striving to keep her composure. She gestured at the vials. "Is that all there is?"

Kindan nodded resignedly. "These cabinets are empty. There's another doorway," he said, pointing to the wall with the drawings, "but it won't open."

"Is it blocked? The rock slide?"

"No," Kindan replied, "I don't think so. We got an echo when we knocked on it." He shook his head. "Either the mechanism's broken or . . ."

Lorana waved away his explanation and strode over to the drawings. "So we've got these, and those vials?"

"That's it," Kindan said.

Lorana bent to peer closely at the drawings. "These are very detailed." She traced the spiraling patterns of one, bending down and peering closer. "This *must* mean something—someone went to an awful lot of trouble to make these."

"Mmm." Kindan's response sounded more like the noise of someone falling asleep than the noise of someone listening attentively. Lorana turned around just in time to catch him nodding off; he woke up again just as his head bobbed down to his chest.

"You should get some sleep," she told him. "You're no good here."

"What about you?"

"I'll be up most of the night anyway," Lorana said morosely. "Arith's not sleeping well."

"I'm sorry," Kindan said miserably.

Lorana shook her head. "You can't help if you're asleep on your feet." She pointed to the door. "Go."

Kindan entertained a rebellious look for a moment before sighing resignedly and shuffling toward the door. "I'll be back first thing in the morning."

Lorana had already turned back to the drawing and was examining it intently, so her only response was a negligent wave of her hand over her shoulder.

When she had finished examining the first drawing, Lorana repeated her inspection on the next. She stopped as she noticed some patterns in the new drawing and went back to look at the first. She sighed. There were not only similar patterns between the two drawings but also similar patterns within each drawing. It reminded her of some strange beadwork. For a while she entertained the notion of getting some colored beads and stringing them in the spiraling triangles that were represented by the drawings. The beadwork would be pretty enough, she mused, but she couldn't see how it could help the dragons.

She shook her head to clear the thought and turned to the third drawing. Again she found similar patterns and repeated patterns in the drawing. She turned her efforts to the fourth drawing—and stopped dead in her tracks. Four drawings, four vials.

Lorana straightened and turned to the tabletop where the four vials were placed. Did the four patterns match the four vials somehow?

Were the patterns supposed to tell someone which vial to use? Could it be that the knowledge represented by those drawings had been so common when they were first drawn that no one had ever considered that the method of reading them might be forgotten and that was why there were only the vials and the drawings? Read the drawings and pick the vial?

But Lorana couldn't read the drawings. And Arith was dying. She knew it, she tried to deny it, and she would never think it while Arith was awake and might hear her thought, but it was so. No dragon who had gotten the sickness had survived.

Four vials. Four drawings. Four illnesses? Was one of the vials the one that could cure the dragons?

Lorana felt Arith stir, could sense which cough was hers among the several that punctuated the deep night.

I'll be right there, Lorana told her dragon, racing from the room. Time is running out, she thought fleetingly as she left the room that held Arith's only hope.

She stopped in the doorway and turned back to the four vials. *Arith?*

I'm all right, the young queen lied valiantly.

Lorana's response was not spoken or thought, but just as clearly as if she had spoken aloud, Arith knew that Lorana had seen through the lie and had known the reasons for it.

Will it hurt to die? Arith asked Lorana, her tone both fearful and curious.

Lorana bit her lip, her face a mask of pain and tears as all the love and hope she had for her dragon tore through her.

You'll be all right! she swore fiercely, with all the strength of her being, willing the stars to change courses, the seasons to halt, and all the pain that was both today's and tomorrow's to stop.

No, I won't. Arith responded firmly, sadly. *I'm dying. Will it hurt?*

Lorana found that her hands were clenched tightly into claws, that through her tears her face was contorted in anger. I will not let this happen, she swore. But as the thought formed in her mind, she realized its futility.

Arith was right—she was dying. Just like all the other dragons on Pern. And in the Oldtimer Room were four drawings and four vials. Lorana turned back to the room.

Maybe you don't have to die, Lorana told her dragon fervently.

As she explained the Oldtimer Room to Arith, Lorana reentered and went to the cabinet against the wall. She opened each drawer in turn, pausing to examine the contents carefully. She found what she was looking for in the third drawer. The syringes were in a sealed rectangular container. Lorana was surprised at the hiss of air rushing into the container when she opened it. There were five syringes.

Lorana marveled at them. They were much smaller and more delicate than the syringes her father had used to inject serum into young calves. She remembered the first time she had helped him, how nervous she had been at the thought of squirting liquids into a young calf.

The contents of the vials were powder. Clearly they needed to be liquefied.

Arith, there may be a cure, Lorana told her dragon. *There are four vials here; I think one of them has the cure.*

Which one? Arith asked.

Which one, indeed? Lorana asked herself. She could try all four one at a time, but how long would she have to wait between each dose to know if it worked? Would Arith have enough time to wait between each dose? How could she decide?

Lorana swallowed and shook her head fiercely. This was not a decision she could make alone—there was more than her life involved.

Maybe we should wait, Lorana thought.

No, Arith responded, and Lorana could feel her dragon's sense of foreboding, her sense of despair. *I think we should do it now.*

Which one? Lorana asked her.

All of them, Arith responded. *If the others are wrong, they won't hurt, will they?*

I don't know, Lorana told her truthfully.

Let's try just a little of each, then, Arith replied. The young gold gave a mental chuckle. *You know, you can hear all the dragons. I think I can hear more of your thinking than other dragons can. There's no time to try them one at a time, is there?*

No, Lorana replied, pulling out one of the syringes. *There isn't any time.*

I'll meet you at the entrance to the Hatching Grounds, Arith told her.

Lorana searched through the cabinet, found an empty, sealed beaker, and opened it. Nervously, she turned to the four larger beakers. How much of each? Less than for a full-grown dragon because Arith was not full grown, Lorana guessed, but how much?

There were five needles, she reasoned, so perhaps each held enough for a full dose. She would need half that much for Arith.

B'nik was shoved roughly awake. He tried to squirm away from his tormentor, but the shaking continued.

"Get up!" Tullea shouted in his ear.

"Mmph, what is it?" B'nik asked blearily. He turned on his side, facing Tullea, his eyes blinking furiously as he tried to see in the dim light.

"I need to talk to you," she told him.

"Can't it wait until daylight?" he asked.

"Of course not," Tullea snapped. "It's about Lorana."

"What about her?"

"I don't want her going to the Oldtimer Room," Tullea said. "She's to be kept away."

"Why?"

"For her own good," Tullea snapped back. Her eyes darted to her dressing table. B'nik's sleep-muddled mind recalled that she had been playing with something silver and small before she'd gone to bed. He didn't recall her having a silver brooch or jewelry box.

"What harm could she get into?" he replied, sitting upright.

"I don't know," Tullea said, not meeting his eyes. "I just don't want her there. It's not her job anyway."

"She knows something about healing," B'nik protested. "She's been helping K'tan—"

"Let her help with the injured dragons," Tullea said. "But she's not to—"

"Shh!" B'nik said, raising a hand. "Someone's coming."

Tullea bespoke her dragon. "It's Lolanth, from Ista Weyr,

and his rider, J'lantir," she said, frowning. "It's awfully late to wake anyone."

Behind her, B'nik cocked an ironic eyebrow, but wisely refrained from saying anything. He sprang from the bed, pulling a robe over himself and thrusting Tullea's toward her.

"He wouldn't be here if it wasn't important," he said. He turned to the food shaft and called down for *klah* and snacks for three, then strode quickly to the doorway to greet J'lantir.

"Weyrleader B'nik," J'lantir said in relief when he saw him, "I'm sorry to wake you."

B'nik waved the apology aside. "Quite all right," he said, "I was not asleep." He gestured toward the Council Room. "If you'll step this way, I'm having some *klah* and snacks sent up. Weyrwoman Tullea will join us shortly."

J'lantir blinked in surprise. "My apologies to your Weyrwoman," he said. "This is a very late hour for me to come here but—"

B'nik gestured him to a seat. "You wouldn't be here at this hour if it wasn't important," he repeated, trying to calm the older rider.

J'lantir drew a ragged breath. "I don't know how badly the illness has hit your dragons—"

"Badly, I'm afraid," B'nik said.

"I'm sorry to hear that," J'lantir replied feelingly. "Perhaps this is a fool's errand, after all."

"At this hour?" Tullea drawled from the doorway. She carried in the tray of *klah* and snacks that B'nik had ordered earlier.

B'nik flushed at her tone of voice, but his reaction was mild compared to J'lantir's painful wince.

The Istan Weyrleader licked his lips. "We have lost seven more dragons in the past day to the illness," he announced.

Tullea and B'nik exchanged horrified looks.

"Thread falls at Ista Hold in less than two days' time, and we have only forty-six dragons fit to fly it," J'lantir continued.

"Then you shall have Benden flying at your side," B'nik announced. Tullea gave him a scathing look, but B'nik ig-

nored her. "We have six full wings of dragons, and our next
Threadfall is not for another twelve days."

"Three wings—one flight—would be more than enough,"
J'lantir said, his face brightening with relief. "It's a night fall,
as you know, and won't last too long."

"Very well," B'nik said. "I'll ask M'tal to be the flight
leader—you've worked with him before. He'll report to you
in the morning."

J'lantir's smile widened into a broad grin. "That would be
excellent!" He rose and grabbed B'nik's hand in his. "Thank
you! Ista will ride with you anytime."

"I'll look forward to it," B'nik replied. "Would you like
some *klah* before you depart?"

"No, no," J'lantir said, shaking his head. "I've been beside
myself trying to figure out how—and I didn't want to—"

"I understand," B'nik interrupted, nodding fervently. He
knew how hard and humiliating this decision must have been
for the older dragonrider. "We are all living in hard times—"

A shriek from the Bowl outside cut through the evening air.

Lorana's hands were trembling as she mixed the serum.
Each time she scooped in powder from the next vial, the
mixture would change color and then slowly return to a clear
liquid. If the proportions were too small, she would have
wasted the precious powders. Perhaps the Oldtimers had
known this and made their powder behave this way on purpose. Lorana hoped so. She hoped that she was supposed to
mix all four vials together. That she had the right quantities.

She was done. Outside, in the distance, she heard Arith
scrabbling from the Bowl into the Hatching Grounds. Lorana took a deep, stilling breath and then carefully filled the
syringe with the contents of the small beaker. She gently
squeezed the air out of the needle until a small spurt of the
precious liquid dripped out. She was ready.

I'm ready, Arith told her.

Lorana didn't remember walking back to the Hatching
Grounds. She did remember stopping in her tracks as she

caught sight of Arith, small and fragile, standing in the dim light that leaked through to the Hatching Grounds.

It is our *decision,* Arith said. *I am young. I am strong. If this works, we can help the others.*

Lorana forced herself to move again. She showed the syringe to Arith.

Will it hurt? the gold dragon asked.

Don't look at it, Lorana cautioned. She found a spot on Arith's neck, felt for and found a large vein. She paused then, overcome by the enormity of the moment.

Is it over? Arith asked hopefully. With a sigh, Lorana gently plunged the needle in and slowly pushed the plunger down.

Now it's over, she told her dragon. She quickly removed the syringe and then, realizing she had nowhere to put it, held it numbly in her hand.

Good, Arith said. *I don't feel any different.* She sneezed.

Lorana jumped.

No, it's—Arith stopped, her eyes whirling to red. She turned her head from one side to another. *I don't feel good.*

Lorana looked at her in the dim light. Arith's skin looked splotchy, different. The young queen made an irritated noise and turned to snap at her side.

It itches! Arith yelled. *Lorana, it burns!*

I'll go get some numbweed, Lorana declared but her feet were rooted to the spot. *I'll call for help.*

It's—it's—oh, it hurts! Arith wailed. *It's wrong, Lorana, it's wrong!* And then, suddenly, she wasn't there.

Arith! Lorana shouted, reaching for her dragon. She reached *between,* dove after her, found a fleeting glimpse in the distance, but it was too far. Frantically, she reached for all the other dragons of the Weyr and followed Arith, desperate to bring her dragon back. Arith fought to get away, pushed against her call, against the strength that Lorana had called from the dragons of the Weyr, fought, and fought—and, suddenly, she found a place where she could go—

No, no, no!

Arith was gone.

Lorana had one fleeting glimpse, one sliver of a feeling that Arith had felt some other calling—and then she was gone.

With one last, heart-tearing scream, Lorana collapsed, unconscious, on the floor of the Hatching Grounds.

*Any Eridani Adept willing to change an ecosystem must com-
mit her bloodline to maintaining that ecosystem eternally.*
    — *Edicts of the Eridani, XXIVth Concord*

Chapter Seventeen

College, First Interval, AL 58

LIGHTNING TORE through the sky over the College, with
thunder following right on its heels in vengeful intensity.
Wind Blossom turned over in her bed, willing herself to
sleep in spite of the noise outside. She needed her rest, she
knew it. But her mind, traitorous in the night, insisted on
turning over and over the problems she would face in the
morning.

What did it matter that fire-lizards sometime in the future
had gotten sick? Would the same illness affect dragons? Kitti
Ping and she had tried to guard against that, even while
knowing that nature and environment would work against
them.

How could she convince the Weyrleaders and the Holders
to devote their energies to guarding against some unseen future that might never come to pass?

"In the morning." Kitti Ping's saying came back to her.
"There is always enlightenment in the morning."

Her mother was right, Wind Blossom knew. Often the
problems that plagued her in the night would be solved in the
morning. She often wondered how much of the solution
came from her worrying and how much from a good night's
sleep.

Sleep was harder to come by these days, she mused. With
this lightning and thunder, it would be a wonder if she would

have *any* energy come the morning. She closed her eyes and tried to will herself back to sleep once more.

A thunderclap, loud and without lightning, startled her completely out of sleep. There was something more, something special, urgent, like a voice crying in the night. Electrified, she threw off her covers and raced down the stairs to the courtyard, despite the pouring rain.

Tieran was there, too, with his fire-lizard—Wind Blossom remembered that fire-lizards did not like the rain—skittering and chittering above him.

"Look!" Tieran shouted above the thunder and the rainfall. He darted out from under the courtyard tunnel and onto the roadway that led from the College.

Wind Blossom followed him. She looked up. There was a shape high up in the air, falling. Before she could react, the shape hit the ground in front of them with a sickening thud.

It was a dragon. Wind Blossom peered at it through the rain and dark night until another lightning bolt illuminated it. She gasped in horror.

"Rouse the College!" she shouted over the rain. "Get the agenothree!"

"Wind Blossom, what is it?" a voice called from behind her. She recognized it as Emorra's. "Get the agenothree! We must burn this corpse. We must burn it now!"

"It's infected?" Emorra asked, gesturing to the others behind her and quickly issuing orders.

"And worse," Wind Blossom agreed, as teams formed up with barrels of agenothree. "Pour it on. Don't stop. All of Pern depends on this."

As the first agenothree hissed over the young dragon's corpse, Tieran rushed forward, his belt knife in his hand.

"Tieran!" Wind Blossom shouted, her voice merging with Emorra's at her side. "What are you doing?"

Quickly Tieran cut a part of the dragon's riding harness, tore off a silver buckle and retreated toward the others. He nodded curtly at one of the groups carrying a barrel of agenothree and, jaw clenched against the pain, plunged his hands into the acid.

"What are you doing?" Wind Blossom shouted again.

"It's all right," Tieran said, showing her his hands. They were pitted and raw from where the acid had burned through the oils of his skin. He waved the piece of metal at them. "This will tell us whose dragon this is."

He gritted his teeth and closed his eyes as the pain from his hands burned through the adrenaline that had carried through his wild act.

"Besides," he added, gasping in pain, "it doesn't hurt as much as wher-bite."

When the cold, gray light of morning finally broke through the scattering clouds, Wind Blossom was still hunched beside the steaming remains of the dragon. The agenothree had eaten all its flesh and left only bleached bone. As each barrel of the nitric acid had burned another layer of flesh and muscle away from the dead dragon, Wind Blossom had felt herself similarly stripped, her emotions laid open and raw to her as they never had been before.

The stream of green mucus that had been forced from the dragon's nostrils on its impact with the ground had made it crystal clear to Wind Blossom that the dragon had been infected with the same illness as the two fire-lizards.

Over and over again her mind replayed the instant when she had *known* that she had to go outside, that something was coming. Over and over her memory showed her the images of the dragon appearing, faintly, high in the sky and falling uncontrollably to the ground—dead. The sickening sound of the dragon's body hitting the ground still made her shudder.

Again she replayed the memory in her mind, fighting with herself to slow it down, to bring every detail into sharp relief. She sighed angrily as she once again failed to determine the precise feeling she had the instant she had *known* she had to go outside. She had felt it before, when the fire-lizards had appeared. Some connection, something.

Bitterly, Wind Blossom shook her head to rid herself of the problem. There were other problems.

She expected M'hall and maybe even Torene to arrive

presently. She wouldn't be surprised if every dragon on Pern arrived. She had started workmen digging a grave large enough for the skeletal remains of the young dragon. The grave would be lined with lime; even though Wind Blossom was certain that the infection itself had been destroyed by the agenothree, she was not certain *enough*.

All those images and memories ought to have been enough to keep Wind Blossom awake through the night.

But there was one more. And it alone had kept her up, had kept her from accepting anything more than a winter cloak and hot *klah*.

It was the image of the dragon's skin, mottled, patchy, and pockmarked, as though it were changing consistency. She had only seen it for a moment and in the gray of night. The image bothered her for a reason she couldn't explain. Deep inside her, she knew that what she had seen held some special significance, but she couldn't identify it. That bothered her—and kept her awake through the night.

"Mother?" Emorra's voice startled her. "Have you been up all night?"

Wind Blossom nodded. "I'm trying to remember something."

"Well, come to breakfast—perhaps you'll remember better when you're warm," Emorra suggested.

"M'hall and the others will be here soon," Wind Blossom said.

"I'll stay," Tieran said, walking up with a breakfast roll in one hand. "I . . ." He trailed off, unable to finish his sentence.

Wind Blossom turned and smiled at him understandingly. Emorra added her smile, as well.

"Go on," Tieran said. "I'll direct any dragonriders to you and keep watch here."

"Thank you," Wind Blossom said, her throat unexpectedly tight.

Tieran nodded and turned back to survey the charred remains of the dead queen dragon.

To keep watch.

And honor the dead.

Thread scores
Dragons scream.
Thread burns
Freeze between.

Chapter Eighteen

Benden Weyr, Third Pass, 12th Day, AL 508

"I WILL STAY with her. You go get some rest," Salina declared, shoving Kindan out of Lorana's quarters.

It had been two days since the Weyr had been jolted awake by Lorana's *grab* of all the dragons, by Arith's horrific cry, and Lorana's soul-torn shout.

"She's wasting away," Kindan cried. "See if you can get her to eat something."

"I'll try," Salina told him. "You get some rest, Kindan. It's your strength she needs now."

"Go on," M'tal declared gruffly, entering the room. "She's right."

Kindan gave the dragonrider a wary look that settled as it registered in his sleep-numbed mind that M'tal had comforted Salina on her loss.

"You're all worn out," M'tal said, patting the harper on the shoulder as he passed by. "Get a good night's rest. We'll call you if she stirs."

After Kindan left, M'tal spoke to Gaminth, who replied miserably, *She won't hear me. She won't hear any of us.*

M'tal crouched down by Salina. "Gaminth says she's blocking the dragons' voices," he told her.

"Can you blame her?" Salina asked, her voice blurred

with sorrow. "I can only imagine how much that would torment her."

"It would have helped so much today," M'tal said. He had just returned from flying Fall over Ista. "Two dead, eight injured, three seriously," he told her.

"That's good," Salina murmured approvingly. "In a normal Fall I would have expected five times that many casualties."

"Ista's losses were worse," M'tal continued, grimacing. "Three dead, nine injured. They have only thirty-four dragons left fit to fly."

"J'lantir must be beside himself with worry."

"B'nik pledged that, as long as there are dragons at Benden Weyr, Ista would have them at their side," M'tal said, his voice full of adamant approval.

"He does you proud," Salina said, grabbing his hand and clenching it tightly.

"He does us *all* proud," M'tal agreed. "He always had the makings. He's risen marvelously to the challenge."

"If only we could say the same of Tullea," Salina said. Beside her, M'tal nodded mutely.

The sound of boots outside the doorway alerted them and they looked up to see K'tan enter.

"I've come to check on her," he told them. He looked around the room. "Has Kindan finally left for some rest?"

"I sent him on his way," M'tal said. He asked Gaminth to get one of the weyrlings to check on the weary harper.

K'tan nodded wearily. "Good."

He gestured entreatingly to Salina, who stood up and moved away from Lorana's bedside to give him room to examine her. K'tan listened to her breathing, took her pulse, and then straightened up again.

"Has she eaten anything? Drunk anything?" When Salina shook her head twice in response, K'tan grimaced. He pursed his lips thoughtfully. "You know yourself better than any what this is like. What made *you* decide to live?"

M'tal gripped Salina's hand tightly. The ex-Weyrwoman's

eyes shimmered with tears, which she wiped away hastily before explaining, "I couldn't go. I was *needed*."

M'tal circled behind her and hugged her tightly against him. K'tan nodded, uneasy in the presence of their intense emotions.

"Then let's hope that Lorana feels as needed," he said softly. He looked up at Salina, his lips showing the hint of a smile. "I'm glad you decided to stay—it would have been much harder without you."

M'tal felt Salina stiffen in his arms and, through years of intimacy, correctly interpreted her gratitude at the healer's words. The ex-Weyrleader eyed the healer, however, with the eyes of a leader of dragonmen.

"You need to take your own advice, K'tan, and get some rest."

"Lorana was the last of the charges I needed to check on," K'tan said.

"One of us will stay with her," Salina promised.

She will not hear us but she knows we are here for her, Gaminth told M'tal.

"Drith says the dragons are doing what they can to comfort her," K'tan added.

"Gaminth also," M'tal said. He gestured K'tan out the door. "Get some rest, Healer."

K'tan, intent on rousing Kindan from his depression, paused outside the Benden Weyr harper's door at the sound of the harper singing:

"A thousand voices keen at night,
A thousand voices wail,
A thousand voices cry in fright,
A thousand voices fail.

You followed them, young healer lass,
Till they could not be seen;
A thousand dragons made their loss
A bridge 'tween you and me.

And in the cold and darkest night,
A single voice is heard,
A single voice both clear and bright,
It says a single word.

That word is what you now must say
To—"

Kindan paused, intent, trying to remember the next words. With a growl of disgust and a ragged jangle on the guitar's strings, he threw the instrument onto his bed.

"Harper, you sing a mournful tune," K'tan said loudly as he entered Kindan's rooms.

Kindan turned to face the Weyr healer, scowling and shaking his head. "I *can't* remember it!"

"Is it so important?" K'tan asked mildly.

Kindan bit off a quick retort and paused before giving K'tan a thoughtful answer. "I don't know," he admitted. "It just seems to fit the times we're in."

"How could anyone know about the times we're in?" K'tan mused, shaking his head. "I think it's just a song. Perhaps it was written after a fever or plague—"

"But that's just it!" Kindan protested. "There hasn't *been* a fever or plague that affected dragons—you know that. We've looked through all the Records."

"Perhaps it was . . ." He trailed off as he caught sight of Kindan's expression.

The harper bounded beyond him, grabbing the guitar back from the bed, and shouting, "That's it!"

Triumphantly, he strummed and sang:

"That word is what you now must say
To open up the door
In Benden Weyr, to find the way
To all my healing lore."

"I remember now, I remember it all."
With a wince of pain, the Benden Harper continued:

"It's all that I can give to you,
To save both Weyr and Hold.
It's little I can offer you,
Who paid with dragon gold."

"That's great, Kindan," K'tan told him, clapping him on the back. "That's marvelous. I'm glad you've remembered the song." He paused. "But what does it mean?"

Kindan's cheerful look faded. "I don't know," he admitted sadly. "Only . . . I'm sure it means something." He frowned in thought.

The drums on the watch heights sounded sharply and Kindan held up a hand for silence as he strained to hear the incoming message.

"What is it?" K'tan asked, not knowing the drum codes as well as the harper.

"It's a message from Fort Weyr," he said. "They flew Threadfall last night over Ruatha and the Weyr itself."

Still listening, the harper gasped and smiled, eyes alight. K'tan bottled his curiosity up until the Weyr drummer sent back his acknowledgment.

"And?" he asked then.

Kindan smiled at him. "And the watch-whers fought the Fall," he said, taking delight in the way the healer's eyes grew wide with astonishment.

"Nuella led them," Kindan went on cheerfully. "Looks like Wind Blossom's creatures have more of a purpose—"

"What?" K'tan asked, catching the surprised look on Kindan's face.

"The song," Kindan said slowly, in amazement. "I remember the title."

K'tan urged him to go on, but Kindan was transfixed in thought.

Finally, the healer said, "The title, Kindan, what is it?"

Kindan shook himself out of his musings and gave K'tan an apologetic look.

" 'Wind Blossom's Song.' "

* * *

"I said get out!" Tullea shouted for the third time at Tilara. "I'll call you when you're needed."

With a worried look toward Lorana, Tilara retreated from Tullea's anger.

"It's not like she needs a whole guard," Tullea muttered to herself as she heard Tilara's feet hasten down the corridor. "Probably going to tell Mikkala. Well, let her. *I'm* the Weyrwoman. Not even Salina can criticize me."

She looked down at Lorana, lying on her back, motionless, in her bed.

"I tried to keep you away," Tullea said, almost apologetically. "But you had to do it your way. Wouldn't tell anyone. The first we hear is you and your dragon shrieking in the middle of the night."

Her voice rose as her anger grew. "You didn't deserve that dragon, you know? You were so sure, so certain, so willing to risk everything. You deserved to lose her, do you hear? You *deserved it*!" Tullea realized that she was shouting at the top of her lungs into Lorana's ear and pulled back, both appalled at her own behavior and amazed by Lorana's unresponsiveness.

"You can't die," Tullea said. "Salina was with her Breth for ten times more Turns than you had months with your dragon, and she didn't die.

"You can't die. You're not allowed, do you hear me? It wouldn't be right. You're not allowed, you're not . . ."

Tullea found herself on her knees at Lorana's bedside, cradling the woman's head in her arms, her tears falling onto Lorana's hair like rain.

"*Please* don't die," Tullea whispered, begging. *"Please."*

For all his Fort riders' work, K'lior was certain that some Thread had fallen through to the ground in the night Fall over Southern Boll. He shuddered at the thought of what the ground might look like in the morning.

Take us to the Hold, Rineth, K'lior said. *I must speak with the Lord Holder.*

Contrary to K'lior's fears, Lord Egremer was effusive with his praise of the dragons and their riders.

"We'll have ground crews out at first light, I promise," Egremer said. He looked nervously northward, toward where Thread had fallen. "How bad is it, do you suppose?"

K'lior shook his head. "We did our best," he said. "But the warm weather meant that every Thread was alive. The watch-whers were overwhelmed and we'd never trained with them, so our coordination was lousy."

Lady Yvala's eyes grew wide with alarm.

"We'll have sweepriders out at first light," K'lior promised. "As soon as we see anything, we'll let you know."

"I'd hate to lose the stands of timber to the north," Lord Egremer said. "They're old enough to be harvested, but I was hoping to hold off until mid-Pass, when we'll really be needing the wood."

K'lior nodded. "We'll do our best," he promised.

"And we're grateful for all that you've done," Egremer replied.

Wearily, K'lior mounted Rineth and gave him the image for Fort's Bowl.

The morning dawned gray, cold, and cloudy. Even Cisca was subdued.

"The reports are in from T'mar on sweep," she said as she nudged K'lior awake, handing him a mug of steaming *klah*. "Five burrows."

K'lior groaned. Cisca made a face and he gave her a go-on gesture.

"Two are well-established. They'll have to fire the timber stands."

K'lior sat up, taking a long sip of his *klah*. He gave Cisca a measuring look, then said, "Casualties?"

Cisca frowned. "Between the illness and Thread, twenty-three have gone *between*. F'dan and P'red will be laid up with injuries for at least the next six months. Troth, Piyeth, Kadorth, Varth, and Bidanth are all seriously injured and will also take at least six months to heal. There are eleven other riders or dragons with injuries that will keep them from flying for the next three months."

"So, we've what—seventy dragons and riders fit to fly?"

"Seventy-five," Cisca corrected, emphasizing the difference. "And we've got over three sevendays before our next Fall. I'm sure that we'll have more dragons fit to fly by then."

"Three sevendays is not enough time," K'lior grumbled, rising from their bed and searching out some clothes.

"No you don't," Cisca said sharply, getting up and pushing him toward the baths. "You smell. You're getting bathed before you do anything else."

K'lior opened his mouth to protest but Cisca silenced him with a kiss.

"If you're nice," she taunted, "I may join you."

K'lior tried very hard to be nice.

Lord Holder Egremer scowled at the line of smoke in the distance. Forty Turns' worth of growth, gone. Three whole valleys had been put to flames before the dragonriders and ground crews could declare Southern Boll Hold free from Thread.

The rains would come soon and the burnt land would lose all its topsoil. He could expect floods to ravage the remnants of those valleys. In the end, there might be a desert where once there had been lush forests.

It would be worse for his holders. They had expected years of work and income culling the older trees, planting new, and working the wood into fine pieces of furniture. Now Southern Boll would be dependent upon its pottery, spices, and the scant foodstuffs it could raise for trade with the other Holds.

The Hold would take Turns to recover.

"I'm sorry, Egremer," a disconsolate K'lior repeated. "If there's anything the Weyr can do to help . . ."

Egremer sighed and turned back to the youthful Weyr-leader. K'lior was no more than ten Turns younger than he, and while Egremer wanted desperately to blame someone, he knew that it would be unfair to blame the dragonrider.

Egremer forced a smile. "I appreciate that, K'lior," he replied. "And there might be more that you can do than you know. If I could have the loan of a weyrling or two, to help scout out the damage and maybe haul some supplies . . ."

"Weyrlings we have aplenty," K'lior said. He shook his head. "It's full-grown dragons that are scarce."

"I'd heard that your losses are high from the illness," Egremer replied. "Is there anything *we* can do for *you,* my lord?"

For a moment, K'lior made no reply, staring off into space, thinking.

"Time," he said at last, angrily. "We need time for the weyrlings to grow up, time for the wounded to heal." He shook his head. "I'm afraid you cannot give that to us, my lord."

Egremer's face drained. "How long do we have, then, my lord?"

K'lior's face grew ashen. "Fort is lucky. We don't have another Threadfall in the next three sevendays. We'll probably be able to fight that." He shook his head. "But I can't say about the Fall after."

The despair that gripped the Weyrleader was palpable. Egremer looked for some words of encouragement to give him but could find none. It was K'lior who spoke next, pulling himself erect and willing a smile back on to his face.

"We'll find a way, Lord Egremer," he declared with forced cheer. "We're dragonriders—we always find a way." He nodded firmly to himself and then said to Egremer, "Now, if you'll excuse me . . ."

"Certainly!" Egremer replied. "I'll see you out. And don't worry about those weyrlings, if it's too much bother. Having them would only save us time."

K'lior stopped so suddenly that Egremer had to swerve to avoid bumping into him.

"Time!" K'lior shouted exultantly. He turned to Egremer and grabbed him on both shoulders. "That's it! Time! We need time."

Egremer smiled feebly, wondering if the dragons' sick-

ness could affect riders, as well. K'lior just as suddenly let go
of the Lord Holder and raced out of the Hold.

"Thank you, Lord Egremer, you've been most helpful," he
called as he climbed up to his perch on Rineth.

"Any time, Weyrleader," Egremer called back, not at all
certain what he had done, but willing to use the Weyrleader's
good cheer to elevate that of his holders, rather than depress
them more by looking at the Weyrleader as if he were mad.

"Cisca, it's time!" K'lior yelled up from the Bowl to their
quarters as soon as he returned *between* from Southern Boll.
"That's what we need—time!"

Cisca stepped up to the ledge in Melirth's quarters and
peered down to K'lior. "Of course we need time," she agreed,
mostly to humor him.

"No, no, no," K'lior shouted back. "The weyrlings and the
injured riders, they all need *time* to grow and recover."

"Make sense, K'lior," Cisca returned irritably.

K'lior took a deep breath and gave her a huge smile.
"We'll time it. Send them back in time somewhere so—"

"So they can recover!" Cisca finished with a joyful cry
and a leap. "K'lior, that's brilliant!"

When K'tan approached M'tal and Salina at dinner that
evening, M'tal gave Salina a worried look.

"Salina, may I talk with you?" K'tan asked, his eyes
pleading, his face pale. "It's about Drith."

Salina responded with a weary smile and a small shake of
her head. Really, she *was* getting used to this, although she
hadn't expected K'tan to be the next dragonrider to ask to
speak to her alone.

M'tal leaned back in his chair, reflectively fingering a
glass of wine on the table. Salina rose from her chair and
gave him a peck on the cheek before following the Weyr
healer out of the Living Cavern.

"How long has it been?" she asked K'tan as soon as they
were out of earshot.

"Over two sevendays," he replied grimly, his face lined

with the pain of so many burdens piled on top of each other—the dying, Lorana, and now his own dragon's sickness. "I keep telling myself that the next potion, the next herbal infusion will turn the tide but—"

Salina laid a hand gently on his arm. K'tan took a shuddering breath.

"I must go check on Lorana," he said finally, ducking away from Salina's gaze. He turned back, eyes puzzled, and told her, "I see her body shudder every time a dragon goes *between,* but she makes no sound."

"I know," Salina replied softly. "I think she *feels* every dragon's death." She looked up at him. "You must know something of how she feels, for all your years healing."

"Is it terribly lonely, losing your dragon?" K'tan asked, fighting to keep his voice steady.

"It's the worst feeling there is," Salina told him honestly. She grabbed him and hugged him tight. "But as long as you have people to live for . . ."

Overwhelmed by her words and enveloped in her comforting embrace, K'tan's composure broke in one soft, heart-torn sob. Clumsily he pushed himself away.

"I'll be all right," he declared. "Thank you."

"I'm sure you will be," Salina agreed, accepting his lie.

K'tan turned quickly, saying, "I must check on Lorana."

"Give her my love," Salina called as the healer strode off deliberately.

By the time K'tan arrived in Lorana's quarters, he had his emotions back under control. After all, he chided himself, he had had Turns of consoling the bereaved, of keeping quiet watch as sick and injured slipped away forever; he should be used to this. And he owed it to his patients and weyrmates. Those who were suffering deserved no less than the best he could give them.

He heard a voice from inside Lorana's quarters and quickened his pace, arriving breathless. Perhaps—

"What are you doing here?" he demanded abruptly, spotting the Weyrwoman as he entered Lorana's quarters.

"My duty as Weyrwoman," Tullea snapped, her cheeks

flushing. She stood up from Lorana's bedside, hands clenched by her side. Her features tightened severely as her anger grew.

"Let me relieve you, then," K'tan said crisply.

Tullea glared at him through narrowed eyes, then spun on her heels and was out of the room before K'tan could react.

He couldn't, for a moment, imagine that Tullea was watching Lorana out of any concern or compassion for the dragon-less woman. He knelt beside Lorana, took her pulse, and checked her temperature and breathing, assuring himself that she hadn't suffered from Tullea's attentions.

K'tan searched the room for a chair, found it, dragged it up beside Lorana's bed, and sat in it, leaning back and stretching out his legs in readiness for a long, patient wait. The room smelled of fresh high-bloom flowers. Had Tullea brought them? Probably Salina, K'tan decided.

As long as you have people to live for. Salina's words echoed sourly in his memory. Who did Lorana have to live for? Her family was gone, she was new at the Weyr, and Tullea, the senior Weyrwoman, clearly had no love for her.

Kindan? The harper was certainly a possibility, K'tan decided, although his blunder in singing "Wind Blossom's Song" may have soured Lorana on him.

The dragons? K'tan snorted his opinion of that prospect. While he got the impression that Lorana was more in tune with the dragons than anyone he'd heard of, even in the Ballads, he couldn't see them, dying in such droves, providing her with a reason for living.

And what of me? K'tan asked himself.

You will stay, Drith told him groggily. Even in the distance, K'tan could pick out Drith's raspy cough from all the others. *You will stay, she will stay. You must. Both of you.*

K'tan was surprised at his dragon's fierce tone.

The answer is here, Drith continued. *You and Lorana must find it.* K'tan wondered how much of Drith's conviction was simply a reflection of K'tan's own beliefs.

We will find it, he promised his dragon. *Lorana will recover soon, and we'll find it. Rest up, old friend.*

In the distance, K'tan could hear Drith's answering rumble turn into another long, raspy cough.

K'tan shot out of his chair and headed for the door. *I'm coming, Drith!*

No, Drith responded. *I must do this now while I still can.*

"No!" K'tan shouted both out loud and in his mind.

I will always love you, Drith told him fondly.

And then—he was gone.

"No!" K'tan shouted again, reaching with his mind to follow Drith. He jerked as he felt another *presence* join him, searching in the darkness of *between* for the brown dragon. Together they roamed, searching all that they could find— but there was no sign of Drith.

Gasping for breath, K'tan found himself once again feeling his body. "Drith, no!"

"Come back!" Lorana cried in unison with him.

Across the room, K'tan—Ketan—locked tear-soaked eyes with Lorana.

"I tried," Lorana called to him, struggling to get out of her bed. "I tried, K'tan, but he fought me. He wouldn't come back."

Ketan stumbled back to Lorana's bedside.

"I'm sorry," she said, shaking her head. "I *tried.*"

Ketan grabbed one of her hands and stroked it comfortingly, his need to reassure her overcoming his own grief.

"I know, lass, I know," he told her. "I felt you there with me." He closed his eyes and reached once more for his beloved Drith. Nothing. For a long moment, Ketan wished he could follow his dragon, realized he would have ridden Drith on that last journey *between* if he'd had the chance. With a chilling shock, Ketan realized that Drith had known that, too. "We must end this."

Lorana's hand tightened on his, and the ex-dragonrider opened his eyes again to see a look of fierce determination in her red-rimmed brown eyes.

"We *will* end this," she promised.

Symbiont: A life-form that lives in harmony with its host, often performing valuable functions for the host, e.g.: E. coli in the human gut.

Chapter Nineteen

College, First Interval, AL 58

TIERAN SPOTTED M'hall and Brianth circling through the clouds above and sent Grenn up to them.

"Tell them it's safe, but to land at a distance," Tieran told his fire-lizard. Grenn gave him a *chirp* to show that he understood and flew on up to the huge bronze dragon.

Moments later, Brianth landed, cautiously far from the still-smoldering remains of the young queen, and M'hall approached on foot. The Benden Weyrleader's jaw was set, and his eyes bleak.

"Did Wind Blossom order this?" he asked Tieran as he neared.

"Yes," Tieran said. "The queen fell from the sky and was dead either from the impact or before that."

M'hall peered closely at the remains. "It seems small for a queen. Are you sure it wasn't a green?"

"It was a queen," Tieran replied firmly. "Not just from the color but there"—he pointed at the blackened skull—"you can see from the shape of the skull and the teeth that it's a young dragon, months old, probably less than six—"

"Less than six?" M'hall was amazed. "And that big? A six-month-old queen shouldn't be *that* big."

"But it was," Tieran replied. "That would be about the size expected at about the thirtieth generation, or so."

"The thirtieth generation?" M'hall repeated, amazed. "How would you know?"

Tieran shrugged. "Wind Blossom explained it," he said. "There were limits on the original work they had done and they knew that the first generations would be smaller than the final generations. That," he added, pointing to the skeleton, "is close to as large as they get, though."

"Where is its rider?" M'hall asking, looking around for another burn circle.

"There was no rider," Tieran told him.

"Could it have been an accident? A queen so young going *between*?" M'hall asked in vain hope.

Tieran shook his head. "I don't know," he answered. "But if it did, then it was sick with what looked to be the same thing this one—" He reached up to stroke Grenn, who had perched again on his shoulder, reassuringly. "—was ill with.

"Thirty generations would be over four hundred years from now," he added.

M'hall whistled in awe. "You're saying that this dragon and your fire-lizard come from four hundred years in the future?"

Tieran nodded, opening his hand. "I pulled this off the dragon's riding harness."

M'hall gave Tieran a questioning look and, at the young man's nod, picked up the small object and peered at it intently.

"That's the Benden Weyr mark," he said instantly, pointing at a small section on the silver oblong. "Those other marks look like"—he glanced up incredulously at Tieran—"the same ones on your friend's beadwork! Animal healer."

"That's what I thought," Tieran agreed.

To his surprise, Tieran did not find himself on duty escorting all the various craftmasters, holders, and Weyrleaders past the newly-raised mound that marked the queen dragon's final resting place and on into the College's Dining Room, hastily rearranged as a meeting place. Instead, he found himself bustling back and forth between Wind Blossom,

Emorra, and Janir, carrying notes, bearing messages, and generally being run off his feet.

The undercurrents in the room were deep and numerous. Just from his own hearing, he knew that the Lord Holders not only warred with themselves over the disposition of Colony resources but also had numerous issues of trade to resolve. The Weyrleaders seemed united, if somewhat restless, willing to follow M'hall's direction.

But the real issue was Wind Blossom's. Those who hadn't actually seen the dragon's burnt skeleton were dubious of the claim, although not quite willing to voice out loud their lack of faith in Wind Blossom's reasoning or abilities.

It promised to be an interesting and perhaps contentious session. Tieran caught a whiff of the snacks Moira and Alandro were baking and was surprised when his stomach gave a disgusted heave. Apparently this interesting session meant more to him than he was willing to admit.

The tables of the Dining Room had been arranged in a large oval. Emorra and the other collegians were gathered at the end nearest the kitchen. Opposite them were the Weyrleaders. In between, on the left and on the right, were the leaders of the Holds.

Tieran was surprised when the first person to speak was Emorra.

"Does everyone have a copy of the agenda?" she asked. Hearing no dissent, she continued. "Very well, I propose we start with the first item: the issue of the queen dragon and Wind Blossom's findings—"

"It seemed awfully small to be a queen," Lord Kenner of Telgar noted quaveringly, glancing around the room nervously, his beak-like nose bobbing this way and that.

"That's because it was an immature dragon," Tieran responded. "Judging by its teeth, it was under six months old, probably as little as two."

"And you agree with this assessment?" Mendin asked, looking pointedly at M'hall.

M'hall nodded. "Yes."

Mendin turned back to Tieran and nodded for him to continue. Tieran looked at Emorra and raised an eyebrow.

Emorra continued. "It is our opinion—"

"Whose?" Mendin demanded challengingly.

"The medical staff and faculty at this College," she replied testily. "Kindly let me continue uninterrupted."

Mendin looked ready to argue the point but desisted after catching sight of M'hall's glare.

"It is our opinion that the queen dragon was a hatchling from somewhere between the thirtieth and fortieth generation," Emorra said. The Lord Holders gave her blank stares, while the Weyrleaders who hadn't heard this before all sat bolt upright in their chairs.

"Emorra, could you tell us what dragon generation we are at now?" Malon of Tillek asked courteously.

"The newest generation is the sixth generation," Emorra answered.

"So the dragon came from the future," K'nel of Ista said.

"How can dragons travel through time?" Kenner asked.

"It is a property of their ability to teleport," Wind Blossom replied. "Any movement through space implies a movement through time."

Kenner looked politely confused.

"Space and time are the same," M'hall expanded, taking pity on the old Holder. "We've done it."

"You have?" Mendin blurted.

"Yes," L'can, High Reaches Weyrleader confirmed. "It is quite draining on the rider, though."

"We estimate that the dragon came from more than four hundred years in the future," Emorra told the group.

"Well, that's a relief," Mendin declared. "We've got nothing to worry about, then." He looked expectantly around the room. "So what's the next item on the agenda?"

"I don't think we should move on so quickly," M'hall replied. He turned to Emorra. "Is there any danger to our dragons?"

"I don't think so," she replied. "The young queen was immediately bathed in acid, so all microorganisms should have been destroyed."

"What about that fire-lizard?" Mendin asked, pointing at the brown fire-lizard curled on Tieran's shoulder.

"I would not have released the fire-lizard from quarantine had I considered it still a possible source of contagion," Wind Blossom spoke up from behind her daughter. She met Mendin's eyes squarely. "The fate of all Pern is at stake."

"Is?" Mendin repeated. "I thought you said the fire-lizard isn't a threat?"

"We don't know why the fire-lizard or the queen dragon found their way back to us," Emorra replied. "They both appear to have come from about the same time, and there are indications that they had the same human partner."

"And that the partner was a rider at Benden Weyr," M'hall added.

"Somewhere in the future, dragons are dying," L'can marveled mournfully.

"But that's not an issue for us!" Mendin declared. "I'm sorry to hear about it, but we have issues we need to deal with today."

"And this is one of them," Emorra declared fiercely. "Twice now we've been lucky." She nodded toward M'hall and the Weyrleaders. "Every Weyr is now on guard against any other dragons falling out of the future, but it just takes one and the illness could spread here."

"No, it can't," Tieran said to himself. He flushed as the others all looked at him. He shrugged. "If the illness spreads here, then there will be no dragons from the future."

"Could you explain?" M'hall asked, gesturing invitingly.

"If the illness comes back in time," Tieran replied, "there are two possibilities—either all the dragons will succumb and there will be no more dragons in the future, or the dragons will get better and pass their immunity on, so there will be no sick dragons in the future."

"I'm afraid there is a third possibility," Wind Blossom said. Everyone turned to her. "It is possible that the queen from the future is a modified watch-wher."

"What?" Mendin shouted. "A watch-wher?"

"I have only completed some preliminary evaluations," she continued unperturbedly, "but I have noticed signs of genetic manipulation in the queen's genetic code."

"But if our descendants could manipulate genetic material, wouldn't they be able to cure this illness in the future?" Mendin asked.

"You are supposing that detailed knowledge of genetics, particularly Pernese genetics, and the tools to manipulate Pernese genetic code would be available four centuries from now," Emorra said. She turned to him. "Tell me, Lord Mendin, how many base-pairs are there in the Pernese genetic code?"

"Why would I need to know that?" Mendin spluttered indignantly.

"Precisely," Emorra replied. "Why would anyone need to know that four hundred years in the future?"

Mendin waved a hand to the Weyrleaders. "Perhaps *they* would know it."

"I don't know it now," M'hall confessed. He glanced at the other Weyrleaders, who also professed ignorance. "I am more concerned with fighting Thread and maintaining a Weyr than the genetic code of the dragons." He glanced at Emorra. "It would seem that the College would retain this knowledge."

Emorra shook her head. "I doubt it, Weyrleader," she said. "Even now there are only three people in this room who can answer my question: myself, my mother, and Tieran."

"What about Janir, surely he knows this!" Mendin objected.

Janir shook his head. "I know a little about terrestrial genetics, but I specialize in human medicine."

"Statistically, if only three people know something now," Emorra said, "then there is a very high likelihood that that knowledge will not survive into the next generation, let alone four centuries from now."

"So the dragon from the future *can't* be genetically modified," Mendin declared. He sat back in his chair and looked around at the other Lord Holders triumphantly.

"That is not necessarily so," Emorra replied.

"How so?" Mendin demanded, sitting upright once more.

"It is possible," Wind Blossom began, then paused, looking at Emorra for her consent. "It is possible that the genetic modifications were provided by one of us and not used until this future time."

M'hall made a thoughtful face. "Are you suggesting that we dragonriders bring one of you forward in time four centuries?"

"Is that even possible?" Mendin murmured.

"It is possible," Wind Blossom conceded with a nod. Then she turned her gaze to M'hall and the Weyrleaders. "I don't think it is advisable."

M'hall gestured for her to enlighten them.

"You have observed that there is a great deal of physical stress associated with traveling *between,* particularly *between* times. I do not think that I could handle such a prolonged strain," Wind Blossom said. She glanced apologetically at Emorra and Tieran before adding, "And while I don't doubt their efforts, I believe that neither Tieran nor Emorra would be up to the scientific challenge."

She paused to give Tieran and Emorra a chance to demur. When they remained silent, she went on. "Also, there is the fact that the equipment and knowledge base we need are here, now, at the College and may not be available four centuries in the future."

M'hall stroked his chin, nodding. "Even with what the dragons could carry, I imagine there could always be one important thing that would be left behind."

"And it would be a one-way trip," Tieran pointed out. The others looked at him. "We couldn't risk accidentally bringing the illness back in time with us."

Mendin threw up his hands, leaning forward again in his chair. "So it's impossible, then." Tieran turned to Mendin and the other Holders. "I think we should move on to the next agenda item—the disposition of the remaining stonecutters."

"I believe that I have the agenda," Emorra said blandly. Mendin flushed and then gestured angrily at her to proceed.

"The fact remains that there are signs of genetic manipulation," Wind Blossom spoke out. "If we believe that our descendants could not have done this unaided, and we agree that we cannot journey forward in time to aid them, then it is clear that we must choose—must, indeed, have already chosen—a third course."

Mendin glared at the old geneticist and only brought his emotions under control by firm exertion of will. "With all due respect," he said, though none could be heard in his tone, "did you not say that your results were preliminary?"

Wind Blossom nodded.

"And you conducted these tests yourself?"

Again, Wind Blossom nodded.

"It is a fact that you are the oldest person now living on Pern," Mendin noted. "Could it be possible that you were mistaken?"

Roland, Southern Boll's Lord Holder, who had been puzzling something silently, suddenly piped up, "How did you figure this out? I thought we'd lost all our technology!"

"We did," Wind Blossom agreed. She shifted uncomfortably in her seat as though recollection pained her. "Many of our finest instruments were lost in a storm when we crossed from Landing." She looked directly at Mendin. "Including most of the equipment specifically tuned to manipulate Pernese genetic code." She glanced over at Malon and M'hall. "It was only after the quarantine of the fire-lizards that a chance comment by M'hall caused me to wonder if some of the equipment might have survived."

The other Lord Holders exchanged surprised looks.

"I was lucky enough to retrieve some useful equipment off the shores of Tillek Hold," Wind Blossom continued.

"And power packs, too?" Mendin asked, mentally upping the amount of stonecutting he could do.

Wind Blossom shook her head. "These units all have their own internal, nonremovable power supplies. They are all highly-specialized equipment of Eridani origin."

Janir cleared his throat and asked in a small voice, "Could this equipment have helped us in the Fever Year?"

Wind Blossom pursed her lips and shook her head sadly. "It was only tuned to the Pernese genetic code," she told him. "We used it to help us design the dragons."

"But that leaves us no nearer to solving your conundrum," Mendin said.

"I do not agree," Wind Blossom said. "I believe that we have evidence not only that we *will* do something but exactly *what* we will do."

"And that would be?" Roland asked.

"It is clear to me that we must come up with a way to preserve our equipment and knowledge in such a way as to help our descendants," she replied.

"You would have to not only provide them with the equipment but teach them how to use it," Mendin declared angrily.

"That *is* what we at the College are supposed to do," Emorra replied evenly.

Impression:
Mind to mind
Heart to heart
Breath for breath.

Chapter Twenty

Benden Weyr, Third Pass, 22nd Day, AL 508

IT WAS STILL DARK outside, but Benden Weyr's Bowl was filled with the activity of dragons and riders preparing for the Fall. The air in the Bowl was filled with predawn fog, wisping up in swaths through the dark.

Lorana was both surprised and pleased at the reception she received from rider and dragon. Beside her, she could feel Ketan's renewed mourning as he experienced the Weyr preparing for the first Fall he wouldn't be flying.

"Healer," B'nik called softly out of the darkness. He stepped closer, emerging from the foggy dark.

"Weyrleader," Ketan replied politely.

B'nik, discarding any thought of commiseration, stepped close to clasp the healer on the shoulder. "I hope you won't have much work when we get back."

Ketan smiled. "So do I," he said. "Fly safe."

In the darkness a dragon coughed. Lorana lurched against Ketan and straightened, mumbling an apology.

"Perhaps you should still be resting," B'nik said to her, his voice full of concern.

"I'm all right, I just lost my footing," she lied. "Besides, I wanted to offer my help. M'tal thought that my ability to speak to any dragon might be useful."

"It would be very useful," B'nik agreed immediately, surprised at her offer. "I—I didn't think that you'd—"

"I would be happy to help," Lorana told him firmly.

"Then I shall happily accept your help," B'nik replied cheerfully.

"Retanth says that all is ready," Lorana said.

"Tell him to have the Weyr assemble up by the Star Stones," B'nik replied. "Hopefully there'll be no fog up there."

"The watch dragon reports that the air is clear and the sun is just visible on the horizon."

"Excellent!" B'nik said, already seeing the value of Lorana's abilities. The one thing neither he nor M'tal could figure out was how to direct the wings and keep in contact with the Weyr at the same time. He turned back to his dragon. "Caranth, let's ride."

"Good Fall, Weyrleader," Lorana called after him. She and Ketan could not quite make out his parting wave in the growing light.

"So," Ketan said when the last of the dragons had cleared the Bowl, "suppose you tell me which new dragon has the sickness?"

"Caranth," Lorana replied mournfully.

"Are you sure you have the coordinates right?" B'nik asked his dragon anxiously as they prepared to guide the Weyr *between* to Threadfall over Bitra.

I am sure, Caranth returned unflappably. B'nik was reassured by his dragon's calm manner but still toyed with the idea of asking M'tal to have Gaminth guide the Weyr to the Fall. *I am just coughing, not confused.*

"Very well," B'nik said, letting out a deep sigh. "Let's go, Caranth!"

Following the visual image from the Weyrleader, one hundred and seventy-four fighting dragons went *between*.

Lorana didn't realize that she had tensed up until she felt Caranth's calm report of the arrival of the Weyr over Bitra—

and then she found herself gasping in a deep lungful of fresh air.

Ketan gave her a surprised look, then nodded in realization. "You were worried about Caranth?"

"B'nik was worried about Caranth," Lorana said. "Caranth seemed fine to me. Sick but still clearheaded, able to fly. Eager, even."

Ketan cocked his head at her in curiosity. "Do I gather that if *you* were worried about Caranth, you might have stopped him from bringing the Weyr *between*?"

Lorana allowed a ghost of a smile to cross her lips. "I might."

"Lorana," Ketan began, cautiously choosing his words, "you *do* understand that the Weyrleader is responsible for the fighting dragons, don't you?"

Lorana cocked her head at him. "Are you asking whether I know my place in the Weyr, Healer?"

Ketan pursed his lips uncomfortably. "I doubt if anyone knows your place just now," he said judiciously.

"I agree," she said with a small nod. "But I think it would be wrong, don't you, if I knew that Caranth was too sick to give good coordinates not to stop him." A small crease appeared between her brows. "What *would* happen if Caranth gave bad coordinates and the Weyr followed him?"

Ketan shuddered and his face went white. "They would be lost *between*."

"Oh," Lorana said, her eyes going wide. Ketan's expression answered her question better than words.

B'nik was bone-tired and bone-cold when, six hours later, Caranth relayed that the sweepriders had reported the end of the Fall.

"Send the other wings back to the Weyr," he told J'tol, "and have half our wing check for burrows."

J'tol waved in acknowledgment and veered off, his wingmen following in close formation.

B'nik was glad that he had listened to M'tal's advice and had kept his wing in reserve during the fighting. He had been able to quickly order his riders to fill gaps in other wings when needed—which had not been as often as he'd feared.

M'tal sends his congratulations, Caranth relayed.

Tell him thank you, B'nik responded, grinning unabashedly. While he hated the reason for it, he had to admit that it really *was* nice to have an ex-Weyrleader available and willing to give him honest praise when he earned it.

Let's go chat with the Lord Holder, he added, his grin disappearing as he imagined the sour expression of Gadran, Bitra's aging Lord. Even if no burrows were found, he was sure that Gadran would find some reason to moan or bicker.

J'tol reports three deep burrows in the northern valley, Caranth told him. *He says they'll have to fire the forests to contain them.*

"Is something wrong?" Gadran asked, taking in B'nik's worried expression.

"I'm afraid there is," B'nik told him. "We fought the Fall as best we could, but my sweepriders report that three burrows are well established in the valley north of here."

"Well established?" Gadran echoed, licking his lips nervously and peering to the north, as if expecting Thread to crest the ridge at any moment. "How well established?"

"I'm afraid we'll have to fire the valley to contain it."

"Fire the valley?" Gadran looked crestfallen. "All those trees?"

"The trees are what has let the burrows establish themselves so rapidly," B'nik explained.

J'tol wants to know if they can fire the valley now, Caranth relayed, with a note of anxiety.

"Tell J'tol to fire the valley," B'nik answered aloud.

"What?" Gadran shouted. "I did not give you permission—"

"I could not wait," B'nik replied. "The burrows were spreading too rapidly."

The first wisps of smoke started to rise from the valley to the north, the wind carrying it southward.

"There hasn't been rain here in months," Gadran said

quickly. "There's a danger that the fire might spread into this valley."

"I'm afraid that's a danger we'll have to risk," B'nik said. "I would prefer to lose a valley to fire far more than lose a Hold to Thread."

"It's not your decision to make!" Gadran snarled.

"On the contrary, as Weyrleader, it is absolutely *my* decision to make," B'nik replied, simmering with anger. He wondered how often M'tal had cursed this fool Holder and hoped that his heir would have more sense.

He gave the Lord Holder a curt nod. "I have to attend to the injured," he said, turning back to his dragon and mounting before Gadran could respond.

"No, I'm afraid Gadran's always been like that," M'tal said when B'nik approached him that night at dinner.

"What about Gadran?" J'tol called, striding into the Living Cavern, knocking soot off his riding gear. "He was red-faced and screaming when I left him. Is there more already?"

B'nik shot his wingsecond a look of alarm.

J'tol grimaced in response. "The fires got out of control; the winds up there were vicious," he said. "We had to set backfires on the slopes above Bitra Hold itself before they were contained."

"I should have stayed," B'nik groaned.

"What would you have done?" M'tal asked calmly. He nodded to J'tol. "J'tol's worked with fires before and shown his ability. I doubt anyone could have done better."

B'nik gave J'tol a consoling look and nodded. "You're right," he said to M'tal. "All the same," he added with a grin for his wingsecond, "I could have spared you his ravings."

A chorus of dragon coughs echoed in from the Bowl outside. All conversation stopped.

J'tol waved a dismissive hand at the noise. "Some of that's *our* dragons—they've got smoke in their lungs," he assured the others. "It'll clear out soon enough."

Lorana gave B'nik a probing look and raised her eyebrow

inquiringly. B'nik returned her look with confusion until, with a sudden start, he realized that she knew about Caranth.

"There are more important things to consider," she said to him. She paused to give him a chance to respond and continued only after it was clear that he would not speak. She gestured to Kindan. "Kindan says that he's discovered the words of his song. Did he tell you?"

B'nik shook his head. "We haven't had time to talk until now."

"And you shouldn't be talking, you should be eating," Tullea quipped, seating herself beside him. With a glare at Lorana, she urged B'nik to eat his dinner. "How was the Fall?"

B'nik found himself with a mouthful at her urging, desperately trying to swallow in order to answer her question.

M'tal took pity on him. "The Fall was not bad and was well flown." He nodded to B'nik. "We lost seven, all the same, and another eighteen were injured."

"There are only five wings fit to fly," B'nik added.

"It won't be long," Kindan murmured to himself.

Tullea heard him all the same. "It won't be long before what, Harper?" she demanded.

Kindan shifted uneasily in his seat. "It won't be long before there will be no dragons to fight Thread," he told her softly. He turned to B'nik. "Which is why I think it's vital to get the miners back to find a way beyond that second door in the Oldtimer Room, or another way into wherever that door goes."

"And kill more dragons?" Tullea asked scornfully. She gestured to Lorana. "Would you have more people sacrifice their loves and sanity?"

"Would you lose *all* the dragons of Pern?" Lorana asked in response. Tullea stared at her.

"We cannot say what lies beyond those doors," Lorana told the group. "But if we don't find out, we will have denied ourselves any chance of curing the dragons."

"How do you know?" Tullea protested.

"I don't," Lorana admitted. "But think about it—those

rooms were built for a reason. They were built with Oldtimer skills—to what purpose?"

"To create the dragons," Tullea replied, waving her hand dismissively. "Everyone knows that the Oldtimers created them from the fire-lizards."

"But they created them in the Southern Continent and fled north," Kindan remarked. "These rooms would not be where they made the dragons. In fact, since Benden was the second Weyr founded, these rooms would not have been made until long after our ancestors moved north."

M'tal, J'tol, and B'nik looked thoughtful.

"All the miners' hammering will disturb Minith," Tullea protested. "I won't permit that!"

"She's not ready to lay her clutch yet," Ketan observed. "If the noise bothers her, you could move the queen's quarters to the northern side of the Bowl. There's a nice set of quarters with a connection into the Hatching Grounds—that might prove useful for when you want to visit."

Tullea looked momentarily interested in the proposition, then brushed it aside. "What makes you so sure that these rooms have the cure?" she demanded of Lorana.

"I don't know," Lorana replied honestly. She chewed her lip hesitantly, then glanced at Kindan. "Although if that song, 'Wind Blossom's Song,' was meant for our times, then there would have to be a reason that I was to come to Benden Weyr," she added. "And those rooms are the most obvious reason, aren't they?"

B'nik looked troubled. Lorana caught his gaze. "How many more dragons will die?" she asked him pointedly. He flinched.

"Will this Weyr be emptied of all dragons?" She turned to the others. " 'Dragonmen must fly when Thread is in the sky,' " she quoted. Shaking her head, Lorana continued, "I don't see any other way to cure this sickness. I've tried—and I know Ketan has tried—every remedy we've ever heard of that could help. This sickness is new to dragons. I think that without help from the past, all the dragons of Pern will perish."

She turned to B'nik. "Weyrleader, bring the miners back. Let us find the other rooms. They might be our only hope."

"And if they aren't," M'tal added glumly, "then at least we'll know the worst."

B'nik raised his eyes bleakly to M'tal. "Send for the miners, please."

"T'mar!" K'lior exclaimed as the bronze rider dismounted from his dragon, a grin spread from ear to ear. K'lior hurtled over to the other rider and grabbed him in a gleeful hug.

"How did it go?" K'lior asked, pushing himself back from the grinning bronze rider, oblivious to the rest of the Weyr surrounding them and hanging on their every word.

T'mar's grin slipped, and K'lior noticed for the first time the deep bags under the bronze rider's eyes. K'lior stepped back and took a thorough inventory of the rider and the rest of the dragonriders who had returned from their three-year sojourn *between* back in time to the empty Igen Weyr of over ten Turns ago. T'mar looked fit, tanned, and healthy—but bone-weary.

"I would never recommend it, Weyrleader," T'mar replied, fighting to keep on his feet, "except in direst circumstances.

"The dragons were fine, but even the youngest riders felt . . . stretched and constantly drained," he went on. "I even had fights among the injured riders, tempers were that frayed by timing it."

He gave his Weyrleader a strained look.

"We were in the same time for too long, we could hear echoes of our younger selves, it was—" He shook his head, unable to find further words.

"But you're here now," K'lior said, surveying the full-strength wings landing behind him in the Bowl.

T'mar straightened and smiled, his hand sweeping across the Bowl. "Weyrleader, I bring you one hundred and twenty-two fighting dragons."

"Good," K'lior replied firmly, clapping T'mar on the shoulder. "Get them bedded down and then get some rest." He spoke up for the crowd. "We've Thread to fight in three days' time." He turned back to T'mar. "I can let you rest tomorrow, but we'll have to start practicing the next day."

"Thread in three days?" T'mar asked, puzzled. "Did I time it wrong?"

"No," K'lior replied. "You timed it perfectly. We're going to help Ista Weyr." He beckoned to his wingsecond, P'dor, to join them.

"In fact," he said as P'dor drew close, "we're going to help all the Weyrs." He nodded to P'dor. "Let them know what we've done and discovered."

P'dor jerked his head in acknowledgment and turned away.

"Wait!" T'mar called after him. "You'll need my reports."

K'lior raised a hand to dissuade him, but T'mar shook his head, lifting his carisak from his side. "I wrote 'em out before we left."

"Excellent!" K'lior replied enthusiastically. Then he wagged a finger at the exhausted bronze rider. "Now, get some rest."

"I'm sorry, J'ken, but I can't risk it," B'nik said solemnly to the stricken bronze rider. "Turn your wing over to T'mac."

"But it's just a cough!" J'ken exclaimed desperately, turning to M'tal, Ketan, and the others for support. "And you need every fighting dragon—"

"Exactly," B'nik cut across him. "I can't risk any accidents. That's why J'tol and half my wing aren't flying, either. Limanth has the sickness, so you and he won't fly Thread."

"I made the mistake once," M'tal added. "And you remember what a disaster that was."

J'ken hung his head in resignation.

"You can help with the weyrlings," B'nik offered consolingly. "That will free up P'gul to fly with Kirth."

J'ken gave him a stricken look, swallowed, and nodded wearily.

With a jerk of his head to M'tal, B'nik strode away to supervise the rest of the Weyr in its preparation for Threadfall over Benden.

Ketan and Lorana exchanged looks. He cocked his head

toward B'nik and raised his eyebrows at her questioningly.
Lorana sighed and strode off after B'nik.

"B'nik!" she called out. The Weyrleader stopped and
turned back to her, waving M'tal along.

"This is the last time," B'nik promised, answering her unspoken question, his expression bleak, his hands raised
halfway in entreaty. "M'tal will lead the next Fall."

Lorana nodded and grabbed his hands in hers. "Be careful."

"I will," B'nik promised. "For all our sakes."

"And when you get back, you'll tell Tullea," she said.

B'nik let out a deep sigh and nodded. He turned away
from her, toward his dragon.

"Weyrleader!" she called after him. "Safe Fall!"

B'nik raised his arm in salute.

Lorana was surprised to find, after an hour's searching,
that Kindan was in the Weyr's Records Room once more.

"I thought we'd exhausted this approach," she remarked as
she entered the room and dropped into a chair.

Kindan looked up from his reading and flashed her a hesi-
tant smile.

"We did," he agreed. "I was just looking for maps of the
Weyr to show to Dalor."

"No luck with that other door, then?"

"No," Kindan said, shaking his head ruefully. "But Dalor
doesn't want to use force just yet—he's afraid of jamming
the door shut."

"Wise," Lorana agreed. She gestured toward the Records
spread out in front of him. "Any luck?"

Kindan shrugged and slumped further into his chair. "Not
yet."

Dalor stuck his head in the door just then. "There's a rock
slide down the corridor here, did you know?"

"Yes, that's the one we talked about the last time you were
here. It's been that way for Turns," Kindan replied. "Probably
happened during the last Pass."

"I'd like to try to clear it," Dalor said. "It might not be the right way, but it's not far above the Oldtimer Room and the corridor walls look smooth, like the walls to the Oldtimer Room."

"It's worth a try," Lorana agreed.

"Tullea won't like the noise," Kindan said.

"She'll change her tune when B'nik tells her," Lorana murmured.

"Tells her what?" Dalor asked. Kindan just looked at her.

Lorana frowned, sighing. "Caranth has the illness."

An uncomfortable silence fell.

"We'll find the way through that other door," Dalor declared firmly. With a nod, he turned and left, calling out orders to his miners.

"He'll make a good Masterminer," Kindan said fondly.

"Are you always plotting for your friends?" Lorana asked, grinning.

"Only the good ones," Kindan replied with a grin of his own. His mood changed. "Lorana, I want to apologize—"

Lorana raised a hand and shook her head, silencing him. "We have more important things to consider."

"Not for me," Kindan declared, looking her squarely in the face. "I love you. I—"

"Kindan," Lorana said softly. She rose from her chair and walked to stand behind his. In a flash, she leaned over and wrapped her arms around his neck.

"I love you, too," she murmured into his ear. Then something on the Record he had been perusing caught her eye.

"What's that?" she asked, cocking her head critically and pointing to the lower corner of the Record.

Kindan bent over to peer closely at the spot, then sat bolt upright. "That's it! Those are the Oldtimer Rooms!"

"It looks like there are three," Lorana remarked, peering over his shoulder.

"And it looks like the corridor that Dalor's excavating should lead right into the big one," Kindan agreed.

* * *

"Words are not enough to express our thanks, Weyr-leader," J'lantir called as K'lior and three full-strength wings of Fort dragons burst into the air over Keroon.

"You'd do the same if our roles were reversed," K'lior replied with a dismissive gesture. "After all, 'Dragonmen must fly—' "

Piyolth reports the leading edge of Thread, Lolanth relayed. *Gaminth sends his regards.*

J'lantir peered and could see a group of Benden riders, with a bronze in the lead. He waved back to M'tal just before the Benden riders went *between* to return to Benden Weyr. The number of Benden dragons looked terribly small.

"You've the greater number," J'lantir called, turning back to K'lior, "would you lead the Fall?"

K'lior inclined his head gracefully. "It shall be my honor." He relayed his orders to the riders of the combined Weyrs. As one, dragons turned their heads to their riders, and riders fed them firestone. As one, the fighting dragons of Ista and Fort Weyr rose to defeat the deadly Thread.

"Have M'tal give the coordinates back to the Weyr," B'nik told a coughing, exhausted Caranth.

I think that is wise, the dragon agreed. *Gaminth says that M'tal asks if you're all right. I told him it was me. He said to be careful and asked if we should just fly straight back.*

"Perhaps," B'nik said out loud, patting Caranth's neck fondly. "Are you up for it?"

Another cough wracked Caranth. *I think I would be better going* between. Another cough and a cloud of green ooze engulfed B'nik. *I don't want to fly right now.*

B'nik thought furiously: If they went *between* and Caranth got lost, then they would be lost together; but if they flew straight back, Caranth might get even worse from the extra strain. *Very well,* B'nik told his dragon. *We'll follow Gaminth.*

Lorana says that she'll be waiting, Caranth told him. *She asked,* the dragon volunteered before B'nik could upbraid him. *She says you'll have to tell Tullea.*

B'nik closed his eyes tightly at the thought.

* * *

"Take this to Caranth as soon as they land," Lorana said, pointing out the line of steaming buckets to the weyrlings. There were only two injured dragons, and both had minor injuries. On the other hand, two dragons had not returned from the Fall and eleven more were coughing with the sickness. "Make sure that B'nik gets him to drink them all, no matter how awful it tastes."

"Latest concoction?" Kindan asked, striding up to her from his conference with Dalor above the Records Room.

Lorana grimaced. "It's the same old concoction," she admitted. "Only I added more menthol to ease their breathing—and a bit of coloring," she added.

Kindan quirked an eyebrow.

"Well, sometimes just thinking that something's going to work can make all the difference," she explained forlornly.

Kindan patted her comfortingly on the shoulder. "You're doing your best," he told her.

"Then why are dragons still dying?" she cried, burying her head against him.

"Lorana! Lorana come here now!" It was Tullea. Judging from the look on B'nik's face, he'd just told her his grim news.

"So how long have we got?" B'nik asked, looking around the table in the Records Room at Kindan, Ketan, Lorana, and M'tal.

Kindan was the only one who would meet his eyes. He peered down at the slate in front of him, reluctant to hand it over to the Weyrleader.

"What's that?" B'nik asked, catching Kindan's motion.

"Well, it's not complete," Kindan temporized, "and the numbers are not in agreement, so I suspect some people must have ignored the first signs—"

B'nik cleared his throat loudly and gestured for Kindan to get to the point.

"It's a list of the dragons we've lost," Ketan said. "With

guesses as to how long it was between the first signs of symptoms and when they . . ." his voice trailed off sadly.

Kindan spoke into the awkward silence that followed. "As I said, I suspect that some of these numbers are off because the riders didn't report the symptoms immediately."

"Three sevendays looks to be the longest," Lorana said in a dead voice, looking up to meet B'nik's eyes. "Since Caranth has already been coughing for a while . . ."

"At least a sevenday," B'nik told them quietly. He sat down quickly, resting his head on his hands, eyes closed. Lorana knew that he wasn't talking with Caranth. A moment later he looked up at M'tal, eyes bright. "If anything happens, I want you to take over the Weyr."

"I would prefer it if events do not make that necessary," M'tal responded, gesturing toward B'nik as though to hand back the privilege.

"In any event," B'nik continued, nodding gratefully to M'tal for his support, "I shall need you to lead the next Fall." His mouth worked soundlessly for a moment before he forced himself to say, "Caranth is not up to it."

Lorana let out a sigh of relief. B'nik smiled glumly at her and turned his attention back to M'tal. "There aren't that many fit to fly left."

"I know," M'tal replied. He cast a glance at Ketan.

"We lost another ten dragons last night—five didn't even make it *between,* and their bodies are still in their weyrs," the healer said. "At this rate, we'll lose another twenty from the sickness before next Threadfall."

The others were too shocked to respond.

"Tell him the rest," Kindan said with a wave of his hand.

"We've identified seven more sick dragons this morning," Ketan said.

"Seven!" B'nik was astonished.

"It could be good news," Lorana said hopefully. The others looked at her. "It could be a sign that the infection has peaked and that, after this, the numbers of new dragons catching the sickness will decrease—"

"Only because there won't be any dragons left," Tullea interrupted sourly from the doorway. She strode in, glaring around the room. "Why wasn't I informed of this meeting?"

"You were resting," B'nik explained.

Tullea turned her attention to Lorana. "What are you doing here?"

"She's here at my request," Kindan told her, his voice edged.

"And mine," B'nik added, gesturing for Tullea to take a seat. She remained standing.

"How long has Caranth got?" Tullea demanded of Lorana.

Lorana gestured to Ketan, indicating that he was properly the one to answer.

"I'm asking *you*, dragonkiller," Tullea snarled.

"Tullea!" B'nik shouted, his voice carrying over the angry growls of the others. "You will apologize."

"Why?" Tullea responded silkily. "She killed her dragon, there's no denying it."

"She was looking for a cure," Kindan told her, his eyes flashing in anger.

"If I had known, I would have done the same," Ketan added. He nodded apologetically toward Lorana. "And she's paid the price in full already, without your sniping."

Tullea bridled, clearly not anticipating the outrage she had provoked. "I am Weyrwoman here. You owe me allegiance, Healer!"

Ketan stood up slowly, arching his fingers on the tabletop and leaning on them. "My duty to you, Weyrwoman, was the honor that bound a dragonrider to the rider of the senior queen," he said, spitting out the words. "As I am no longer a dragonrider, who holds my allegiance is now subject to question." He nodded to Lorana. "This lass has made the supreme sacrifice that a queen dragonrider, any rider, can make for the Weyr—she has lost her dragon trying to save us all."

He stood, pushed his chair back and made a half-bow to Lorana before turning away from the table. "My allegiance does not require me to share a room with someone who will disparage her actions."

And without turning back, he left. Kindan got to his feet immediately behind him, dragging a stunned Lorana along.

B'nik broke the shocked silence that followed. "What do you think you were doing?" he shouted at Tullea. "That was completely uncalled for!"

The blood drained from Tullea's face as she looked from B'nik to M'tal and back again, the full impact of her words registering as she absorbed their angry expressions.

When Tullea went looking for Lorana the next day to apologize—after a night of arguing with B'nik—she was infuriated to discover that Lorana's quarters were empty, completely cleared out.

"She's moved," Mikkala reported when Tullea upbraided her about it.

"Where?" Tullea demanded.

Mikkala was reluctant to answer; she bent over her stew and gave it a vigorous stir.

"Mikkala," Tullea repeated, her voice edged with a rising temper, "where is Lorana sleeping?"

"I believe the harper offered her quarters," Mikkala finally replied.

With a frustrated groan, Tullea stamped her foot and rushed out of the Kitchen Cavern toward the harper's quarters. Halfway there, she discovered Lorana, Kindan, M'tal, and B'nik clustered together in conversation.

"What's going on?" she demanded suspiciously, her peace mission forgotten.

"News from Fort Weyr," B'nik told her, his face bright and smiling.

"From Fort?" Tullea barked. "I thought we'd agreed that no more dragonriders should come from other Weyrs."

"Lorana heard it from K'lior's Rineth directly," M'tal explained.

"She can talk to any dragon, you know," B'nik reminded her.

Tullea's expression was sullen. "So, what did Rineth have to say?" she asked Lorana.

"Fort Weyr's weyrlings and injured dragons timed it," Lorana told her.

"So?"

"So they went back to old Igen Weyr, Turns before the start of the Pass, and spent three Turns there. They fought Thread at Keroon two days back."

"Weyrlings? Fought Thread?"

"Not weyrlings any longer," Kindan corrected. "Which is why K'lior had his Rineth contact Lorana. He asked her to spread the word to all the Weyrs. He suggests that if we follow his plan, we'll be able to share time back before the Pass, get our injured dragons healed and weyrlings aged in time to fight the next Threadfall."

"If we sent back the older weyrlings—they should be able to time it—and the injured, we could add nearly two full wings of fighting dragons," M'tal observed.

"Why not send the younger weyrlings?" B'nik asked. "There are more of them."

"Too risky," M'tal responded. "We might lose more on the jump *between* than we can afford."

B'nik nodded in agreement.

"Ketan says he's up for it," B'nik repeated, raising his voice to be heard above Caranth's raspy coughing.

"He just lost his dragon!" Tullea declared angrily. "What makes you think he cares?"

B'nik bit back angry words before he hurled them irretrievably at Tullea, but he couldn't hide the fury in his eyes.

"What will you do if Caranth dies, B'nik?" Tullea asked. "Who will fly Minith then?"

B'nik gave her a pleading look. "She hasn't laid her clutch yet," he told her. "It will be a long while before she rises to mate again."

"Ketan should stay here, continue working for a cure," Tullea persisted.

"Tullea," B'nik said reasonably, "if Ketan goes with the weyrlings and injured dragons, he'll have Turns to work on a cure *and* we'll have fit dragons to fight the next Fall."

B'nik did not point out that, as he was sending only the weyrlings and injured dragons, Ketan would have no sick dragons to work with. But that had been B'nik's plan—to let Ketan recover from his loss, helping healthy young dragons grow to maturity.

"You do what you want," Tullea told him after a long moment sulking in silence. "You're Weyrleader."

"Yes," B'nik declared firmly, "I am."

"Where are you going?" she called as he strode out of their quarters.

"To let Ketan know my decision," B'nik replied, turning back in the doorway. "We've got a lot to arrange and little time."

"I thought you said they'd be gone three whole Turns," Tullea retorted.

"*They* will," B'nik agreed. "But *we'll* only have two days."

Kindan found Lorana in the Supply Caverns, supervising the movement of medical supplies assigned for the injured dragons who were designated to go back in time with Ketan. He waited until he could catch her alone and said quietly, "How do we know we aren't sending sick dragons back in time?"

"We don't," Lorana admitted, grimacing. "Ketan and I have screened all of the dragons carefully and not one of them has any signs of the sickness, but . . ."

"So could *we* have brought the sickness back in time and infected the Weyrs?" Kindan asked pointedly.

Lorana creased her brow thoughtfully. She shook her head. "It had to start somewhere, so I don't think it came back from now to then," she decided in the end. "Besides, it's not so much a question of where it came from as it is how to cure it."

Kindan shrugged, acknowledging her point.

"How are the miners doing?" she asked, waiting for a group of sweaty weyrlings to haul their burdens past them.

"They're doing well," Kindan replied. "Dalor tells me that he thinks the same thing happened on the upper passage as on the lower. If he's right and it's just a rock slide, they won't have more than a spear-length of rock to remove."

"So another day or two?"

"Yes, about that," Kindan agreed.

"That will be just about when Ketan and the weyrlings return."

"Right in time for the Fall over Nerat," Kindan agreed.

A weyrling approached Lorana, wiping sweat out of his eye and giving her a questioning, if hopeful, look. Lorana smiled at him. "No, that's the last of it, J'nor."

She gestured for him to rejoin the Weyrlingmaster and then jerked her head at Kindan, inviting him to follow her out of the Supply Caverns and up into the Bowl.

The part of the Bowl nearest the Supply Cavern was busy but organized. P'gul, the Weyrlingmaster, had taken charge, delegating some work to Ketan and the more able of the injured dragonriders. He, B'nik, and M'tal were conferring together.

"Now," B'nik was saying to P'gul as Lorana and Kindan approached, "You'll take care to return precisely in two days' time just before dusk."

"That's cutting things tight, isn't it?" P'gul asked.

"It can't be helped," B'nik replied. "I don't want you or any of the others coming back too soon—I'd hate for you to meet yourself coming or going, and the weyrlings—"

"Won't be weyrlings when we get back," P'gul observed.

"That's true," B'nik replied. "And I'm sure they'll be well-trained in all the recognition points. But just as I expect them to be trained, I expect them not to be trained in timing—or else one of them will try it on their own before they're ready."

"There is that," P'gul admitted.

"Good man!" B'nik replied, smiling and clapping the dour Weyrlingmaster on the back. "It'll be three Turns for you, but only two days for us."

P'gul nodded. "I just wish that we knew more of what to expect when we go back in time."

"Rineth reports that it doesn't bother the dragons at all,"

Lorana said, inserting herself into the conversation with an apologetic look at B'nik. "But the riders are all confused and get very irritable."

M'tal nodded, then stopped, looking thoughtful.

"Is there something you want to add, M'tal?" B'nik asked.

"Hmm?" M'tal roused himself, then shook his head. "No, no, just an odd thought that crossed my mind."

For a moment B'nik considered whether to press M'tal for details, but then he decided against it. He turned back to P'gul.

"Well, I envy you the peace and relaxation you'll have with those weyrlings," he said to the older dragonrider, eliciting a humorous snort from all around.

"I'll try to remember that, Weyrleader, when I'm relaxing in the warmth of the Igen sands," P'gul replied, with a faint smile. He waved to the group, then mounted his brown dragon and signalled to the rest of the weyrlings and injured dragons.

"Good flying!" B'nik shouted to everyone.

His words were drowned out as wave after wave of dragons took to the air and circled up to the Star Stones.

When all the dragons were properly aligned, P'gul gave a signal—

"Lorana, don't try to follow them," M'tal said urgently as he saw her close her eyes.

—and the dragons winked *between*.

Lorana opened her eyes and looked at M'tal.

"I don't know if your mind wouldn't get lost *between* times," he explained.

Kindan looked from M'tal to Lorana and grabbed her hand tightly in his. Lorana squeezed his hand in reply.

"This is utterly untraditional!" D'gan declared in outrage to his wingleaders as they met at Telgar's Council Room. "I cannot believe that an ex-dragonrider would have the nerve to address herself to my *dragon* and not me."

"What did she say?" D'nal asked.

"Kaloth tells me that she said that Fort Weyr has successfully sent their injured dragons and riders back in time, along with their weyrlings, to the abandoned Igen Weyr," D'gan replied with a sniff.

"Really?" L'rat exclaimed, his eyes going wide. "That explains the fires we saw Turns back—do you remember, V'gin?"

The Weyr healer nodded reminiscently. "We thought perhaps they were traders or something using the Weyr."

"And *why* wasn't this reported to me?" D'gan asked archly.

"I'm sure it was," L'rat said. "But it would have been just about the time of the Plague, if memory serves. I'm sure we all had other things to worry about."

"They went back in time," V'gin said quickly, "to what purpose?"

"Why, to heal, of course," D'gan responded, as though it should have been obvious to all of them.

"But they could have healed just as easily here," L'rat remarked, frowning.

"But they *timed* it," D'gan snapped. "So that they were gone only days in our time while they spent Turns."

"So their weyrlings grew up and their injured recovered," V'gin surmised, nodding at the neat solution. "That's very clever." He looked at the Weyrleader. "Did you say K'lior at Fort had the idea?"

D'nal shot him a sharp look. Everyone knew that D'gan had no time for Fort's Weyrleader, nor any other Weyrleader, for that matter.

"So what else did this Lorana say, D'gan?" L'rat asked quickly, hoping to avert another of the Weyrleader's outbursts.

"She said—and this I cannot countenance—that Benden was going to use the three Turns starting nine Turns back and she advised us to consider going back six Turns if we wanted to use it," D'gan replied angrily. "As if Benden could dictate how we use our Weyr!"

"Well," L'rat replied honestly, "it's not really our Weyr anymore, is it?"

D'gan's eyes bulged at the Wingleader's pronouncement.

"We're Telgar riders now," V'gin declared, nodding in agreement with L'rat's declaration. "We have no claim on Igen."

"I think it's more important to consider whether it would help us," D'nal said, trying to defuse any needless argument. "If we had all our injured dragons and riders ready to fight at Upper Crom, we'd have more than twice the strength we have now."

D'gan sat down in his chair, his lips thinned angrily, but his eyes were thoughtful.

"If you added the older weyrlings—it wouldn't do to send the youngest ones back, they wouldn't survive the trip—then there would be another full wing on top of that," V'gin added. He looked up at the others, eyes gleaming. "Why, we'd nearly be back to full strength!"

"That's true," D'gan agreed, still looking distracted.

"I make it nearly three hundred and thirty fighting dragons," D'nal said, totting up the numbers in his head. "And today we've only got a bit more than one hundred and twenty."

"Food's no problem," D'gan declared. "This Lorana person said that Fort had left them with plenty and they'd pass on the favor." He snorted. "I'll bet Fort just herded up the beasts we'd let run free."

D'nal and L'rat exchanged satisfied glances.

"So shall we do this, then?" V'gin asked. "I must say, it seems an excellent idea."

"Yes, it does," D'gan agreed sourly, silently berating himself for not having thought of it on his own. While it galled him to admit that K'lior had had a worthwhile idea, he could tell by the looks of his Wingleaders that he had no choice but to go with it. He leaned forward, determined. "Very well, we'll do it."

He turned to D'nal. "I'll want those dragons back in time to fight at Crom."

"I understand, Weyrleader," D'nal replied, realizing that

the job had been delegated to him. "Should I take D'lin with me?"

L'rat and V'gin gazed curiously at D'gan. D'lin was his eldest son and had Impressed a well-bred bronze more than a Turn ago; they were all sure that D'gan was grooming him as his eventual successor. Having the lad time, it would put him in a position to take over from his sire in short order, should anything untoward happen to Telgar's Weyrleader.

"D'lin?" D'gan asked, amused at the question. He shook his head. "No, he'll stay here with me. He still needs seasoning." Having made his decision, he rose, dismissing the others and terminating the meeting.

L'rat and D'nal exchanged nervous glances as they headed toward the exit of the Council Room. Next door they could hear the unmistakable coughing of a dragon suffering from the sickness—D'gan's own Kaloth.

"I thought you should have the honors," B'nik said softly to Lorana. They stood at the end of the newly-cleared corridor.

Dalor had been right: The rock slide had only blocked part of the way. Once the miners had removed the fallen rock, the corridor was clear and open, running straight along until it stopped in front of a set of stairs leading down.

At the bottom of the stairs, another short corridor led to a door. At the side of the door the miners had discovered another square plate, just like the one Tullea had discovered in the first room.

B'nik hefted a long stick—a liberated broom handle—and offered it to Lorana.

"You might want to stand back and use this, in case the air is bad," he suggested.

Lorana nodded and gratefully took the stick while B'nik waved Dalor, Kindan, and Ketan back up the stairs.

"Push it and run back," Kindan called down to her.

Lorana grabbed the stick in both hands to steady it, then leaned forward and pushed the plate.

For a moment, nothing happened. Then a groaning noise

could be heard from beyond the door. Slowly the door slid open, revealing a well-lit room beyond. Entranced, Lorana forgot to run: She peered in, and the bad air caught her.

When she awoke later, Kindan was leaning over her; his look of concern vanished into one of sardonic humor the moment her eyelids fluttered open. She realized she was in his quarters, lying on his bed.

"I thought you were going to run," he chided her.

Lorana shrugged. "I was trying to see what was inside." She pushed herself up.

"You would have seen sooner, if you'd run," he told her, helping her to her feet. "But B'nik decided to wait until you were able before letting anyone into the room."

"That was nice of him," Lorana said.

Kindan considered this. "I'm not so sure he intended to be nice as much as he wanted to be sure that we did not repeat the mistakes we made last time." He paused. "Tullea has not been invited."

"Let's go," Lorana said, feeling a sense of urgency.

"Why the rush? The room has waited all this time, it can wait a little longer."

A cough from up high near the Weyrleader's quarters echoed harshly across the Weyr Bowl—and then was repeated by dozens of other dragons.

"The dragons can't," Lorana said hoarsely.

Mutualistic: A symbiotic relationship in which each species benefits.

Chapter Twenty-one

College, First Interval, AL 58

"WELL, THAT WENT WELL," M'hall murmured in Emorra's ear as the gathering broke for lunch.

"I thought it was a shambles," Emorra replied.

M'hall smiled and shook his head. "You haven't seen the Weyrleader's Council." His smile vanished. "So what's next?"

Tieran, who had seen them from across the room, approached and suggested, "Perhaps we should eat in the faculty room?"

M'hall looked around and noticed that, while they were not the only group gathered in the room, they were the group gathering the most attention. He waved a hand toward the door. "Lead on."

In the faculty room they found Wind Blossom and Janir, heads close together in soft but intense conversation. Wind Blossom paused to wave, but immediately resumed her conversation with Janir.

"The question is, how do we teach people we don't even know?" Tieran said as they found a small group of seats.

Emorra disagreed. "I think the question is, what can those people do?"

"I think the most important question is where they'll do their work and how we'll keep the wrong people away from it," M'hall observed.

"Well, it'll have to be Benden," Tieran said in an offhand

manner. He turned back to Emorra. "Surely if we can teach them, then it won't matter what they can do."

"Excuse me," M'hall interrupted, "but why do you think it'll have to be Benden?"

"Because whoever rode that queen obviously came—will come—from Benden," Tieran replied. "We don't know how people will travel then, and her queen was too young, I assume, to take her anywhere yet—"

"You're right, there," M'hall confirmed. "Although she was so big . . ."

"I think that carrying a rider is a question more of bone and muscle maturity, particularly bone, than of size," Emorra observed. M'hall acknowledged this with a nod and turned his attention back to Tieran.

"So, I think that Benden's the right place," Tieran concluded.

"Don't you have some nice geothermals there?" Emorra asked.

"We do," M'hall agreed. "Although how long we can keep the active systems alive is a good question. We're already having parts problems with the electrical distribution."

"So it'd have to be passive, then," Emorra noted. "If my memory is correct, the power supplies on the Eridani equipment are rated for centuries when not in use."

"How long will the power last when they're *in* use?" M'hall asked.

"They'll support decades of continuous use," Emorra said. "From what Mother told me, the Eridani try to engineer their equipment for the long term."

M'hall was impressed. "Four centuries is definitely 'long term.'"

Tieran shook his head. "Wind Blossom said that the Eridani think in millennia and more."

The door to the faculty room opened and Seamus O'Connell peered in. M'hall smiled and waved him over.

"I was wondering when you'd come wandering by," M'hall said as his youngest and largest brother pulled a seat over to join them.

"The Lord Holders have been on to me about the stone-cutters," Seamus began with no preamble. "It occurs to me that you might want them yourself for this project."

"It didn't seem clear to me that this project has been approved," Emorra remarked.

Seamus glanced at M'hall for confirmation. M'hall laughed. "My little brother is making his feelings on the notion quite clear."

Tieran looked thoughtfully at the two of them. "You mean, where Benden leads, who will fail to follow?"

"Only when Benden is right," Seamus added in his soft, deep voice. He gave Tieran a frank look. "It's a risky proposition, but . . ."

"Our parents thrived on similar 'risky propositions,'" M'hall finished.

"The dragons," Tieran guessed.

"So it seems fair that we should entrust their deliverance to the same family that has guarded them so well," Emorra said with a nod toward M'hall.

"It's not that," Seamus demurred. "Benden makes more sense." At the others' questioning looks, the big engineer explained, "I've looked over the survey maps of the Weyr. There aren't many places to hide a new structure. But there is one good place, except . . ."

"What?" M'hall prompted.

"It is situated near a fault line," Seamus replied. "I can almost guarantee that the rooms will be cut off from the Weyr by a rock slide within the century." He winked at them and added conspiratorially, "Or sooner, if need be."

"But why—" Emorra began.

"Oh!" Tieran interrupted. "I see." He turned to Emorra. "We build the rooms and then cut them off from the rest of the Weyr so that no one will disturb them until they're needed."

"But how will anyone know about them?" Emorra asked. Tieran shrugged.

"So you'd be wanting the stonecutters, then?" Seamus

asked. He looked at each of them in turn, then added, "Because if you do, you'll have to fight Mendin to get them."

Mendin consoled himself that he still had two of the stonecutters and that possession was nine-tenths of the law. All he needed was to find sufficiently trained personnel to use them—and quickly. He could see himself apologizing oh-so-obsequiously to the Weyrleaders: "Oh, I am sorry! If only I'd known beforehand that you wanted them."

Yes, that apology would do nicely, Mendin decided. He was about to call over one of his minions when he was distracted by a commotion at the door.

It was his oldest son, Leros, whom Mendin had left to mind the Hold.

"The stonecutters are gone," Leros whispered when they were seated and the others in the room had returned to their own conversations. "Dragonriders from Benden Weyr took them."

For a moment blind fury coursed through Mendin's veins. How dare they!

He reasserted an iron grip on himself before his emotions were displayed on his face.

"I see," he said aloud, furiously racking his brain for a way to turn this to his advantage. He looked up at Leros. "I think that Fort Hold should throw its full support behind this project."

He turned to the others and raised his voice so that all could hear. "I can see now that this will be a great legacy to our descendants and nothing less than they would expect of us. Just as our ancestors bequeathed us the dragons for our defense, so we should bequeath these medical rooms for the defense of the dragons."

The other Lord Holders exchanged looks as they digested this change of tack on Mendin's part.

"I agree," Malon of Tillek seconded firmly. "Pern is nothing without the dragons."

And so it was decided.

* * *

"You are the most well-trained doctor we have," Wind Blossom began again, hoping that somehow repetition might alter Janir's response.

"In human physiology, Wind Blossom," Janir protested again. "I know nothing of the dragons or the Pernese genetic code."

"But you've learned so much that is applicable through your medical training," Wind Blossom replied. "It wouldn't take you long to pick up on the Pernese genetics."

"But I am the head physician," Janir objected. "I will never have the time you'll need." He took a deep breath and shook his head in wonderment at her obstinacy. "I will have too many patients to deal with and there is no substitute. In fact, I should be training my replacement this very moment."

Wind Blossom raised her eyebrows.

"I should be training *three* replacements," Janir corrected himself in response to her unspoken query. "And *that* will also eat into my time." He glanced over at Emorra and Tieran. "You are going to have to use them—they know more about this than I do."

Wind Blossom deflated with a sigh. "I suppose you are right," she conceded. "But if I cannot convince them . . ."

"Then ask M'hall," Janir replied. "I think he'll convince them."

"If he can't, then I want to know that you'll take their place," Wind Blossom declared.

"If they won't work with you, Wind Blossom, we'll talk again," Janir replied.

Just then M'hall entered the room, wearing a victorious look.

Late that evening, well after the Holders and Weyrleaders had unanimously agreed to use the last of the stonecutters to create a medical laboratory at Benden Weyr, and had agreed that Wind Blossom would be responsible for its contents, Emorra found herself in the faculty lounge along with Tieran. Wind Blossom had gone to her bed much earlier, after informing Tieran and Emorra that she would require their help on the project.

Cool, clear Benden wine had been poured liberally in celebration.

"Tieran," Emorra said as the effects of the wine belatedly registered on her, "I've drunk more than I should. We'll need our rest. Mother will be certain to want to start early in the morning."

Tieran looked reluctantly at his half-full glass, tossed it back in one gulp, and rose. "May I escort you to your room?"

Emorra dimpled, and allowed Tieran to help her to her feet.

Tieran realized that he was taller than Emorra; he couldn't remember when that had happened. Her cheeks were flushed with wine and her eyes—her almond eyes were warm and enticing.

"If I made a pass at you," he suddenly asked, "would you mind?"

"No," Emorra said softly, leaning toward him.

Tentatively, Tieran leaned forward and kissed her.

In the two days since the council, Wind Blossom appropriated a classroom, turned a surgery into a lab, and slept for a grand total of six hours—Tieran knew because he'd gone to sleep *after* she did, and he'd gotten a bit more than five hours of sleep.

They were in the classroom now. Wind Blossom was at the blackboard, chalk in hand, writing down their suggestions.

"The dragons must save themselves," Wind Blossom pronounced. Tieran bit back a retort as he noticed the look of intense concentration on her face.

"Are you saying that they will build an immunity?" Emorra asked as Wind Blossom's silence lengthened. "But we have no way of knowing the mortality rate of this infection."

"We do not know enough about this illness," Wind Blossom declared. "The people in the future know about it, but we do not."

She paused to let the others comment, but Tieran and Emorra only nodded in wary agreement.

"We know how to alter the genetic code of the dragons, and we know how to create specimens and map genetic material, but they do not."

Again, she paused for comment and again, there was none.

"They cannot bring their knowledge to us without also bringing the infection itself," Wind Blossom continued. "So we must bring our knowledge to them."

"But M'hall said the dragonriders couldn't—" Tieran protested.

At the same time Emorra cried, "That would infect our dragons, too!"

Wind Blossom rapped the chalk on the blackboard, the noise echoing harshly around the room, until the other two were silent.

"We will teach them," she declared. "We will teach them how to collect specimens, use the mapper, and construct genetic code."

Tieran sat back again in his chair, his brows furrowed thoughtfully. Beside him, Emorra gnawed her lip unconsciously, her eyes closed in concentration.

"You mean we'll make classrooms?" Tieran asked after a while. "To teach people chemistry, biology, and technology?"

He shook his head. "I don't see how we can do it."

Wind Blossom frowned at him. "Teach them how to identify the infection and how to engineer an antigen," she said. "That is not hard."

"So you mean to explain everything in layman terms," Emorra said. She cocked her head in consideration. "It could work."

Tieran gave Wind Blossom a penetrating stare. "It bothers me that there has never been a report of illness in the fire-lizards. I thought it was an axiom that an ecosystem will always evolve."

"You're saying that something should have come up in eight years?" Emorra asked, frowning in disbelief.

"No, in fifty years," Tieran answered. "In the same time, we've had a major epidemic nearly wipe us humans out, and yet the fire-lizards, dragons, watch-whers, wherries, and, for all I know, tunnel-snakes seem not to have suffered from any form of viral, bacterial, or fungal assaults."

"I see what you mean," Emorra replied.

"You are forgetting Pernese genetic code," Wind Blossom said, shaking her head in disappointment.

"No, I'm—" Tieran said hotly, only to cut himself off. "Oh," he admitted, going slowly pink, "I am."

"What about it?" Emorra asked, looking from Tieran to Wind Blossom and back for an explanation. Wind Blossom gestured to Tieran to answer.

Tieran took a breath. "Well, you have to remember how Pernese genetic code differs from ours."

"Mmm?" Emorra murmured, gesturing for him to continue.

"Well, our genetic code is composed of two strands of DNA joined in a double helix," Tieran said. "Whereas Pernese genetic code is composed of three strands of what we call PNA joined in a twisted triangle.

"Two of the strands complement the major strand," he went on. He walked up to the blackboard and gestured to Wind Blossom, who surrendered the chalk. With a nod of thanks, Tieran turned to the blackboard and began to draw. He drew a series of triangles stacked on top of each other, each twisted slightly out of line with the one preceding it. The corners of the triangles he filled in with dots. He proceeded to label the dots: A, A', N; B, N, B'; C, C', N.

On another part of the board he drew the long-familiar double helix of DNA, creating a twisted ladder and labeling the "rungs" on one half of the ladder, A, C, G, T while labeling the other side of the ladder T, G, C, A.

Tieran jabbed a finger at each of the letters in turn. "A stands for adenine, C for cytosine, G for guanine, and T for thymine.

"They are grouped in threes and each group of three is called a codon," he said. "Each codon codes either an amino acid or is a special marking signifying the start or end of a genetic sequence.

"Because there are four possible amines taken three at a time, there are sixty-four possible variations, but terrestrial DNA only encodes twenty amino acids along with one start and one stop codon."

"I remember now," Emorra said. "It always seemed wasteful."

"It allows room for expansion," Tieran said. "It also allows for errors or mutations to creep in. Typically there are six to seven hundred mutations in each newborn."

"So that's why we get sick," Emorra remarked.

"More because the viruses and bacteria that attack us mutate than because of our mutations," Tieran replied. "But sometimes it is our mutations that cause problems."

He turned to the twisted triangle of the Pernese genetic code.

"Here, A, B, and C are only simple names for the different Pernese amines that make up their genetic material," Tieran said. He pointed to the dot marked A'. "A-prime, here, is merely the amine that binds to A, and so on for B-prime and C-prime."

"So what's N?" Emorra asked. "Null?"

"Exactly," Tieran agreed. "One of the fundamental differences between Pernese genetic material and terrestrial DNA is that instead of having two strands that are mirror images of each other, PNA has a main strand and two other strands that alternately mirror the main strand."

"So does PNA have four pairs in a codon?" Emorra asked.

Tieran shook his head. "No, just three like our DNA."

Emorra raised her eyebrows at that. "So that means that PNA can only code twenty-seven variations."

"That's right," Tieran said. "Of course, we only need twenty-two out of the sixty-four that can be coded with DNA, so PNA is actually more efficient."

"They code twenty amino acids?" Emorra asked, looking at Wind Blossom.

"No, they code twenty-three amino acids," Wind Blossom corrected.

"They also code two different START and STOP sequences," Tieran remarked. "That leaves no spare codings."

"The combination of the three strands makes it harder for PNA to be split," Wind Blossom said.

"Wouldn't that be bad?" Emorra asked. "As I recall, whenever genetic material is accessed, the strands are separated and a segment is copied."

"That's not exact," Wind Blossom replied chillingly. "But it is sufficient for our current discussion." She waved for Tieran to continue. Stifling an impulse to argue with her, he turned back to Emorra.

"The fact that Pernese genetic material—"

"Didn't you say to call it PNA?" Emorra interjected.

"—PNA, then, is harder to separate means that mutations in the PNA are less likely than in terrestrial DNA," Tieran said. He looked at Wind Blossom and asked, "Is that why you think there haven't been any illnesses? Because PNA is so much less prone to mutations than DNA?"

"It is just as prone," Wind Blossom corrected. "However, the rate is slower."

Tieran waved away the correction as meaningless.

"There is a big difference," Wind Blossom persisted. "It means that over time, PNA will have mutations."

"It still means that in the same period of time there will be more mutations in DNA than in PNA," Emorra said, coming to Tieran's defense.

"That's not all," Tieran said. "The very resistance to change means that PNA is less able to deal with unwanted mutations."

"Oh, I think PNA deals with mutations quite admirably," Wind Blossom said dryly.

Emorra looked to Tieran for enlightenment.

He shrugged. "She means that most mutations will be fatal immediately."

"And PNA is the same for everything Pernese?" Emorra asked. At Tieran's nod, she mused, "So whatever is affecting the fire-lizards and dragons in the future could be as simple as a symbiont that's mutated into a parasite?"

"It could be," Wind Blossom agreed.

"But how does that alter our problem?" Emorra asked. "Regardless of the origin, we have to teach our descendants how to effect a cure."

"And you will undertake to teach our distant descendants how to use the mapper?" Wind Blossom asked.

"Of course," Emorra said. "But I'll need Tieran."

"*I* shall need Tieran," Wind Blossom countered.

"We'll share," Emorra said as a compromise.

"Agreed," Wind Blossom said, with a faint triumphant light in her dark eyes.

Tieran looked from mother to daughter and back again and, wisely, kept his silence.

Tieran and Emorra stood on either side of a blackboard with identical expressions. They had managed to fill the blackboard twice with just the highlights of the materials they had to cover.

"If this were a lecture, how long do you think it would take?" Emorra asked Tieran.

The young man frowned thoughtfully before shaking his head. "I don't know. Perhaps more important is how long they can afford to sit still just learning."

"What, are you afraid that they'll race ahead and start using the materials before they properly know how?"

"Wouldn't you, in their situation?" Tieran asked.

"We'll have to come up with a way to slow them down, then," Emorra said. "Some sort of test, a hurdle they have to pass before they can move on."

Tieran pursed his lips thoughtfully. Before he could reply, the door to the classroom burst open. It was Carelly.

"Come quickly, Wind Blossom needs you!"

The two exchanged alarmed looks and raced out the door to follow.

Upstairs, they found Wind Blossom lying in bed. Never before had they seen her looking so pale, so feeble.

"What is it, Mother?" Emorra asked, grabbing a chair and looking down worriedly.

"We have failed," Wind Blossom said. "The gene mappers cannot store all the data."

"What?" Tieran barked in surprise.

"There is too much data," Wind Blossom repeated. "With all the information on the various immune codings, there is at least three times more data than the mapper can store."

"So we eliminate some," Emorra suggested, matter-of-factly.

"What if we eliminate the wrong data?" Tieran asked her, shaking his head.

"So, we don't," Emorra replied.

"And how can we do that?" Tieran demanded. "Are they just supposed to tell us what they need?"

Emorra's eyes widened as she absorbed Tieran's words.

"Yes," she said. "And that will be the key to opening the second door in the classrooms."

Harper, teach.
Miner, mine.
Smith, forge.
Healer, cure.
Dragonrider, protect them all.

Chapter Twenty-two

Benden Weyr, Third Pass, 26th Day, AL 508

KINDAN SMILED at Lorana as she paused at the bottom of the stairs leading to the Oldtimer Rooms.

"It's all right," he told her. "I've been in them." She cocked an eyebrow at him. "And I touched nothing."

"We should get Ketan," she said.

"Right behind you!" Ketan called out, clattering down the stairs to join them. He and the weyrlings—now grown dragons and riders—had returned the day before, exhausted. Of the lot, the weyrfolk without dragons had fared best, Ketan included. "I saw you headed this way."

Reassured, Lorana moved in front of Kindan and was the first in the room. The sound of a disembodied voice stopped her in her tracks.

"Welcome," it said. "I am Wind Blossom. If you have come to these rooms for an emergency involving the dragons, then please step inside. If not, please leave immediately."

Eyes glowing, Lorana turned back to the other two, who stood poised in the doorway.

"She said her name was Wind Blossom," Lorana called, gesturing excitedly for the others to enter.

"The song was right," Kindan whispered, entering the

room and peering cautiously around, as though afraid that his gaze might damage some unknown treasure.

"Indeed it was," Ketan agreed, pointing to the far wall. There was a door outlined, but no sign of a square plate with which to open it. Instead, written on the door in strange paint was:

"That word is what you now must say
To open up the door
In Benden Weyr, to find the way
To all my healing lore."

The voice changed to another's. "I am Emorra, Wind Blossom's daughter. Please, if you have come here to learn how to conquer the dragons' illness, go to the first cabinet labeled 'A' and take the booklets there—one copy for each of you." The voice paused. "When you have done that, please take one of the chairs and we will continue."

Lorana gave Kindan a nervous look, but he nodded firmly to her and the cabinet.

"Apparently we are to be schooled," Ketan surmised as Lorana passed a booklet to him. He glanced at it. "This may take a while."

"Then the sooner we start, the better," Lorana declared, seating herself.

Before she could open the booklet, footsteps on the stairs outside caught her attention.

"May we join you?" M'tal asked, as he and Salina appeared in the doorway.

Lorana, Kindan, and Ketan exchanged looks. "I don't see why not," Lorana replied.

"The more help, the better," Ketan agreed.

"Excellent," M'tal replied, nodding his head in thanks. "And Kiyary has promised to bring down refreshments in two hours."

Ketan smiled. "I hadn't thought of that," he admitted. Neither, from their sheepish looks, had Kindan or Lorana.

"There are booklets in that cabinet behind us," Lorana said, gesturing. "We were just getting started."

"It was the most amazing thing," Ketan added. "When we first entered, the voice of Wind Blossom herself greeted us."

M'tal and Salina looked both surprised—and somewhat disappointed at having missed it.

"When everyone is ready," the voice of Emorra spoke from the ceiling above them, "please have someone close the door. Instructions will be played while the door is closed and everyone is seated. If you wish to take a break, simply either all stand, or have someone open the door. The instructions will resume from where they left off when the door is again closed and people are seated.

"Please note that there is no way to know how many of you are present, so if one of you must leave, be sure to leave the door open until that person returns, or she will miss parts of the instruction." There was a pause. "Now, the first thing to do is to read the first chapter of the booklet. If you have problems reading the text, you will have to see if you can locate someone who can read it for you. If you *do* have such problems, please leave the room immediately. The power required to light this room and provide my voice is limited and will eventually fail.

"At the end of the first chapter you will find instructions on how to indicate that you have finished the first chapter and understand it."

Kindan's furrowed his brows in puzzlement. "That will be some trick," he said.

"You may start reading whenever you are ready," Emorra's voice said. "Please do not stand on courtesy, as I am not present—this is merely a recording of my voice."

All five of them exchanged astonished looks, and Ketan mouthed the word "recording" to himself, trying to grasp the full flavor of its meaning. But Lorana was less interested in the Oldtimer skills than she was in finding a cure for the dragons. Avidly, she opened the booklet and began to read.

"The dragons and watch-whers of Pern are modifications of the indigenous fire-lizards," the booklet began. "It was possible to make the much larger dragons and watch-whers from the fire-lizards because all living things contain a set of instructions telling the creature how and what to grow to make a complete living being.

"These instructions are embodied in a genetic code," the booklet continued. Lorana leaned forward and immersed herself in the wonders of genetic codes.

An hour later, she got up from her seat, stretched, and walked to the cabinets. She opened the one marked B, pulled out a tray of equipment, and returned to her seat.

"What are you doing?" Kindan asked, looking up from his book.

"Well, I'm ready to start the first experiment," she explained. "You know, the one at the end of chapter two."

"Chapter two?" Kindan said in astonishment. "You're already done with chapter two? I'm still trying to finish chapter one."

Before Lorana could reply, Ketan piped up, "No, don't wait up for us, Lorana. If we don't catch up soon, maybe you'll explain it to us."

Lorana nodded and resumed her seat. Immediately she turned to the beginning of chapter three and started working with the equipment.

The bulk of the equipment consisted of small colored objects, about the size of the tip of her thumb. They weren't quite balls, being planed off and grooved on four sides—top, bottom, and two sides that met in a corner—the booklet said that they represented the fundamental genetic material. The blue object was for the A molecule, the red object represented a B molecule, the green a C molecule; the purple object represented a C-prime object, the magenta object was for B-prime, and the yellow object was for A-prime. There was a seventh object—a beige one—that represented the N or Null molecule. There was also a pencil and a tablet of paper, which she was to use to record her answers.

Lorana quickly assembled three of the objects—blue, yellow, and beige—into a triangle. In short order she had built another triangle—red, beige, and blue—and carefully slid the two triangles one on top of the other. With a gentle movement, she twisted the top triangle slightly and felt it lock into place.

Delighted, she gave a cry of joy, which startled the others. They looked up at her and then gathered around in wonder.

"What is it?" M'tal asked, eyeing the object eagerly.

"Are you building a sequence?" Ketan asked.

Salina craned her neck to get a better view. "Is it a START sequence or a STOP sequence?"

"Ahem." Kindan cleared his throat loudly. "Some of us are still reading."

"Some of us are *slow,*" someone—it sounded like Ketan—murmured in response. Kindan reddened and bent his head back over his booklet, pointedly ignoring them all.

The sound of footsteps outside heralded the arrival of Kiyary and several others from the Kitchens with refreshments.

"Is it lunchtime already?" Kindan asked in surprise.

"We can eat while we work," Lorana said, helping Kiyary place a tray on the workbench in the rear of the room. Kiyary muttered a quick thanks, her eyes wide as she peered around the room in awe.

"So the Oldtimers made these rooms for us?" Kiyary asked.

"We heard the voice of Wind Blossom," Ketan told her. "Her mother created the dragons."

"And they can help us now?" Kiyary asked.

"That's the hope," M'tal said, helping himself to a mug of *klah* and some sweetrolls.

"And if they can't?" Tilara asked, crossing the room with another platter. She set it down beside the one Kiyary had brought. "What then?"

Ketan and Lorana exchanged looks. "We will find a cure," Lorana told the older woman firmly. "By ourselves, if necessary."

Tilara gave Lorana a probing look and, satisfied, nodded. "I'd heard that you felt the death of every dragon," she commented.

Lorana nodded, her eyes dark with sorrow.

"Then no one has a better reason to find a cure than you."

She turned away from Lorana and started bustling around the platters and chivying Kiyary to get everything just so. When she turned back again, her eyes were bright with tears and she had a plate with several sweetrolls on it.

"You haven't eaten yet," Tilara said, thrusting the plate at Lorana. She gestured to one of the chairs. "Sit, and eat."

"But—"

"You'll learn nothing with a growling stomach," Tilara insisted.

"She's right, you know," M'tal agreed, stuffing another sweetroll into his mouth.

"And if you choke to death, you'll do us no good, either," Tilara scolded the ex-Weyrleader. Salina added a quick murmur of agreement, giving her weyrmate a dark look.

Lorana's attempts to bolt her food were also thwarted.

"I spent more time making them than you are eating them," Tilara told her reprovingly. "Stop to taste them, at least, girl!"

Lorana reddened, but she did slow down, and as she did so, she realized that Tilara and Kiyary had outdone themselves in making the sweetrolls. They were pungent, sometimes spicy, with thin slices of wherry meat, some sauce that Lorana didn't recognize, and thin-sliced vegetables artfully mixed in. Some were cold and others were hot, and all together they were more of a meal than a snack.

When they were all full and the sweetrolls gone, Tilara bustled Kiyary into collecting the used plates back onto the trays.

"We'll leave the *klah* here for you," Tilara said. "It won't get cold for a while—I've put a warmer over it." And with that she headed back to the kitchens, Kiyary in tow.

By evening they had made far more progress, but it was not enough for Lorana.

"We're still no nearer to figuring out how to open that door," she said, jabbing her finger toward the poem-decorated door on the far wall of the classroom. "And we've no better idea how to save the dragons."

"Mmm, I'm not so sure about that," Ketan disagreed. "We know that dragons, like fire-lizards, have natural defenses against disease."

"So?" Lorana demanded.

"And we know that this disease overwhelms those natural defenses," Ketan added.

"That's all we do know," Kindan snapped, sharing Lorana's disappointment and anger.

"And we know about PNA and how it contains the codes for all the vital operations of the dragons, and all Pernese lifeforms," Ketan continued. "I think that's more than enough to learn in one day."

"I agree," M'tal announced. "My brain is feeling quite ruffled with all this. I'll be glad to have a night's sleep in which to settle and soothe myself."

Despite herself, Lorana chuckled in appreciation.

"Very well," Kindan conceded, "I suppose we could do with a rest."

"We'll be back before dawn," Lorana added firmly.

"*At* dawn," M'tal corrected, "and after breakfast."

The next morning, they met in the Kitchen Cavern for breakfast. M'tal noticed how the dragonriders politely avoided them and how the cooks—Kiyary in particular—went out of their way to be sure that they ate a good meal.

"Kindan, what are you doing?" Ketan asked as he downed his second mug of *klah*.

M'tal and Salina smiled at each other. They, too, had noticed the harper's tapping on the table, but it was a well-known fact that the Weyr's healer always required *two* mugs of *klah* to wake up in the morning.

"Oh, sorry," Kindan said absently, dropping his hands to his lap. A moment later, one was up again as he took another mouthful of oatmeal. Shortly after that, both of Kindan's hands were on the tabletop again, tapping softly.

Lorana gave him a look but shook her head.

"Kin—" Ketan began again, but Salina's look cut him

short. The ex-Weyrwoman was looking intently at Kindan's fingers.

Lorana noticed her look and frowned, closing her eyes in concentration. A moment later, she opened them again and exclaimed delightedly to Kindan, "You did it! You learned the sequence!"

Kindan, startled out of his reverie, gave her a surprised look. "I did?" he asked. As her words registered, he shook his head. "No, I was just practicing some drum codes . . ." His voice trailed off thoughtfully. "The drum codes are sounds."

"But they're grouped the same way as the PNA sequences," Lorana insisted. Tentatively, she tapped out a sequence and then looked challengingly at Kindan.

"That was the START sequence," Lorana said.

"No, it was the ATTENTION sequence," Kindan corrected her. He frowned in thought and quickly tapped a different sequence. "What's this?"

"That's the STOP sequence," Lorana answered promptly.

"It's the END sequence for the drum codes," Kindan told her. "What's this?" He tapped a set of sequences.

"ABC, CBA, BCA," Lorana translated.

"You're right! PNA is based on drum codes!" Kindan declared.

"I'd say it's the other way around," Ketan remarked after a moment.

Kindan frowned. "I suppose you're right."

"But it makes sense," M'tal said. "The genetic code is designed to store the most information possible in a group of three, so for simple drum codes it would be just as efficient."

As they returned to the Learning Room, Kindan explained, "I had this strange dream that someone was trying to tell me something, some message."

"Now you know what it was," Ketan said.

Kindan, inspired by his new understanding, soon caught up with the others. Several times, in fact, they turned to him for guidance in difficult sections. He would close his eyes in thought and tentatively tap out a sequence, and correct it.

"How do you know whether it's right?" Lorana asked when they'd solved one particularly difficult problem.

"I've been drumming for Turns," Kindan told her. "It wouldn't sound right unless it *was*."

By evening the next day, they had all graduated from constructing simple codons to working through replication and the creation of proteins.

"So the PNA controls how all of the cells in the dragons are created, grow, interact, and die," M'tal found himself explaining to a bemused B'nik at dinner that night. "And PNA contains the fundamental instructions for building defenses against disease and infections."

B'nik, whose duties kept him from what everyone had started to call the Learning Rooms, struggled to keep up with the old Weyrleader. "So, if we can figure out which infection is affecting the dragons, we can build a defense against it?"

"That's the hope," M'tal replied, surprised at B'nik's quick grasp. "But we haven't finished the study books, and we know that there's another room between this one and the first one we discovered."

"What's in it?"

M'tal shrugged. "I don't know," he said. "I suspect, given all that we've learned, it is probably a room where we can experiment and observe. Perhaps it has instruments to allow us to actually *see* the infection."

"But I thought you said the infection—that 'bacteria' or 'virus' you were talking about—is too small to see," B'nik protested.

"It is," M'tal agreed, "with the eye alone. But there are hints in the books that there are tools that make such small things big enough to see."

"Hmm." B'nik leaned back in his seat, mulling over this revelation. Then he leaned forward again and beckoned M'tal to come close to him. "Caranth is getting worse," he confessed. "How long do you think—"

"Are you asking if we can find a cure in time for Caranth?" M'tal asked gently.

"And the others," B'nik added quickly.

"We'll do our best," M'tal replied. "I know what you're facing."

B'nik gave him a bleak look. "Do you think——" He found that he couldn't go on and swallowed. He took a deep breath and began again. "I'd like you to take over the Weyr if anything happens to Caranth."

M'tal gave B'nik an encouraging smile and slapped the younger man on the shoulder reassuringly. "It won't come to that, B'nik," he told the young Weyrleader fiercely. "Not if I can help it."

B'nik looked long into M'tal's eyes and then nodded slowly. With a husky voice he said, "Thank you."

Loudly, Kindan closed his book and looked up at the others.

"Done!" he crowed. His grin faded when he saw that M'tal, Salina, and Ketan had already closed their books. He was surprised to see that Lorana was still reading. Indeed, she looked like she was just at the beginning of the book. Kindan gave Ketan a questioning look.

"She's rereading it," Ketan explained. *"Again."*

With a frown, Lorana slammed her book shut and looked up angrily at the others.

"So what do we know?" M'tal asked. "We know how the immune system works both against specific and nonspecific assaults."

"We know that sometimes the immune system can attack symbionts," Salina added, still surprised that there were tiny creatures that lived in harmony with the dragons.

"And even the body itself," Ketan added.

"And we have a vague idea of how to build new responses to attacks," Kindan said.

"But only by changing PNA," Lorana added glumly. "We can't make one of these 'antibiotics' or 'antivirals' to directly assault the disease."

"But once we can engineer a change," M'tal corrected, "we can build a 'retrovirus' to correct all the genes of all the cells in the dragons, so that they can correctly fight the infection."

"And once we get it right with *one* dragon," Salina added, "we can take ichor—the dragon's blood—from it and inject it into other dragons, and the cure will spread through the circulatory system."

"And," Ketan added ominously, "it'd be best to use the cure on a queen who's close to clutching—the cure would be carried to the hatchlings."

M'tal and Salina exchanged disturbed looks. There was only one queen near to clutching and that was Minith.

"But we still are no closer to identifying the infection," Lorana protested. She turned toward the still-closed door. "And we have no idea how to open that door."

"Except what's written on it," Kindan said.

"Does anyone know how to talk with people who have been dead for over four hundred Turns?" Lorana asked acerbically.

"There must be a way," Salina said, "or they wouldn't have put that verse on the door."

"Or built these rooms," M'tal added.

"How do we know that?" Lorana asked. "Perhaps these Learning Rooms were meant for others? Perhaps they've already been used and we're not supposed to be here."

"No," Kindan answered firmly. " 'Wind Blossom's Song' could only refer to you. These rooms were made for us." He pursed his lips thoughtfully and muttered, "Or you."

"Then why," Lorana cried, her arms flung out in despair, "don't I know the answer?"

Ketan looked at her sympathetically. He knew that she was right, that they could just be chasing a phantom hope. But that was the only hope left. If the answers to their problems weren't behind those doors, then the dragons would all die, of that he was certain. And if the answer was behind the door, then he was equally convinced that Lorana had to be the "healer lass" mentioned in the song. One look at Kindan convinced him that the harper was just as certain.

In the silence that filled the room after her question, M'tal rose from his chair and stretched. "Let's go," he said, "and sleep on this. Tomorrow we may have more answers."

"Tomorrow, Thread falls over Nerat and Upper Crom," Lorana protested. "How many more dragons must die before we can open that door?"

"I don't know Lorana," Salina said, rushing over to the younger woman and hugging her fiercely. "But you can only do so much."

"I know," Lorana said miserably, burying her head in the other woman's shoulder. "But—"

"Sh, sh," Salina said soothingly.

"We must leave now, Lorana," Ketan said. "We need our rest, and M'tal will be flying Thread tomorrow."

"And we'll be tending to injured dragons," Lorana noted. "We won't be here tomorrow."

M'tal shooed them all out of the room. As they climbed the stairs back up to the second level, he said, "A day's rest from this will do us all good."

"At least we'll have enough dragons to fight with," Kindan added.

"That's true," M'tal rumbled agreeably. Judiciously, he added, "They're all a bit more green than I would have liked but—"

A sharp intake of breath from Lorana interrupted him. "What?" he asked.

"It's Caranth," Lorana said. "He's not feeling well." She glanced at M'tal. "I don't think B'nik should lead the Fall tomorrow."

As they crested the top of the stairs, a loud barking cough echoed down the corridor from the Weyrleader's quarters.

M'tal's face darkened and he picked up his pace.

"Well, now, this is *much* better," D'gan declared as he flew slowly in front of the ranks of dragons arrayed in front of him. The ones who had timed it still looked a bit off-color, he admitted to himself with a frown, but they represented over two-thirds of the Weyr's fighting strength.

"Today we'll show them how it's done, won't we, Kaloth?"

he asked, reaching down to pat his bronze dragon affectionately. As if in response, the dragon gave a long, rattling
cough, arching his neck and not quite unseating his rider.

I'm sorry, Kaloth apologized meekly.

"Not to worry," D'gan grumbled. "It's that addled
healer—he should have worked up something to help you by
now." He peered over Kaloth's shoulder and spotted K'rem
below, preparing his brown. "Take me down and we'll talk to
him."

K'rem glanced up at Kaloth as the bronze dragon landed
and his rider slid to the ground. As D'gan strode toward him,
the healer carefully schooled the frown off his face.

"Kaloth's cough sounds worse," K'rem commented as
soon as D'gan was within hearing. "I had hoped that the last
herbal would have helped."

"It didn't, obviously," D'gan replied sourly.

"Weyrleader," K'rem began hesitantly, trying to choose
his words carefully, "perhaps it would be best if Kaloth
rested today—"

"What? Deny him the chance to lead the full Weyr?"
D'gan cut him off loudly. "No, just because your fardled
medicines don't work, doesn't mean that my dragon can't fly
when Thread is in the sky."

With a pleading look, K'rem came closer to the irate
Weyrleader. "D'gan, he's sick. He needs rest."

"Find a cure, Healer," D'gan ordered, turning back. "Find
a cure *after* we fight this Fall."

As D'gan returned to mount his dragon, his son, D'lin, approached him eagerly.

"The Weyrlingmaster says Aseth is ready, Father," D'lin
called. "Which wing should we fly with?"

D'gan shook his head immediately. "No," he said, "you're
not flying the Fall today."

D'lin's face fell. "But, Father . . ."

"Next time, D'lin," D'gan told him brusquely. "Today I
want you here, ready to ferry firestone and be a messenger."

"Yes, Father," D'lin replied woodenly, and turned away,
shoulders slumped, toward his dragon.

For a moment D'gan thought of calling his son back, of telling him how proud he was and how much he loved him. But then he shook the notion off, reminding himself that the boy had to learn to handle disappointment with discipline. As far as D'gan was concerned, D'lin was a dragonrider first and a son second.

As the sun crested the heights of Benden Weyr, it illuminated a Bowl already bustling with activity. The younger weyrlings, who had not timed it, were busily bagging firestone and building piles of supplies. Dragonriders, up early and already well-fed, were checking riding gear, or were gathered in knots talking tactics with their Wingleaders.

In a corner not far from the Living Cavern, Ketan and Lorana were setting out supplies and organizing for the inevitable injuries that occurred fighting Thread.

Caranth peered down morosely from his weyr over the proceedings, occasionally joining the cacophony of dragon coughs, which echoed eerily around the Bowl. Minith's worried croons to her mate were answered by soothing noises from Caranth, which fooled no one.

M'tal and B'nik moved from wing to wing, talking with riders and Wingleaders, presenting a calm, united presence that reassured and relieved everyone they met.

"They're up too early," M'tal remarked to B'nik as they moved away from one group.

"I know," B'nik agreed. "But you know how it is, the morning of a Fall."

"Well, I do *now*," M'tal agreed. "After all, we've had what—all of *five* Falls so far."

B'nik furrowed his brow. "I hadn't really counted," he admitted. "It almost seems like we've *always* been fighting Thread."

"It's been only four sevendays," M'tal remarked. "How will we be after Turns of this?"

B'nik shook his head. "I don't know," he said reflectively. He twisted his head to try to locate a cough from one of the sick dragons, failed, and turned back to M'tal. "But if we don't find a cure soon . . ."

M'tal clapped B'nik on the shoulder. "I know," he said somberly.

B'nik glanced at him, gave him a small nod, and then turned to the group they were approaching, calling with forced cheer, "So, J'tol! Ready to lead the wing?"

The fighting dragons departed an hour before noon—one hour before Threadfall was due at Nerat.

Lorana watched as the dragons winked *between*. A nudge from Ketan got her attention; he cocked his head toward B'nik and they both watched as the Weyrleader's shoulders hunched—and hunched further as another wracking cough from Caranth rent the late morning air.

"I could—" Lorana began.

"Why don't you and Kindan see if you can learn anything more," Ketan suggested.

Lorana looked at Kindan, who nodded in agreement.

"Have someone call for us when we're needed," Kindan said over his shoulder as they raced off toward the stairs to the second level. Ketan waved in acknowledgment.

They were both puffing from exertion as they reached the stairs leading down to the Learning Rooms.

"It'll be easier when we can get that door open," Kindan remarked. "Then, presumably, we'll be able to come in from the Hatching Grounds."

"And all that's needed to do *that* is for me to figure out what word I'm supposed to say and how I'm supposed to tell someone who is hundreds of Turns dead," Lorana said bitterly.

Kindan ducked his head and concentrated on getting down the stairs and into the first of the Learning Rooms, which he had dubbed "The Classroom."

Inside, Lorana seated herself and began once again to study her book.

It took Kindan longer to settle down in the icy silence that had spread between them. In the end, too full of nervous energy to stay seated, he got up to pace the room, earning a disgruntled look from Lorana. He flashed a smile in apology, was rewarded with a frown and a sigh, and turned his attention to the writing on the door.

"You know," he said after a moment, "we're going about this the wrong way."

Lorana slammed her book shut and peered over her shoulder at him. "What should we do, then?"

"We should concentrate on what we know first, and then worry about what we don't know," he said. Lorana's look was not encouraging but he pressed on. "For example, what would this word be?"

Lorana's face relaxed into a thoughtful frown, and she turned away to get into a position more comfortable for thinking.

"Maybe they need to know if the infection is bacterial or viral," Kindan suggested.

Lorana shook her head. "I don't think that's it," she said after a moment's further thought. "The textbook hints that the problem is one of data reduction. It would seem that there wouldn't be all that much difference between antibacterial and antiviral methods.

"It must have something to do with how the disease is spread," she said softly to herself. She got up and walked over to where Kindan stood in front of the door, once again reading the inscription on it:

> *"That word is what you now must say*
> *To open up the door*
> *In Benden Weyr, to find the way*
> *To all my healing lore."*

"Well," Kindan commented as he followed the lines with his eyes again, "at least it's not the most disturbing part."

Lorana cocked an eye at him, and Kindan sang,

> *"A thousand voices keen at night,*
> *A thousand voices wail,*

A thousand voices cry in fright,
A thousand voices fail."

As he sang it, Lorana's eyes widened with fear and she started shivering.

"What is it?" Kindan asked, grabbing her shoulder with his hand. "Lorana, are you all right?"

But Lorana wasn't hearing him.

"D'gan, *no!*" she shrieked.

D'gan looked over his shoulder one final time at the arrayed dragons of Telgar Weyr. Beneath him Kaloth shook with a long gargling cough. He saw K'rem turn to look at him and, impatient to get at Thread, he ordered Kaloth to take them *between*.

Just as the cold of *between* enveloped D'gan, he felt Kaloth give another shuddering cough.

Not long now, he told his dragon. Kaloth coughed again. D'gan began to think that perhaps he would keep Kaloth back on the next Fall. Let D'nal or L'rat lead—it would do them good.

Kaloth coughed again. A chill ran down D'gan's spine, colder than the cold of *between.*

Between *only lasts as long as it takes to cough three times,* D'gan recalled.

Kaloth had coughed three times.

Kaloth coughed again—and in that instant, D'gan realized his error.

All the dragons of Telgar Weyr had gone beyond *between.*

The Weyrs! They must be warned! D'gan thought in terror as the last of his consciousness seeped away.

D'lin swallowed hard as he watched the dragons of Telgar wink *between.* He had worked hard for his first chance to fight Thread. Soon, he thought to himself, the Weyr would appear over Upper Crom, ready to flame the deadly menace from the sky.

Aseth turned his huge head to stare down at his rider. *Our turn will come soon.*

Of course, D'lin agreed fervently, not wanting his beautiful Aseth to think for a moment that he was in any way less than the most perfect dragon ever hatched on all Pern.

I do not hear them, Aseth thought a moment later, craning his neck up high in the sky.

And then the world collapsed. D'lin felt as though someone had punched him both in the stomach and just as hard in the brain, if that were possible. He was overwhelmed by pain and fear.

The Weyrs! They must be warned! D'lin heard the thought as though it were his own. Aseth bellowed in horror and defiance. Without thinking, D'lin leapt on his dragon and urged him up, out of the Bowl.

Benden will be nearest, D'lin thought, his sight masked by the waves of tears that were streaming down unchecked.

Come on, Aseth, between*!* And with that, overwhelmed by despair, hopelessness, and pure courage, D'lin urged his dragon *between*—

—without envisioning his destination.

Two thousand Turns later, their bodies would be discovered, entombed in solid rock at Benden Weyr.

M'tal looked back with satisfaction at the wings behind him. Every wing, including those who had gone back in time, was formed up neatly.

Thread ahead, Gaminth informed him.

I see it, M'tal replied, signaling the wings behind him to rise up to meet the incoming Thread. And then—

—a wave of horror, wrenching loss, and fear wracked him. Gaminth bellowed in pain, his cry echoed by every dragon.

What is it? M'tal asked his dragon fearfully.

D'gan and Telgar, Gaminth replied, sounding shaken in a way that M'tal had never heard before. *They're gone.*

All of them?

All the fighting dragons, Gaminth confirmed.

And Thread? M'tal asked, as he envisioned Thread falling unopposed on the ranges of Upper Crom. But he already knew the answer.

"Lorana!" Kindan shouted, catching her as she slumped toward the floor. In the distance he could hear dragons keening. "Lorana, what is it?"

A dragon's bellow rent the air, answered by another more plaintive one.

"Is it Caranth?" Kindan asked.

Lorana opened her eyes, shivering. "It's Telgar," she told him dully.

Caranth? she asked, but the dragon was already aloft, riderless, beating toward the watch heights. In an instant she guessed his intention. *Caranth, no!*

Lorana felt the bronze go *between,* chasing after the dragons and riders of Telgar Weyr. With a cry, she reached out to grab him, bring him back—and found herself dragged along instead.

"Lorana?" Kindan called softly. But her eyes had gone vacant, just as they had been when she had lost Arith. Kindan's own soul cry was echoed by Minith. The dragon repeated her cry louder—and then the cry was cut off.

"Lorana, Minith's gone after Caranth," Kindan said, hoping that she would hear the words in her lifeless state. The only response Lorana made was a gasp, as though she'd had the breath knocked out of her.

A rush of feet echoed down the stairs and Ketan and Salina burst into the room. They looked from Kindan to Lorana and back.

"She must come back," Salina rasped. "She can talk to all the dragons. She can bring them back."

"How?" Kindan asked, but Salina had moved beside him and grabbed Lorana. With palm wide-open, she slapped Lorana's face.

"Lorana! Lorana, you must come back, come back *now,*" Salina begged. She swung for another slap just as Lorana's

eyes fluttered open and she raised a hand feebly to ward off
the blow. "Call them back, Lorana. Bring them back."

"I can't," Lorana said, her voice choking on tears. "I tried
that with Arith and it didn't work."

"You must, Lorana," Salina said fiercely. "You *must*. Call
all the dragons of Pern. Bring them back."

Lorana took a deep steadying breath, glanced at the old
Weyrwoman, and nodded slowly. She closed her eyes and
reached out, as she had done before when Arith had gone *between*.

This time, however, she stretched beyond the confines of
the Weyr, reaching first to Gaminth, then to all the dragons of
Benden and then beyond—

—to Ista,

—to Fort,

—and to High Reaches.

There were not enough dragons at High Reaches and she
found herself feeling a strange echo. It reminded her somewhat of the echo she'd felt before, but that other echo had
had a feeling of *old* about it—this one didn't.

Mentally, Lorana shook the strangeness aside, desperate
to find Minith, Caranth, and the dragons of Telgar. She
searched, forcing all the dragons of Pern to follow her will,
to search with her.

They were willing accomplices. She felt the presence of
Bidenth, the senior queen at Ista, and suddenly all the dragons of Ista were behind her, aligned with the direction of her
mind. And then she felt Melirth, the queen of Fort Weyr, and
again the strength of the dragons merged with her. For a
moment Lorana felt as though she were exploding, being
stretched beyond all imagining. She fought a moment of
panic, won, and redirected her efforts back to Minith.

There! She found a faint echo, a spark of the queen
dragon. And beside it, she felt Caranth. She tugged at them,
battling them, willing them to obey her and ruthlessly chan-
neling the power of all the dragons of Pern to her aid.

She could feel Caranth resist, try to slide away from
her. She fastened on to him tightly and pulled against him,

pulling him back to *here.* She felt his resistance crumble, felt a shadow of B'nik as he, too, added a call to his dragon. Relieved, Lorana allowed her mind for just an instant to range further, searching for the dragons of Telgar.

She felt a faint echo, a response, and turned all her power toward it, compelling Minith to order the dragons of Benden behind her, and weaving Caranth indissolubly into the mix. She reached—

—and felt a shock, a stab of familiarity. Not the dragons of Telgar, but something different, something she'd felt before.

Garth? she called. And just then she felt something else, some other presence. Lorana felt herself opening a door, using all the strength of the dragons to push it open.

For only a brief instant she felt she had a connection.

Dragons? The question came to her more as a feeling than a thought. *Sick? How?*

And in that instant Lorana knew the answer. Across the link, with the greatest effort she could muster, she shouted out loud and in her mind, *"Air!"*

Kindan felt Lorana go limp and caught her.

"The door!" Ketan exclaimed in awe. "Look at the door!"

The door to the second Learning Room was sliding open.

Parasite: A life-form inimical to its host, often killing the host to ensure its survival.

Chapter Twenty-three

College, First Interval, AL 58

"THERE'S NO WAY we can be *sure* that our future student will be able to *tell* us which vec—" Tieran halted midword and cocked his head to listen.

"It's just thunder," Emorra chided him irritably. "You can't use that as an excuse to get out of this argument."

"Kassa said the weather would be clear tonight," Tieran replied, still puzzled.

"And Kassa is always right," Emorra observed tartly.

"About the weather, she is," Tieran said. He started toward the door. Grenn met him, chittering wildly.

"Where are you going?" Emorra demanded.

"I'm going to check on your mother," Tieran replied, following Grenn as the little fire-lizard scouted ahead. "Something's not right."

"I'll come with you," Emorra said.

"She's not been looking well recently, has she?"

Emorra frowned. "She's been pushing herself too hard."

"It's not like she's still young," the two said in unison and then stared at each other in surprise. Tieran broke the moment with a chuckle and they started up the stairs toward Wind Blossom's quarters.

"Air!" Wind Blossom shrieked.

How Tieran covered the remaining distance to Wind Blossom's room, he could never recall, but he was in the room and at her side instantly. Emorra arrived only a fraction later.

Wind Blossom looked up at them, panting for breath.

"It must be a seizure!" Tieran declared.

"No, a heart attack," Emorra said.

Wind Blossom pierced them with her gaze. "I heard her," she told them. "I heard her, she said *air*!"

"Who said air, Mother?" Emorra asked.

"The girl from the future," Wind Blossom said. "She found me. She was so *strong*. I have never felt such power. She must have harnessed all the dragons of her time." She glanced at them, eyes saddened. "She was looking for missing dragons. A lot of missing dragons—"

"A thousand?" Emorra asked fearfully.

Wind Blossom ignored the question, concentrating her strength on asking, "She *knew*, somehow she knew that I had a question—how did she?"

Tieran and Emorra exchanged looks.

"I'll write a song, Mother," Emorra said. "I'll write a song to ask the question."

Wind Blossom brightened. "Yes, a song!" she agreed. She smiled up at her daughter. "Write a good one, love."

The breath left Wind Blossom's lungs and she fell back to her bed with a surprised look on her face. Feebly she beckoned Emorra toward her.

"Mother?" Emorra cried, arching forward, her ear close to Wind Blossom's lips.

"And then you'll be free," Wind Blossom whispered. Her last flickering thought was triumphant: There, Mother! I have freed them from you and the Eridani curse.

For a long while afterward, Emorra stood over her mother's bed, eyes streaming with tears.

Then, without saying a word, she moved to her mother's dresser, opened the top drawer, searched quickly, and pulled out the yellow tunic. She returned to her mother's side and gently lifted the lifeless body, deftly maneuvering it until she had exchanged the yellow tunic for the white one in which Wind Blossom had died.

"I *did* notice," Emorra whispered, tears streaming down

her face. Tieran laid a hand on her shoulder, and she grabbed it tightly with her own.

"I don't understand. Why did Wind Blossom need this clue?" Seamus asked M'hall. Everyone from the College and the Hold had gathered to mourn Wind Blossom's passing, and Seamus had joined his brother, Torene, Tieran, and Emorra to find out what was going on with their research.

"The gene mappers can only store so much information," M'hall explained. "In order to eliminate unnecessary information, it was necessary to know whether the disease is spread by air, food, or water."

"And how do we know that this future rider understood the question correctly?" Holder Mendin, who had wandered over in time to hear the conversation, asked with a smirk.

"We don't," Tieran answered. "If we find more dragons or fire-lizards dropping in on us, then we'll find out that we're wrong."

"If we do nothing," M'hall added, "then we'll only find out when our dragons become infected."

Mendin smiled, waving a hand toward Tieran and Emorra. "Well, surely these two marvelous youngsters will be able to whip up a cure in no time."

"No," Tieran said. "We'd have to relearn what the future rider already knows—and we don't know how long it's taken her—"

"Her?"

"She rode a queen, Holder Mendin," Emorra reminded him.

"So our only hope for the dragons of Pern is to trust that you two"—Mendin gestured to Tieran and Emorra—"can complete the work that Wind Blossom had only just begun before her untimely demise."

"I'd say that they are the only hope for *all* of Pern," Torene replied.

Mendin quirked an eyebrow in amazement. "Indeed? And have they got the training that Wind Blossom did not?"

"Wind Blossom had started on a line of inquiry which is

proving quite fruitful," Tieran said. "And, as always, she had a fallback plan prepared."

"Really?" Mendin asked. "And why not just use this fall-back plan and save yourselves more trouble?"

"Because the fallback is a method to make a watch-wher into a dragon," Tieran replied. From the looks of the dragon-riders, and Mendin himself, Tieran regretted his impulsive-ness. "And that assumes that the watch-whers prove immune to whatever is attacking the dragons."

"So why would she do that?" Mendin asked. "If the watch-whers could succumb to the same illness?"

"Well, they might not," Emorra said. "Mother made some alterations to the watch-whers to make them somewhat more self-sufficient than the dragons."

"In case something happened to the dragonriders?" To-rene murmured.

Emorra nodded glumly.

"Wise," Torene decided with a firm nod.

"So, as you can see," Tieran said, "we still have to provide a cure for the dragons."

"Hmm," was all Mendin said in response, his eyes flicker-ing darkly as he wandered away.

M'hall waited until Mendin was out of earshot before he turned back to Tieran and Emorra. "Can you do it?"

"Well . . ." Emorra began, temporizing.

"We can do it," Tieran declared. Emorra gave him a sur-prised look, which he quelled with a firm look of his own.

"Good," M'hall said, even though the byplay was not lost on him.

"I've been thinking of some things that might help," Sea-mus interjected.

"We'd be glad of anything," Tieran replied.

"Help how?" Emorra asked.

"Well, there are several things," Seamus expanded. "I've got one of the old RTG's stored away. It's not much use by it-self because it's low-powered, but there is one storage array still working, so I think I can couple the two of them—"

"Excuse me, what's an RTG?" Tieran interrupted.

"Radio Thermal Generator," Emorra replied. When she saw Tieran's confused look reflected in the faces of M'hall and Torene, she added, "It's a power generator with a long-lasting supply."

"But the overall power's not that great," Seamus said. "So it's not much use for most things. I think it'll be ideal as a power source for these Training Rooms, however."

"Then we can run lights, right?" Tieran exclaimed happily.

Seamus nodded and opened his mouth to say more, but Emorra cut him off.

"You said there are several things—what else?" she asked.

"Well . . . I've managed to save some of the old powered doors," Seamus replied. "And I noticed that your mother recovered a voice recorder. I've been thinking of ways we could hook that up to a loudspeaker—"

"Why would you want to do that?" Tieran asked.

"So that we could speak to our students," Emorra answered immediately.

"I got Wind Blossom to show me how to use it," Seamus added. He pulled from his pocket a small object that fit in the palm of his large hand. "She agreed that it would be an excellent idea, and she even recorded a short introduction."

He pressed a button on the object's side.

"Welcome," it said in Wind Blossom's voice. "I am Wind Blossom. If you have come to these rooms for an emergency involving the dragons, then please step inside. If not, please leave immediately."

"Will that do?" Seamus asked, looking up at the others.

Tears streamed from Emorra's eyes.

"That will do fine," Tieran said emphatically.

"Can you make three rooms for us?" Emorra asked through her tears. "We'll have one for the lectures, one for lab work, and the final one for constructing the cure."

"How big do you need the rooms to be?" Seamus asked, pulling on his chin thoughtfully.

Emorra and Tieran exchanged looks.

"How many people would you say?" M'hall asked them.

"I doubt more than fifteen," Emorra said. "Any more would be too many."

"Fifteen's a lot," Tieran said dubiously. He pursed his lips for a moment and then nodded. "Fifteen's the upper limit, then."

"No one's used the stonecutters in a decade," Seamus said, temporizing his answer. "But all the same, I think we can do that."

"Excellent," M'hall replied, clapping his younger brother on the shoulder. "When can you start?"

"Those doors," Tieran interjected suddenly. "Can you control when they open?"

Seamus frowned. "I could, but there's always the danger that the controls would freeze," he replied warily. "Why do you ask?"

"I don't think it's a good idea to let our students into the lab or the workroom until they know what they're doing," Tieran replied.

"So you want some way to test them before they get in?" Emorra asked.

Tieran nodded. "Exactly."

"Well, we know what to use for the key to the lab," Emorra said.

"What?" The others asked in chorus.

" 'Air,' " Emorra replied. "The only one who should know that answer will be our queen rider."

"Ex-queen rider," Torene corrected sadly. M'hall met her eyes and they both shuddered in sympathy for that future rider.

"She must be quite something," Seamus agreed.

"We can't let her down," Emorra declared. She turned to Tieran. "Let's get to work."

It's all that I can give you,
To save both Weyr and Hold.
It's little I can offer you,
Who paid with dragon gold.

Chapter Twenty-four

Upper Crom Hold, Third Pass, 28th Day, AL 508

THE SUN WAS WELL past noon but the air above Upper Crom Hold was cold with winter winds blowing from the mountains to the north. Thin wisps of cloud were visible high up in the sky.

A moment later, the wisps of cloud were smeared with other shapes. The shapes slowly resolved themselves as they descended. Thread.

The air was not so cold that Thread froze. Slowly, silently, Thread streamed from the sky, floating on the winds and down toward the unsuspecting ground below. Once there, it would burrow, sucking all the life out of the land and spreading voraciously across the continent.

The holders were all in their holds, well barred against Thread, waiting for the all-clear from the dragonriders of Telgar Weyr, sworn to protect them.

There were no dragons.

Those dragons had gone *between* and would never come back.

Thread fell lower, into warmer bands of air near the ground. Soon they would touch and—

A gout of flame licked the sky, then another, and another. Suddenly, the air was filled with flaming dragons and charred Thread.

"Take a wing low!" D'vin ordered as the riders of High Reaches Weyr fanned out, weary from their jump a day into the future. Hurth roared, adding his own emphasis, and D'vin slapped his bronze dragon affectionately.

"You tell them!" he roared out loud, grinning from ear to ear. She was right, he thought to himself.

She is a queen rider, Hurth said, as though that were all that needed saying.

D'vin nodded and turned his attention to the Thread in front of him. He was a dragonman, and this was his duty.

No Thread would fall on Crom Hold while there were still dragons left at High Reaches Weyr, D'vin swore to himself.

"Lorana?"

Lorana opened her eyes. Kindan's anxious face swam into view. She was lying on her back on something hard. Cold, too.

"Are you all right?" Ketan asked, leaning over her.

Lorana rolled to her side and raised herself on her arm.

"No, no, stay put!" Kindan ordered.

Lorana ignored him with a shake of her head—a move she regretted as the room swirled before her eyes. She closed them for a moment, opened them again and stood up.

"Lorana!" Kindan begged, looking at her anxiously. "You need to rest. You passed out!"

Lorana shook her head in disagreement. She reached out with her senses, touching Minith. She felt Caranth sleeping fitfully.

"No," Lorana said feebly. "No, I've got to work."

"No, you're too ill," Kindan said.

"I'm not ill," Lorana replied testily. She quickly explained what had happened, how she'd grabbed for Minith and Caranth, using the dragons of the Weyr, and then, when she felt the dragons of Telgar Weyr being lost, had tried to grab them, too—and had failed only to discover herself connected to a distant someone, the Oldtimer she'd felt before, and how she'd answered the Oldtimer's question.

"I'm not ill," Lorana repeated when she had finished.

Without giving him a chance to answer, she moved past him, through the doorway that her word had opened and into the room beyond.

Lights came up in the new room as she came in, but no voice greeted her. She looked around the room and her eyes lit up with wonder.

"Kindan, come look!" she cried excitedly, heading toward the benches placed on one side of the room.

Kindan followed her, with Ketan trailing behind. Salina paused in the doorway, taking in every part of the room in silent wonder.

"Look, there's the other door!" Ketan declared, pointing to a door on the far wall. "And it's got the same press plate as the others."

He ran across the room and pressed the plate. The door slid open, revealing the first room they'd discovered.

"We couldn't open this door from the other side," he said.

"I think we were supposed to come *this* way," Salina remarked. "I think the first door we came through was just for emergencies."

"So the rock slide activated it?" Ketan asked.

"Well, we might as well get working," Lorana said. "M'tal will be back from the Fall soon enough." She looked at Ketan. "There are some injured dragons coming back now."

Ketan was surprised. "So soon?"

"Everyone was disturbed when Telgar was lost," Lorana replied.

"Those who could still hear dragons," Ketan said, his eyes full of sorrow. He saw Lorana's look and hastily added, "I would not have wanted to have been you just then."

Lorana managed a small, sour smile and shrugged. "If I hadn't been—"

"Our ancestors would never have known our peril," Kindan finished briskly. He gestured around the room. "Where should we start first?"

"I'll go tend the dragons," Ketan said, turning to leave.

"You'll be quicker going through that door," Lorana said, pointing to the door leading to the Hatching Grounds.

"So I will," Ketan agreed in pleasant surprise. As he headed off, he called back over his shoulder, "I'll send for you if we need help."

Salina waved acknowledgment and sauntered over toward Lorana.

Lorana gravitated toward the cabinets on the left wall. There were three, just as in the first room. The nearest was also marked A. She opened it and drew back in awe.

On the middle shelf of the cabinet was an ungainly object.

"I know what that is," Kindan declared.

"It's a microscope," Lorana said, gently cradling it in her arms and placing it on the countertop behind her. She looked it over carefully, angled the reflecting mirror at the bottom to catch the light from overhead. She frowned for a moment, turned back to the cabinet, and then murmured happily as she found what she was looking for. "Here are the specimen slides!"

"What have they got?" Salina asked.

"What sort of magnification does that microscope have?" Kindan added.

"Sixteen hundred," Lorana answered, peering at the different lenses at the base of the barrel. She looked back at the slides, selected one, and slid it under the calipers on the microscope's table, firmly holding it in place.

She bent down over the eyepiece and very carefully adjusted the focus. With a gasp of surprise, she drew back.

"What is it?" Salina asked.

"A human hair," Lorana replied, gesturing for the older woman to look. Kindan was next and just as impressed.

They spent hours working with the microscope, examining the prepared specimens and commenting to each other about their findings.

"So what we need now is a sample from one of the sick dragons," Kindan said finally, looking up from the last of the bacteria specimen slides.

Lorana looked ready to agree and then her face took on a distant look.

"That will have to wait," she told the others. "M'tal is back and Ketan needs help."

Salina gave Lorana a nervous look. "No," Lorana assured her, "he and Gaminth are just fine. But there were many injured in the Fall."

"I think we can leave everything where it is," Salina said as they left the room and headed toward the Hatching Grounds. "But should we shut this door?"

"I'd advise against it," Kindan said. "We don't know how much power it takes to open it again."

Salina and Lorana nodded in agreement.

As they entered the Bowl from the Hatching Grounds, two sounds came to their ears simultaneously. One was Tullea calling imperiously for Lorana. The other was a dragon's cough—Minith's.

Kindan was surprised to see Lorana's face light up in excitement: He would never have considered her spiteful. Her words immediately erased his unease and left him feeling chagrined. "Minith must have just come down with the illness," she said. "If we can get a sample from her—"

"We could identify the disease," Salina finished excitedly.

Then Lorana's shoulders drooped. "Or maybe not," she said. "It's also possible that Minith has been sick for quite some time and is only now at the stage where we notice it."

"So the beasties we find might not be the culprit?" Kindan asked.

"Perhaps just some secondary infections," Lorana agreed.

"It's better than nothing," Salina said. She stopped as she looked at the injured dragons and riders covering the Weyr Bowl floor. She turned to Kindan. "You get the sample while Lorana and I help Ketan."

Kindan bit back saying, "Me?" Instead, he mutely nodded and headed up to the Weyrleaders' quarters.

It was past dinner when Lorana and Salina finally made their way back to the Learning Rooms. There they found Kindan and B'nik peering over the microscope.

"Look," Kindan said, gesturing. "I made up a slide. There are thousands of them!"

Lorana and Salina both took long looks through the microscope.

"I made out about ten different bacteria before I gave up," Kindan said. He gestured to a pad beside the microscope. "I did my best to draw them."

Lorana looked at them and nodded. "Yes, very good, Kindan," she said. She flipped to a clean page and grabbed the pencil, leaning back over the microscope. In moments she had drawn three more shapes. Then she, too, stopped and relinquished the microscope.

"Those little things are killing our dragons?" B'nik asked, both amazed and angered at the size of the dragons' attackers.

"There are many such small things," Lorana said. "Most of them are beneficial—they help to protect the dragons. We have similar bacteria ourselves."

"But these bacteria have turned nasty," Kindan added. "Or they always were, and the dragons' natural defenses have been overcome."

"They caught this from the fire-lizards," B'nik said, looking at the others for confirmation.

"We're pretty certain of it," Kindan agreed.

"Although it could be something that the dragons gave to the fire-lizards," Lorana added. "They're so closely related it could go either way."

"It's a pity the dragons are so much like the fire-lizards," B'nik remarked, his lips tight. "They seem so big, I would have thought that difference alone would have protected them."

"If anything, their size works against them," Lorana said, shaking her head. "Their lungs are so much bigger than the fire-lizards' that there's that much greater a chance of an infection taking hold."

"And this," B'nik gestured around the room. "With this you'll be able to find a cure?"

"We'll try," Kindan promised.

Lorana caught the nub of B'nik's question. She met the Weyrleader's gaze squarely. "Weyrleader, I'll do all in my power to make sure that not another dragon of Pern dies from this illness."

B'nik returned her gaze. He nodded gratefully, then smiled ruefully. "Just make sure you get enough sleep," he ordered, wagging a finger at her.

"I can sleep when we've got a cure," Lorana protested.

"I think we could all do with a night's sleep, given the day's events," Salina said. She quelled Lorana's rebellion with an admonishing look. "We'll start again first thing in the morning."

The next morning Salina was not surprised to find Lorana already in the Learning Rooms, engrossed in her studies. Salina placed the tray she'd brought with her on the countertop far from the microscope and Lorana's work, carefully poured a mug of *klah*, and deftly interposed it in Lorana's hand when the younger woman absently searched for a pencil.

Lorana gave a squeak of surprise and looked up from the microscope to smile sheepishly at Salina.

"Where's Kindan?" Salina asked, taking the sketchbook from Lorana and looking it over.

"He was asleep when I left him," Lorana replied.

Salina noticed that there was another, smaller piece of equipment on the table, beside the miscroscope.

"What's that?" she asked.

"This is a sequencer," Lorana said. "I've managed to confirm the presence of several likely bacteria." She made a face. "I think, in the old days, they would have used something else instead of the sequencer to identify bacteria."

"Perhaps that's all they had left," Salina suggested, eyeing the small device carefully. It looked sturdy enough, just small—a bit smaller than her jewelry case.

"That's what I thought, too," Lorana agreed. Her frown deepened. Salina gave her a questioning look. In answer, Lorana said, "It's just that if this is all they had left, will it be sufficient?"

The little unit chimed softly and Salina noticed that a yellow light had gone out, to be replaced by a green light.

Lorana peered down at the top of the unit and grinned. "The sequencer has located a common gene among the bacteria it's sampled."

"What's that mean?" Salina asked.

"In this case, I programmed the sequencer to look for a common gene sequence that we could use to prevent the bacterial infection," Lorana replied. She held up a textbook, gestured to the middle cabinet, which was now open and stocked full of books, and then said, "This book here showed me how to do it."

"So we have a cure?" B'nik asked. Lorana turned to see the Weyrleader standing in the doorway.

Lorana hesitated before replying. "I can't say for certain," she told him. "It looks promising, but I haven't tried to work out how to build the defense into the dragons."

B'nik gave her a puzzled look. Before Lorana could draw breath to explain, M'tal, Kindan, and Ketan arrived.

"Did we miss something?" M'tal asked.

"Lorana's found a cure," B'nik said, barely restraining his excitement.

"Perhaps we should all get comfortable and let Lorana tell this once," Kindan suggested as he brushed by Ketan to find a seat and turn it toward Lorana and the workbench.

So Lorana began her explanation again. She told them what she'd seen in the microscope, how she'd learned to get the sequencer to search for matching gene sequences that could be used to block the bacteria, and how she'd found one.

"How does what you're doing connect with that?" Ketan asked, gesturing to the diagrams on the walls. Lorana followed his gaze and her face fell.

"I don't know," she admitted. She walked around the bench and over to the wall to peer at the diagrams. "These are diagrams of the dragons' genes for lungs, breathing, and lung protection," she said after peering at them for a while.

"Was it meant as a clue?" B'nik asked, rising from his chair to study the diagrams himself.

"Could be," Ketan agreed, standing beside B'nik and peering at the gene maps in turn. He looked to the right. "But what's this?" he asked, pointing to the second map. "It almost looks the same."

Lorana peered at it for a moment. "It's the map for the same areas on the fire-lizards."

"Perhaps we were to construct a cure for them, too," Kindan murmured.

"They're almost identical," B'nik remarked. He peered closely at the two maps. "No! Here's something different."

Lorana looked back and forth between the two maps. "I think that codes for size," she said after a long silence.

"So there's really not all that much difference between the two," M'tal said. "I can't understand why they'd bother to draw both maps."

"Perhaps we do have to find a cure for the fire-lizards," Ketan mused. "After all, it seems like what affects them, affects the dragons, too."

"So if the fire-lizards ever get sick again, the dragons will get sick, too?" B'nik asked. "But why hasn't this happened before?"

"Because it takes time for bacteria to mutate," Lorana replied distractedly. She was looking vaguely at the diagrams without really seeing them. "After a while, the parasites that kill will have to mutate into symbiotes."

"Symbiotes?" B'nik repeated blankly.

"Germs that live in harmony with their host," M'tal explained. "Like the bacteria that flourish in our gut."

"Or on our skin," Ketan added. "We have bacteria that help protect us from infection."

"But it seems like people are always getting sick," B'nik said. "Well, not so much the dragonriders, as holders and such."

"It comes in cycles," Lorana said in agreement. She thought of all she'd learned about mutations and genetic codes. She sighed and looked at Salina.

"We could cure this illness, but what about the next?" she asked.

"The next?" B'nik asked nervously.

"Don't worry, it probably won't happen for another hundred Turns or more," Kindan said reassuringly.

"But it *will* happen," Ketan pointed out. He looked at Lorana. "And then what? Can we preserve these rooms for our descendants?"

"I don't think there'll be enough genetic material left to build a cure," Lorana replied. "In fact, I think there'll be enough for four doses, at best." She paused. "Of course, there is the watch-wher cure."

"Pardon?" M'tal asked.

Lorana bit her lip before answering. "One of the vials was specially marked," she told the others. "I read about it this morning. It was made by Wind Blossom herself, just before her death. It was meant only to be used as a last resort.

"It would turn a watch-wher into a dragon," she said. Her face clouded as she continued. "What I gave to Arith was a mixture of all four." She sobbed, "That's what killed her!"

"You don't know that," Salina said firmly. "She was sick."

"She would have died without it," Ketan added. His words and expression reminded her of his loss—and Salina's.

Lorana found herself caught in a strange, sad bond with the two other ex-dragonriders.

The mood was broken as the sound of footsteps echoed from the corridor into the room.

"Lorana!" Tullea screamed, crashing into the room, her eyes ablaze. "You—so clever! How dare you? There were five stillborn in Minith's clutch! *Five!*"

She advanced on Lorana, hands raised in outrage, fury obvious to all. Unconsciously, M'tal, Salina, and Ketan put themselves between the two women. Kindan moved himself around Lorana, to block her from Tullea's view.

"You!" Tullea turned to B'nik. "What are you going to do? You let this happen!" She turned her fury on him, slamming her fists into his chest.

"Tullea, Tullea, what's wrong?" B'nik asked.

"Did you *hear* me? Five of our eggs never hatched! How

can we hope to replace the lost dragons if the eggs don't hatch?"

"Hatched? She clutched already? But the others?" B'nik asked, startled. "They were all right?"

"Yes," Tullea snarled, staring past him toward Lorana. "No thanks to you, I'm sure!" She turned back to B'nik. "I want her turned out. I don't want her in my Weyr. Send her back to her people."

"*We* are her people, Tullea," Salina said, drawing herself up proudly.

"She stays with the Weyr," M'tal added.

"Hmmph!" Tullea said. "Neither of you are Weyrleader here!" She turned back to B'nik. "She should go before she kills more dragons." Viciously she snarled at Lorana, "Dragonkiller! You should be *between* with your dragon and all the others you killed—"

"Tullea!" B'nik shouted, grabbing her and propelling her out of the room. "That's enough!" Brusquely he manhandled her from the room.

"But five, B'nik! We lost five!" Tullea wailed as her voice faded in the distance.

There was a moment of silence while the others collected themselves.

"I'm sorry, Lorana," Kindan told her. "I was hoping we could shield you from that."

M'tal nodded sternly. Then he stopped and looked up at Ketan. "When did Minith clutch?" he asked.

"She hasn't," Ketan replied, his face showing his surprise.

"That's it!" Lorana exclaimed, oblivious to the others. "We must build a shield."

Salina turned to her. "A shield?"

"To slow down the parasites," Lorana explained. She looked at the others and then turned to the larger map. She grabbed a marker and circled several choice spots. Frowning, she crossed out one or two.

"Look, as long as the dragons share this much similarity to the fire-lizards, any disease that affects the fire-lizards will affect the dragons," she explained.

"Only if the fire-lizards get near the dragons," Ketan objected. "And now that they've been banished, what's the likelihood?"

"True," Lorana agreed. "But some day they might come back, and we can't be sure if the dragons couldn't just as easily pick up diseases from other Pernese organisms."

"I suppose," Ketan allowed reluctantly.

"But if we can change this, right here," she said, pointing to her circle again, "then all the bacteria and viruses will have to mutate before they can assault the dragons."

"You want to change the coding of the START sequence?" Kindan asked incredulously. "Will it work? Can you do it?"

"Well, there are enough unused sequences in the PNA," M'tal observed thoughtfully.

"And we don't have to change them all," Salina added.

"No," Ketan objected. "I think we should change them all."

"But that would only work with new dragons," Kindan objected. "Today's dragons have this START sequence."

"I think we can do it," Lorana said. "We'll have to build a mechanism to convert all the dragons' genes and hormones to use the new START sequence—"

"We could probably insert a change so that it occurred during cell mitosis," Ketan suggested. Then he frowned and added, "And meiosis."

"But not the START sequence," Kindan objected. "The STOP sequence. That way any retrovirus will just code in junk that will be rejected."

They spent the rest of the morning discussing the solution. By lunchtime, they had agreed on the approach. The problem now was the actual execution.

"We're going to have to produce a short-term solution, too," Salina pointed out. "It won't do any good to prevent future infections if the current one isn't stopped."

"Of course," Ketan agreed, wondering why Salina had raised the issue.

"Do we have enough of the basic material to construct both changes?" the ex-Weyrwoman asked.

"I don't know," Lorana replied. "Let's start by looking at how much genetic material we'll need to code the protection of the lungs."

The others agreed and they started another round of long discussions, which didn't end until hours later.

"By my calculations," Lorana said, "we can do it, just barely."

"But there'll only be enough for one dose," Ketan said.

The others nodded glumly.

"There's no other choice," M'tal said finally. "Let's do it."

Lorana carefully set up the sequencer. "Get the vials," she told Kindan. "Just the red, green, and blue ones."

Kindan looked at the vials and saw that each had a colored dot drawn on them. "How did you find out which one was which?"

"I ran a small sample through the sequencer," Lorana told him.

"The yellow is for the watch-whers?" Ketan asked. Lorana nodded.

Kindan returned with the vials. Lorana slowly emptied each one into the hopper on the top of the sequencer.

"Are we sure?" she asked the others, her finger hovering over the "Start" button.

"Do it," Ketan said.

Lorana pushed the button.

"How long until it's complete?" M'tal asked.

"About four hours," Lorana replied.

"And then what?" Salina asked. "When will we know if it works? Who should we give it to?"

Lorana shuddered, knowing the answer.

Salina's eyes widened. "Minith?" she asked.

"She would be best," Lorana said. "If she hasn't clutched already, then the immunity would be passed on to her eggs."

"She can't have clutched yet," M'tal replied. "We would have known. Tullea must have had a bad dream."

"What would happen, though, if the cure didn't work?" Ketan asked.

"She'd be no better off than she is," Kindan said.

"Possibly worse," Lorana corrected. She met Ketan's eyes. "If we're wrong, she could easily die like Arith."

"She is the last queen of Benden, I won't permit it!" Tullea exclaimed when they found her in the Weyrleaders' quarters later. She and B'nik were eating a late night snack. "Isn't it enough to kill your own dragon?"

"Tullea, she's trying to help," B'nik said scoldingly.

"Fine, let her try it on your dragon," Tullea snapped.

"If we give the cure to Minith, it will be passed on to her eggs," Salina told her. "We only have the one dose."

"And Benden has only the one queen!" Tullea snarled in reply.

"Yes," Lorana agreed. "Minith is Benden's last hope."

You say my eggs will live, if I do this? Minith asked Lorana.

I hope so, Lorana replied honestly.

I can do this, Minith told Lorana.

"No!" Tullea jumped up, scything toward Lorana with her nails. B'nik rose and clutched her, keeping her from striking Lorana. "No, I won't let you! You are not Minith's rider! Minith, go *between*! Now!"

No, Minith replied firmly. Tullea's eyes widened in surprise. *I am Benden's last queen, it is my duty.*

"Minith says she will do it," Lorana calmly informed the others.

"No," Tullea protested. She turned to B'nik, pleading, "You can't let her. She killed her dragon and now she wants mine!"

This is our only hope, Minith said. From her weyr, she bugled loudly. Her sound was interrupted by a sharp cough. *This is* my *only hope.*

"She's right, Tullea," Lorana said.

"We've tried everything else," Ketan agreed.

Minith ducked her head in from her sleeping quarters. *What do I have to do?*

"I will inject you with this," Lorana said, holding up a syringe.

"Well, do it then," Tullea growled. After it was done, she speared Lorana with a glare. "You can talk to all the dragons, can't you?" She didn't wait for a response. "Do you hear them die?"

"And feel them," Lorana admitted quietly.

"Good," Tullea replied heartlessly, storming from the room into her dragon's quarters. "Then whatever happens to Minith, I hope it hurts you as much as anything."

We have to do this, it is our duty, Minith told her rider as Tullea scrunched down between her dragon's forelegs. From the farther weyr, Caranth rumbled his agreement, which partway through turned into a long hacking cough.

"And she never said anything more about the clutch?" M'tal asked B'nik as they sat in front of one of the fires in the Kitchen Cavern. M'tal had managed to lure B'nik away from the vigil over Minith late in the evening after Tullea had finally nodded off.

"No," B'nik answered. "When I mentioned it she called me a liar and started shouting." He shook his head sadly. "She didn't use to be like this. She's as bad as some of those who timed it."

M'tal's eyes lit. "She is, isn't she?" he said slowly. His brows furrowed in thought.

"What is it?" B'nik asked.

M'tal looked up at B'nik. "I need you to come with me," he said finally. He raised his hand to forestall any of B'nik's questions. "We'll take Gaminth. We won't be long."

"What for?"

"I'm not sure," M'tal admitted, rising. "But if I'm right, I know why Tullea's acting this way."

"Wake up!" Tullea's voice carried across the room to Lorana. "Wake up, dragonkiller. It seems your precious potion hasn't worked."

Lorana stood up quickly and looked at Minith. The gold queen was nearly orange; her head hung listless and her breathing was labored.

"So, you've killed my dragon, too," Tullea said, rising menacingly.

"That's not so!" B'nik's voice startled them. They turned to see him enter with M'tal a step behind. "The cure will work."

From the pouch hanging on his side he took a small syringe, twin to the one Lorana had used before, and went to Caranth's weyr. Quickly, he woke his dragon and, talking softly all the while, injected him.

M'tal had a very smug expression on his face. "You know," he said blandly, "I never could figure out why High Reaches became so rude several Turns back."

Footsteps behind him announced the arrival of Kindan, Ketan, and Salina.

B'nik grinned impishly at the old Weyrleader. Lorana's look of puzzlement faded.

"Where I have just been, you are known as the dragons' savior," M'tal told her softly.

"High Reaches!" Kindan exclaimed, slapping his forehead.

"Yes," M'tal agreed. He turned to Lorana. "Your cure worked. But it is not enough to hatch healthy dragons—"

"They have to be old enough to fly," Lorana exclaimed with a groan.

"Tullea, it's time to go," B'nik said. He gestured behind her to Minith.

"She's not able to fly!" Tullea protested.

"She is, and she will, because she *has,*" M'tal corrected her.

"Where am I going?" Tullea asked.

"To High Reaches," B'nik said. "Three Turns back in time. You must warn them and convince D'vin to close the Weyr."

"Back in time?" Tullea repeated, looking from B'nik to M'tal. "To High Reaches?"

"The sickness will not reach there, because you'll get them to close the Weyr," M'tal explained.

"I can't go alone!" Tullea cried, looking around.

Ketan stepped forward. "I'll go with you," he told her.

Tullea had hardly left, and the astonished remainder had barely gotten into the Kitchen Cavern for an early breakfast before they felt the arrival of a dragon from *between.*

Lorana rushed out into the Bowl.

"Minith!" she cried. "What are you doing back so—"

Tullea jumped down beside her dragon. The queen rider was smiling and more relaxed than Lorana had ever seen her.

And she was *older,* Lorana realized.

Tullea gave Lorana a measured look, then smiled. "Lorana," she began, "I know it's only been a moment for you, but—" She stopped, her voice catching in her throat.

"You have saved the dragons, all the dragons of Pern," she said finally. "You saved my Minith." She gestured fondly back at her dragon.

"I'm sorry for all the terrible things I said and did to you—you didn't deserve any of it," she told Lorana contritely.

"She was in two times at once, for over three Turns," Ketan explained.

"I felt like I was always torn apart, stretched!" Tullea told the group. "But it was worth it. Ketan has serum for all the dragons here at Benden," she went on happily. "And riders have been dispatched to Fort and Ista, as well.

"The serum is dragon's blood," she explained. "Ketan says it's not like human blood—that's why we call it 'ichor.' The blood alone will provide the cure for the other dragons."

She smiled at Lorana. "You did it! You saved them all!"

Tullea paused and reached into her wher-hide jacket. "This is yours. I took it from the first Learning Room."

She pressed a small object into Lorana's outstretched hand.

A burst of cold air announced the arrival of another dragon from *between*. It was a bronze dragon, full-grown, larger than any Lorana had seen.

I am Kmuth, the dragon told her. Above him, his young rider bowed deeply. *I greet you.*

Lorana looked at the object in her hand. It was some sort of case. The top was covered with a very old version of the Masterhealer's mark. She turned it over and gasped as she saw that the bottom had her own Animal Healer mark carefully drawn on it.

There was another burst of cold air and a brown dragon appeared. *I am Aloth, Lorana.*

Oh, you're beautiful, Lorana told the brown, who flapped his wings in pleasure.

An enormous burst of cold from *between* announced the arrival of the largest dragon ever seen at Benden Weyr.

I am Tolarth, the newest queen dragon of Pern told Lorana proudly.

"Open it," Tullea said, her voice wavering with emotion.

Lorana looked up and was surprised to see tears rolling down Tullea's cheeks.

"Please, you'll see," Tullea pressed.

Lorana opened it. She gasped and cried out loud. Kindan heard the noise and rushed to her side.

"Look!" she said, showing the case to Kindan. "See?"

Inside the case was a three-linked locket. Lorana lifted it out and opened it up. The middle link was made of Arith's saddle star.

"Where? How?" Kindan asked in amazement.

Lorana didn't hear him. The other two links in the locket had pictures in them. She looked at the first one—it was a small painting of a very ancient woman with a very compassionate face.

"Is that—is that Wind Blossom?" Kindan asked in awe. "And who's this scarfaced man?"

Lorana turned to look at the second locket and cried out loud.

"What is it?" Kindan asked, wrapping an arm around her comfortingly.

"It's Grenn!" Lorana cried, pointing to the small fire-lizard perched on the man's shoulder, tears of joy streaming down her face. "That's my fire-lizard! He lived! He made it back in time, and he *lived*!"

And the children shall lead you.

Epilogue

"I'VE ALWAYS FELT that there was something missing," Tieran mused to his companion.

"You are a romantic," she said.

"Where to put it?" Tieran muttered to himself, searching the room. "Someplace not too obvious . . . ah! Here." He put down the locket.

"What do you hope to gain with that?"

"I want her to know that *we* knew her pain. That we understood."

"Tieran, whoever it is won't be born for hundreds of Turns. We have no way of knowing that this will even work."

"It'll work," Tieran said assuredly. "I know it."

"How?" Emorra asked. "My love, sometimes I think you are too much of a dreamer."

"Daddy!" a small boy's voice called.

"We'll be right there," Tieran replied.

"Really, Tieran," Emorra shook her head.

"Did you ever wonder how she touched your mother? Did you wonder why this clever one—" He stroked the fire-lizard affectionately. "—appeared? There was a bond."

"Yes, I agree."

"A familial bond. Whoever she is, she is one of our children's children."

Emorra pursed her lips and nodded. "I've always agreed with you on that, love."

"Mommy!" the boy cried impatiently.

"We'll be right there," Emorra replied, cocking her head at Tieran and then in the direction of the boy.

Tieran smiled triumphantly at her as he caught her hand in his and they turned to go to their son. "And have you ever known one of us *not* to get our way in the end?"

ACKNOWLEDGMENTS

This book is the first book written solely by someone else in Anne McCaffrey's Pern universe. I would like to thank Ms. McCaffrey—"Thank you, Mum!"—for letting me do so. I was thrilled to get a smiley face ☺ from her on my outline, as well as all her encouragement and her bravery in letting someone else play in her very special sandbox.

The quality of that outline was dramatically improved by the comments of Michael Reaves, Brynne Chandler, and Jenna Scott.

I would also like to thank my sister, Georgeanne Kennedy, for her insightful comments and questions, and for her unfailing support in my efforts to write this novel.

This novel would not have happened at all without the encouragement, understanding, and keen insight of my editor, Shelly Shapiro, of Del Rey Books. She not only encouraged me when I needed it but also challenged me to stretch to greater heights—the true hallmark of a great editor.

While too many cooks may spoil the broth, it is amazing how many sets of eyes can gaze over the same mistakes—and miss them. I am very grateful to Judith Welsh, my editor at Transworld, for catching errors that no one else noticed.

I would also like to thank Don Maass of the Donald Maass Literary Agency for his steady support, keen insights, and quiet encouragement.

I would like to thank Harry and Marilyn Alm for their prompt replies to questions regarding Threadfalls and particularly recommend Harry's Threadfall charts for anyone seriously interested in figuring out what goes where on Pern—at least when it comes to nasty stuff.

I am also indebted to Dr. Natascha Latenschlauger for her help in dealing with illnesses and genetic material, no matter which planet it comes from.

I want to thank my early readers, Sonia Orin Lyris, Angel Hanley, Harry and Marilyn Alm, and—of course—Anne McCaffrey (Mum) for all their comments, suggestions, and insights without which this book would not be.

Finally, I would like to sing the praises of my copy editor from Del Rey, Martha Trachtenberg, who caught or questioned countless errors in the original manuscript and whose songwriting knowledge made "Wind Blossom's Song" vastly superior.

Any mistakes, errors, and omissions still found are all mine.

Read on for a sneak peak at

DRAGON'S FIRE,

the second exciting collaboration
by Anne McCaffrey and Todd McCaffrey . . .

Flame on high
Thread will die
Flame too low
Burrows woe.

"COME ON, JAMAL, you'll miss it!" Cristov called as he weaved through the Gather crowd. He looked over his shoulder and frowned as he saw that the distance between him and his friend had widened. Jamal hobbled after him gamely on his crutches. Cristov stopped, then turned back.

"I could carry you, if you want," he offered.

"I weigh as much as you do," Jamal said. "How far do you think we'd get?"

"Far enough," Cristov lied stoutly. "It's only a few dragon-lengths to the edge of the crowd."

Jamal shoved Cristov away. "It'll take forever with these," he cried, waving at one of the crutches with his arm. Jamal had broken his leg a sevenday before and would be on crutches for at least two months.

"Then I'll carry you," Cristov persisted, trying again to grab hold of his friend.

"You couldn't do it even if you were the size of your father," Jamal said. Cristov hid a sigh; even if he were the size of Tarik, he'd probably not be big enough to carry Jamal.

"You'll be the proper size for the mines," Tarik had said once when Cristov had complained that all his friends were taller than he was.

"I can still try," Cristov persisted. Jamal groaned at him and tried to shake off Cristov's aid.

"There's your father," Jamal said in a low tone. Cristov

looked back to the edge of the Gather and saw Tarik. Their eyes locked, and Cristov's heart sank as his father beckoned imperiously to him. "You'd better go. He looks like he's in one of his moods."

"I'll be back," Cristov said as he started away. Not hearing any comment from Jamal, he turned back, but Jamal was already hobbling away, nearly lost in the Gather crowd. Cristov wanted to sprint after him, to turn him around, to meet his father with a friend at his side but—

With a grimace, Cristov turned back to the edge of the Gather crowd and caught the look on his father's face; seeing Tarik repeat his impatient, beckoning gesture, Cristov knew why Jamal had left.

"I just wanted to spend some time with Jamal," Cristov said as he neared speaking distance.

"Never mind him," Tarik growled impatiently. "You'll make new friends up at the Camp; you won't need worry about that cripple."

"He'll be fine when the cast's off," Cristov protested. For all the ten Turns that Cristov had lived, his father had found fault with anyone that Cristov had tried to befriend.

"That's neither here nor there," Tarik grunted. "He's a cripple now and I'm glad you won't be around him." He snaked a hand onto Cristov's shoulder and pulled him tight against him.

"This is Harper Moran," Tarik said, gesturing to the young man in blue beside him. Cristov nodded politely to the Harper.

"Look! The dragons are starting the games!" Moran exclaimed, pointing up to the sky.

Cristov craned his neck back but found himself bumping into his father's chest. He squirmed forward to give himself enough distance to look straight up into the sky.

"It's a nice day for it," Moran said. "Not a cloud in the sky."

"I hope Telgar wins again," Cristov said. Crom Hold was under Telgar Weyr's protection; it would be the dragons from Telgar who flamed Thread from the sky when it fell. Cristov knew that Thread wasn't due for nearly another seventeen Turns; having only nine-and-a-half Turns of age himself, Cristov could hardly imagine such a distant future.

"Of course they'll win again," Tarik growled. "They won last year, because of their new Weyrleader."

"He came from Ista Weyr, didn't he, Father?" Cristov asked, still amazed that a whole Weyr had been abandoned.

"There wasn't much else for them to do," Harper Moran remarked, "given the drought down that way and that their last queen had died."

"Their loss, our gain," Tarik said. "Telgar Weyr's got nearly twice the dragons the other Weyrs have."

"And twice the duty, too," Moran said.

Cristov lost the sound of their voices, intent only on the dragons flying into view above him.

One group, all golden, burst into view high up above them. The queen dragons.

Moran pointed. "They're going to throw the first Thread."

"Thread?" Cristov gulped. He knew from that Thread would burn through and consume anything living, would voraciously spread, and could be destroyed only by a dragon's fiery breath.

"Not real Thread," Tarik growled. "Just rope."

"Made to look like Thread," the Harper added. "For the games."

"Oh." Cristov turned back around and craned his neck skywards, relieved.

A wing of dragons suddenly appeared in the sky well below the queens, and moments later the loud *booms* of their arrival shook the air.

"Light travels faster than sound," Harper Moran murmured. Cristov wasn't sure if the Harper meant to be heard or was just so used to teaching that he never stopped.

"They look small," Cristov said, surprised.

"They're Weyrlings," the Harper said. "They're just old enough to fly *between* and carry firestone."

"Firestone?" Cristov repeated, unfamiliar with the word.

He made a face and turned to his father. "Is that another name for coal?"

Instantly Cristov knew from his father's angry look that he'd asked the wrong question. Cristov flinched as he saw his father's arm flex, ready to smack him, but he was saved by the Harper.

"No, it's not another name for coal, more's the pity," the Harper said, not noticing or choosing to ignore Tarik's anger. "You've never seen it, though you might remember it from the Songs."

"I did," Cristov confessed. "But I always thought it had to be coal."

Tarik glared at him.

"You said, Father, that Cromcoal makes the hottest fire there is. I thought for sure that the dragons had to use coal for their flames," he explained, wilting under Tarik's look. Feebly, he finished, "I was sure they'd only use the best."

"Your lad's a fair one for thinking, Tarik," Moran said with an affable laugh. "You can't really fault his logic."

"It's his job to listen to his elders and learn from them," Tarik replied. "He doesn't need to do any thinking."

Moran gave the miner a troubled look. "Thinking comes in handy for Harpers."

"He's not going to be a Harper," Tarik replied. "Cristov's going to be a miner. Like his father and my father before me." He gave the Harper a grim smile and held up a hand over Cristov's head. "We're built the right size for the mines."

"I imagine that thinking will be important for miners, Tarik," Moran said, shaking his head in disagreement. "Times are changing. The old mines have played out; the new seams are all deep underground. Mining down there will require new ways of thinking."

"Not for me," Tarik disagreed. "I know all I need to know about mining. I've been a miner for twenty Turns now— learned from my father, and he'd been a miner for thirty Turns. It was *his* father that first opened our seam, seventy Turns back."

A ripple of overwhelming sound and a burst of cold air

announced the arrival of a huge wing of dragons, flying low over the crowd.

"Telgar!" the crowd shouted as the dragons entered a steep dive, twisted into a sharp rolling climb, and came to a halt, their formation intermeshed with the Weyrlings so perfectly that it looked like the two wings of dragons had been flying as one, even though the fighting wing was head to head and a meter underneath the Weyrlings.

Cristov gasped as a rain of sacks fell from the Weyrlings only to be caught by the riders of the great fighting dragons. Looking at the jacket worn by the bronze rider leading the fighting wing, he saw the stylized sheaves of wheat set in a white diamond—it was the Weyrleader himself!

As one, the fighting wing of dragons turned and dove again, flawlessly returning to hover in the same place where it had come from *between*. As the dragons hovered, their great necks twisted and their heads turned back to face their riders, who opened the sacks they had caught from the Weyrlings to feed the firestone to their dragons.

"Nasty stuff, firestone," Cristov heard the Harper mutter behind him. "Nasty stuff."